MONTE CARLO MASQUERADES
A NOVEL

# MONTE CARLO MASQUERADES

*A Novel by*

## MONTE RENFRO

SPRAGUE PUBLISHING COMPANY
VANCOVER, WA

ISBN-13: 978-1520113937 ISBN-10: 1520113935

Library of Congress Control Number
2017902764

Sprague Publishing Company
P.O. Box 873934
Vancouver, WA 98687 USA
Spraguepublishingco@gmail.com

V20

Monte Carlo Masquerades is available in paperback & as a Kindle eBook exclusively at
Amazon.com
Amazon.co.uk
Amazon.fr (boutique: livres anglais)

Cover design: BookCoverExpress.com

*To Tom Kingzett*
*Friend, Critic, Friend*

Now what else is the whole life of mortals but a sort of comedy in which the various actors, disguised by various costumes and masks, walk on and play each one's part until the manager walks them off the stage?

—Desiderius Erasmus (1466–1536)

# Thursday, March 12, 1914
## HÔTEL DE PARIS

*ENTER, PURSUED BY A BEAR.* FOR NO EXPLICABLE reason, repeating this twist on Shakespeare's stage direction had become the spot of salve Lily Turner applied to her smarting pride and growing frustration each morning just before she knocked on the door to report to work.

"Come in. Come in," Mrs. Murphy ordered when she opened the door. "We've been waiting for you."

Lily hesitated as her mind sought to sort out the anomalies in the scene. In the first place, it should have been the maid, Bridget Rose, who answered the door. In the second place, Lily, who measured 5'10" in her stocking feet, could see beyond her employer's shoulder that the cousin, Ted Wycliffe, was present. While he was allowed unfettered bowing and scraping during Mrs. Murphy's leisure hours, he was never admitted to the inner sanctum while she managed her business affairs.

Despite those curiosities, Lily knew the impatience wasn't because they needed a fourth for Bridge, so she assumed an appropriately penitent aspect and stepped forward. At the same time, a thin, angular man with the deportment of an undertaker was emerging from the door on the left that led to Mr. Murphy's bedchamber.

Wycliffe answered the unspoken question, "Lily, allow me to introduce Chief Inspector Gautier of the Monaco Sûreté Publique."

Gautier made a small bow from the waist, keeping his intense dark eyes continuously on her. Lily's confusion deepened. Whatever this man was here for, it wasn't to celebrate Mrs. Murphy's safe return from five days of dumping money in Cannes.

"Chief Inspector Gautier, may I present Mrs. Murphy's secretary, Miss Turner," Wycliffe said. "As they say, two heads are better than one. She will be my assistant."

This time, Lily couldn't arrest the puzzlement before it invaded her face. Assist this toadstool of a man with what? She had had little to do with him since he boarded the Murphys' private Pullman in Chicago on the party's way to Monte Carlo, but she had observed more than enough during his two visits to San Francisco during her tenure there over the past nine months.

Her lips parted, ready to blurt out an objection, but Mrs. Murphy preempted her. "Joe has been shot dead in his bed. You're going to help Teddy."

Lily's jaw dropped as the breath rushed from her body. Fixing her stare on Chief Inspector Gautier, she mechanically extracted the stenographer's book from her bulging workbag and removed the freshly sharpened pencil tucked within its pages.

"Yes, ma'am," she murmured.

Trailing Mrs. Murphy, Lily was the last to enter the bedroom. The first thing she saw was the perfectly still form on the bed, but it was impossible to keep her eyes on it. Her gaze went hurrying across the top of the elaborate white headboard until she came to the adjacent white-and-gold table in the style of Louis XVI. There, a dark-green book lay beside a tumbler. The book appeared new or lightly used. The glass was filled with something that looked like whiskey. Yet even with her eyes locked on that tableau, from that one glimpse, she knew Mr. Murphy reclined on his right side on top of the counterpane, facing an interior wall, his back to her and to the door, his head at an unnatural angle on the pillow. His left arm was flung outward, reaching beyond the mattress' edge. She also knew that he was clad in black trousers with only an undervest covering his torso, that his loosened braces were bunched at the back of his waist, and that a cream-colored spread had left one bare foot uncovered.

She heard Wycliffe say, "Someone was either a very good shot or else Joe was shot at point-blank range."

Still fighting to hold back the panic which was threatening to overwhelm her, Lily concentrated on the book. Its cover faced down, so she strained to read the title on the spine without appearing to do so.

"Probably went straight into the heart," Wycliffe added.

In spite of herself, Lily looked towards the bed, her grip on the pencil and tablet tightening. Wycliffe was leaning over, inspecting Mr. Murphy's back. There indeed was a conspicuous dark spot on the white jersey. She had never before seen a man after he had been shot in the back, but for some reason, she would have expected more blood. For that matter, she realized, she had never seen a dead person before. She used to think she had. Back at Effie's big house in Chicago, a body had been brought around the side of the building twice, to be loaded onto a wagon waiting at the garden gate. Lily had watched from the kitchen window, and Piedmont instructed her to put her hand over her heart as the body went by, as though she were saluting the flag. But those were wrapped in quilts, and nothing of the persons within had been visible.

3

"If you please, Monsieur, do not touch anything," Gautier said.

Other than withdrawing his hand, Wycliffe didn't move. At the same time, Lily's confusion was lifting, and the situation's potential was soaking into her consciousness and starching her courage. She was in the company of a real detective and this was a real murder. If she was going to need a fainting couch at the sight of her first crime scene, she might as well resign herself on the spot to spending the rest of her days crossfooting mind-numbing columns of numbers while measuring her minutes in eraser crumbs and quantifying her hours in triplicate: white, pink, and yellow.

A soft rapping at the exterior door diverted everyone's attention in that direction. Glad for a break in which to further square herself, Lily slid the pencil above her right ear and left the room.

When she opened the door to the corridor, a diminutive man announced in French, "Good day, I am Doctor Fournier."

Behind the doctor stood another man, light-haired and close to her own height. She looked down at the older man's plump face. That concerned expression was going to be wasted on this patient.

"Is Chief Inspector Gautier here?" Fournier asked. The distinct smell of alcohol accompanied the question.

Responding in French, she said, "Yes, in the bedchamber," and motioned in that direction.

When she failed to step aside to grant them entrance, Dr. Fournier looked at her with raised eyebrows. "Mademoiselle?" he inquired.

She turned to see Chief Inspector Gautier signaling the newcomers to join him.

When Lily reentered the bedroom, Mrs. Murphy was glaring at the officials as though they were an invasion of

4

rodents. Her cousin was rummaging through a drawer at the bottom of the oversized mahogany wardrobe.

"Monsieur Wycliffe," the chief inspector said, with a heroic lack of irritation in his voice, "you will kindly step away. Dr. Fournier will examine now."

The doctor was regarding the body as though he were called out to inspect one of these every morning at this hour. He pressed his palm against the chest, then pulled a mirror from his pocket and held it close to the lifeless face. Lily was flabbergasted. What antediluvian cave had they dug this man out of? She knew the mirror's purpose. She had read about the technique often enough in the heaps of detective stories she had eagerly devoured since she was ten years old. But this was 1914. Everyone knew stethoscopes had long ago replaced a mirror as the principal tool for detecting life. Perhaps the doctor needed to be brought up-to-date about the advancements in moveable type and the steam engine as well.

"Useless," Dr. Fournier declared, retracting the unfogged mirror.

Lily opened her notebook and entered the date at the top of the page before recording the doctor's name and that of the younger man, whom Gautier had introduced at Duchamp. She drew a line across the page to indicate where she would begin the points to be put into a letter to her friend and business partner, Fran Jameson. She would mention that Duchamp was decidedly handsome. She would also mention that Dr. Fournier belonged with the fossils and skeletons up at Monaco's Anthropologic Museum.

"Madame," Gautier said, "we will want to search the room."

"Not without my representative here, you won't," Mrs. Murphy said.

When Wycliffe straightened to level triumphant eyes on

the chief inspector, Lily could have sworn her new master gained a couple of inches in height.

"As Madame wishes," Gautier replied.

"Lily, I want everyone's name and a signed receipt for anything they take out of here. Teddy, come see me afterwards." She swept out of the room without waiting for a response.

As the doctor extended his hand to close Mr. Murphy's eyes, Gautier approached the French windows leading to the room's abbreviated balcony. Using a handkerchief over the tips of his fingers, he twisted the white-enameled knob. Like a trained parlor poodle, Wycliffe hastened to position himself beside the inspector.

"Lily, make a note the door was unlocked," Wycliffe directed.

She clinched her jaw and did as commanded while her indignation grew white-hot. Mrs. Murphy's handing her over like she was a sack of oats was bad enough, but to be handed over without so much as a by-your-leave to a man of Ted Wycliffe's caliber ....

When he appeared in San Francisco last summer on his first visit from Chicago, Lily had initially been inclined to pity him, not because of his oddly changeable face, which alternated between idiotic and intelligent, or because of his barbaric toupee, which looked like a swatch cut from a buffalo-hide, but because of his halting gait. Sometimes the limp was so severe he seemed barely able to traverse a room. But her inclination to sympathy was soon overwhelmed by disgust. Even though she was mercifully spared from witnessing most of their congress, Wycliffe's fawning over his relative was so self-demeaning and so blatantly transparent Lily had been unable to decide which was the more revolting, his perpetration of it or Mrs. Murphy's unprotesting acceptance

6

of it. In the end, she declared the contest to be a draw.

She turned her back to him and forced herself to take deep, calming breaths. It didn't matter whether it was Clara Barton or Ivan the Terrible who issued the orders. The only thing that mattered was that she earn enough money to keep the door to the Turner and Jameson Detective Bureau open. This must be done even if a whole herd of sycophantic cousins, scurrying along as fast as their hands and knees could carry them, arrived to torment her forbearance and compromise her dignity.

As if made to order, a rush of fresh sea air enveloped her senses and helped to damp her righteous indignation. From the opened door behind, she heard the shout of a coachman to his horses on the road below, the "ah-oo-gah" of a motorcar's Klaxon, and the leisurely spaced "pop-pops" of gunshots from the Tir aux pigeons. Turning, she saw Wycliffe peering over the rails of the miniscule balcony.

"You don't think the killer entered through this door, do you?" he asked Chief Inspector Gautier. "This is the top floor. It's unlikely someone could climb up here."

Gautier intoned a non-committal sound.

"But," Wycliffe went on, "there are cat burglars, are there not, who can scale walls such as these?"

*Cat burglar*, Lily wrote, once in cursive, again in capitalized block letters. That must be the reason she didn't trust cats, thieving little beasts. Below the words, she sketched a cat upright on its hind legs, its eyes outlined by a mask, with a pistol in its paw. At the same time, she remained aware that Duchamp was sifting through the wardrobe's lower drawer. Wycliffe also noticed this activity and abandoned his post beside Gautier to supervise the contents being removed.

The doctor and the corpse he was handling with cool detachment invaded Lily's consciousness once more. He was

7

holding Mr. Murphy's undershirt away from the chest and peering beneath it. She watched for as long as she decently dared but could not tell what held the doctor's attention. Turning again to the chief inspector, she wondered if this were the first time he had taken in the view from the upper floor of the Hôtel de Paris. She doubted it. Surely, at least one of Monte Carlo's notorious suicides had taken place here. His back was to her, so she couldn't tell if his eyes looked outward or inward. In the distance, the morning sun danced across the sea's surface, which caught and reflected the light like thousands of tiny mirrors shifting and swaying in a majestic dance of light and color, a perfect counterpoise to the morbid scene inside.

Having finished with the wardrobe's drawer, Duchamp patted the pockets of Mr. Murphy's overcoat, which had been folded over the bed's footboard. His face displayed heightened alertness, and when he raised his hand, a large piece of jewelry was looped around his fingers. Lily took a step towards him. It was Mrs. Murphy's emerald and diamond necklace. Although its center stone was the size of a quarter-eagle coin, as great gems go, the piece was relatively modest. Nonetheless, Mrs. Murphy swore that because of its sentimental value she would not trade it for the Star of Africa. This assertion, Lily seriously doubted.

"Your cat burglar is not a good one," Duchamp said flatly.

Wycliffe was gaping as though the man were holding a lighted stick of dynamite.

After taking the necklace from his colleague's hand, Gautier balanced it in his palm for several seconds, then held it up so it could be backlit by the windows. Frowning, he extracted a loupe from an inner pocket and studied the piece at length, giving special attention to the larger stones. Lily made a note that she and Fran would want to learn a few jeweler's skills. She hoped the New York City Public Library had a text on the subject. Their firm couldn't afford a one-page pamphlet, let alone another book.

"It is not genuine," Gautier pronounced, "an excellent piece of paste, first-rate, but not genuine."

Lily looked at her new master. He appeared too dazed to hear anything that was said.

"Place this in a box," Gautier said, indicating the glass of whiskey on the bedside table. Lily's French vocabulary, though good, did not include the word the inspector used to his assistant, but she guessed it meant fingerprints.

Gautier picked up the book lying next to the glass and fanned its pages, then stopped and turned them more deliberately. From her perspective, Lily glimpsed words underlined in ink and occasional notes in the margin before Gautier slipped it inside his jacket.

Wycliffe's eyelids fluttered as though he were Snow White coming awake. "What is that?" he said.

"A German dictionary," Gautier answered.

"You're taking it?"

"Yes."

"Let me see it first," Wycliffe said.

When Gautier responded with the greatest of mildness that it would be returned with the other things, Wycliffe turned pink, then red, then purple, but said nothing, possibly because magma had melted his vocal cords. Lily decided she would ignore the brewing Vesuvius until the eruption and recorded the glass and dictionary as items removed.

"Let me have your pencil," Wycliffe said. Pulling a fistful of papers from a sidepocket, he selected one while the rest drifted to the floor.

As Lily waited for the pencil to be returned, it suddenly occurred to her to question who found the body. Michael

Gallagher, nominally Mr. Murphy's valet, was nowhere in sight, nor had she seen his wife, Bridget Rose, who should have answered the door. Considering that back in San Francisco one butler was released from service because a piece of cork, so minute it could be seen only by the mistress of the household, had been detected in a glass of champagne and that a parlor maid was fired without notice upon the discovery of a water-spot on a teaspoon, it was difficult to imagine the fate of the servant so negligent as to leave a dead husband on top of the counterpane.

"So that's your conclusion?" Wycliffe said. "You think the murderer entered through that balcony door?"

Gautier did not respond.

"I hope I scarcely need to point out that my cousin, Mrs. Murphy, should be above any suspicion in this matter. She was, after all, in Cannes until only just this morning."

Before Wycliffe could receive or demand a reply, his attention was again diverted by Duchamp, who was unfolding a packet of papers removed from a gutta percha collar-box. As Wycliffe lunged towards him, Duchamp barely managed to raise the bundle over his head in time to keep it from being ripped from his hand.

"What is it?" the chief inspector asked.

Once more Lily admired his calm demeanor. If she were in charge, Wycliffe would have been hog-tied and tossed from the room long ago. Then again, the chief inspector was easily twice her age. By now he had probably seen so much astounding stupidity and unalloyed absurdity that such things no longer excited his amazement.

"They are tickets for passage," Duchamp answered, keeping the prize beyond Wycliffe's reach. "Quite the journey, a number of segments. By rail and steamer to Cherbourg, to Liverpool. I don't know, finally to Belfast."

Because the detective had answered in French, Wycliffe referred his gaze to Lily. "But that's ridiculous," he muttered after she translated.

Duchamp hesitated before lowering his arm, but Wycliffe had again descended into a trance and didn't notice the packet was within his reach.

Finished with his examination of the body, Dr. Fournier had remained beside the bed, apparently to catch the show's succeeding acts. He now snapped shut the clasp on the black satchel and pulled the spread over Mr. Murphy's head. He then crossed the room to say a few quiet words to Gautier. While students at Bryn Mawr College, Lily and Fran, certain of their destinies as detectives, had spent hours practicing lip-reading with one another. Unfortunately, they had not done this in French.

Gautier looked down at the doctor but made no reply to his comments. Lily wished he had covered poor Mr. Murphy's bare foot. The air seeping through balcony's partially opened door carried with it a remnant of the night's chill. She knew her concern was irrational, but that didn't prevent her feeling it.

After Dr. Fournier left, Wycliffe came around and started demanding particulars about the tickets. When were they purchased? How many persons? What dates? What class? The chief inspector assured him all those things would be included in the report. At this, Wycliffe lapsed into yet another deep reverie. Maybe he was summoning Madame Blavatsky to ask her what to make of these questions. Not that Lily had a ready answer either. Of one thing she was certain: Mrs. Murphy would never, not even if she were drunk or drugged or both, consent to visit Ireland.

Lily's pencil halted in mid-air. Mrs. Murphy would never go to Ireland, but someone else might. Yes, a petite, pretty, young blond might go to Ireland. Since arriving at the suite, Lily had been occupied with following and recording the activities. Consequently, she had put out of her mind that which had perplexed her earlier today. Now, however, she made the undeniable, quite disturbing connection: Joseph Murphy had been shot dead, and this morning, Little Beauty had not appeared, as she should have, to take her exercise in the garden below Lily's room.

# Thursday, March 12, 1914
## LA CAVE DU RENARD

PAUL NEWCASTLE STARED AT THE CARDS BEING DEALT and questioned why he hadn't given up an hour ago and returned to his room to grab some badly needed sleep before reporting to his other job this afternoon. In the past fifty minutes, he had given more money to that foul-mouthed Corsican than such an execrable creature deserved to see in an entire lifetime. Even for a place such as this, whose denizens were more likely to attack each other with the empty wine bottles than return them to the proprietor and where advantages in etiquette were calculated only by a diminution of savagery, even for this place, the Corsican had set a new standard for boorishness, not for any particular offense but by the cumulative effect.

He had appeared here at Pierre Vioget's drinking and gambling hole for the first time this morning. Standing at the thick plank of wood that served as the bar's counter, he demanded an *ordinaire* and the day's meal. He gulped the soup and ripped at the beef with his few remaining teeth, pausing every now and again to pick his nose or wipe his mouth on the back of his filthy sleeve. He then released a volcanic belch, hawked in the dish, and farted odiferously before announcing to the men engaged in a card game that he was ready to relieve them of their money. His statement had not been nearly so delicately nor as diplomatically worded. For Paul, such scenes were one of the drawbacks of making this dingy establishment his home port, but it was also the reason he had chosen it. Monaco was smaller than Hyde Park, and a man had to work hard to keep free from prying eyes, yet Paul never worried about anyone from the Casino accidentally coming across him at Pierre's.

Compounding Paul's antipathy to the lout was his need to study his cards with the intensity of a man who needed to remove his shoes to sum to twenty, an estimation bolstered by the fact that he did not know the Battle of Waterloo had been concluded a hundred years ago. On those infrequent occasions when Paul claimed the bank, the nasty beast proceeded to describe in such telling detail the acts Paul performed with diseased camels that one could only assume the man himself had been intimate with the *genus camelus*. When he felt particularly aggrieved by a game's outcome, he would go on to chronicle the mating habits of English mothers. If Paul were in a better mood, he might have admired the man's astuteness in perceiving his origins since his French was flawless and he never spoke anything other here. Yet, what grated most about the man's brutish hostility was his ingratitude. Paul not only was taking small banks, he was losing overall.

Because it had taken him some time to find this game, which had enough money changing hands to make it profitable but not so much as to make it remarkable, Paul managed his net gains and losses at La Cave du Renard with the precision of a Chinese embroideress. He knew exactly how much money he wanted to clear over several weeks' time but took pains to win and lose in a manner that could not be detected as systematic, at least not by the amateur gamblers and professional drunkards who rotated through the place. Perhaps Pierre had figured it out, perhaps not, but Paul had already fouled enough nests in his life, and the last thing he wanted was to have to look for a new game now. Another two months and the score for which he had waited a lifetime would be his at Antibes. With that cache secured in the hold, he was going to set off, all sails unfurled, to end his exile in this gilded wilderness and to begin life anew in a faraway land.

From the corner of his eye, he saw the Corsican was about to let loose again. Without looking up, Paul pushed a Napoléon to the middle of the table. It was a ridiculously large wager, and he regretted it the moment his fingers released the coin. Even without the lout's taunts, he was having trouble concentrating. He couldn't count his fingers let alone the cards, not when his mind wouldn't stay on point. It was bad enough that he had begun patting down his pockets for spectacles anytime he wanted his eyes to stay focused. Today, congestion choked his chest, and a searing throat was burning holes in his thoughts. Although throat maladies usually plagued him with memories of his father's fatal visitation of the King's Evil, it was the cough he had entertained for nearly two weeks that had him covertly checking the color of his handkerchief several times a day.

Muttering an oath, the Corsican sent his chair clattering onto its side and made a vulgar announcement of his need to relieve himself. It took several seconds for Paul to realize he had won the round in spite of himself.

"Next one?" Pierre inquired, his eyes sweeping across Paul and the other three men at the table.

Paul acceded with a vague motion of his hand. Scylla or Charybdis? La Cave du Renard or the Monte Carlo Casino? When one was in hell, the name on the doorplate was irrelevant. It was as impossible to see the outdoors from the Rooms as it was from the lowest gambling den, and while nothing could stave off the stink of stale beer and centuries of spilled wine permeating every surface in this hole, unlike at the Casino, a sliver of breathable air did manage to edge in alongside the scrap of light admitted by the rock wedged at the door's bottom. Granted, the Rooms sported thicker upholstery and their denizens could boast of better tailors, but British aristocrats, Russian royalty, or rancid sailors, they were all one and the same to Paul. If pressed on the point, however, he would have to admit that he did take a degree of comfort from being among men with only real things to worry about: enough food, enough wine, and not getting their throats cut. Besides, at the other job he had to be on his feet from two o'clock in the afternoon until midnight, an increasingly troublesome feat since his right knee had begun presenting him with yet another intermittent complaint. Failing eyesight, a faltering knee, hair going white at the temples, all these represented what Paul Newcastle saw as his besetting problem: at forty-three, he would soon be too old to stay in the game, but unless Antibes could be safely landed, he could not afford to get out of it.

The Corsican paused on his way back to spray vile remarks at Sylvie, the girl with heavily laddered black stockings, henna-colored hair, and bad teeth. She had recently begun spending her mornings at Pierre's, sharing coffee and bread with two other prostitutes who rented a room nearby. "Syphilitic whore" was among the Corsican's more benign remarks. Paul stiffened and instinctively looked about for a weapon. It should be impossible for him to remain perched like an anchovy on a salad while a lady's honor was being impugned. Fortunately for him, however, Sylvie proved capable of handling the lout herself. As fast as the insults were lobbed, she batted them back with a forceful display of language which featured detailed descriptions of her attacker's deformed member and the inadequacy of his testicles.

As the barbarian lumbered across the room with Sylvie continuing to hurl epithets at his back, Paul finally understood what Bruno the Oak saw in that girl. Bruno, whose biceps would snap a knife-blade before it could break the skin, had a moon-shaped face, a nose as flat as an anvil's top, and tiny eyes that gleamed with puppy-like adoration every time he found Sylvie in attendance at Pierre's.

Retrieving his chair, the Corsican delivered a stream of dark saliva at the floor.

"Next one?" Pierre asked.

Paul shook his head. It was not for want of trying that the lout had missed Paul's shoe. Rising from the chair, he suddenly remembered the other reason he needed to return to his room at Madame Piggot's pension. Yesterday afternoon, he had felt too sick to make a copy of this week's list of hotel-guests, but it must be done before tonight.

"Tomorrow?" Pierre asked.

"Probably not," Paul answered. But then, that was what he always said.

On his way to the door, he stopped beside the table where the three women had resumed their conversation. Sylvie's large, suspicious eyes reflexively turned inviting when she looked up to see Paul standing beside her. With an elaborately wide and slow sweep of his arm, he brought his hat to a place over his heart and gave her a deep, reverential bow.

# Thursday, March 12, 1914
## HÔTEL DE PARIS

WHEN LILY FOLLOWED THE DETECTIVES BACK TO THE sitting room, another unfamiliar Frenchman had joined Mrs. Murphy. He stood in front of the windows, nervously fingering a gold watch-fob while his head bobbed from side to side as if attached to a coiled spring. His face, notched by heavy black eyebrows and scored by numerous tiny lines, was that of a man with many vexations. His lips were stretched tightly as his eyes traced the movements of the waiter clearing away the luncheon dishes. Apparently, Mrs. Murphy's lunch had been served promptly at one o'clock. From the look of the dishes being stacked on the tray, she had managed to stomach most of the meal in spite of her husband's indisposition. And if the right gastronomic and culinary stars were in alignment, maybe it had been unnecessary for more than one or two items to be sent back to the kitchen as "unfit for human consumption."

The detectives had remained in Mr. Murphy's bedchamber for over an hour after Doctor Fournier left. They removed the contents from all the drawers and searched the pockets in each article of clothing, setting aside collections of flasks, gold cigar cases, pocketknives, bootjacks, bootlace hooks, and several sets of opal cufflinks. Gautier shook the flasks next to his ear before removing the tops and sniffing the contents. The felt-lined shoe trunk, its brass-fittings gleaming like 24-karat gold, drew special interest. Each boot and shoe was scrutinized, with extra attention given to the soles by twisting their heels, apparently to see if they contained hidden compartments. Lily wondered if this was standard procedure in Monaco. Wycliffe's behavior continued to bounce among daft, dissociated, inquisitive, and in far too many instances, obnoxious. At times, she found her affiliation with him to be so humiliating she was tempted to terminate it by defenestration, his.

With everyone gathered again in the sitting room, the freshly cut roses spilling out of a dozen vases had taken on a funereal aspect. The new widow was installed with magisterial bearing on a sofa. She had exchanged her traveling costume for one of her new Worth day-gowns, a deep-blue silk, trimmed in black lace with details of iridescent green. She looked like a giant tree-swallow, an impression further enhanced by her ample bosoms. Because she always wore gloves, even in situations where a lady might be excused for not doing so, the tan kid-leather gloves worn earlier had been replaced by a pair of thin black silk. Lily had often thought it was a shame Mrs. Murphy hadn't had an Effie to advise her back when it could have made a difference.

"Age tells first in the hands," Effie used to advise in every letter, as if Lily could possibly have forgotten the other ten-thousand times she had been forewarned of this Fate Worse Than Death. In fact, Effie always went to bed wearing cotton-gloves encasing the pounds of cold-cream lathered on her delicate fingers. Lily believed she would have stuck them inside a freshly slaughtered pork-belly if that would have better served the purpose. But the regimen worked. The last time they'd been together, almost twelve months ago, Effie had been thirty-four, approaching a woman's middle-age, and her hands had looked as youthful as Lily's twenty-year-old ones.

When Chief Inspector Gautier addressed the man with the bobbing head as Monsieur Barousse, Lily jotted down the name, but her mind stayed with Duchamp, who was taking his leave along with the items removed from the bedchamber. In answer to a question from Gautier, Barousse produced a key.

"If you will lock the door until my men can return for Monsieur Murphy," Gautier directed.

For the second time today, Lily was on the verge of blurting out an imprudent objection. Tears blistered her eyes, but she sucked them back, like a sponge wicking water, and stiffened her knees beneath the ankle-length gray skirt. She understood that her fulsome sadness was unwarranted. Then again, even though she hardly knew the man, he had been consistently genial to her. She had every right to mourn the loss of the one and only bright spot in this tenuous and tedious job.

Gautier said, "Madame, is there anything there you need?"

"I didn't need anything in that room, including him, even when he was alive."

While Barousse hurried over to secure the door, Lily drew in a long breath and held it as she wrote, in shorthand, *Mr. Murphy not needed.* Gautier took the time to record something in his own notebook.

Ted Wycliffe, balanced like a tripod on his rhinoceros-horn walking stick, was blinking rapidly and making jerky movements with his free hand. Surely his distress was caused by his cousin's frankness, not the sentiment. Although the Murphys occasionally pantomimed civility, anyone familiar with them knew their discourse was habitually marred by rancor. *Uxorious* could no more describe Mr. Murphy than *submissive* would his wife.

Mrs. Murphy pulled an angora scarf from one of the boxes lined with lavender tissue paper sharing the sofa with her. "I want to know what you think, Teddy. What color is this?"

This time, he appeared only moderately discomfited by the inappropriateness of the question. "Maroon."

"I think it's more a burgundy, wouldn't you say?"

Gautier allowed the cousin to chime his agreement before reentering the conversation. "Madame," he said, "did your husband usually carry cash?"

She refolded the scarf and placed it on her lap before answering, "Cash? Of course he carried cash. He insisted on cash, never used bank drafts. I told him time after time he shouldn't carry all that money on him. Teddy, you heard me. I knew he would be mugged for it one day, but it made him feel important. Always asking if someone could change a hundred-dollar bill just so he could make a show of how thick the wad in his money clip was. He always kept a thousand-dollar bill tucked in his wallet too, in case he wanted something extra."

"There was no cash, no money clip, no wallet in his room," Gautier said.

"That figures. He might as well leave me the same way he met me, not a penny on him."

Lily kept her gaze locked on her stenographer's book. That last statement had taken her aback. She had assumed the barge-loads of furs and diamonds and mountains of *bric à brac* were the bribes Mr. Murphy paid his wife to stay out of his way and to act as an advertisement for his success. She knewlittle about the couple's finances, but she thought he was engaged in several large-scale enterprises, such as mining and shipping, while his wife enjoyed a private fortune of her own. In the correspondence leading up to the job, queries concerning Lily's bookkeeping skills had raised the hope that she would be given responsibilities which required more than a knowledge of the alphabet. She did verify, record, and file the invoices for the household expenses and epic shopping adventures, but she had no idea whose disbursements funded their disposition. To this day, Mrs. Murphy continued to write her own checks and balance her own accounts, and all her husband's affairs were managed by his personal accountant and attorney.

"Do you think it was a robbery, Chief Inspector?" Wycliffe pressed. He beamed with expectation, like a child trying to guess what he was getting for Christmas.

Gautier kept his eyes on the widow. "You believe someone killed him for his cash?" he asked.

She snorted rudely. "In Monte Carlo? I'm supposed to know? You tell me."

"He was found by his valet?" Gautier asked, still addressing Mrs. Murphy.

"I already told you exactly that. I was in Cannes the last five days and returned this morning by train. A terrible trip, terrible, all the way home." She turned to glower at her cousin. "*All* the way home. More will be said about that later, Teddy." She took a long pause, either to allow the full extent of her trauma to settle into her cousin's consciousness or else to rewind the stem of her indignation. "The first-class car, full of Germans or French, something foreign, yapping and pointing, all of them sounding like they were gargling phlegm. And all of it for nothing." Another fierce glare at Wycliffe put the full-stop on the statement.

"I can tell you, there's nothing worthwhile in Cannes, not even if you count the Russian royalty who are supposed to be there in droves. You couldn't prove it by me. And the shops are miserably stocked, not one decent Sèvres jardinière. I did send for the dressmaker recommended by the Baroness Ephrussi de Rothschild." The mention of this name was accompanied by a scowl in Barousse's direction. "I ordered three traveling costumes to be made up and sent over." She straightened with satisfaction, as if this purchase constituted the equivalent of a decisive hit with her foil.

Despite the announcement that Cannes held nothing worthwhile, Lily was estimating how long it would take to sort, proof, and record receipts from a five-day expedition. She wouldn't know until instructed which purchases were to be delivered to the hotel and what would go into storage for shipping later. With someone else, half the jumble could have been dumped into the Mediterranean, and it would never have been missed. But Mrs. Murphy would have noticed if a demitasse spoon went astray. She regularly audited the swelling inventory. Once, she caught an error in the number of pieces in a silver service, and several times she had provided the details for an illegible document.

The complaint rolled on. "And then I get home, or here, back to here, and what? This. I was exhausted from listening to those Germans or Russians or whatever they were. I certainly didn't need to be greeted by this."

Lily assembled a look of compassion. How inconsiderate of Mr. Murphy to go and get himself shot when he must have known his tender-half would return distraught and depleted from days of spending enormous sums of money, hours of traveling first-class with persons who didn't speak English, and God only knew what other travails of the body, mind, and spirit.

"You traveled to Cannes alone?" Gautier asked.

"No, I went there with the Sturdivants, the Henry Charles Sturdivants, I shouldn't need to say, of New York City. That's in the United States, you know. We traveled in their private railway carriage." She focused again on her cousin. "Teddy, remind me to tell you about the places they've been, all of last year sailing around the world on his yacht. He named it the *Caraway*. That's how clever he is. He sent the yacht back to America, and they're taking the White Star home. I told them they would be sorry. I told them about that vile trip we had coming over. I told them they should take the Hamburg Amerika Liner not the White Star. It's sure to be smoother."

It was a pity, Lily thought, Mrs. Murphy hadn't known before they left the States that the flag the vessel flew controlled the weather and the seas.

Although Mrs. Murphy might believe the Sturdivants' around-the-world itinerary and numerous ports of call to be the sum of all imaginable good, no one else in the room seemed to share this opinion. Wycliffe managed to appear only mildly discomfited by her pattering-on while Barousse nodded at the ornate plaster-ceiling like a craftsman about to give a bid for its restoration. For his part, Gautier waited with sublime patience for this digression into the irrelevant to end, his sober eyes fixed all the while on the speaker. Lily sneaked a look at the watch pinned to her bodice. No wonder her stomach was rumbling.

She drew herself back to full attention when Mrs. Murphy's trumpeting of the Sturdivants' triumphs came to an end.

Gautier allowed the silence to soak in before asking, "The valet, Michael Gallagher, was here when you arrived?"

Another withering glare placed the blame for the man's unbearable persistence in dwelling on that unpleasantness squarely on her cousin. "Didn't Mr. Wycliffe tell you what happened?" Mrs. Murphy said.

Her tone would have made an iceberg shiver, but Gautier

looked like a bored lecturer waiting for the answer to the same question he had put to his students dozens of times before. "If you would please to tell me yourself," he said.

She expelled an exasperated breath and ostentatiously turned her head to gaze out the window, a pose clearly intended to comment on the incalculable depths of the man's stupidity. The chief inspector, however, was equal to the occasion. His features remained placid as his eyes focused steadily on her. Forgetting her gnawing stomach, Lily counted the number of seconds that elapsed during the impasse.

After ninety-six seconds, Mrs. Murphy shifted her back and straightened the lace around her collar, then said, "Mr. Wycliffe already told you. I found that man standing by the window over there and, if this can be believed, smoking a cigarette." She again selected her cousin to protest this outrage to. "Smoking in *my* sitting room. He told me I should send for the police because Mr. Murphy had been shot."

Gautier said nothing, waiting for her to play out her own scene. If the role were Lily's, she would have put a small quiver in her voice at the end of the last sentence. Certainly, a little more sorrow and a little less offended convenience might have gone a long way in helping her case with the inspector. But Lily had worked for Mrs. Murphy long enough to know she was not deliberately being offensive. Madeline Murphy sincerely believed that everyone not her social or economic equal was a helot. Therefore, she saw no reason for squandering any agreeableness on Gautier.

"I sent the insolent incompetent away. I sent him to fetch Teddy, Mr. Wycliffe."

Once again, Lily thought of Bridget Rose. Had she reported for work as usual this morning, or had Michael Gallagher waylaid his wife beforehand? She hoped no one would bring up the question now, not before she had a chance to eat. Her stomach's rumbling was growing louder.

"Did you go into Mr. Murphy's room?" Gautier asked.

"Mr. Wycliffe came, and he had you called," Mrs. Murphy said. Her hand was stroking the angora scarf as if it were a cat.

Gautier appeared willing to wait until sunset for a direct answer to his question when Barousse audibly cleared his throat. "I-if Madame would like to be moved to another suite," he said, "I shall be pleased to see what is available."

"Moving is too much trouble," she said. "But I'm not paying for those rooms." She tilted her chin in the direction of her husband's chambers. "No one's using them."

Barousse's professional demeanor altered not a whit although a flash of something electrical passed between him and Gautier. This, Lily deciphered as agreement over the woman's meanness, in every sense of that word. At the same time, it was difficult to understand how Mrs. Murphy could seem utterly unfazed by the fact that a man had been shot in the suite she occupied. That, even without taking into account that the man was her husband.

"O-of course," Barousse said, "I shall see to it."

Half-listening to Gautier tell Barousse he would also want to speak to the valet. Lily made another note, to review the charges for Mr. Murphy's room when she filed the week's statement from the hotel. She placed a question mark beside the date. Beginning last night or today? That thought set her adrift in her feelings once more. Mr. Murphy had died, very recently, yet no one seemed to be expressing the smallest interest in the simple sadness of that fact. She had been the last to leave the bedchamber. First, she latched the balcony door. Then, still perplexed by the lack of a sketch artist on the scene, she assured herself that the doctor had already disturbed the body's original position. Therefore, despite her mingled feelings of embarrassment, dread, and futility, she had passed close enough to the bed to reach out and spread the cover over the exposed bare foot.

Gautier turned abruptly to Mrs. Murphy and said, "Madame, do you have your train ticket?"

Barousse's head came to a standstill, and Mrs. Murphy's hand on the scarf froze. She looked up with the air of a person who has been goaded beyond all endurance. "Don't be an idiot," she said. Her eyes shifted to Wycliffe, as though he were supposed to pull the item from his pocket. In return, his eyes seemed to plead with her. She turned back to Gautier's unwavering gaze. "Am I compelled to produce it?" she asked.

"If you please, I wish to see it."

"No."

"I beg your pardon, Madame. Do you mean that you do not have your ticket or that you decline to satisfy my request?"

"I? I? I satisfy *you*?"

"Inspector," Wycliffe interjected, "if you please, Mrs. Murphy's ticket will be sent over as soon as it has been located. But is this necessary right now? After all, you must know my cousin has endured a terrible shock."

Lily dutifully recorded a reminder about the ticket and forced back her reflections on the widow's manifestations of terrible shock. While Wycliffe's proposal lingered in the air, her pencil drew small circles beside the completed notation. The circles grew larger and larger. The pencil slowed. She was thinking like a docile servant, not like a detective. What if she were not willing to give her employer the benefit of the doubt? The thought of Little Beauty returned and along with it, another startling possibility. The girl had not appeared in the garden today. She always took morning walks in the garden when Mrs. Murphy resumed residency at the hotel.

The thought was unthinkable, but Lily allowed it. What if Little Beauty had been murdered too?

It was at this moment the chief inspector chose to raise the matter of the paste necklace found in Mr. Murphy's overcoat.

# Thursday, March 12, 1914

NEARING THE COMPLETION OF HIS ASCENT FROM LA Condamine, Paul paused to catch his rasping breath. To his left was the Hôtel de Paris. Directly ahead were the tall black, gold-festooned doors that were the entrance to Garnier's Monte Carlo Opera. Down a short run of steps on his right, the Casino's lengthy terrace overlooked another, wider promenade where throngs of Kodakers and daytrippers streamed, arm in arm or beneath parasols. Beyond the gleaming white balustrades, the hills of the Italian coast, smudged blue by distance, gave the scene an enlarged context, like the painted backdrop of a stage. A short distance offshore, a flock of seagulls circled like buzzards above a small launch wallowing in the tide. The muffled sounds of gunshots arose from the Tir aux pigeons, the large, graveled semicircle constructed on the rocks below the railroad tracks and used for trapshooting live pigeons. It was said that every now and again, one of those bespoke birds succeeded in defying its fate by wheeling out over the sea and escaping, but Paul had never witnessed one of those miracles.

He might have observed that the sea was in a lazy mood this afternoon, shifting and rolling, seldom rousing itself to white-fringe a breaker, but the sea's changing temperaments had long since ceased to interest him, just as he had come to disdain all the surrounding excrescences of the landscape—the hotels, the villas, the promenades, the Casino, the killing-ground beneath. Granted, he hadn't felt that way the first time he saw this bijou of a country, nearly four years ago, but at that time, he would have embraced the Somali Desert as the new Eden.

He released a cough against the rumpled handkerchief and checked it for blood before returning it to his trousers and pulling out his pocketwatch. Twelve minutes after two, twelve minutes late. Two more months, perhaps less, and his life would no longer be strapped to the minute-hand on someone else's watch. But two more months, perhaps less, did nothing for the present. Brushing his fingertips along the pale scar just below his left earlobe, he resumed the climb.

Arriving at the Casino, Paul ignored the office where supplicants applied for admittance to Monte Carlo's *raison d'être* and approached the *vestiaire*, removing his overcoat and at the same time ensuring there was no loose change in the pockets.

"Good day, Raoul," he said to the boy behind the counter. "Who is here this afternoon?"

"The Gand Duke Red-and-Black, if you can believe it."

"Grand Duke Red-and-Black" was the *nom de jeu* conferred by the Casino personnel on a nobleman whose surname was one of those twelve-syllabled Russian affairs. Paul lifted his eyebrows to signal his appreciation of Raoul's amazement. In the pantheon of the profligate, any member of the Russian aristocracy would have to be ranked above Zeus. Their love of losing huge sums at the tables, limitless as that seemed, nevertheless was surpassed by their love of staying drunk. Most of them remained strenuously employed during the afternoons downing superhuman quantities of port, to ease themselves into shape for drinking gallons of spirits and magnums of champagne all night. To find one of them in the

Casino before dark was as rare as finding one of them sober.

"You don't say," Paul responded, smoothing back his hair with his hand as he gazed around. Since the Sporting Club and the Salon Privée, the more exclusive gambling venues, were not open at this hour, even such a spectacularly first-class personage as the grand duke was in danger of being swallowed by the numbers of Cook's tourists who populated the Rooms in the afternoons.

"But yes," Raoul said, "and wait until I tell you." He drew his tongue along his upper lip. "With him, La Belle Otero."

Paul's smile was indulgent. He liked this boy, a little gossipy, perhaps, but as a nephew of Olivier Broliquet, he came by that honestly. "Pull your tongue back into your mouth," Paul said. "You cannot afford the spit to polish one of those jewels on her breastplate."

He interrupted himself to deliver a deep bow to the white-haired woman shuffling past, bent by age and leaning heavily on a walking stick. She was his favorite among the elderly creatures who arrived early at the Rooms to lay claim to a seat. Once settled, she would assiduously mark down the runs of the game as though pursuing a complicated strategy of play. Later, after the crowds thickened around the table, she would sublet her chair to the first person who casually slipped a Louis into her palm. Several times, this charming old lady had asked Paul if they had ever been lovers. Each time, he answered they had not. "To my everlasting sorrow," he always added.

A voice from behind prevented his addressing her this afternoon. "Monsieur Barousse wishes to see you in his office, immediately."

Paul didn't have to turn to know which doorman had spoken. It was the one who always looked like he was fighting back a smirk. Knowing it was a facial tick, not an emotion, made it no less annoying. Raoul passed back the coat and hat as Paul sorted through the implications of the summons. He had received his weekly flogging from Barousse only yesterday, and the copy he had made of the current list of the Society's hotel guests was in his pocket, thank God. He couldn't remember anyone particularly noteworthy on it. A few minor European and Russian royalty, several fabulously wealthy Americans, the usual constellations of British aristocrats. Whom had he overlooked? Regardless, it was decidedly a bad day to be called upon to defend himself, his brain a lump of lard. If he were lucky, Barousse was demanding this extemporaneous audience just so he could rough up his underling for a little sport – easier, no doubt, than shooting trapped pigeons.

# Thursday, March 12, 1914
## HÔTEL DE PARIS

Outside the gilt-lettered door to the manager's office, Paul finished another round of coughing before rapping. He usually entered his tormentor's lair with a smile nailed down so tightly not even a typhoon could rip it loose, but he discovered he couldn't engineer this feat twice in one week, not this week at any rate. It was enough just to keep the curiosity out of his expression when he saw that a man and a woman were with Barousse. All were standing. Without glancing in Paul's direction, Barousse pulled out his watch, studied it longer than necessary, then snapped the case shut and cleared his throat.

"Monsieur Wycliffe," he said, "m-may I introduce to you Monsieur Newcastle, one of the subdirectors for the Commissariat of Surveillance at the Monte Carlo Casino."

Upon hearing himself introduced by his official title, Paul was heartened. Possibly the affair, whatever it was, concerned Casino business, and it wasn't going to be like two weeks ago, when the problem was a duchess with an incontinent borzoi that needed an outing each morning.

Recalling that Wycliffe was a guest at the Hôtel de Paris, Paul ran the American through the baffles of his mind. He had appeared in the Casino only two or three times during the past few weeks. He was neither a person of importance nor a big spender. The Surveillance crew had tagged him as unlikely to be trouble. Even though he hadn't attracted attention with his betting, he was hard to miss. For one thing, there was the twisting gait, as though one leg were shorter than the other, and that toupee never failed to startle.

This afternoon, Wycliffe wore the same pepper-and-salt waistcoat Paul had previously seen him in. The make of the suit and the leather of his shoes pronounced him a man of adequate means. The missing metal ferrule on the horned cane still had not been replaced.

While the counterformality of introducing Wycliffe to Paul was being extended, he took in the young woman. If she had been in the Casino, it was when he was not present because he was certain he had never seen her before. Unlike those women who fall just short of beauty, this one had overshot the mark in every way. A couple inches shy of six feet in height, she towered over her companion. Her thick-lashed eyes were theatrically large and set too far apart, and the dark eyebrows would have benefited from a tweezing. The mouth was overly generous, and he admired the effort it must take to maintain that severe expression. The slightest movement of her lips carved a deep dimple in each check and had the effect of softening her appearance almost to beauty. A rail-straight back held broad shoulders above a narrow waist. Strong hips were suggested beneath the slim skirt. She wore no gloves or jewelry, and her straight brown hair was pulled into a bun. No one troubled himself to introduce her.

"W-we had an unfortunate incident with a guest," Barousse said, nodding agreement with himself. "Monsieur Joseph Murphy of San Francisco was found expired in his room."

Paul slapped a clamp on his neutral expression and

waited. Had they been discussing a connection between Joseph Murphy and himself before he arrived? Impossible. Wycliffe's mouth was pinched, like he had been charged with a distasteful but necessary duty. His gaze remained on Barousse, but when the woman's eyes connected with Paul's, she did not avert hers. Paul, to his own consternation, did, a sure sign of his uneasiness. Impossible, he told himself again.

Barousse continued, "T-the Sûreté Publique have taken charge. Monsieur Wycliffe is a relative of Madame Murphy. She wishes him to be a part of any investigation. The question of a robbery has been raised. As you know, the Society's hotels never have robberies, so we want to help our guests settle the question to their own satisfaction."

So that was all it was. Paul was being detailed to play nanny to a tribe of Americans, so Chief Inspector Gautier wouldn't be bothered by the meddlesome fools. This could be worse than watching a whole pack of borzois relieve themselves.

Barousse said, "Monsieur Newcastle, you know the guest to whom I am referring, yes?"

Didn't he just? Of all the guests who had to decide to die this week, why did it have to be that one? "Yes," Paul said, using a minimum of breath in order to avoid inspiring more coughing. "I shall be pleased to be of assistance."

"G-good. I expect you will ask the other men at the Casino what they saw," Barousse said.

"Mr. Barousse," Wycliffe said, "Mrs. Murphy appreciates your cooperation in this matter, but I told you I don't need assistance from your staff. I will handle this on my own."

"T-thank you, but I fear I must insist," Barousse said. "Monsieur Newcastle is the best our organization has. He has proved himself to be excellent at resolving complicated situations in the past."

Considering that Barousse usually treated the organization's best like he was a mange-blighted pariah, Paul thought this praise distinctly lacked sincerity. Besides, he had caught the flash of triumph in the manager's eyes. This assignment wasn't about Murphy. The couple either had a rack borrowed from a medieval torture-chamber or else they had erected a stake and laid by a fagot in anticipation of roasting him alive. There would have been a place in the Grand Inquisition for Barousse.

"I'm sure he's excellent," Wycliffe said, his tone plainly expressing the opposite belief. "As they say, the proof will be in the pudding."

Cannibalism, it was then. Paul had always suspected the Americans of exactly that.

# Thursday, March 12, 1914
## HÔTEL DE PARIS

WHEN TED WYCLIFFE THREW OPEN THE DOOR AND stepped aside to allow his two guests to enter, Lily's first thought was that this sitting room must be the despair of the hotel's chambermaids, if they ever set foot in it. Corner to corner, wall to wall, the floor was strewn with stacks of pasteboard boxes, newspapers, magazines, albums, valises, and all manner of other, undifferentiated clutter. The chairs, sofas, tables, any and every flat surface, bore more piles. A few stacks were bundled with twine, but most evinced no discernible attempt at organization.

Kicking aside a clump of newspapers in front of one of the sofas, Wycliffe said, "Take a seat, Paul."

"Much obliged, Mr. Wycliffe," Newcastle said, without moving towards the proffered spot.

"Call me Ted. Take a seat." It was more command than invitation.

Picking her way through the jumble, Lily saw more papers spilling from the half-opened drawers of the writing desk. The lid was off the inkwell; the blotting mat was a solid stain. The only things that appeared to have been arranged with deliberation were the playing cards laid on the breakfast table for an unfinished game of Patience. She positioned herself at a distance from the men, her arms pressed against her stomach to keep it from howling like a wolf.

The Casino man was looking around like a prospective buyer, oblivious to the slovenliness, interested only in the room's dimensions and window-casements.

Wycliffe was rooting around in a box atop a tottering tower of folders. The stack swayed beneath his furious stabs and probes, but to Lily's amazement, it didn't collapse. Without uttering another word, he disappeared behind a door that presumably led to the bedchamber.

She turned back to Newcastle, who stood with a smile tugging at the corners of his mouth.

"I regret I have not had the honor, Miss ...."

"Lily."

His silence indicated he was waiting for the rest, but she refused to gratify him with a surname. Let her new master's abysmal manners remain unredressed.

"Lily," he conceded with a nod. "Enchanted, I'm sure."

Although his face remained serious, his dark eyes gleamed with merriment, leaving her with an inchoate sense of being mocked.

"Perhaps you have discovered that, over here, persons are not introduced as a matter of course as they are in your country," he said.

She made no response.

"Miss Lily, would you be so kind as to excuse my sitting while you stand?"

"Certainly, Mr. Newcastle. Do make yourself at home."

He placed his homburg and folded overcoat on the back of the sofa before taking a seat. "Paul. If you like, Miss Lily."

Earlier, in Barousse's office, Lily had thought Paul Newcastle appeared ordinary, even nondescript. Now upon closer inspection, she could see that, despite the tell-tale signs of advancing age, he was an attractive man, firm-jawed with clear-cut features. The reddened nose and puffiness around the eyes might be attributable to the cold he obviously suffered with, yet it was equally possible he was fraying from dissoluteness. His collar and cuffs were brightly starched. The suit was well fitted. The full head of dark hair was graying at the temples in the distinguished manner. He was probably vain about his hair. Men that age who weren't balding usually were.

Wycliffe lurched back into the room and stopped behind the second, unoccupied sofa. He gripped the back with such ferocity it was difficult to tell whether he was holding himself up or the furniture down.

"Here, take this," he said, offering Lily an accountant's journal in his outstretched hand. "I want you to keep notes for the investigation in this, not in that stenographer's notepad of yours. I want them in longhand in this journal."

When she pointed out that her records would be more accurate and comprehensive if taken first in shorthand and later typed, it seemed to take him several long seconds to work out her meaning.

"All right," he answered, "take them in shorthand, but transcribe them by longhand into that journal by the end of every day. That's the form I need them in."

Lily regarded him with open astonishment. Did the great William Burns have to take orders from a Luddite? There was a thin logic in his directive. Among this welter, a journal might be marginally easier to locate than stray sheets of paper or even a file folder.

"Start with your notes from this morning. And I want you to talk to Bridget Rose before the police do. Disgruntled servants are a dangerous source of domestic intelligence. She's likely to say anything."

Mrs. Murphy hadn't taken her maid with her on the most recent trip to Cannes. It was the first excursion for which she had failed to do so. Five days ago, Lily had put it down to her employer's tiring of the woman's churlish temperament, but now she no longer was sure.

Wycliffe said, "I want to know exactly what she saw and heard. Write it all down in that book like I told you. You may need to help her remember exactly what she saw and heard. Make sure she knows what to say and what not to say to the police. Make sure she knows it's not necessary to be perfectly forthcoming about the Murphys' private lives, especially when that has nothing to do with the matter at hand. Maddie doesn't need some charwoman giving the officials the wrong impression."

Lily pretended to write something in her notebook. What kind of idiot would place the suggestion that the truth needed to be hidden directly into Paul Newcastle's ears?

"Record only the facts," he continued. "This is not the place to express your opinions and prejudices. Your job is to discover the truth, not to invent it. Give me the facts. I will draw the conclusions."

A good thing, too, if he didn't want her opinion. Moreover, she would speak with Bridget Rose. She had her own questions she wanted answered. But she would *not* encourage the woman to lie.

"In due time," Wycliffe added, "I will need you to send some telegrams for me."

She continued scribbling nonsense. Eventually, she looked up but made no other acknowledgement of the insulting dictates.

"I don't have a journal for you," Wycliffe said to Newcastle. "I wasn't expecting you to be working for me."

The Casino man's stiff upper-lip was nothing short of a

marvel to behold, not the slightest hint of the soul-shattering disappointment that announcement must have provoked. On the other hand, it was hard to believe there wasn't a trainload of journals stashed in the crush surrounding them.

"Like I told Barousse, I don't need help from his establishment. As they say, too many cooks spoil the soup. There might be something you can do. I'll have to think about it."

Wycliffe pushed himself off the sofa, slowly straightened his back by pressing his palm against a spot above his waist, and made his way to the table holding the siphon and decanters of liquor. As Lily's eyes followed him, she could feel Newcastle's attention on her. In Barousse's office, she believed he had calculated the precise weight of her workbag and the exact number of buttons on her gray dress, but she hadn't flattered herself that his interest came from attraction or admiration. Rather, she thought he had attempted to read the situation through her. She turned her gaze back to him, canted her head, and gave a half shrug.

"Drink, Paul?" Wycliffe said.

"No, thank you."

Lily decided she might as well set some ground-rules right away. "I'll have a whiskey and soda, if you please, Ted," she said. She couldn't know if the look he returned was brought on by her request for liquor or her presumption in using his Christian name. Whatever was behind the look, she enjoyed it. Her pleasure, however, was cut short by guilt. With the cane, he would have to make two trips to carry two glasses.

"Here," he said, indicating the glass he had set, none too gently, beside the bottles on the table.

She should have known such a gallant would never permit a lady to suffer pangs of remorse over her lack of consideration.

After Ted made his way back to the sofa, it took him several extensive maneuvers to place the tumbler of whiskey on the table, to lower himself onto the cushion along with elaborate assistance from his cane, and to position the cane at the perfect angle against the cushion's edge before again embracing the tumbler. It was better than watching a circus contortionist.

Leaning forward, he said, "There's something that needs to be cleared up here at the get-go, Paul. Barousse said Mr. Murphy *expired*. In point of fact, he was shot."

The whiskey hit the bottom of Lily's empty stomach with a scorching blast. She barely stopped herself from releasing a sharp whistle as she rocked forward. So much for showing Ted Wycliffe what she was made of.

Newcastle said, "Whatever that question is, I assume it has been given to the Monaco police. Mr. Barousse said they had taken charge."

"They have, and I'm not going to interfere with their investigation unless it becomes necessary to get it done right. I'm willing to wait and see what they come back with. But, as they say, dead men tell no tales. Take my word for it. Joe's murderer will be caught – and punished."

Placing the glass on an unopened carton of blotters, Lily began a letter in shorthand to Fran to capture the day's events she didn't want to forget. Turner and Jameson had paid their $15 for *Frederick Wagner's Detective Agency* correspondence course, but much of what she had observed today wasn't included in its "ten lessons and seventy-five methods." For instance there was the loupe Gautier carried and the attention given to the shoes. There was his equanimity when handling Wycliffe and Mrs. Murphy. Sherlock Holmes' unflappability made good reading. Gautier's was true restraint. And there was that superb timing in dropping the bombshells about the railway ticket and the necklace. And the necklace, yes, there was the necklace, Lily's private patch for sleuthing.

"Now see here, Paul," Ted said. "Don't think you're dealing with some rank amateur. Barousse didn't make my credentials perfectly clear. I am a detective by profession. Reluctant as I am to, as they say, blow my own horn, you should know I was the top operative for the Pinkerton National Detective Agency for over ten years. Surely you know what Pinkertons is?" Receiving no answer, he went on, "If you know anything at all, you probably think of them as bounty hunters and tamers of the Wild West–Jesse James and all those characters. But that was in the early days. The history is too voluminous to go into here and now. Suffice it to say, Pinkertons has more active agents than the U.S. has soldiers in its army. Our operatives have always gone where the criminals go. We infiltrate their organizations, and we dispatch the scum ourselves when necessary."

Lily forgot her hunger. For the first time since she had laid eyes on this man, he was saying something interesting. She hadn't been included in the accusation of total ignorance concerning the Pinkerton Detective Agency, but that was because Ted Wycliffe didn't consider her at all. Had he done so, he would have been wrong. She knew a good deal about the organization.

Behind the explosive labor disputes in Pennsylvania's anthracite coal fields in the 1870s were the years of merciless exploitation of men, women, and children by cabals of greedy employers, crosscut with episodes of retributive violence and internecine betrayal. The magnitude of villainy, disloyalty, corruption, and bloodshed encompassed within that saga would have done honor to the House of Borgia. The events spanned years and ended with spectacular murder trials, yet they had not rated so much as a paragraph in the history books at Mount Saint Joseph Academy. Nevertheless, each year, Sister Ignatius required her new pupils to prepare a twenty-page essay on the subject. The Catholic clergy had been active in the conflict, and Lily suspected the old nun had been peripherally involved and was unwilling to allow the memory to grow extinct. While most of the students centered their assignment on the Molly Maguires, Lily focused on the Pinkerton agent who was accepted into that collection of murderous thugs or martyred saints, depending upon the perspective, and whose testimony led to the executions of their leaders. It was in researching the infiltrator, James McParlan, that she had tripped across Kate Warne, Pinkerton's first female detective and the woman who, in an instant, set fire to Lily's life's ambition.

"I am quite well known and highly respected by the Chicago Police Department," Ted was saying. "They call me in on the QT whenever a case has them stumped. I field inquiries and requests for help from all around the country, but I don't work outside Chicago. It has quite enough bank jobs and blackmailers to occupy my idle hours.

"Have you heard of the Drawdown Gang? That was a big case, Lake Forest Savings Bank. I'm the one who led the police to John Shinburg. I can't tell you the details without revealing trade secrets, but suffice it to say, when his rooms on Randolph Street were searched, they not only found a complete workshop for manufacturing burglar's tools and making wax impressions of keys, but over $50,000 in stolen bonds as well. Once again, the criminals learned that, as they say, crime does not pay, especially when the right man is on their trail."

"Just so," Newcastle said. "Now, about the robbery here at the Hôtel de Paris, what's missing?"

Ted looked blankly at Lily. Clearly, this was not the expected response to an account of his Olympian feats.

"A necklace," she prompted.

"Necklace. Yes, a necklace, the necklace," he said.

Fighting back an audible expression of exasperation, she said, "It's a diamond necklace with an emerald centerpiece. A paste copy was found in Mr. Murphy's coat."

"That's right," Ted said. "That could be, that's where you might be of use, Paul. The necklace must be recovered. It is, as they say, a pearl of great price." He gave his head a shake. "But it's not a pearl. It is an emerald. Diamonds, too. It belonged to my grandmother, my father's mother. It was given to my cousin's father because he was the first to marry, that's all. This is where you can be useful. You can find out what happened to my grandmother's necklace. Someone must be trying to sell it. Find out who that someone is."

Lily felt the distinct sting of resentment. As long as she was stuck in this hateful job, she had decided she might as well churn butter. She intended to convince Ted to use her as something more than a scribe, and she had laid claim to the mystery of the necklace. She was going to ask around about it. She had a heart-wrenching tale of the beloved, dead mother and the scoundrel of a stepfather who must have pawned her only heirloom. Better than the melodrama, however, was Little Beauty. She was the person most likely to know something about the genuine necklace, and Lily was the only person in the room with a bead on her—for what that was worth.

The final thought brought her back to earth. What might the discovery be worth? Flexing her muscles as a detective was one thing, but what she needed was money. The partnership was two months behind with the rent for the space Fran used as an office during the day and as a bedroom at night, and the landlord wasn't the only creditor with whom they were in arrears. Richard Parr received a bonus of $100,000 for tracking the culprits in the famous sugar case, but Lily's recovering the necklace probably wouldn't merit a "thank you." On the other hand, it might lead to a few extra months of employment. After examining the handwriting in the files and the rate at which these changed, she deduced that being Mrs. Murphy's secretary was akin to being Mrs. Bluebeard. She had already outlasted all her predecessors by more than a month, and the firm of Turner and Jameson could not afford for her to be without a paycheck even briefly.

"What makes you think it was stolen?" Newcastle asked.

"It's not there, is it?" Ted said.

"Jewelry changes hands often in Monte Carlo."

"Like I told you, a large emerald center stone with diamonds. I'll get the precise description from Mrs. Murphy."

"Value?" Newcastle asked.

"I'll get that from her too. I told you, the sentimental value is priceless."

"In that case, you should offer a ransom."

Lily's hand flew to her mouth, to hide her smile. She doubted Ted noticed, but she couldn't escape the feeling that the Casino man kept watching her from the corner of his eye. She camouflaged her action by drawing her fingers across her forehead as though troubled by a headache.

"That's ridiculous. We shouldn't have to pay to get back what belongs to us," Ted said.

"How much of a ransom, Paul?" Lily asked. The figure couldn't be too large.

He glanced at her but gave his answer to Ted. "If its value is sentimental, a deal more than it can be pawned for."

"That's ridiculous," Ted repeated.

Newcastle seemed indifferent to the response. "One necklace?" he asked. "Nothing else?"

It was a good question, the answer to which should have put paid to the idea that anyone other than Mr. Murphy had taken the authentic one. Mrs. Murphy kept dozens of pieces of jewelry in a strongbox in her room. Why would an outsider take only the one?

Before Ted could answer, Lily said, "Paul, how does one advertise such a ransom?"

"Many of these kinds of negotiations are never advertised. Sometimes the criminals take the initiative and contact the owners or their insurers. In fact, this happens more often than victims are apt to admit. Not only jewels, but bearer bonds, antique coins, stamps, incriminating letters, all manner of valuables. Perhaps Mr. Wycliffe would want to tell you about Pinkerton's role in recovering Pierpont Morgan's *Duchess of Devonshire*."

When Ted ignored this suggestion, Paul repeated his former question.

"No," Ted said, "it wasn't just the necklace. There's also the matter of some cash. A solid-gold money-clip and a wallet that had over a thousand dollars in it."

When Paul excused himself in order to cough, Lily returned to contemplating the anomaly with his nose which she had noticed each time he turned away. Viewed straight-on, it looked classically straight, evenly proportioned, but in profile, it appeared stubbed and flat, like a pugilist's. An interesting effect, it gave his appearance an unalloyed masculinity seldom found in very handsome men.

"Pardon me," Paul said, returning his handkerchief to his pocket. "How may I be of assistance with that?"

"Isn't it obvious?"

"Enlighten me, if you will."

"Do I need to tell you everything you're supposed to do? I thought Mr. Barousse said you were some kind of expert."

Lily rolled her lips inward. Even a child would understand the futility of recovering currency.

"Cash is fungible," Paul explained. "Nothing is easier to get rid of without a trace. So that takes care of the cash. As for the clip, I doubt I will be permitted to go about turning out men's pockets on the off-chance they might have Joseph Murphy's money-clip."

This time, Lily focused on the posh accent. Possibly pure gold. Possibly pinchbeck. She was incapable of detecting the slips in diphthongs or variations in vocabulary that betrayed the metal's baseness. The large number of British subjects in Monte Carlo had provided her first extended exposure to their language. She strained to hear the rhythms and the subtleties in the sounds, but when she tried to imitate them, her words came out like clotted cream.

"So," Ted said, "what you're saying is that it would be like looking for a needle in a haystack. That should not be impossible for a skilled detective."

"I would say it's like looking for hay in a haystack."

Enough of this silly parrying. Lily wanted to eat, finish her work with Mrs. Murphy, and still have time to visit Little Beauty.

"Paul," she said, "you told Mr. Barousse you were familiar with Mr. Murphy. What had he done to attract your attention?"

His eyes, when turned on her again, were devoid of their former gaiety, and there was an ever-so-slight hesitation before he answered, "Nothing, Miss Lily. It is my job to know who our esteemed guests are. The Société des bains de mer owns the Casino concession and several of the better hotels. They are understandably concerned that their guests should enjoy their visits without suffering undue anxiety about the safety of their possessions."

She looked at Wycliffe. Having tossed back the last of his whiskey, he was occupying himself by rolling his cane back and forth between his hands, as though this exchange were irrelevant.

"How do you know who the hotels' guests are?" she asked.

"Many of the wealthier clients stay a month, often longer. Most of them return again and again. We know who they are, as do all the thieves and confidence men."

It was now that Lily recalled following the two men out of Barousse's office and across the hotel's lobby, beneath the enormous chandelier and past the equestrian statue of Louis XIV, with its much rubbed knee. Like a good squaw, she had maintained the requisite ten paces behind her braves until they arrived at the elevator. There, the operator's white-gloved hand pushed aside the clattering accordion gate with its iron fretwork to allow a tall, black-haired younger man to emerge from the gilded cage. She noticed Paul Newcastle take a step back, his eyes widened by alarm or surprise. The man glanced at the three of them but displayed no signs of recognition. Nothing to do with Mr. Murphy, she was sure, maybe someone Paul knew to be a crook or a con artist.

"Let me make this clear," Ted said before she could ask another question. "I'll take care of the murder. Your only concern, Paul, is the money and my grandmother's necklace. I certainly hope Mr. Barousse has not misplaced his confidence in you." His tone was one which might have been applied to a particularly dimwitted stable-boy or bootblack.

Paul Newcastle got to his feet and gathered his belongings. "Just so," he said.

The doorknob was turning in his hand when Ted added, "Be here again the day after tomorrow, Saturday, two o'clock. That should give you plenty of time to come up with something."

When Newcastle turned back, he looked at her, not Ted. "Until Saturday," he said. "Miss Lily, it has been a pleasure."

And, with a dip of his head in her direction, he was gone.

# Thursday, March 12, 1914
## MONTE CARLO CASINO

"Good day, Raoul," Paul said, handing over his hat and coat for the second time today.

"Good *evening*, Paul," Raoul said, lifting his chin towards the door and the gloaming of the spring day beyond it.

Leaving the vestibule, Paul entered the first gaming room, the Salon Renaissance. Its denizens were nothing like those pictured in the literature which relentlessly promoted the Casino's glamor. Tonight, he felt like a charter-member of this club, at one with the drooling invalid in the wheelchair, the consumptive woman with the claw-like hands, and the man with the missing arm, victim or villain of a distant war. The day had done as much to Paul, starting with that foul-mouthed Corsican, followed by the unscheduled meeting with Barousse, brought on by Joseph Murphy's death. Then there was the assignment to that American hyena, Wycliffe, and it wasn't over. There was still the need to lay eyes on the *bête noire* and dispose of the copy of the guest lists.

Realizing that he had been staring too long at the bald man whose red beard met his chest, Paul returned to the vestibule. He wasn't ready to undertake the night's work. In a day crowded with unsettling events, he had yet to come to grips with the most disturbing one. Hands down, that distinction went to the young man exiting the lift at the Hôtel de Paris. Was the bloody cold causing hallucinations? He didn't want to believe it was Sophie's boy. It couldn't be. He had put the *paid* stamp on that colossal disappointment over three years ago. It was more than a little irritating to think it should turn up again, here. However, after a lifetime of sizing up people with a glance, Paul trusted his instincts. Hundreds of thousands of pleasure-seekers swept through Monaco each season, part of the winter flood washing downward to escape the bitter cold in the north. Jonnie could have been caught up with the rest of the flow. He would never recognize his uncle, but Paul wanted to be prepared before another encounter and not overreact as he had this afternoon. Tomorrow, he would go out to Cap d'Ail and see about getting a definitive answer. Even without that question, however, he needed to pay a visit to Hervé Andreas.

The first time Joseph Murphy came into the Casino, he struck Paul as a rather unassuming man to be occupying a large suite at the Hôtel de Paris. Other than opal cufflinks, his appearance offered no flamboyant signs of wealth. However, in addition to a distorted right shoulder, which made his carriage noticeably lopsided, the American had made himself conspicuous by asking around for a place where he could go to play deep. He claimed he didn't like the Casino's 6,000-franc limit.

Most of these "explorers" Paul left alone, but Murphy had made noises about other requirements, and these made Paul decide the man would be worth steering in Hervé's direction. The referral was made anonymously, in a handwriting unlike his own, and because Paul was as talented at inserting items undetected into a man's pocket as he was at removing them, there was nothing to connect him with Murphy. He didn't even know if the American had taken the suggestion. Nevertheless, an important guest's desire for a greater challenge outside the Casino, while not uncommon, would have guaranteed the attention of the other *commissaires,* or surveillance men. Accordingly, an impromptu visit to Hervé's villa was required, to make sure there were no corners to be squared there.

Satisfied with this plan, Paul ambled across the Salon Renaissance and Salle Mauresque with their acres of gilding. He minutely straightened his shoulders and tilted his chin fractionally higher as he passed beneath the wide arched portal into the Salle Garnier. She was there, there at her usual table in the corner, sitting as she always did, facing the entrance where Paul stood. It was the first moment of something like happiness, or the first release of tension, he had felt all day. Even though his eyes continued to sweep the room like an auctioneer searching for bids, he could see her gold-chain purse lying on the green felt and her white-gloved fingers, already revealing signs of soil from handling coins. She must have arrived early tonight–a promising sign.

"Zero-three!" came the croupier's announcement of the last roll of the wheel. Faster than most eyes could follow or minds could comprehend, four miniature rakes shoved the coins and plaques toward the winners and swept the losing stakes off the table to take their place in the Society's coffers. Within seconds, the invitation for the next roll was issued, "Gentlemen, make your wagers!"

Nearing forty years of age, Céline Claudet remained a slim, attractive woman. Tonight, she wore the emerald-green gown which set off her green eyes, and the dark curls piled on top of her head were secured by a gold-filigreed comb. She pushed out a single Louis. The crinkling at the corners of her eyes sent Paul's hopes soaring, but when she withdrew her hand, it remained at rest on the green baize instead of touching the corner of her lips with the tip of her little finger.

Too bad. Very much, too bad. He could not think of a single night since their affair had begun last November when he would have appreciated those hours in her bedroom more. The bad mood he had been kneading earlier swelled and twisted until it contorted itself into an unwonted anger. He had never objected to the terms of their arrangement, to the circumstance of her life, but tonight, he not only resented the refusal, he resented the reason for the refusal most of all.

"Nothing more!" declared the croupier. The red-and-black wheel was spinning, the ball was clattering. No more stakes could be placed.

Paul remained at his post for four more spins of the wheel at Céline's table, allowing his anger to subside while his bored gaze tracked the movements of the persons at the room's other three tables as well as those of the onlookers pressing in. Because he was an undercover employee and she another man's mistress, they rarely spoke to one another here, and he never initiated a conversation. They did not have to feign ignorance of each other, only indifference. All the men on his team undoubtedly knew of the night at the beginning of the season when she had arrived after eleven o'clock, intoxicated and on the verge of making a scene. Paul had drawn up beside her and wordlessly guided her outside; whereupon, she descended into a crying jag. He had hailed a motorcab and accompanied her to a small villa at nearby Cap d'Ail. He returned to work immediately after seeing her home. However, what his men did not know was that, on her doorstep, she invited him inside.

"Next time," he said. And the next time, he had.

Moving from Salle Garnier to the first of the two Salles Touzet, his disheartenment was made complete by the sight of the man with the wild beard and severe underbite. His presence was not unexpected, but Paul wasn't capable just yet of downing another choking swallow of humiliation. His posture remained at ease and his face expressionless as his gaze slid off the bête noire like water off glass.

Since the age of five, when he had come to understand the danger to his accumulated wealth that lay in truthfully answering his father's interrogations about his street-earnings, Paul had been honing his skill at allowing his face, his eyes, his hands, his entire body to say exactly what he wanted them to say and no more. As a child, it had taken him a full year to settle on the correct level of inattention, somewhere between studied indifference and ostentatious distraction, which should be displayed around a person whose pocket he intended to pick. This evening, he spent a full and pleasant minute admiring a demimondaine in a revealing evening-gown before turning his back on the malformed leech sharing a space with her.

After completing his first orbit of the six gambling rooms, with a deliberate pass beneath *The Florentine Graces* so he could satisfy his habit of arching an eyebrow in their direction, Paul was ready to escape the Rooms' stifling heat and bad air. Upon entering the atrium, he immediately caught sight of Marcel Absel doing his imitation of nonchalance beside one of the beige-pink marble columns supporting the gallery overhead. Absel was Paul's counterpart in the Salon Privée. Because that newest room, constructed in 1910, claimed not only a more exclusive clientele, but superior ventilation as well, Paul determined Absel was here for a reason other than better air. After a short delay, Paul followed the other man up the staircase next to the *vestiaire*.

Absel exhaled a billow of gray smoke as Paul closed the door to a room reserved for employees, then announced, "The Commissariat arrested that one who was passing the false Louis and handed him over to the police."

"Was it was the one you identified?" Paul asked as he eased himself onto a chair.

Absel replied with a single nod.

Many of the Casino's personnel swore that, after a fortnight, they saw nothing but the same people coming around again and again, like the troops of a stage army. This could never be Absel's complaint. He did not see people merely as general types, such as tall or stout or old, but was adept at fastening on specific physical attributes, such as bulging eyes and nostril size, which could not be altered with make-up, lifts, or padding, and on minor decorative accoutrements, such as the height of heels, the quality of gloves, and brand of cigars. Add to this aptitude a remarkable memory, and the outcome was an outstanding *commissaire*, like Marcel Absel.

Lighting a second cigarette from the stub of the first, Absel went on, "The fool changed his suit coat each night, attached false beards and moustaches, used dyes, toupees, and glasses, wore lifts in his shoes, the works. He played at different tables, sat sometimes, stood at others, played left-handed, then right-handed, did everything he should have except for two things. He always wagered precisely two Louis, the false one beneath the true one, thereby halving his losses and doubling his gains, and he had a Masonic emblem on his watch-chain. It was usually out of sight, but he made the mistake now and then of checking the time. It took only three nights after we detected the first false Louis to pinpoint him as the source. The tables with the man who always wagered two Louis and wore a Masonic emblem were invariably the tables turning up with counterfeit money. Monsieur Maubert had him turn out his pockets. The false Louis exposed him completely."

Paul was listening, but at the same time he was trying to

come up with a way of asking Absel if a tall Englishman in his late twenties had been seen in the Privée Salle, without doing so in a way that would draw attention either to Jonnie or to Paul's interest in him.

Absel said, "Maubert has not fired Yvan Laurent. You must be shielding him."

"He's coming along."

"I was certain he was going to fire him after last week."

"He's coming along."

Absel ground out the cigarette in a gold-rimmed ashtray. "You are only forestalling the inevitable," he said without looking up.

Back in Salle Schmidt ten minutes later, Paul wandered purposefully between the tables, where people were stacked two to four layers deep behind the chairs. With each fall of a ball, waves of elation and dejection passed across the players like a wind through a field of tall grass. He weaved through the crowd, shifting sideways to make room for a couple squeezing their way in the opposite direction, stepping back to avoid a waiter. At one table, he concentrated on the players' hands, at another, on their eyes, at another, their mouths, automatically noting who was playing methodically and who was placing his bets with wild abandon. He remained on the lookout for anyone who appeared to be on the verge of becoming overtly peevish about having lost his last sou.

Paul slowed to observe a squat German woman's system. It was scarcely elaborate. After three spins, she placed her plaque on the color that had come up on the third roll. He watched her lay down another plaque and lose. She might as well be counting the number of women wearing crimson. From the tail of his eye, he saw the *bête noire* clear the bottleneck clogging the portal and, in his splay-footed way, start closing the distance between them. The earlier snub must have nettled. Cyril Phelps' protruding jaw was quivering with such fury he seemed to have forgotten the need to be circumspect.

The time had come to confront that inevitable. Paul turned to face Phelps, now less than six feet away, then pivoted on his heel and headed for the gentlemen's W.C.

# Friday, March 13, 1914
## GIORGIO'S CAFÉ

THE SUNLIGHT PIERCING THE GNARLED BRANCHES OF the ancient olive trees which lined the terrace of Giorgio's Café came to a rest in the middle of Paul's throbbing brain. A cup of coffee sat untouched while he used his right hand to shield his eyes. This morning, he had been tempted to overlook appearing for this daily command performance. It wouldn't have been the first time, and he could always blame his oversleeping on the ague. He never enjoyed wasting time here, but today he was impatient to get to Hervé's, to make sure his friend was prepared for possible inquiries about Joseph Murphy. Paul continued telling himself this was the principal reason even though he had stopped pretending he wasn't equally keen to learn whether that was Sophie's son. Another pretense. He refused to consciously think of Jonnie as his nephew. He was only Sophie's son.

Giorgio placed a glass of clear, viscous liquid beside the coffee cup. "Monsieur Phelps suggests Schnapps, Paul."

Paul lifted his sheltering palm long enough to signal gratitude with the flick of a finger. Years of experience had left him with the settled conviction that, no matter how bad things were, they could always get worse. Yesterday had proved that thesis tenfold, and any hopes for an improvement today were pipped at the post by the sight of Cyril Phelps lounging at a table in the corner of Giorgio's terrace. The *bête noire*'s presence meant he wanted to talk. What now? Too few members of Burke's Peerage on the guest-lists? Wants them in block letters or copied twice?

Cyril rose, tucked a newspaper under his arm, and picked up his coffee cup.

Declining to look up at the form hovering beside him, Paul said, "You're standing in my light."

Cyril sat and placed the newspaper in the middle of the table, aligning his cup directly below it. He hesitated several seconds before selecting the spot on which to place the top hat. "Does Diogenes have a hangover?" he said.

His voice was high-pitched and never whine-free. As often as Paul had heard it, he was always startled by its sound. It was like hearing a violin shriek when the kettle drum was struck. Cyril's appearance was no less discordant. The smartly cut frock coat and sharply creased trousers were at odds with the rest of his person. His head was too large for the narrow shoulders; the nose overpowered the face; and the nostrils prevailed over the nose. His bulbous lips were as tough-skinned as an African explorer's, and the jutting lower chin made it impossible for the bottom teeth, three of which were gold, to escape notice.

"No," Paul said, "I have a headac –" The word was cut short by renewed hacking.

Cyril shifted his eyes to the empty tables around them. "You were late to the Casino yesterday," he said.

Paul lifted the glass. "Much obliged. I have a cold." He always used a flat, classless English accent here. Cyril hadn't put down the money for the cut-glass version.

"Who doesn't know that? You've been sitting over here making more noise than a gaggle of geese."

Some of the sharper edges had also been knocked off Cyril's speech, but it was still as jagged as an oyster shell. Paul knew the hat Cyril had situated with solicitude carried a Lock's of St. James's label and that he not only had another hat from that prestigious firm but that his irreproachable morning coats bore the name Henry Poole and Co., clothier to the courts of England and France. While Paul made a point of living below his means, Cyril Phelps most certainly was living beyond his. Another thought of Jonnie edged its way around Paul's defenses. At least he, or his *doppelgänger*, had been well turned out, not as expensively as Cyril, but well enough.

Cyril said, "I had a few glasses of wine with Dr. Fournier last night. Sober or not, he plays the coroner in Monaco. Says he was called out yesterday to look at some dead American shithead at the Hôtel de Paris."

Paul didn't bother pretending he didn't know what Cyril was talking about. "Yes, American. Should be of no interest to your British readers."

In spite of the disadvantages of his appearance, Phelps was *The Times'* correspondent in Monaco, a position Paul believed he must have blackmailed his way into just as he had blackmailed Paul into providing access to the lists of the Society's hotel guests.

"Never can tell," Cyril said. "The man was Irish. Might be somebody's cousin. Those R.C.s, they have hundreds of cousins, thousands, half of them in the United States." These words were accompanied by a look filled with dark, suggestive meaning. Cyril frequently gave off looks filled with dark, suggestive meanings. "At any rate, looks like the American shitbag was allergic to bees and that's what killed him. But that doesn't change the fact someone else wanted him dead too. He was shot, you know."

The news of Murphy's true cause of death barely ruffled Paul's interest. Obviously, The Hyena hadn't known about it yesterday. But Paul had no reason to care one way or the other, not before he learned whether Murphy had created a nexus with Hervé.

"Ordinarily," Cyril said, "my money would be on the wife. *Cui bono*, you know. Probably already emptying out his cabinets and drawers. Matter of fact, she wasted no time over the death certificate. Wants Fournier to wire an attestation to San Francisco. But there's more to this one than a greedy wife and an allergy to bees. Dr. Fournier says the man had tickets to Belfast and a German dictionary in his room."

Wycliffe hadn't mentioned any tickets or a dictionary, but this omission meant nothing to Paul either.

Cyril chose a piece of bread from the basket after pinching everything in it and helped himself to Paul's personal jar of orange marmalade. He sucked the excess preserves from his fingers as he chewed, the gold teeth flashing. The bushy black beard vibrated like a tremulous old man's, but Cyril wasn't old. He was thirty-nine, four years younger than Paul himself.

When Cyril reached his fill, his beard and lapels were liberally adorned by crumbs, and chunks of bread littered the table. These, he brushed onto the ground. This was Giorgio's cue to rush out with his broom. By now, anyone who wasn't fatally obtuse would have found the hint in the rapidity with which Giorgio arrived. No café owner wanted to attract scavenging pigeons and seagulls. For an insanely long moment, Paul found himself wishing he could drag Jonnie here and introduce him to this noble representative of England's Fourth Estate, this thing that properly belonged at the bottom of a bog. He wished he could show Jonnie what his objections were based upon, show him how despicable those rumormongers and graverobbers were, those authors and engineers of sensationalism, men who exploited the plights of the miserable, hacks who shoveled nourishment into the mouths of the monsters who battened on their neighbors' sorrows.

Cyril unfolded the newspaper and swept an index finger across *The Times'* headline. "Look at this. Lloyd George has declared the universal end of representative government and the abolishment of all civil liberties if the Irish don't get Home Rule. Accuses the inhabitants of Ulster of hypocrisy. The Tories have given a carefully worded response: 'Hogwash.'"

He studied another article for longer than the couple of inches of length should have required before raising his head. "A member of the Downing Street staff has let it slip that the Tsar will be in London later this year, part of the visits being exchanged among the heads of the Triple Entente. It's rumored to go deeper than that. The *Daily Citizen* claims they want to force Germany to make the Triple Entente a quadruple alliance. Try that: Germany, France, Russia, and Great Britain, all allied. Makes you wonder, doesn't it, what fairy tales those men feed on?"

He licked his overstuffed thumb and turned the page. Paul noted where the page was touched, so he could avoid placing his own fingers there. "Here's one that's right up your alley," Cyril said. "Ernest Hooley has been sentenced to prison for misappropriating the money he raised selling stock in the Dunlop Pneumatic Tire Company. Those Americans make me want to vomit. Half of them millionaires, and they have to defraud their investors for more. Makes you want to unbutton and piss on them all, doesn't it?"

Paul didn't respond. It didn't matter whether the proposed retribution referred to stock defrauders in particular or the entire nation. This recapitulation of the news was not a normal part of their meetings. Cyril must be miffed about having been put off last night.

Cyril launched his next assault on the bowl of olives. "Let me tell you something else," he said, spitting two olive pits into his cupped hand. "You should know this without me telling you. There's a guest at the Hôtel de Paris who has to wash the blood off his money before he spends it. What do you think of that?"

"Must be hard on the linens."

Paul understood full well that Cyril was referring to the international arms-dealer Basil Zaharoff. He knew the man by name, by face, by reputation, but he never came into the Casino, so there was no reason to give his presence in Monte Carlo any thought.

"Perhaps you can afford to make light of this, but some of us cannot," Cyril said. "There are things about this Murphy that are troubling. Like I said, he was Irish."

"I thought you said he was American."

"Ireland is in the bones, not on the passport. There's something else of significance. He owned merchant ships. You know what merchant ships do, don't you?"

"Float."

"They transport things. Big things. Tons of big things."

"I'm obliged to you for clearing that up for me."

Loading his mouth with more olives, Cyril grunted his disapproval.

For Paul, that was the one redeeming feature in this unwelcomed association. The best con artists had to be superb actors. They were required to feign complete surprise, agonizing worry, unsurpassing delight, profound sorrow, any number of emotions, all of which were usually the exact opposite of what they were feeling. But with Cyril, Paul never had to trouble himself with disguising how much he disliked the man's company.

"Winzig Krenz," Cyril said. "Do you know who Winzig Krenz is?"

Paul knew him to be a fat Berlin nightclub entertainer and comedian who kept a villa near Villefranche and was said to be a prolific host and a prodigious lover. To the question, he said nothing.

Cyril again surveyed the empty chairs around them before leaning forward, his voice a grating whisper. "A couple of weeks ago, I accidentally saw Murphy getting into Krenz's motorcar. Not just getting into it, but acting very suspiciously too. It was around ten o'clock at night, behind the Hôtel de Paris. Behind it, not in the front, where the motorcars are supposed to wait. After that, I watched more closely. Two nights later, he again left around ten o'clock and again made a point of walking to the back side of the hotel where Krenz's chauffeur waited." Cyril's eyes were unnaturally bright, like those of a man under the influence of absinthe. "Let me repeat the names: Basil Zaharoff, Winzig Krenz, and Joseph Murphy. Can you not see the sinister implications there?"

What Paul saw with crystal clarity was that his hopes of keeping Cyril away from the Murphy affair were dust and dung.

"Let's start again with Murphy," Cyril said. "Yes, he was an American, but aren't their Irish patriot societies the wellhead of armed rebellion in Ireland? Everyone knows the Fenian brotherhood was founded there to supply weapons and money for the freedom movement, just like everyone knows the American Fenians were behind the dynamitings in Britain in the 80s. One might argue those are distant events, but the feelings behind them are current. Parliament finally passed a bill authorizing Home Rule in January, but it hasn't been implemented. And let me tell you, there are large numbers of men with violent tendencies for whom Home Rule is not a satisfactory solution."

When Paul signaled to Giorgio for a second glass of Schnapps, Cyril seemed not to notice. He went on, "I'll speak it plainly. Murphy was an Irishman with money and merchant ships. Zaharoff is a man with guns to sell. It is no accident they are in Monte Carlo at the same time and staying at the same hotel. Murphy was negotiating with Zaharoff to buy weapons to smuggle into Ireland on his ships. I know you don't believe me, but I'm certain of it."

No, Paul did not believe it, no more than he had believed the other risible espionage schemes concocted by Cyril, such as the itinerant sidewalk artist who offered paintings of Monte Carlo with underpaintings which were drawings of the new British fortifications at Gibraltar or the one about the Pedro Murias cigars, favored by a certain Austrian diplomat, which were disguised incendiary bombs, timed to flame out in fifteen days, well after a military cargo ship had left port for the middle of the Atlantic.

Paul had never held truck with spies or their ilk. He invariably turned a deaf ear to the vaguest overture from someone mired in that shameless, soulless world. As far as he was concerned, the entire network, friend and foe alike, was like a country-house party for Edward the Caresser's set, with the participants creeping up and down the back stairs, peeping in keyholes, listening at doors, and bribing the servants, while everyone knew perfectly well who is sleeping with whom, everyone that is, except a pair's legitimate mates at the dinner table.

He said, "Have you ever known anyone to pass through Monte Carlo who wasn't plotting against some government or other? Last year, according to you, King George and

Kaiser Wilhelm were conniving to overthrow the Tsar of All the Russias, so England and Germany could divide his navy between themselves. If I am not mistaken, after the showing in Japan, the Russian navy comprises a scull and a cruiser that cannot cruise. So Murphy and Zaharoff have suites at the Hôtel de Paris. What of it? So do Lord and Lady Beresford and the Duke of Leeds. So Murphy went to a bacchanal at Krenz's. What of it? Is Winzig an apiarist?"

"A what?"

"Never mind."

"You sit around in this pampered paradise and never see what's going on right under your nose. These days, there's two factions in Germany. There's a peace party and a war party. Krenz undoubtedly is in the latter. He provided a place where Murphy could collude with Zaharoff on behalf of the Irish revolutionaries. Something went wrong, and not knowing he was dead, the conspirators shot him to silence him."

Paul contemplated what a marvelous way that would be to silence this hound from hell. He could have asked why anyone in Germany, outside the Krupp family, might be interested in this fantastic transaction. However, the photograph in his inner-pocket was growing heavier, so his impatience for leaving took charge.

He said, "Sounds like you've got this Murphy chap all buttoned up."

"Not by a long shot. I've put together what I could from the facts I have. There is no question about it. He was up to something, and I, the Home Office, *we* need to know exactly what he was up to. We need to get to the bottom of it."

Paul forced a cough to cover his genuine reaction. Of course it was time to bring in the British Secret Service. It was the cudgel Cyril hauled out every time Paul failed to satisfactorily answer his helm. He had his doubts about Cyril's connections with that murky organization. He would have thought the Secret Service preferred gentlemen for its agents and more discreet ones at that. At best, Cyril had probably given himself a field-promotion from paid-informant to official agent. Either way, it didn't matter. Paul did not remain stuck like hoof-glue to a man he abhorred in order to render service to the Crown. He suffered this fool neither gladly nor willingly but grudgingly and only because, back in Liverpool, a young Cyril Phelps had known George Chandler, and worse, he remembered that George Chandler had been a wanted-felon when he fled there twenty-five years ago.

Cyril's voice abruptly fell silent, as though the man seating himself beside them had been the subject of their gossip. Well stricken in years, the man was heavily stooped, as if his torso were encased in chains, like Houdini.

"And you want me to do what?" Paul asked, reaching for his homburg.

With one hand, Cyril closed the newspaper while spitting olive pits into the other. "Read it yourself. It's the latest edition."

Two men descended on a nearby table and laid out a chessboard, causing the dog dozing beneath it to leap awake, barking hysterically.

The unrebuked clamoring set Paul's headache to hammering again. He got to his feet. "Good day," he said, picking up the newspaper.

"Always a pleasure, Old Man." Cyril said, reaching for the last olive.

# Friday, March 13, 1914
## POST/ TELEGRAPH OFFICE

INTERCEPTING ANOTHER LOUD SIGH AND BLISTERING grimace from the beefy man in the chair opposite, Lily brought her foot's drumming to a hard, final slap against the wood floor and returned a venomous look of her own. He was no study in tranquility himself, squirming around on his heavy haunches and snorting like a rutting rhinoceros. Now, he was making a show of rolling his neck-of-many-chins and stretching his back. She positioned her feet so she could wriggle her toes inside her boots, a less obvious but also less satisfying expenditure of excess energy. It took conscious determination not to send her fingers drumming across the cover of her stenographer's book. The tether to her patience, having restrained her for over two hours within the narrow space provided for the public at Monte Carlo's telegraph and postal office, had been gnawed and scraped and stressed until only the thinnest of threads remained.

Behind a heavy wire screen to her right, two clerks sorted envelopes and scribbled notes on forms, interrupting their activity now and again to enter a number or a name on a blackboard covering one wall. A third man in the cage had his chair balanced on its back legs and a desk supporting his feet as he read the *Menton and Monte Carlo News*, which he lowered occasionally to stare with significant irritability at the two clerks. The supervisor, no doubt. She aimed a few daggers in his direction for good measure. The cross mood with which she had begun the day had escalated to all-out belligerency.

After leaving Wycliffe's room and returning to the suite yesterday afternoon, Lily had first been required to listen to a lengthy lament over the crippling inconvenience Mrs. Murphy had suffered due to her secretary's absence. Any disinterested observer would have concluded it was Lily's selfish caprice alone which led her to disregard her duty in favor of spending the afternoon in the company of that repellent-looking cousin and coughing Casino man. Then with a suddenness that would have snapped the neck of the guest of honor on a hangman's scaffold, Mrs. Murphy broke off her harangue and fell to dictating a series of telegrams. This was scarcely the first time Lily had observed her employer carrying on one minute as though she and a serious thought had never been on the same continent on the same day and then, without warning, metamorphose into a hard-headed business woman who breakfasted on balance sheets and saw the world through the single telescopic lens of her financial affairs. The transformation fascinated Lily. Not even Effie could match it.

Last night, Mrs. Murphy had outdone even herself. The dizzying speed with which orders were barked often overwhelmed Lily's painfully learned shorthand, and she had to later rely on her memory to fill in the blanks. The first wires were to go Mr. Murphy's attorney and accountant demanding, by return-cable, details of his will and a complete listing of his assets, including a statement of their costs and current market-values and where the titles of ownership were held. Their client's bank accounts and securities were to be itemized and the process for transferring ownership begun. All property leases must be identified, so they could be renegotiated or terminated. The next wire went to Mrs. Murphy's attorney, directing him to compile a list of her assets which would be affected by the change in her legal-status from wife to widow. Another wire went to the housekeeper of the Murphys' mansion on San Francisco's Nob Hill, Mrs. Dunworthy, instructing her to assemble Mr. Murphy's belongings—suits, overcoats, shirts, hats, shoes, walking sticks, shotguns, pistols, golf clubs, watches, cuff links, anything and everything in his rooms — and have them transported to Butterfield's Auction House. Next, a wire went to that enterprise directing it to send a copy of the inventory to Mrs. Murphy's accountant and an estimate of the auction-proceeds in a separate wire to her. In what seemed like an afterthought, another message was directed to Mr. Murphy's attorney instructing him to draft an obituary and send it for approval before placing it in the San Francisco newspapers.

Last night's sole compensation had come when Mrs. Murphy unfolded the note Wycliffe sent over. In it, he recommended she offer 20,000 francs for the return of the necklace, no questions asked. After slashing the amount to 10,000 francs, she agreed to the proposal. Twenty-thousand francs would have been magnificent, but Lily was quite willing to settle for ten.

When she had crawled into bed around 2:00 a.m., her mind continued sorting through her orders, but permeating all these thoughts was the haunting image of poor Mr. Murphy's body. Several times, she drifted into a shallow sleep, only to be shaken awake by thoughts of what she might find, what she might say, what she might learn when she made that call on Little Beauty today.

A swirling gust of frigid air preceded a new customer into

the post office. Lily felt a ridiculous nudge of disappointment when it wasn't the detective Duchamp. The woman who entered went to the cage to fill out a telegraph form. Her action seemed to stir something deep within The Rhinoceros' musical soul. He set off a maddening litany of noises, running through them like the scales on a piano, "Humprh! Bruhprh! Uh! Er! Uh! Ugh! Humprh!"

This time, instead of directing her animosity towards his flapping dewlap, Lily brazenly glared at the swatch of shirt visible between the point where the white silk-vest, hopelessly inadequate to its burden, fell short and his trousers began.

"Humprh! Bruhprh! Uh! Er! Uh! Ugh! Humprh!"

She stopped wriggling her toes and curled them under, in a hidden version of a fist. She might as well have that Casino man here, hacking and blowing his nose, or Ted Wycliffe, fondling his cane and stroking his toupee.

She leaned over to extract an envelope from her workbag, so she could read the letter once more, just in case she had missed a word or a comma the other ten times she studied it. Posted eleven days ago and arrived this morning, Fran's letter said they had a prospective client who, if landed, would provide their first substantial fee. Fran had been tantalizingly sparse with the details, saying she feared jinxing the arrangement if it were presented as a *fait accompli*. There was nothing in the letter or in the realm of rational thinking to suggest there would be anywhere near what Dorothy Anderson's father paid detectives to look for his daughter, but Lily's thoughts kept drifting towards that stratosphere.

The next thing she knew, she was on her feet, staring helplessly at the door. It was the fifth time she had found herself like that. She still had nowhere to go. She had been ordered to wait for three hours, and if no replies were received, the telegrams to the attorney and the accountant were to be retransmitted. She placed the order to resend these at the same time she submitted the first because she knew no replies would be forthcoming. The time-difference meant the first telegrams would arrive in California somewhere around midnight. She hadn't pointed this out last night. If instructed to telegraph God for answers to the same questions, she would have likewise complied without demur.

She checked her watch. Twenty-three more minutes. She caught the eye of one of the clerks, crooked her head towards the door, and held up her hands, all fingers spread apart.

Outside, her pacing initially resembled that of a palace guard. A number of steps in one direction. An about-face. An equal number of steps in the opposite direction. Another about-face. Gradually, the number and length of her steps expanded until she was taking long, comfortable strides along the terrace skirting the sea while she pondered the reality of the status quo. She had a prospective ten-thousand-franc reward and Fran had a prospective prosperous client. It was the proverbial "two in the bush" with nothing in the hand. And the landlord took only what came from the hand.

She halted beside the concrete balustrade and faced the sea, allowing the wind to sweep the loosened strands of hair off her face while her eyes tracked a steamer headed up the coast towards San Remo. The patient slapping of the waves below served as a counterpoint to her mood.

When Effie refused to pay the tuition at Bryn Mawr unless Lily first completed business school, she had objected that she didn't want to be a secretary. Effie's response had been, "It sure beats mangling and ironing."

At that time, Lily had stifled her arguments but she didn't quell her ambitions. Because she had been excluded since birth from membership in any order of the orthodox, she had never seen herself settling for a life fashioned from a

Butterick pattern. As a young girl, she sifted through books and magazines like a 49er panning for gold, seeking accounts of women who succeeded outside the bounds of conformity. Her imagination was stirred by such real-life adventuresses as Annie Oakley, Annie Smith Peck, Mary Kingsley, Olga de Meyer, even Belle Starr.

After the initial discovery of Kate Warne, Lily soon learned that Mrs. Warne was not only Pinkerton's first female detective, she later became the superintendent of a whole division of female detectives. Throughout the rest of her school years, Lily kept her daydreams nourished by a long line of female sleuths in dime-novels. She understood that Loveday Brooke, Judith Lee, Dorcas Dene, and Dora Myrl were fictional women, but that didn't keep her from recognizing what they represented. They said a woman could find work that was mentally challenging, physically demanding, socially unconventional, and financially rewarding, all the things Lily thought she needed for a satisfying career.

It was a long, narrow, and brittle limb she and Fran had ventured onto, and Lily would have sold herself into White Slavery before she would have confessed to Effie the gamble they had undertaken. There was no need to invite her scorching scorn and predictions of failure. Nevertheless, Lily remained convinced the gamble could be won.

The sounds of St. Charles' bells tolling the Angelus declared her release. In a matter of seconds, she had the door open and was signaling the clerk to transmit the second telegrams. She bestowed her most winning smile on the fat man before sticking out her tongue at him and closing the door.

# Friday, March 13, 1914

FLIPPING OPEN THE NOTEBOOK, LILY'S EYE immediately went to something she had put out of her mind for three hours. Even though Mrs. Murphy was never above discussing something as vulgar as cost, in this instance, she had delegated the job of bargaining with the local undertaker to her secretary. Lily calculated there should be adequate time for lunch and for making inquiries about a mortician before she reported back to work at two o'clock. As she continued flipping the pages, checking for other tasks, her speed increased, first to a rapid walk, then a trot, and by the time she was passing the Hydropathic Establishment, she was practically running.

Suddenly, she bounced off something solid. Next, her legs were wrapping around themselves and becoming tangled in her long skirt. She felt moist earth on her cheek, and the smell of humus filled her nostrils. She was lying face-down in one of the painstakingly trimmed flowerbeds that fringed Monte Carlo's pathways. Her instinct was to leap to her feet while praying that only a few doddering dowagers had witnessed the spectacle, but she couldn't get her skirt, legs, ankles, feet, and God-knew-what-else unsnarled. She also didn't know what her right hand was pressing against until, with horror, she realized it was a man's shoe. She jerked back, swiping at the hair spilling over her eyes, grinding more mud onto her face.

"Oh," she exclaimed. Oh God, don't let it be him, not Duchamp, not now.

"Oh," she repeated, gazing up at the man's face, which wore a droll smile as an accessory to his own astonishment.

"Oh," she moaned, recognizing the man to whom Paul Newcastle had reacted at the elevator.

"I say there. That's quite the attention grabber," he said. "Are you all right?"

The only response she could manage was to squeeze her eyes shut. To her dismay, he was still there when she opened them. He again extended his arm, motioning that she should take his hand. Instead, she wiped soil off her nose with the back of her sleeve.

He knelt beside her and lifted her hair to press his handkerchief against the left side of her face. His eyebrows were pinched with concern. "Your cheek is bleeding," he said.

She didn't realize she had gone deaf for several long seconds until the sounds of chirruping birds resumed as loudly as crashing cymbals.

"It must have been that rose brush," he said. "I'll see to it that it is drawn and quartered and cast into the sea."

Still she said nothing, did nothing, except sit like a dumb cow, staring into those intensely brown eyes. The skin pulled downward at the corners gave them a melancholy appearance, but that was more than offset by the lop-sided grin.

"*Parlez vous anglais?*" he asked. "*Je parle français, un peu. Ce va?*"

"I'm sorry," she mumbled.

"You should be," he said. "My plan of eclipsing Belmonte as the greatest matador of all time has been shattered. I am a ruined man. What is to become of me now?" The grin spread across the rest of his face.

Lily realized she had expected the British accent, but not

that damned grin, mocking her defenseless embarrassment. "I'm sorry," she said again. "I was running. I wasn't watching where I was going. I'm terribly sorry. I really am." She was babbling like an empty-headed schoolgirl. She knew it and couldn't stop.

"Seriously, no apology is needed. I have always hoped that someday I would knock a beautiful woman off her feet although, I admit, this is not precisely the way I had it pictured." He pressed the handkerchief against her cheek again.

"Don't bother," she said, batting his hand away. "I doubt it's a severed artery."

She was drowning in a Niagara of shame. He was trying to help, and she responded like a shrew. Her focus went to the pencil at the base of the rose bush.

"Here," he said, passing her the handkerchief as he retrieved the pencil and brushed damp soil from it.

Steadfastly refusing his assistance, she struggled to her feet with all the gracefulness of a water buffalo laboring to extricate itself from quicksand. Straightening to full height, she shook clumps of damp earth out of her shawl and looked around for the rest of her belongings: her notebook, her workbag – her dignity.

"May I introduce myself? Jonathan Chandler of *The Daily News,* at your service any time you need a target for lawn bowling. I've seen you before, have I not, at the Hôtel de Paris?"

Just when she was about to get on top of the situation, she was slammed back into confusion. Had he been more observant than he appeared at the elevator, or had he seen her another time? She doubted the latter. She would have noticed him even without Paul Newcastle's reaction.

"The Hôtel de Paris, yes. Are you there too?"

77

"No, I am slumming at Beausoleil. There's quite a number of the unyachted up there."

"I see." She followed this with an inane half-laugh. It might as well have been a giggle. She wanted to kick something, him preferably. By now, he must have her pegged as an escapee from the local lunatic asylum. She held her breath, counted to five, then to ten. She needed to assemble her thoughts and disassemble her feelings. She scrutinized the handkerchief like it was an outsized tumor on her palm, shoved it towards him, then immediately retracted it. At last, her brain had picked itself up too.

"How rude of me, Mr. Chandler. I'll have it laundered and ironed. Where may I have it sent?" Before he could reply, she added, "Please allow me to introduce myself, Lily Turner."

She held out her arm for a handshake. Instead, he gently turned her palm downward, brushed off the dirt and pieces of shriveled leaves with a touch that was pure caress, and bent to kiss the back of her hand. A slow-burning fire seared up the veins of her arm, suspending her breathing in an altogether delicious way. It was the first time she had known a man's lips and touch in over a year.

He released her hand. He had not held it indecently long. "Please forgive me if that was too familiar. I wasn't trying to be impudent."

"Then congratulations are in order. Apparently, you can achieve it without trying."

Her churlish remark provoked the reappearance of the impish grin. This time, she was very sure she wanted to kick him.

"If you insist upon laundering the handkerchief, would it be impudent of me to suggest we meet Sunday and you return it then?"

There was work to be done. There was always work to be

done. But tomorrow was Saturday, and Mrs. Murphy would be away most of the day. She had proudly announced she would be visiting friends aboard their yacht today and would remain overnight. Even with the added complication of a recently deceased husband, all the outstanding tasks could easily be finished by Monday morning.

"I would like that," she said and immediately regretted her reply. What was she thinking, or not thinking? There was no money in an idle flirtation. What if Little Beauty wanted to see her again after today?

"Where may I call for you?" he said. "At the hotel?"

This time, she caught the danger before stupidly agreeing. "The post office. I'll meet you at the post office. I'll have business to do there."

"The post office?"

"Yes, it's down there." She indicated the direction with a flourish of her hand.

"But it will be Sunday."

Of course it would be Sunday. She knew that.

"May I propose the horticulture exhibition at the Palais des Beaux Arts?" he said. "It's official. Anyone willing to sign a pledge promising not to assault the plants will be granted entry."

She clenched her shawl more tightly about her waist and hitched her workbag higher on her shoulder. Above all, she wanted to get out of here before she was gobbling more mud.

"Fine," she said. "I'll meet you there, one o'clock."

"May I accompany you to the hotel?"

"Why, thank –" Alarm choked off her voice. "Uh, no. Uh, errands. I mean, that is, no, no thank you. I have errands. That is, I must ...." A singe was creeping up her neck and invading her cheeks. "The other direction. I'm going the other direction."

Rather than stamping her feet and trying to redeem this final stupidity, she wheeled and hurried away, back down the path she had been ascending when she blundered into him.

# Friday, March 13, 1914
## VILLA ACHILLES

SUCKING AIR LIKE A FREIGHT ENGINE, PAUL PAUSED BESIDE two brass Coqs Gaulois bracketing an opening in a stone wall, behind which lay a rock-lined path threaded beneath orange and mimosa trees and leading to a low, white villa overlooking the Mediterranean Sea. He removed his hat to run a comb through his hair and sop the moisture off its edges with his handkerchief. He hated showing up looking like he had been chased out of town by gendarmes, dirty and sweaty, trousers sprung at the knees, as apt as that image might be. Yet before he had finished removing the grime accumulated during the descent from Monaco and the climb to Cap d'Ail, another passing lorry was smothering him in dust once more. Why couldn't these places tar their roads the way the Principality did? He replaced the hat, brushed his fingertips along the facial scar, and started down the tree-lined path.

The young man who answered the door was not the same as last time. This one, Italian judging from the accent, had unusually long arms, hair that looked like it was plastered down with butter, and a painfully executed smile, possibly aiming for debonair but striking grimace. He scampered off after Paul announced himself, leaving the visitor to hang his own hat and coat.

Hervé burst into view with a shout that should have knocked all the bats off the rafters. "Old friend, I did not know you were coming." He rushed forward, arms spread wide for an embrace, and planted two enthusiastic kisses beside Paul's cheeks.

"Antonio," he called over his shoulder, "kill the fatted calf. He is home. Come, come, my friend. You must see what I've done with the place."

At forty-five years of age, Hervé carried not a pinch of sag or fat. His face looked older than his body, but the lines around his eyes were like the sun's rays in a child's drawing, radiating warmth and good humor. One might have thought that three years in the notorious La Santé prison would have bludgeoned away all traces of geniality from a man. It would have done so for Paul.

Hervé kept his arm around Paul's shoulder as he guided them into a salon well lit by a lantern skylight and where a fire crackled in a Provençal tiled fireplace. The star-patterned parquet floor was polished to a crisp with beeswax, and the exterior wall was lined by four floor-to-ceiling French windows, beyond which a walled courtyard held statuary and potted bonsai trees. Two somnolent cats, one yellow, one white, took their leisure on a concrete bench with lion's feet. They might well have been drugged just to complete the perfection of the tableau. Paul took a chair next to the divan where Hervé had seated himself. Antonio hovered in the middle of the room.

"Champagne, the best," Hervé directed.

When Paul quit fighting the building cough, his quondam partner drew back in mock horror. "You are sick with the lung fever, and you have come to me for a cure? I am touched by your confidence, but alas, the last time I was a doctor, you were with me, in Vienna. This is how long it has been. I regret that my knowledge of the healing arts has atrophied in the intervening years."

While they waited for Antonio to return, Paul contemplated the revolution which had occurred in the room's décor since he last called at Villa Achilles, four months ago. At that time, green was the predominant theme. Now, it was red. Red-and-white striped divan, red Venetian crystal, red lamp-shades, red candles. The silver tea-service had been replaced by a beastly red samovar, which Paul studied specially. After St. Petersburg, when they had barely escaped with their toenails, let alone their skin, he would have assumed a permanent aversion to anything Russian.

Antonio crossed the room balancing two filled coupes on a tray, his mouth ajar and footwork self-consciously precise. A string was tied on his right index finger. Was that to remind himself not to trip over his own feet?

With an elegant sweep of his arm, Hervé held his glass in Paul's direction. "Red is the color of the day, but since Waterford went out of business, I have not been able to get them to produce new coupes exclusively for me. Therefore we must make do with these."

"You could serve red wine in them," Paul said.

"Prostitute the finest crystal in the world? Is that what they are doing in Monte? You must get away from that crass circus more often."

Using this as a springboard, Hervé launched into the conventional diatribes against the evils inherent in the neighboring fiefdom of Mammon, siren to the deluded, corrupter of morality, ruination of unfortunates, where men guzzled champagne from silver pails and gorged on black oysters while their families starved. He waxed positively lyrical on the tragedy of the suicides—the promises unfulfilled, the careers and countries unserved, parents bereaved, wives stricken, infants unborn, children orphaned.

Paul tossed back the mediocre champagne, hoping it would remove the remnant of his headache. He understood the purpose of the exercise. While waiting for Antonio to return with the bottle, Hervé was tuning up the same way an orchestra did, by giving off fractured sounds that said nothing about what was on the program.

"You see more of that than I," he continued, "exiled as I am at the outskirts of that Sodom by the Sea. Yet even here where I sit, one cannot avoid breathing the diseased air. For centuries, every strain of debased, deranged, rapacious pirate has infected this coast, Phoenicians, Romans, Moors, Genoese. Today, it is the decomposing English, the remorseless Russians, and those felons in top hats, the Americans, who pollute the air with their greed and cupidity."

Antonio reappeared with a champagne bucket containing an opened bottle of Möet. He set the bucket on the table, then held up the bottle for Hervé's veneration. Paul ignored the ceremony. The wine and whiskey he and Hervé served were always undeserving of the names on the bottles.

"Thank you," Hervé said when Antonio showed no signs of abandoning his post. "We require nothing more at this time."

At the sound of the closing door, Paul said, "New majordomo?"

Hervé glanced in the direction of the door and, changing to English, said, "I know. He is remarkable chiefly for his lack of virtues. Be patient. At least he has stopped putting the bottles between his legs to open them. The larger problem is his Socialist leanings. I assure him I have no essential objection to that system. Have I not worked all my life for the redistribution of other men's wealth? But I must continually remind him to lower his voice because we are sitting here in the cornucopia of capitalism, not in some Bohemian commune."

Certain the Italian had his ear pressed against the door, Paul moved his chair closer to Hervé, who stubbed out the cigarette without drawing on it again. That much hadn't changed. A cigarette was still principally an accessory for the gold holder.

"What is it?" Hervé said in a subdued tone. "You, here in the bright light of day. Have you grown bold? I know you have not grown careless."

"A couple of things."

"Not something you could put in a note."

"The less written, the less intercepted."

Hervé uncurled his fingers in a motion that said, *of course.*

"First, I think I saw Jonnie yesterday."

"Jonnie? Here? At the Côte d'Azur?"

"Here, at Monte Carlo."

"Are you certain?"

"No, I can't be, but it looked like him, and I can't be asking around myself."

"He is not staying at one of the Society's hotels, I take it."

Paul shook his head. "I saw him getting off the lift at the Hôtel de Paris, but I checked. He's not registered at any of the Society's hotels, not under his own name."

Paul withdrew the photograph from his inner-pocket. Hervé lifted a pince-nez from the table to peer at the four young men gripping tennis racquets and smiling hugely.

"But yes. I remember this," Hervé said. "When was it? Berlin? No, Budapest. You had it when we were in Budapest."

"It was taken eight or nine years ago at Cambridge. It came into my possession when I crept back to England to sneak another look at him before his graduation." Paul pointed to a man on one end. "He's much the same. About

85

six-foot one, 175 pounds or so. You see. Black hair, dark brown eyes."

Hervé looked at the picture, then up at Paul, then back at the picture. "He's better looking than you are."

"Show it to whomever you have to," Paul said. "But don't let go of it. I want it back."

The lines around Hervé's eyes softened. "I understand." His brow furrowed. "You mentioned a falling-out."

Paul turned to study the slumbering cats.

"It must have been a long fall," Hervé persisted.

"Mt. Everest."

After a minute or two passed, Hervé said, "And if Jon is here?"

"I'll decide it then."

Paul set his empty glass on the table to punctuate the end of that topic. "There's something else we should talk about. I referred an American to you two or three weeks ago. Around fifty years of age, about 5'7", on the stout side, not balding, hair black, full beard, all probably colored, name of Joseph Murphy."

Behind Hervé's eyes, Paul saw a drawbridge being raised.

"Do you know whom I'm talking about? Did he take up the lead?"

"He did, and he took away a few more coins than he arrived with. I thought he would be back by now. But, light come, light go."

"He was here only the once? When was this?"

"I cannot remember. What is today?"

"Friday."

"Last week, I think, Monday or Tuesday. I can ask Antonio."

Or tell Antonio.

"Has that man caused trouble?" Hervé's tone was a shade too nonchalant.

"You could put it that way. He died rather unexpectedly at the Hôtel de Paris."

Paul believed he was the only person on earth who would have caught the barely perceptible tightening of Hervé's mouth as he reached again for the cigarette holder. He studied his friend while he went through the ritual of selecting a tall lighter from the collection of gold objects on the table at his left.

"When did he die?" Hervé asked.

"He was found Thursday, yesterday." Paul related the information about the bee-venom and the gunshot, then he said, "I don't care if he was stung by a bee or swallowed by a crocodile. The point is, the police have been called in. I was only the swivel, but can anything lead him to you? How did he get here? How did he contact you?"

Paul had to pursue these questions. Although there was nothing concrete to connect him with Hervé and Murphy, he could not afford any loose ends, no matter how short or solitary. Too much was at stake. He was too close to the final pull on the knot at Antibes. All the way from Monte Carlo to here, he had mentally kicked himself in the rear. In the twenty years they worked together, Hervé never absorbed Paul's need for caution. In terms of loose ends, if left to his own devices, Hervé's operations would look like a rag-picker's floor.

Hervé said, "He sent a note saying I had been recommended and suggested a night for a game. I did not see how he arrived. I had Antonio return him to Monte Carlo in the Vauxhall."

"Who else was with him?" Paul said.

"Pardon?"

"The American. He let it be known he was interested only in a multilingual host. Wanted everything, English, German, Russian, French, maybe Greek and Turkish. Claimed he had cohorts of numerous nationalities. However, if he had friends of those stripes, they cut a wide berth around him in the Casino."

"Perhaps he was saving them for the next visit."

"No doubt," Paul said dryly, waving away the offer of more champagne. "I thought I should mention what's come up with him, in case the police decide to make inquiries."

Hervé's shrug indicated it was a matter of indifference to him. "I should have an answer about Jon by tomorrow night," he said.

Paul was rising from the chair when he recalled the coded message which Cyril, in his incomparable parody of a cloak-and-dagger style, had tucked inside the newspaper. "Can one of your contacts get me the name of someone on Winzig Krenz's staff?" he asked.

Hervé gave a soft chuckle. "Are you thinking of moving up? Herr Krenz can draw people to his villa without paying you to bunco-steer for him."

"The nephew of a colleague is looking for work. He speaks excellent German. If he had the name of someone on Krenz's staff, perhaps he would stand a better chance," Paul lied.

"No doubt," Hervé said dryly.

# Friday, March 13, 1914
## HÔTEL DE PARIS

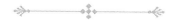

IN FRONT OF THE SUITE'S DOOR, LILY SMOOTHED HER
skirt and allowed her breathing to slow after running up the
two flights of stairs. Following the calamitous encounter
with Jonathan Chandler, she had bathed, applied iodine to
the scratch, and draped her wet hair in front of the radiator.
The nape-bun, however, was damp and the discoloration
from the iodine remained despite vigorous scrubbing. Not
that it mattered. Mrs. Murphy might take to her bed over a
scratch on her Louis IV desk, but she wouldn't be bothered
by a bone-exposing cut on her secretary.

When Ted Wycliffe answered the door, Lily caught sight
of Chief Inspector Gautier. For a wild moment, she thought
she was about to hear that her employer had been shot dead
in her bed.

"Lily's here," Mrs. Murphy announced superfluously from
her perch on the sofa. She wore another of the new frocks,
this one a peach-colored creation with gloves to match. At
some point during last night's marathon, she had explicitly
rejected black, declaring that her new clothes, none of a
mourning-hue, would be out of fashion by next year. New
writing paper, Crane's of course, edged in black, was the one
concession she was prepared to make, but the paper's color

had proved problematic: blue, green, or mauve? That, at any rate, was where it was left last night.

"This is everyone?" Gautier asked.

Wycliffe nodded. He was posted like a sentinel behind his cousin. When Mrs. Murphy was standing, he seldom positioned himself directly beside her. Mr. Murphy, about the same height as Wycliffe and also shorter than his wife, had seldom stood near her either, but Lily suspected it was for a reason other than a wish to avoid the unflattering contrast in heights.

The chief inspector opened a leatherbound notebook and took from it a sheet of yellow tissue-paper covered with lines of typewriting. He addressed the widow, whose expression was as fixed as that of a wooden Indian guarding a cigar store.

"The doctor has presented his report concerning the death of Monsieur Murphy," Gautier began. "The doctor has concluded the cause of death was a fatal allergy to bee-venom. That is to say, he was stung by a bee and died as a result."

"What?" Wycliffe yelped.

Mrs. Murphy looked over her shoulder at him. Her face remained devoid of expression.

"What kind of joke is this?" he demanded. "There was a bullet-wound in the man's back. I saw it. We all saw it. What are you covering up?"

"This is true, Monsieur. But a bullet did not cause the death. The doctor is of the opinion the bullet was inflicted after the unfortunate man was deceased." He paused. "I would prefer not to elaborate in front of the ladies."

"Say whatever you have to say," Mrs. Murphy instructed.

Lily, intensely curious, was glad for the insistence, but Gautier remained silent.

"For God's sake, man," Wycliffe said, "whatever are you talking about?"

"Monsieur Murphy was fatally allergic to bee venom. This is known to occur in certain persons. This appeared obvious to Dr. Fournier yesterday. Naturally, he wished to confirm it. A swollen area on the neck and other ...." His hand made small waving motions. "Other signs indicate the allergy was the cause. For example, the doctor noted a lack of blood issuing from the bullet wound. This would mean ...." His voice trailed off once more.

That his heart was not pumping when he was shot, Lily thought, glad for once for those detestable biology classes.

Mrs. Murphy's aspect remained deadpan, but Wycliffe appeared stricken by the news, no doubt because a solar eclipse had just usurped his day in the sun.

"The whiskey," the chief inspector said.

Lily recalled the glass on the bedside table.

"I ordered it to be analyzed."

"Excellent, excellent," Wycliffe said. "Was it ten-year-old or twelve-year-old scotch?"

"It contained arsenic, enough to kill a person a dozen times over."

At this, the widow spewed a harsh "shewrruff!" As the sound grew into gasping, choking laughter, Gautier's professional demeanor slipped not a millimeter, but Wycliffe's did. He was gaping at her, unblinking, his mouth a wide "O."

"And I wanted to strangle him," she said through sobbing guffaws. "That was him. That was Joe, a man you had to get in line to kill." Her laughter exploded again. "And a bee beat us all to it." She gave herself over completely to hilarity without shielding her mouth with her palm, the way she usually did, to hide her false teeth.

Lily sucked in her cheeks. Her facial muscles were involuntarily straining to join the merriment. "Excuse me," she managed as she rushed towards Mrs. Murphy's bedchamber.

There, she leaned against the wall, shaking her head in amazement. A bullet, a bee, a profligate poisoner. Did this mean the doctor had officially ruled out apoplexy? She took the time to consider the implications to herself. Gautier's revelation may have destroyed Ted's joy, but it should not affect the search for the necklace. The reward was still possible.

When Lily returned to the sitting room, Mrs. Murphy's features had gone slack, and she sat with her feet and legs spread apart, like a country-woman shelling peas. She accepted the glass of water Lily offered without looking up.

The chief inspector continued as if the hiatus had not occurred. "Monsieur Murphy's death has been determined to be the result of natural causes, not a homicide. Therefore, our department is concluding its investigation."

Wycliffe shook his head vigorously. "You can't be. What about the gunshot?"

"It is not a crime in Monaco to shoot a dead man."

Nor, Lily supposed, to attempt to poison one.

"You are saying that Joe – Mr. Murphy – was not murdered. Is that what you are saying?" Wycliffe said.

"He was shot in the back. He was not murdered."

"And you have no interest whatsoever in who shot him in the back?"

"I am saying it is not a matter for us to investigate."

Wycliffe placed his hand on his cousin's shoulder, bowed his head and slowly moved it from side to side, as if the world and all its woes had become too much to comprehend. After a space of several seconds, his hand began a slow, rhythmic patting.

"This is an important development, but don't worry,

Maddie. It may change things but not entirely. As they say, where there is a will there is a way. Justice will be served. You have my word on it. Justice will be served."

"What difference does it make? If Joe's dead, he's dead. I think that's what you mean, isn't it, Inspector? But what about my necklace? And the money, my husband's money?"

Lily forced herself not to drop her eyes in embarrassment over the widow's lack of embarrassment. Perhaps some comfort could be found in knowing there was no longer a need for coaching Bridget Rose about what not to say to the police. If Chief Inspector Gautier did not have an unambiguous picture of the Murphys' marriage by now, he was undeserving of his position.

Wycliffe said, "Tell me, Inspector, can it not be assumed the necklace and wallet and money-clip were stolen by the would-be murderer, or is robbery not a crime in Monaco either?"

Gautier's tone ignored the taunt. "Madame, you stated yesterday that you cannot recall with certainty the last time you saw your necklace but that it was there before you left for five days. Because your husband – deceased husband – had the paste one in his possession, the circumstantial evidence is strong that he took the original. My men will make inquiries, but it is not unusual for persons to part with jewelry and large sums of cash while in the Principality."

"So that's how you're going to treat it? Sweep it under the rug?" she said.

"Maddie, I need, we need, time to think. I promise you, justice will be served," Wycliffe said.

"You can serve justice for dessert for all I care. Are you through, Inspector? I'm expected this afternoon on my friends' yacht. I shall be there overnight, and I do not wish to be disturbed after I leave here."

93

"Maddie," Wycliffe said, "are you sure that's a good idea?"

The look she gave him should have provided both answer and warning. "Why not? And you won't be taking up so much of Lily's time in the future either. She's behind with my work."

That simply was not true, but Lily couldn't feel disappointed by the thought of spending less time studying at the feet of that master. She wasn't seeking the necklace under his aegis anyway. The privacy sign on Little Beauty's door was the most troubling element in the situation. It grew more ominous each time Lily passed. Surely, if there were a body behind it, an odor would have become noticeable. Quite possibly, by now the girl had packed all her things, including the necklace, and lost herself in Paris or London or even Belfast. Maybe she was Irish too.

Wycliffe said, "You may be afraid to pursue Mr. Murphy's murder, Inspector, but I'm not stopping."

Once more, the cataract of freezing disdain failed to faze Gautier. He lifted the box at his feet and placed it on the coffee table. "These items were removed from the bedchamber," he said. "The contaminated whiskey has been properly disposed of."

In answer to Wycliffe's queries, Gautier said the box included the tickets to Belfast and that the fingerprints on the glass matched nothing in the files of the Monaco police. They were also returning the other things they had removed. Lily pulled out her list and hoped her hesitation in touching the items was less apparent to the others than it felt to her. When finished, she looked at the chief inspector.

"There was a German dictionary."

"But yes," he said, reaching for an inner pocket.

The book he handed her was the same color and shape as that taken from the bedroom, but it appeared newer. Its spine was barely cracked, and as she, with feigned carelessness, fanned the pages she could see that many were uncut. Most significantly, the markings and notations she had observed yesterday were absent. She weighed whether to point out the discrepancy. What proof did she have? It would be her word against that of the chief inspector of the Monaco Sûreté Publique. If she had learned nothing else in the past nine months, she had learned to recognize when she was outmanned and outgunned.

She avoided looking at Gautier as she placed a checkmark against the last item and said, "Everything's accounted for."

# Friday, March 13, 1914
## MONTE CARLO CASINO

THE YOUNG MAN'S LEFT ARM RESTED LIGHTLY AGAINST the small of his back, so as not to come familiarly close to the elderly woman when he leaned forward to speak. He was decently, if unremarkably, dressed, a tad heavy on the Brilliantine. She wore a high-necked, long-sleeved black dress with a ruffle of white lace below the chin and heavy pearl pendants on her ears. She had earned Paul's appreciation earlier by being the one who gave his Hélèna her day's Louis in exchange for her chair. The young man's right hand pointed at something behind the woman's back. As her head turned, his left arm began to move.

Paul audibly cleared his throat. The man's eyes widened when they saw the source of the sound. Paul tilted his head to one side, commanding an audience. The man's raised eyebrows deposited deep creases across his forehead. Paul tilted his head a second time. As soon as the man joined him, Paul slid his arm alongside the man's coat, then uncurled his fingers and jangled the coins in his palm. "I believe you will find the air is healthier outside," he said.

In the atrium, Paul stationed himself beside a column and pondered the man he had escorted to the entrance-desk, so his name could be entered on the roll of disreputables not admitted to the Casino. Darwin's thesis had been dealt a staggering blow. Cheats usually evolved along with the Casino's security. But that one was positively Neanderthal. Too young, too inexperienced, too simple, or simply lazy?

Paul watched the other persons loitering in the space, his observations less interested, but no less alert. He had spent a significant part of his shift here, leaning against a marble column, granting relief to his aching knee. He could have taken the tram to Cap d'Ail this morning, but walking was safer, easier to see who was following him, or not. Since leaving there, he had reviewed that session countless times. It meant nothing that Hervé was lying. Hervé never told the truth when a lie would do. The troubling thing was the tension pulling within those lies. Hervé did not worry. That was his strength and his weakness. He never worried. His genius for ingenuity and improvisation was accompanied by a recklessness that approached lunacy. That was what made their partnership successful. Paul's meticulous planning complemented Hervé's audacious schemes. That partnership was another casualty of Marie-Odile's illness. Although spring-loaded reflexes and virtuoso footwork kept Hervé out of most bear-traps, those skills had been known to fail him. Paul was convinced that if he had not been consumed by caring for Marie-Odile, he would have been there, holding the safety net beneath Hervé's high-wire act, and his friend would never have had to suffer the degradations of La Santé Prison.

Paul's gaze lingered on the group of men occupying the opposite corner of the atrium. Uniforms were not allowed in the Casino, but it was never hard to spot Prussian officers with their cropped hair, sculpted moustaches, and the inevitable monocle somewhere in the crowd. Many displayed a montage of *Mensur scars,* or bragging scars, on cheeks clean-shaved in order to show them to best effect. Paul never failed to grasp the irony between the upper-class status the Germans' dueling scars proclaimed and the bottom-class standing that had spelled the genesis of his own.

No sign of Jonnie again tonight. Paul reminded himself for the nine-hundredth time that it was just as well the boy had come a final cropper sooner rather than later. A man should always cut his losses early.

It was this possibility of having to cut his losses that worried Paul about the business with Murphy. He was afraid it would metastasize and fatally infect the long-game he had spent years bringing to fruition, the long-game which was to be his Grand Slam, Triple Crown, and Second Coming, all rolled into one.

In 1902, newspapers on both sides of the Atlantic had heralded the price paid by Pierpont Morgan for a Raphael Madonna. Soon, the press was regularly publicizing accounts of the blizzards of money being spread across Europe by American collectors. Oftentimes, their detractors whispered, the art and artifacts were of mediocre quality, questionable attribution, and dubious authenticity. It would have taken a blindfolded blind man not to see that a market in which the prices ran high, the risks ran higher, and the egotism positively soared was a market heaven-sent for conning.

Paul put months into his plan's conception, ultimately settling on rare books, topped up by an irresistible medieval Book of Hours. In between other jobs, he pieced together the elements. Occasionally, he came across a Caxton available illegally for a pittance. A card game in Brussels handed him a medievalist more heavily weighted by gambling debts than scruples, who exploited his scholarly accesses to photograph genuine treasures. A hungry artist used those and ancient parchment to create an eighty-page book with twelve illuminated miniatures.

Work on the scheme had to be suspended in 1907, when the bottom fell out of the American financial markets. But in 1909, after the U.S. Congress repealed the stiff import-duties on art, another surge of American millionaires chasing after European artifacts soon followed.

However, in 1910, just as Paul was shaking off the dust and about to present the plan to Hervé, the bottom dropped out of his world. Marie-Odile became gravely ill; Hervé was imprisoned; and the rupture with Jonnie occurred. Upon arriving at the Côte d'Azur later that year, Paul could find interest only in taking cover. He assumed a new name, shaved his beard, and shed a stone of weight. Then, for months, he had merely drifted, all canvases folded, until he slowly awakened to the fact that he had landed in a kingdom of Croesuses.

After finally snagging the right American collector, Paul had paid out the line by inches, using the Caxtons and other rare books, before putting out the largest piece of bait: a Book of Hours supposedly painted by Michelino Molinari da Besozzo, an acquisition guaranteed to confer distinction on its owner and inspire envy in his rivals. The bait was taken. The hook was set. The American was to arrive, cash in hand, in May.

To Paul, Antibes was more than a matter of money. Antibes was to be his ticket to the Promised Land, his passage to a comfortable retirement in Montreal, Toronto, or somewhere in the Antipodes. Antibes meant freedom — freedom from the dread of every footfall behind him, every shadow beside him, each knock on the door. Another new name, another new passport from the Spaniard, and for the first time since he was a child, Paul would walk the streets unafraid of being snatched up by the scruff of the neck and flung into a cell. Antibes was life itself.

99

A woman had taken the place vacated by the German officers. She had dead-looking blond-white hair set in rigid waves, a long, thin nose, and led with her chin. Her evening-dress was of cream-colored satin, trimmed with bands of cherry-colored silk. Every finger wore a diamond ring. She raised a jeweled lorgnette and slowly swept the room while peering through it, like an African explorer watching the beasts on the Serengeti. When her focus arrived at the spot where Paul stood, she lowered the glasses to stare at him outright. He watched as the tip of her boa played on her cheek. The smile was unmistakable, but it produced the opposite of its intended effect. It reminded him that Céline Claudet had entered the Rooms about thirty minutes earlier. He bowed to the woman with the boa and left.

Entering the Salle Garnier, he saw that Céline was incandescent this evening. She again wore the emerald-green gown, his favorite. Unlike last night, her dark curls had been allowed to fall loose around her face. Paul smoothed his fingertips along the heel of his palm, recalling the feel of that magnificent hair beneath his fingers as they traced their way along her spine to the concave place in her back and down to caress her bare buttocks.

One night, after the Antibes-deal was set, they had enjoyed a remarkably satisfying session of lovemaking. He had lain with his face buried in the curve of her fragrant neck, which was still moist from the violence of their pleasure. Beneath his cheek, her pulse had not yet returned to normal.

Impulsively, he said, "What if we left here, together?"

"Don't be silly," she answered.

He knew he sounded like a besotted fool. As far as she knew, he had no money, and he dared not mention his prospects. Nonetheless, her rapid, unconsidered response had stung.

As he watched, Céline drew her gloved right hand across the green baize and touched the corner of her mouth before bringing her hand to rest on her left wrist. She was available tonight.

Her sign hit like a blow to the back of his skull. His knees almost buckled beneath the surge of anger. He slumped against the wall, more alarmed than weakened. This reaction signaled how seriously the events of the past two days, The Hyena, Hervé and Murphy, Jonnie — above all, Jonnie — had chinked his armor and burrowed beneath his skin. It was the damned cold, he decided, weakening his defenses. Even the damned headache was threatening to return. A good night's sleep was what was needed. Above all, a good night's sleep was what he needed. Yet it was with a satisfaction bordering on the malicious that, for the first time in five months of meeting clandestinely, Paul sent back his own "Not Tonight" signal.

# Friday, March 14, 1914
## HÔTEL DE PARIS

EASING THE DOOR CLOSED, LILY LISTENED TO THE voices beyond the corner and waited for silence to return after the sound of the elevator's gate closing. Starting forward, she realized she was tiptoeing. Why should anyone else find that odd? She stopped to adjust her attitude and started forward again, then froze at the sound of footsteps approaching in the adjoining corridor. She wished she had brought gloves so she could appear occupied with pulling them on. A porter rushed past her carrying an armload of newspapers.

Over the past twenty-four hours, her prolific imagination had presented one scenario after another of what might lie behind the privacy placard. Most read like the plots of dime-novels. In one, Mrs. Murphy had cottoned on to the infidelity and, not knowing he was dead, shot her husband, then located Little Beauty and shot her too. In another version, Mr. Murphy had disappointed Little Beauty's expectations, so she shot him, tried to poison him, then fled Monte Carlo, or instead of fleeing, Little Beauty committed suicide in an excess of remorse, or she had a second lover who wanted to rid himself of a rival, or Little Beauty and the other lover were responsible for the attempted murders, and he and she were locked in an orgy of champagne and lovemaking, or the other man had strangled her and taken the money and the jewels for himself. Or, or, or.

Lily turned the corner in time to see the service elevator open and a waiter emerge, pushing a cart laden with covered dishes and beverage services. Consciously activating her detective skills, she noted the curly black hair, anemic moustache, and nonexistent chin. To her annoyance, he slowed to a crawl as he approached, sorting through a sheaf of papers on top of the cart. She didn't want to draw attention to herself by abruptly reversing course or by passing him and then reversing, but she could hardly match his inching progress. He glanced in her direction a couple of times as he inspected the pages. She stopped and opened her handbag, making a show of fumbling through the articles inside it.

The waiter arrived at the door with the privacy placard and rapped lightly, announcing "Room Service" in French. She wanted to kiss him.

Drawing up beside the cart, Lily stared straight at the door, but she could sense his apprehensive looks darting in her direction. The key rasping in the lock brought them both on point.

Through the space provided by the partially opened door, Little Beauty, clad in a pink quilted dressing-gown, regarded her two visitors with bewilderment. Her eyes were red and puffy, and her hair, the color of sun-drenched daffodils, fell about her shoulders in a jumble of uncombed curls.

Unsure whether she was more relieved at finding the girl alive or by the alleviation of half the suspicions about Mrs. Murphy, Lily could say nothing for the space of several seconds. "Hello," she managed at last, slipping in front of the cart. "May I introduce myself? My name is Lily Turner. I beg your pardon, but I very much would like to speak with you."

The emotion suffusing the girl's face could have been

confusion, fatigue, or fear. It was impossible to tell. Lily turned to the waiter and added, in French, "In private." He remained with his eyes fixed on Little Beauty, his eyebrows knitted. This was definitely off to a bad start. They were acting as if Lily was going to tie up the girl and rob her as soon as he was got out of the way.

"If you please," Lily said, producing her warmest smile, "it will take only a few minutes. I've seen you before, in the back-garden. My room is just around the corner, number 203." She pointed at the end of the hall.

Looking no less befuddled, Little Beauty stepped back to allow her callers to enter. She surprised Lily by giving the waiter directions in French. Maybe she was from New Orleans. Many sporting girls started out there.

The apartment's floor-plan was identical to Lily's, with a door to a bedroom opening out of a modest-sized sitting room. Here, however, French windows admitted a broad view of the sea instead of looking down onto a garden and out onto other buildings.

As the waiter laid out the cutlery and linens, his seesawing Adam's apple looked like he was dislodging a walnut from his throat. He looked up frequently, first at Little Beauty, then at Lily, then back to Little Beauty. He reversed the arrangement of the salt and pepper shakers, then returned them to their original positions. He repositioned the knife and spoon three times and squared the napkins twice, licking his lips and wiping his hands against the sides of his trousers after each adjustment. Having apparently exhausted his repertoire of stalling devices, he stepped beside the table and stood at attention, like a cadet awaiting orders from his commander.

Lily turned to Little Beauty, whose vacant eyes seemed not to have taken in any of this. "Do you want him for anything else?" Lily nudged.

"No," Little Beauty said quietly. "That will be all," she said more firmly.

Maybe the waiter thought she was talking to Lily, but she doubted it. At any rate, he didn't move.

"I will let you know if I need anything else," the girl said.

Despite this announcement, he dawdled so long Lily was starting to think she was going to have to shove him out the door. After it finally closed behind him, she motioned towards the sofa, where an unopened copy of *The Atlantic Monthly* lay. "Shall we sit?" she said.

The girl obeyed and began twisting the handkerchief clutched in her hands. If she hadn't spoken to the waiter, Lily would have thought the girl was a mute. Choosing a chair perpendicular to the sofa, Lily considered her opening. It needed to sound like a statement, not an accusation.

"You don't know me, but I saw you on the steamer coming over. I saw you with Mr. Murphy, on the boat deck."

Dark creases appeared between the perfectly shaped brows. The hands, surprisingly strong to be so small, had twisted the handkerchief to the size of a paper-straw.

"I – I just happened to see you. I was walking about," Lily said.

As far as it had gone, Mrs. Murphy's description of their February crossing as "vile" was accurate. But Mrs. Murphy had endured the slamming ocean and lashing winds in the relative comfort of a first-class stateroom, and from the many times she had recounted the experience, it was impossible to tell whether her discomfort had been occasioned principally by the punishing North Atlantic winter storms or her parlor suite's lack of a private promenade. Lily, on the other hand, had shared a cabin with three strangers, two of whom spent their days and nights vomiting into buckets beside the berths and a third who lay strapped to her bunk passed out from the Irish whiskey she kept in a flask tucked beneath the thin mattress and snoring at a decibel-level that would have claimed all the prizes in a competition with the ship's horn. Knowing they were sailing on the *Titanic*'s sister-ship did nothing to promote restfulness either. As a consequence, Lily spent a significant part of each night either pacing the third-class promenade or fighting against being bucked out of a chair in the public room.

On the night just mentioned, she was awakened in her chair, not by the violent heaving of the leviathan beneath her but by something more disturbing—an eerie calmness. Wrapped in the deck blanket appropriated for her personal use, she climbed the stairs to the top deck, whose only canopy was the sky. A gibbous moon, nearing the apex of its cycle, was gauzed over by thin clouds. From far below came the sighs of the waves being cast aside by the hull. With the dark blanket draped over her head, whenever she stepped into one of the deep shadows created by one of the four enormous steam-stacks or by the lifeboats rigged along the sides, she was virtually invisible. Upon becoming aware of a couple sandwiched between two lifeboats, her instinct was to clear her throat or shuffle her feet to alert them to her presence. Then she was stunned into inaction. There was something familiar in the man's voice. The woman spoke his name, *Joe.*

It might have been a different Joe. Lily might have been mistaken about the voice. If not, nothing good could possibly come from letting her employer's husband know she had blundered into his clandestine life. She crept backwards slowly, soundlessly, until she was out of their line-of-sight. Claiming the darkness beneath another lifeboat, she had crouched and watched and waited for them to leave.

"I work for Mrs. Murphy," Lily said. "But I haven't told anyone else about you. You see, I don't even know your name."

The girl brushed at the mob of curls flopped across her forehead. "Sally. Sally Holmes." The words, spoken barely above a whisper, were directed at the rug beneath the dainty pink slippers.

Bingo and bull's eye. That night aboard the *Olympic,* other than a fleeting impression of blond hair, Lily had no idea what the woman looked like, and despite certain events she believed were related, such as this girl's appearance in the garden only when Mrs. Murphy was in Monte Carlo and the privacy sign that appeared only when *la femme* Murphy was absent, it was possible these correspondences were coincidental. Life, after all, was fitted out with coincidences. Even though Mr. Murphy took pains to be circumspect about his extramarital affair, by happenstance, Little Beauty and Lily occupied the same floor at the Hôtel de Paris, just as, by happenstance, she had seen the couple on the boat deck.

Sally was working at unraveling the handkerchief.

"I'm pleased to meet you, Sally. I'm very sorry about Mr. Murphy's death." Lily paused to recalibrate her voice, wanting to convey an appropriate level of understanding. "I know it is a great loss for you."

The girl's face, which had been rigid with confusion or fear, melted into sorrow. Her lips pressed inward upon themselves, and her chin trembled beneath a choked-back sob.

Even though Lily was barely twenty-one, next to Sally, she felt years older and worlds wiser. Rationally, she knew that what Sally's kind did to earn a bed and breakfast was no different from what thousands of other women did everyday by becoming wives. But only the enlightened Lily, who had a tendency to disappear at critical junctures, was willing to acknowledge this parity. At the moment, she was finding it difficult to feel compassion for the girl's distress and impossible to feel sympathy for her plight. Even in disarray,

Sally was beautiful. Sensuality poured in streams from her velvety skin. The Gibson Girl mouth curved effortlessly upward, and her large eyes, despite their redness, were a clear, unstained blue, with no allusions to depth. Cleaned up, dressed up, once more deploying her little arts—the sidelong stares, the fluttering eyelashes, the seductive smiles—and she could have a new benefactor in tow by nightfall and be feeding off him like a tick by morning.

Settle down, Lily ordered herself. A good detective could not afford to be hobbled by prejudices. She had read the carbon copy of the police report three times. According to Dr. Fournier's best estimate, Mr. Murphy had died on Wednesday, possibly late in the afternoon or early in the evening. The gunshot had come after that, but there was no way of knowing when the poisoned whiskey was left. One thing was certain: he had died in his own apartment, so that would have been after he had left his mistress.

Might as well plunge right in. "Were you with Mr. Murphy on Wednesday?" Lily said.

Sally swiped at the hair on her forehead and looked back at the service-tray. "Would you care for some coffee?" she said.

It wasn't exactly the response Lily was aiming for, but it was a positive sign. She wasn't being told to leave. She said, "I'll pour if you like. Would you care for some too?"

Sally shook her head.

At the service-tray, Lily took her time. From this vantage point, she could see the bedroom, where a diaphanous beige material was draped over a dressmaker's manikin. Three bolts of fabric were propped against the wall.

"Your room has a pleasant view," she said, taking her chair again. "You must see the sun rise. I look down on the other garden. As I said, I've noticed you there." Quickly, she added,

"Once or twice." She was struggling to bring out the "friend" persona demanded by the occasion. Not just any friend, a *concerned* friend. What did concerned friends say in these kinds of situations? What would Piedmont say?

Piedmont. Dear, dear Piedmont, the cook Effie hired when they moved to the big house, the woman who had taken the place of the mother who had vanished with the move to Chicago. Stereotypically speaking, Piedmont should have been a fat Negress with close-cropped white hair and a permanently clucking tongue. In reality, she had blotchy pink skin, dishwater-blond hair, and was thinner than a needle. During the day, she kept up a mumbling monologue in which identifiable words were discernable only occasionally, like scraps of meat in a thin stew.

"Have you eaten anything today?" Lily asked.

"I'm not hungry."

"You must have been hungry when you ordered a meal. You need to eat. You don't want to go and make yourself sick." So far, classic Piedmont. But the threat of Effie's displeasure wasn't lending muscle to the assertion. "Mr. Murphy wouldn't want you to make yourself sick."

The dam holding back the flood of tears was breached. Lily retrieved a fresh handkerchief from her handbag and pressed it into the girl's hand. Regardless of what Concerned Friend would do, she wasn't about to sit next to Sally and put her arm around her. She wasn't able to muster that level of verisimilitude.

At the age of ten, Lily had been shipped by train to Flourtown, Pennsylvania, to live among a race as alien as Eskimos, to begin her life as an infiltrator, an imposter. At Mount St. Joseph Academy for Girls, she had soon learned there was no salt more pungent than the taste of her own tears. If she had been a tributary, she believed, the Mississippi would have flooded that year. Eventually, the hollowed-out place inside her, paradoxically empty yet brimming with pain, had ceased producing unbearable stabs of grief and embarrassingly timed tears. Yet to this day, someone else's torrent of tears always threatened to pull the lever on her own reservoir of sorrow.

To her relief, the sobbing was cut off in mid-gasp. Sally was visibly fighting to staunch the flow, sniffling loudly, batting her eyelashes, and stifling tiny hiccups. Instead of drying her face with the new handkerchief, she gnawed a corner. Lily leaned back, letting cynicism clear her own eyes. A performance worthy of a standing ovation. The little vamp could probably blush at will too.

"I'm sorry to have to ask," Lily said, pressing the requisite pity into her tone, "especially at a time like this, but I have a few questions I wanted to put to you."

Sally stopped gnawing the handkerchief.

"Is it possible Mr. Murphy was having money difficulties? I mean, did he leave you, as it were, stranded here?"

"What?"

"Had he ...." Lily gathered herself for the blow. "Had he, say, lost money gambling? Let me get to the point. Are you all right financially? This is an expensive hotel. I didn't know if you were worried about how you would pay or get home or –" She stopped herself. It could sound like she was offering to foot the bill. Get to the necklace. But how to get to the necklace? "I want to be honest with you. There's some question about whether Mr. Murphy might have been looking for a way to raise a little money."

This time, there was no doubt. It was fear suffusing Sally's features, but only momentarily. Next, determination filled the blue eyes, the rosy nostrils quivered, and Lily knew she was about to hear a lie.

"I'm sure I wouldn't know," Sally said in a clear, strong voice. Dried tears had left dull traces on her cheeks. "Why are you asking these things if Madeline didn't send you?"

"As I said, I work for Mrs. Murphy. There have been some rather odd inconsistencies associated with –" She almost said *her husband's death*. Accurate, but scarcely politic. "Mr. Murphy's death," she finished.

Then the realization struck. Lily had to bite back a gloating smile. Bingo. Bull's Eye. Checkmate. Game, set, match. How had Sally known Mr. Murphy was dead? It hadn't been in the local newspapers, not yesterday, not today. Lily had looked. And why hadn't Sally asked about the cause of death? And why had no one questioned how a bee could nail a man in a closed bedchamber on the upper floor of this hotel? The suite's windows and balcony doors were never opened. A speck of dust might alight on one of Mrs. Murphy's treasures. And now, now that she thought about it, how unnatural the position of Mr. Murphy's body had been. If he were suffering a fatal reaction to a bee's sting, would he have simply lain on his side and died? Why hadn't she, of all people, seen through it immediately? Mr. Murphy had died in "compromising circumstances." He had died in his mistress' apartment, maybe in her arms, and Sally had done what any mistress would have done. She kept the necklace and the cash and returned the husband to his owner. There were logistics to be dealt with in such situations, namely the inconspicuous removal of the body. How had she managed that? Not alone. That much was for sure. Lily would have to settle that detail later. Sally was eyeing her with open curiosity.

"I apologize," Lily said. "I just realized you must be unaware of the inconsistencies, the oddities, connected with Mr. Murphy's death. He was always so very kind to me. I was hoping I could, well ...." She splayed her fingers in a sign of uncertainty. "Since I had accidental knowledge of your acquaintance with him, I was hoping you could help. Help with these questions, that is."

"What," Sally said in a steely tone, "oddities?"

This, Lily had prepared for, so she slipped effortlessly into a redacted version of events. No mention was made of the missing money or necklace, paste or otherwise. She did, however, include the bee-venom, gunshot wound, and poisoned whiskey, as well as the police's lack of interest in pursuing the matter. Sally's first reaction appeared to be dumb horror, followed by a request for the account to be repeated after which she came up with questions of her own. Yes, Lily told her, these irregularities were going to be investigated, by Mr. Wycliffe, not the police. No, Mrs. Murphy had not yet made arrangements for the body. Yes, Lily most likely would be making them. Yes, Lily would inform Sally once the arrangements were made.

When silence again descended, Sally sat staring at the wall while Lily wished she knew what was going on inside that perfect little head. Her own silence was encased in the satisfaction of knowing she had arrived at the precise place where she and Fran had believed they would have a stockinged leg up on their male counterparts. They had known that women had been acting as spies in the House of Love since the days of Samson and Delilah, but they also divined that the bed was not the only route women could use for access to secret information. Another means could be by befriending the wives and girlfriends of men involved in a plot. Lily knew she was going to have to proceed with delicacy. Sally would never admit she had the necklace or knew where Mr. Murphy pawned it unless she had full faith in her confidante. It didn't take a keen intelligence to detect snobbery, and condescension could be as insulting as contempt.

It was Sally who broke the silence. "Mr. Wycliffe's inquiries, will you know what he learns?"

"I expect to, yes." *Maybe.*

Sally's eyes scanned her visitor from head to toe, lingering on Lily's boots before returning to her face. Recalling the bolts of cloth in the bedroom, Lily resented the appraising nature of the survey. Her gray dress might be plain, but it wasn't a gunny sack, and it had been far from cheap. Nothing she could order from Sears Roebuck would reach her ankles.

"I will pay you to tell me what Mr. Wycliffe learns," Sally said.

"I beg your pardon."

"I will pay you well to tell me what he learns. I want to know who tried to kill Joe. I need to know."

Apparently, the idea that she herself might be in danger had not escaped Sally either. "Do you know who might have wanted him dead?" Lily said.

"Three days ago, I would have said no one. However, you have presented ample evidence that argues to the contrary. Will you tell me what Mr. Wycliffe learns?"

Lily stood to return the cup with the untasted coffee to the service-tray, then crossed to stand in front of the windows. Behind them, the miniature balcony held a pot with a white flowering clematis, bee-bait. She kept her back to the room as her eyes sought the line of demarcation between the gray-blue sky and the gray-blue sea. But this afternoon, the line had blurred into gray invisibility. It was impossible to see where the sea separated from the sky or the sky from the sea.

What, Lily wondered, would she have to sell if she were no longer working with Ted? What could she sell even if she were? What if she uncovered something vitally important on her own? Could she peddle the information to Sally and not tell Mrs. Murphy and her world-class detective cousin?

Those were among the questions nipping at the edges of Lily's conscience while another blasted through it like a cannonball. How much was Sally willing to pay?

Lily returned to Sally but remained standing, uncertain what she was going to say. One of these days, Effie had gleefully predicted, Lily was going to have to broom off her high-horse before she could climb back on it. It was galling to think that prediction was about to be satisfied.

"I cannot retail Mr. Wycliffe's information," she said. Her sense of self-righteous virtue was content with the statement even if her pocketbook was not. "However, I will freely share anything needed to ensure your safety." Sally opened her mouth, but Lily did not allow the interruption. "And I can accept compensation for making inquiries on my own." She leaned down to remove a small gold case from her handbag. "This is my card. I am a partner in a detective bureau in New York City."

As Sally looked at the printed card, her expression quickly went from curiosity to consternation to fury. She turned the card over, studied the blank back, then returned to the printed side. "Who is paying you to follow me?" she demanded.

"No one."

"You said you work for Madeline."

"I told you, I saw you by accident."

"You're not making any sense."

Nor was she. Lily seated herself once more and delivered a brief, straightforward explanation of her situation.

"I see," Sally said. "You're a private detective who just happens to be Madeline Murphy's personal secretary."

That was quite close to exactly what Lily had said.

"Economic necessity," she said.

"Money, you mean. I understand that," Sally said.

I bet you do, Lily thought.

Sally looked down at the card in her hand. "Where –" she began. "What –" she tried again.

Lily felt her disgust rising. She knew what was coming next: *Where is your husband? Send him along. Or your brother will do.* Maybe the "Women Understand Women" slogan they used in their newspaper advertisements should not have been left off their business cards.

"What are your credentials?" Sally said.

Lily spent a couple of seconds mentally changing courses before gathering her answer. She exaggerated only slightly the number and significance of the cases settled thus far, and the Wagner's Detective Agency materials had to be elevated from correspondence course to diploma. "I can provide references," she finished. "But that will take some time."

"What is your rate?"

Lily could hardly hear the question over the sound of her own beating heart.

"For part-time, $25 per week." The same amount she made all month as a secretary. "In advance," she added.

Mrs. Murphy may have introduced Lily to the vocabulary of stockbrokers and demonstrated how to browbeat merchants and lawyers, but Effie had taught her everything there was to know about a cash-up-front business.

Sally's hand slipped between the sofa's arm and the cushion and reappeared with a pocketbook. Counting out the bills in her lap, she said, "There will be a $100 bonus for the name of the person who left the whiskey and another $100 for the name of the person who put a bullet in Joe. Is that acceptable to you?"

# Saturday, March 14, 1914
## HÔTEL DE PARIS

TED HAD ANSWERED THE DOOR IN HIS STOCKING FEET and with two plasters dotting his cheeks. Directing his callers to sit, he then disappeared through the other doorway. Not wanting to stare at her companion, who was reading, or pretending to read, one of the newspapers he had scraped off the sofa, Lily fixed her gaze on the mantle clock. She was eager for this meeting to begin, eager to learn if there were other candidates for the attempted murders besides the ones she had: Mrs. Murphy, Ted Wycliffe, Bridget Rose, and Michael Gallagher. Maybe she would throw in that suspicious-acting floor-waiter. It wouldn't be the first time some lunatic believed himself to be in love with an enchantress and set out to dispose of his arch-rival. She had $200 in bonuses riding on the answers to two attempted murders. Furthermore, there was no telling how long Sally would wait. Girls like her were made for the good times, not for moping around.

Lily had wired all the money to Fran this morning, knowing it would be immediately absorbed by their delinquent accounts but wishing part of it could be used to dig into Mrs. Murphy's background. She remained the prime suspect in Lily's mind. Was she as wealthy in her own right as she pretended to be? Certainly, she was the one who benefitted financially from Mr. Murphy's death, and just as certainly, no one could say she had been prostrated by grief over his demise.

It was too bad, Lily thought, that she couldn't ask Effie about Ted. She would be the perfect person to get the low-down on someone from Chicago. However, not only had Lily never breathed a word in that direction about pursuing a career as a detective, Effie didn't even know Lily had left the United States. Communication between them had ceased when she moved to San Francisco to take the job with Mrs. Murphy. Prior to that, Effie had made it clear she expected Lily to settle closer to Chicago, and she had made her disapproval of Lily's choice of California even clearer.

Looking up, Lily saw Paul Newcastle was regarding her with that infuriating twinkle in his eyes. No smirk, nothing she could put her finger on, just an undeniable feeling of being teased. She was instantly reminded of a man with an annoying grin and a kiss like a soft breeze.

"I was thinking," she said, "that I've not seen anything in the local newspapers regarding Mr. Murphy."

Paul snapped the edges of the paper before refolding it and smoothing the creases until it appeared untouched.

"You will find, Miss Lily, that there is no scandal in Monaco and very little crime. Malicious, even salacious, gossip perhaps, but no scandal and very little crime."

"You don't expect me to believe that, do you?"

"There is an occasional bit of unpleasantness, I grant you. However, such inconveniences are managed with great discretion. It is much like those parents who declare their daughters mad and lock them in the attic. As long as their privacy is honored, no one outside the immediate family needs to be made aware of the unpleasantness harbored there. Now that I think about it, that's not a bad analogy.

You might say the Principality chooses to maintain the same steadfast attitude about crime within its borders as mothers do about the virtue of their daughters."

"Are you saying crime is allowed to flourish in Monaco?"

"Quite the contrary, and I hope you don't think I meant to suggest a lack of virtue is allowed to flourish in young women. Perhaps an example: a few years ago, rumors flew about a Russian aristocrat who was said to have shot a police officer here. There were many whispered versions but never a public acknowledgement. Not long afterwards, Monaco's Commissioner of Police was awarded a ribbon or medal or some such by the Tsar. Completely unrelated incidents, I am certain.

"If anything, Monaco's police are exceptionally competent. If I am not mistaken, Chief Inspector Gautier served for years under the great Goron in the Paris Sûreté. My point is, Monte Carlo attracts miscreants of every class, but it would be dismal advertisement for the gambling Rooms if criminals were officially spotted on this soil, so Monaco prefers to hand off its problems to Scotland Yard or France's La Sûreté Nationale and let them make the arrests. An excellent system, transgressors are dealt with, and Monaco's reputation remains unsullied. There was the notorious Gould affair in '07, but that was too sensational, and there was no other place to send it."

She was about to ask about the notorious affair when Ted Wycliffe flung himself through the doorway. Lily thought he might be having an attack of gout. He was leaning more heavily on his walking stick and moving more stiffly than usual. He also looked heavier around the middle. At the rate he was going, he would soon be unable to tie his shoelaces.

"Let's go over what has been learned since last we met," he said. "Thursday afternoon, was it not?"

Lily obediently nodded while Paul made no response. When Ted assumed a position in front of the fireplace, it wasn't clear what impression he wished to create. Being of insufficient stature to rest his arm on the mantle and project that commanding presence, he leaned on his stick like it was a Pillar of Hercules. Lily got her notepad in place. Despite all her finer instincts, not to mention common sense, she maintained a thin hope that, if the rust and peacock feathers were knocked off, Ted might be able to teach her something about the craft of detecting. Who knew? If she stretched the possibilities all the way to fantasy, someday he might put in a good word for her with Pinkertons.

Apparently satisfied he at last had his audience's attention, Ted said, "Let me begin by telling you, Paul, that some of the things the chief inspector disclosed yesterday have put this case in an entirely different light than what I saw on Thursday. As they say, one should not count his chickens before the eggs are hatched. This is a new case, far more complicated than I anticipated. There is a lot more to think through. But trust me. The outcome will be the same. Justice will be served. First, on the table in front of you, Paul, is an exact description of all the necklace's stones, their cuts and weights. It was prepared for the insurance company. Take that journal too. I want you to put your notes in it like Lily's doing."

The paper would be the one Lily retrieved yesterday from the files in her sitting room. A person unfamiliar with Mrs. Murphy might have questioned why she brought such a document to the other side of the world. In fact, however, the files contained itemized lists of everything brought and bought, so an insurance claim could be filed promptly if anything went missing.

Paul picked up the sheet of paper, then folded and placed it in his pocket without glancing at it.

"You need to get on that right away," Ted said. "We must, as they say, make hay while the sun shines."

Lily couldn't help herself. She rolled her eyes. Here she was, thirsting for the drops of occupational wisdom that would issue forth from the mouth of this crack investigator, and all she got was an observation on the intersection of sunshine with hay-harvesting.

"Mrs. Murphy is offering 10,000 francs for the return of her necklace," Ted said. "Can you remember to put that word out?"

The question, the attitude, and the tone were beyond insulting, but Paul's face remained as immobile as a painting. Lily had to admire his disciplined responses to Ted's insults. Although he revealed flashes of good humor towards her, with Ted, Paul's demeanor never displayed anything other than shallow civility or benign indifference.

Next, Ted launched into a summary of the meeting with Chief Inspector Gautier. Paul's lack of reaction upon hearing the cause of death might have been attributable to his usual opacity. However, Lily was willing to bet Dr. Fournier had spread that news to the rest of Monaco long before Mrs. Murphy was informed. Ted continued with the details he had omitted in the previous session: the whiskey, the tickets to Belfast, the German dictionary. He concluded with the information that Monaco's police no longer believed there was a crime to investigate.

Lily intended to ask Sally about the tickets and the dictionary. They did stand out as peculiarities, especially after Gautier substituted a different book. But why had the inspector said nothing about the fact that Mr. Murphy was moved? Surely, if Lily figured it out, he had too. Maybe relocating a corpse before it was shot was not considered a crime in Monaco either.

"At first, I was inclined to brush those things aside," Ted said. "People get up to all kinds of odd doings when they go abroad. I didn't know then that the whiskey was poisoned. These things have expanded the scope of my inquiries. The tickets to Belfast were third-class, not Joe's usual mode of travel unless he was planning to go incognito, which we cannot rule out. I've spoken to the valet, Gallagher. He swears his master said nothing about the two of them going to Ireland. So we are at a dead-end, so to speak. This doesn't mean we can eliminate Gallagher as a suspect. He is Irish, after all, just like my cousin's husband. The Irish hate all authorities except the Pope. As for the German dictionary, Joseph Murphy was a prodigious reader, but he was not a student of languages. As they say, still waters run deep, but I don't think this is a matter of still waters."

He looked at Lily and, to her horror, produced a smile. "You, my dear Lily, will have a more active role than I originally planned. I trust you will be up to it?"

*My dear Lily?* On the one hand, a more active role was exactly what she wanted. On the other hand, *my dear Lily?* "Yes," she said. "As a matter of fact, I've been thinking I will talk to the chambermaids."

"Why would you want to do that?" Ted said.

"To find out what they saw when they last cleaned the rooms, whether or not the glass of whiskey was there, that sort of thing." She braced for the rebuke which would slap her into her proper place, lower than dirt.

"Right. Exactly. I was going to tell you to do exactly that."

Of course you were, she thought.

"And you, you Paul, are to interrogate the floor-waiters, bootblacks, barbers, the other men on the staff who may have come in contact with Joseph Murphy. I've spoken with Mr. Barousse again. The hotel doesn't care to have word going around that a robbery has taken place on its premises, let alone two attempted murders. He has agreed you will work for me until these matters are resolved to my satisfaction. Do you understand? Check with him if you must. Now, tell me –" He was interrupted by a polite knock on the door.

Ted took the note the porter handed him and read it without closing the door.

He looked at Paul and Lily. "We have to go to Maddie right away. Her suite has been ransacked."

It was hard to read anything other than delight in his expression.

# Saturday, March 14, 1914
## HÔTEL DE PARIS

"YOU THERE! YOU! PUT THAT DOWN. IT NEEDS TO be wrapped carefully, very carefully. Do you understand very carefully? Everything must be wrapped in tissue paper. Everything. I don't care if it's gold or silver or cast-iron. Mr. Barousse, doesn't anyone in this hotel speak English?"

From his position in the parade of hotel staff toting trunks into the Murphys' suite, Paul heard Barousse step into the breach to edify the offender.

"Lily, it's about time you got here," Mrs. Murphy said. "Tell him to put that vase down."

Paul had barely cleared the threshold when the line jolted to a halt. He stepped out of the procession to work his way closer to a wall, beyond that woman's striking range. The room was a mess all right, worse even than Wycliffe's. The furniture's drawers had been removed, their contents emptied onto the floor. A secretary with a marble top had been forced open, much of it smashed to bits. The cushions from the sofas and chairs were sliced. Goose-down, horsehair, and steel springs were scattered throughout the room. Interestingly enough, the multitude of *bric à brac*, some housed within vitrines, others obscuring the tops of tables, were mostly undisturbed. Wedged amidst the disorder, a flotilla of valises, hat boxes, suitcases, portmanteaus, and steamer trucks pasted over with railroad and shipping-line labels awaited the fulfillment of their destinies. Jacques Barousse was installed on the far side of the room, hands clasped behind his back, rocking on his heels like a waiter suffering from an attack of gas. Wycliffe had made his way to his cousin's side and was saying something she seemed to be ignoring.

"Those go in my bedroom," she said. "Take them to my bedroom. I want to separate how they're packaged. For heaven's sakes, why is that man not wearing gloves?"

A keening coming from one of the bedchambers overrode the last question. If that wasn't bad enough, the racket set the three caged birds to squawking at the top of their tiny lungs.

"Lily," Mrs. Murphy shouted over the din, "go with Mr. Barousse. He's to find me a suitable villa by this afternoon. You look at it, and if you agree, take it."

"Madame," Barousse said, the word sounding pinched, "I-I said we would try to find you something. This time of year, it may be difficult. It is the season."

Her hand flicked off the protest. "I know it's the season. Why do you think I'm here? Teddy, you know it's the season, don't you? You're the one who said we must come now." Again to Lily, "I don't care what it costs. The hotel will guarantee it. Won't you, Mr. Barousse?"

No question who had the whip-hand here.

New trunks, untouched by a single sticker, arrived and were huddled next to the others. The wailing recommenced, now sounding more like a braying mule.

"What is that noise?" Wycliffe said.

"Bridget Rose. She doesn't want to go," Mrs. Murphy said.

"I'm not leaving Michael," a tear-choked voice corrected.

"Lily, go stuff a sock in her mouth," Wycliffe ordered.

"Teddy, are you staying here? Your room will be next. What do these people want?"

"Maddie, slow down. Mr. Barousse, will you excuse us while I speak with my cousin?"

Barousse nodded his agreement and continued eyeing the porters. As yet, he had shown no sign of recognizing Paul's presence. The sounds from the bedroom slackened to whimpering, then ceased. More porters arrived with more trunks. A Good Samaritan covered the hysterical birds.

"Tell them to put the new trunks on top of the others," Mrs. Murphy told Barousse.

"Maddie, I implore you. Let Mr. Barousse tell those men to stop right now. I need to look at the evidence before it's further disturbed. Have the police been called?"

"The police? What can they do besides tell me a swarm of bees was responsible?"

Lily returned, clutching her journal and notebook. From this distance, Paul could barely see the cut on her cheek, only half hidden by her hair, which had aroused his curiosity earlier. Somewhat like his scar, a person had to be looking for the cut to see it.

Mrs. Murphy said, "Did you check with the telegraph office this morning?" When Lily said she had and that nothing had been received, Mrs. Murphy said, "Then leave right now, you and Mr. Barousse. I want a villa as soon as possible."

"Maddie," Wycliffe said, bringing her hands to a standstill with him own, "you're overwrought. I want to talk to you about what's happened, just a few minutes. Then Mr. Barousse will find you another room."

Barousse confirmed the statement with a nod.

"I'm not staying here. I've contacted Madame Ephrussi, the baroness Rothschild. Before, at the Casino in Cannes, she offered me the use of her new villa at Cap Ferrat. She has two others in Monaco and doesn't use it much. I can stay there until I find a place of my own."

"But will you be safe? Mr. Barousse, tell her she's better off here, where the police are patrolling the streets and buildings day and night."

"My husband was shot in his bed and barely missed being poisoned in this place. Just how safe do you want to tell me it is?"

The yowling ratcheted up once more. Wycliffe stomped to the bedroom door, his stride significantly improved since he first appeared in his sitting room.

"Bridget Rose," he yelled, "go back to your quarters and prepare your bag. You will be told when to return and finish packing Mrs. Murphy's things. Mr. Barousse."

The manager started forward at the sound of his name, like a horse at the jingle of its bells.

"Could you direct Miss Turner and let us know where Mrs. Murphy can rest in the meantime?"

Having been instructed neither to go nor to stay, Paul remained where he was, waiting to hear from one of his two commanding officers. With luck, contradictory orders would be issued, and the two would be forced to settle the matter with pistols and seconds at daybreak in a field outside of town.

Now silent, a woman emerged from the bedroom and crept along the wall at the other side of the room. Her hair was the color and dullness of ashes. Her defeated aspect and reluctant pace reminded Paul of a public execution. She left the hallway door open behind her, having never once looked at her audience.

After she disappeared from sight, all eyes went back to Barousse. With a few words and gestures, he had the room emptied of porters. As he was leaving, he stepped closer to Paul and said, "Report to my office when you are finished here."

The room settled into silence. Wycliffe placed one of the destroyed cushions upside down on the exposed springs of a sofa and urged his cousin to sit. Ordered to pour two brandies, Paul lined up three glasses. He was heartened to see the suites were outfitted with first-rate crystal. He filled the one for himself to the brim, then looked around for a silver salver. There should have been three or four, if not five.

"Tell me exactly what happened," Wycliffe said, placing the glass in Mrs. Murphy's hand. "I know you're anxious to leave, but we must keep our eye on the ball. Tell me about yesterday."

Mrs. Murphy drank off half the brandy before beginning. "I went out to the Jones' steam-yacht. They just arrived from the West Indies, and I sent my card over right away. He's one of New York's 400, you know, related to the Newbolds. They haven't missed a year in the Social Register since 1888. All the clubs too, the Union, the Racquet, the Tuxedo. We dined at Ciro's then went out to the yacht. It's grand, perfectly grand. Eight staterooms, a crew of twenty-seven, outfitted with tiled bathrooms, four fireplaces, gorgeous china."

"Who knew you were going to be gone overnight?"

"Lily. Bridget. You. I don't know."

"Paul, did you write that down?"

Paul hadn't recorded anything. Any idiot should be able to remember what Mrs. Murphy had said. But he had forgotten Wycliffe wasn't just any idiot. He was a colossal idiot.

"What did you do last night?" Wycliffe said.

"We played cards, Whist."

Paul considered interrupting to ask who won. Surely, The Hyena would want that detail for his collation of clues.

"We rose around ten o'clock and had breakfast. Indescribable. Smoked salmon, omelets, lobster, fresh grapes and strawberries." She stared accusingly at Paul.

"This establishment should think about employing new cooks. They roast their meat to rags. I've fed pigs better."

He lowered his eyes and opened the journal for the first time to write, *Fire chef.* Then he crossed that out and replaced it with *Get pigs*.

"And I return to this. Why would they come back?" Her voice caved with distress. "I've got to get out of here, Teddy. We'll just have to make other arrangements, you and I. People were in here, in my things, in all my things. Thank God, Mother's necklace had already been stolen!"

Wycliffe patted her hand like she was an old-age pensioner. "I know, dear. I need to hear a little more. Then you can go take a rest. Bridget Rose will bring whatever you need."

She flared back to full strength. "How will she know what I need? A woman who's been with me a few scant weeks?"

The brandy had loosened the congestion, and Paul could no longer hold back his cough. Mrs. Murphy swirled to deliver another withering stare. Cyril Phelps might want to pass over the most obvious candidate for the attempted murders of Joseph Murphy in favor of some Greek snake-oil salesman, but Paul was putting his money on the widow. She had the disposition of a boiled cat and probably trained with Annie Oakley. He would credit her with the lethal whiskey as well. That woman would poison her husband's breakfast if he so much as sneezed at an inconvenient moment. However Joseph Murphy met his death, he had obviously taken the easy way out.

After a few more questions and answers passed between the cousins, Paul followed the pair into her private quarters where, absent the archipelagoes of packing boxes, the incursion was even more evident. Again, drawers had been pulled out, contents strewn on the floor. The bed had been stripped, the mattress and pillows sliced apart. Piles of crumpled gowns, confections of satin, crepe, silk, and lace, lay heaped on the floor in front of three opened wardrobes. As in the sitting room, the smaller things, silver and crystal scent-bottles, trays of combs and pins, were untouched.

Paul entered the bathroom. It smelled like a Grasse factory. Milady obviously favored milled soaps, French perfumes, and silver toilet-accessories. The towels had been pulled from the cupboards, but the staggering number of small jars, pill-bottles, and ointments lining the upper shelves were undisturbed. Paul awarded the intruders a plus for thoroughness but a demerit for neatness. The ripping and slicing were puzzling. The poorer classes hid their pathetic treasures under floorboards or hearth stones, but rich men didn't typically sew their money into cushions and mattresses, especially not in hotel rooms. Not that it couldn't be done. With enough time, skill, and the right tools, upholstered furniture could be retacked and a carefully opened seam invisibly repaired. He and Hervé had once turned a place inside out without leaving a sign of their uninvited presence. But they had had a comfortable week. These culprits had to make do with less than a day.

"Is anything missing?" Wycliffe asked.

"How should I know?" Mrs. Murphy said. "I haven't had time to go through everything."

"Where was your jewelry?"

"Except for what I had with me, I had Mr. Barousse put everything in the hotel's safe, barn door and all."

"Maddie, someone thinks you have something they want."

Indeed, Paul thought. And what might that be?

"What about Joe's room?" Wycliffe said.

"Mr. Barousse said it's turned over too. Why didn't they look when they were here to shoot him?"

After the widow took her leave, Paul followed Wycliffe into Murphy's bedchamber. As expected, the room's contents were tossed about and the mattress and cushions sliced. Paul waited in the doorway while Wycliffe paced the room like a claims inspector.

At the end of his third circuit, he said, "Are you aware, Paul, that Monte Carlo is a hotbed of international espionage?"

"Afraid I've not heard that before."

"Well it is, and after what's happened here, I have a lot to think about."

Paul made no reply.

"Be at my room Monday, day after tomorrow, four o'clock sharp, so we can take this up again after I've had time to think." Then, lowering his voice for no reason Paul could discern other than to sound more mysterious, Wycliffe said, "I just told you about the tickets to Belfast and the German dictionary that were found in this room. I'm going to have to work it out. All those things, the murder, the tickets, the dictionary, there must be a connection."

He went on to indicate where the German dictionary and the tickets for passage were found, hovering over each spot as if reliving a beatific vision. From an inner pocket, he produced a book with a green cover. "Can you read German?" he asked.

Paul could but said he could not.

Wycliffe leafed through the book, then made a show of turning it upside down and shaking its pages. It was impossible to think he hadn't done this before.

"Sometimes people hide things inside books," he announced. "This dictionary was in my pocket. The tickets are in my room. It could be, they are what the thieves were looking for."

Paul doubted it. Whatever was being sought was of

sufficient value to make it conceivable a millionaire like Joseph Murphy might stitch it into his furniture. Tickets to Belfast, even if first-class, wouldn't be worth hiding under a cushion, let alone sewing into it.

"I'm starting to think the two things are connected," Wycliffe said.

Possibly, but Paul was fairly certain a man could get by in Ireland without speaking German.

Wycliffe said, "Before you object –"

Paul wasn't about to object. He had had all of this coxcomb he could stomach in one day.

"It's becoming clear to me that Joe Murphy was involved in something underhanded and whatever it was got him shot. Also, whatever these intruders were looking for, they didn't find it. That much is clear to me too."

That much was clear to Paul as well. "Just so," he said, placing his hat on his head and tracing his fingers along its brim. "I'll leave you now. Got to make those inquiries about the necklace."

Furthermore, as a man who never backed coincidences, Paul would also be making an inquiry about this disgracefully sloppy business in the Murphys' suite.

# Saturday, March 14, 1914
## HÔTEL DE PARIS

"TAKE A CHAIR," BAROUSSE DIRECTED, WITHOUT taking his eyes off the page he was writing on.

In honor of his dual roles as Subdirector for the Commissariat of Surveillance and The Hyena's puppet, Paul took two chairs, à la Nathan Rothschild, placing his overcoat and homburg on one and seating himself on another. Barousse blotted the fresh writing, screwed the top onto the fountain pen, squared the edges of the papers before him, and solemnly regarded his visitor without speaking. Paul was used to these long pauses. He suspected the man wanted to give the impression of being sunk in deep, ponderous thinking while, in fact, he was reviewing his supper order.

"I thought you were villa-shopping," Paul said, unwilling to wait longer. He was overdue for reporting at the Rooms, and for all he knew, Jonnie was there gambling away Paul's hard-earned investment in him.

"That is why I have staff. My deputy accompanied Miss Turner." The stammer which launched Barousse's sentences in English was absent in French. He stopped speaking while he removed the top from the fountain pen and refilled it from the cut-glass inkwell. This interruption completed, he said, "I am pleased you will continue working on the

Murphy situation. It casts a grave shadow across our hotel's reputation."

Paul decided he must find out what was in those camphor compresses he was applying to his chest each night because he was certain they were causing hallucinations. First, Jonnie at the lift and now, Barousse acting perfectly civil.

"What exactly have you learned?" the manager asked, trying unsuccessfully to sound casual.

"Nothing Gautier doesn't already know."

"And what is it, exactly, that Gautier knows?"

Paul recited it all: the bee, the whiskey, the gunshot, the paste necklace, the dictionary, the tickets. Most likely, Gautier knew of Murphy's appearances at Winzig Krenz's too. Others must have seen him there. Regardless, Krenz was outside Paul's remit, so he omitted that detail. He did disclose what he would have told Wycliffe about Murphy's looking for a high-stakes game. Paul wasn't the only one who knew about that quest, so there was no profit in keeping it secret. That he had made no progress in the locating the necklace was the truth. That he had made inquiries, not.

"And the family, what have you learned about them? How do you find Monsieur Wycliffe?"

"He has many winning qualities."

"What does he know?"

"The dictionary and the tickets to Belfast seem to have excited his interest."

"What does he make of them?"

"He doesn't know what to make of them."

Barousse put his hand to his nose and pushed up his spectacles, then removed them to polish the lenses with his handkerchief. Another break to consider supper.

"This is an embarrassing situation for all of us," he said, returning the spectacles to his nose.

Paul didn't pretend to agree. The Society dealt regularly with bankrupts, swindlers, blackmailers, thieves, pickpockets, the occasional suicide or suspicious death, and an ever present host of self-righteous moralizers prophesizing earthquakes engendered by a wrathful God. Other than the bee, was anything so different here?

Barousse said, "Mrs. Murphy is determined to quit the hotel, but she is leaving others here on her account."

So that was it. As manager, Barousse was responsible for everything on the surface of the hotel and everything that lay behind it: the housekeeping, the heating, the plumbing, the shops, the kitchen, the restaurant, but always, always, his biggest concern was whether the guests could and would pay, especially if they had invested all their money in the Casino. A corpse in one of her bedrooms would be a perfect excuse for Mrs. Murphy to do the hotel out of her bill. In fact, for her, one of those squawking birds found dead in its cage would probably serve just as well.

"How many rooms are on her account?" Paul asked.

Barousse opened a folder and studied the top page as if he hadn't thought to tally the number before. Paul was ready to snatch it out of his hand and look for himself. There could be no purpose in any of this except to further delay his reporting to work. Then again, perhaps that was exactly the point, to put him in bad odor with management, to get him fired or demoted. This could not be allowed to happen. He had to remain strapped to the Ixion wheel of wage-earning until the deal at Antibes was consummated. Like chickens, big tunas shouldn't be counted until they were safely landed. The hook might be set, but the line could snap, or the catch might be swallowed by a whale.

Looking up, Barousse said, "There is the suite, plus her cousin, her secretary, a man-servant, and a woman-servant. I would like for you to continue to work closely with Monsieur Wycliffe and to keep me informed of what he is doing."

Especially if it looks like he's about to pick up sticks and move? But that made little sense. Barousse had any number of eyes inside the hotel – chambermaids, porters, floor-waiters – who could do that better than an outsider.

"I have spoken with Frédéric Wicht. Effective immediately, he has given you a furlough from your Casino duties."

Paul remained stock still. Why didn't Barousse go to Maubert, the Director of Interior Service, with the request? Why did he approach the general director of the Casino unless it was to make sure he was aware of Paul's dereliction of duty? Paul's face grew as rigid as Agamemnon's death-mask while he internally questioned for the thousandth time the source of Barousse's tireless animosity.

Four years ago, when Paul first landed in Monaco, he had been almost as full of fear as when he had arrived in Paris twenty-five years earlier and for the same reason. About a month after he had begun playing cards at La Cave du Renard, Pierre Vioget observed, "Your hands are very good, my friend. I begin to suspect you can arrange the cards according to your pleasure."

Paul neither protested nor agreed with the assessment. Instead, he passed the deck to be cut.

"My cousin works in surveillance at the Casino and can recommend you," Pierre had said. "They should appreciate your talents. It takes one to catch one, does it not?"

The management of the Casino apparently saw value in Paul's gambling-hall savvy because he quickly rose to supervisor of his shift. As such, one of his duties was to review the lists of the hotels' guest and to disseminate the more notable names among the members of his team. Until two months ago, he retrieved these lists each week from the Front

Desk of the Hôtel de Paris. But in January, this changed. He was told to report to Jacques Barousse for the lists. Initially, this worried him. Were the lists being salted? Did someone suspect they were being handed over to a third-party, such as Cyril Phelps? However, several weeks passed and nothing untoward emerged, leaving Paul to conclude the change had been only to put him at the manager's tormenting pleasure. He no longer was simply handed the lists. He was also expected to be a hewer of wood and carrier of water.

Most weeks, in addition to handing him the lists, Barousse had some demeaning task he wanted Paul to perform before he reported to work at the Casino. Paul chose not to draw attention to himself by making an issue of the matter. He was too close to Antibes to make waves, but this didn't stop him from questioning what he had done to earn the man's disapprobation. He even asked someone to point out Madame Barousse, to ensure he hadn't inadvertently made an overture to her. Ultimately, he decided Barousse was nothing more than a sadistic little prig of a Frenchman who was taking advantage of a chance to torture an Englishman. Paul couldn't say for certain that he wouldn't do the same if the opportunity presented itself.

He got to his feet.

"One more request," Barousse said. "I would like for you to keep me informed, informed in detail, of everything that happens in this matter. I would like to know in detail," he repeated, as if this depth of revelation had not been emphasized before, "everything you learn about Monsieur Murphy and his acquaintances."

"Should not be a problem," Paul said, shrugging into his overcoat. "I'm keeping a diary."

# Saturday, March 14, 1914
## VILLA ACHILLES

BEFORE PULLING THE BELLS BESIDE THE DOOR, PAUL waited on the stoop, listening. He heard strains of music coming from the rear of the villa, but no voices. Even if Hervé were hosting a game tonight, it was early, only seven o'clock.

Left to wait in the unheated salon by Antonio, Paul released a weak cough, more from boredom than from need, and automatically checked the handkerchief for blood. He was annoyed by the chilly discomfort of the room and the lack of refreshment. He wished he could get the answers to the two questions he had left yesterday and be done with it. But it wasn't going to be that easy. They had passed that. The number of persons expressing a strong interest in the recently deceased Joseph Murphy of San Francisco had turned into a full-throated choir, and that Hervé was one had become increasingly obvious.

Antonio returned with a tea service on a tray, which he placed on one of the tables without offering to pour, and turned to building a fire. He was coaxing the flames into fuller life when Hervé rushed into the room, tying a red silk kimono around his waist and smelling heavily cologned. After pouring himself a cup of tea, he gave Paul a significant look then took his place on the divan and proceeded to further stress Paul's endurance by embarking on a lengthy lamentation over the Principality's opera season. Considering that he never set foot in Monte, what did Hervé care if that overdressed Neapolitan, Enrico Caruso, had delayed his appearance there another year? And what did Paul care if that ingrate owed his early success to Monte Carlo or if Stravinsky's absurd *Le Sacre du printemps* had finally put that perfumed circus-ringmaster, Sergei Diaghilev, and his herd of performing seals in their place? Meanwhile, Antonio was torching more holes in Paul's patience by spraying sparks as he jabbed at the logs with the poker. For God's sake, had no one ever told that boy not to play with fire?

For his part, Hervé was still dwelling on Diaghilev and his Russian Ballet, which entertained at Monte Carlo every season. Had Paul not been aching to hear about a more important subject, he might have been more sympathetic to the commentary, especially since it was Hervé who had taught him such things could matter. Paul may have taught himself how to wax over his humble beginnings with an upper-crust accent and society-manners, but it had been Hervé who taught him it was not enough to speak and behave like a cultured man. He had to think like one as well.

WHEN GEORGE CHANDLER, OR WHOEVER HE PRETENDING TO BE THAT week, turned nineteen, he was surviving a second year in Paris by continually shifting, like the hunted criminal he felt himself to be, from one rented room to the next, each place seedier and more steeped in squalor than the last. He set out to learn the new language by hanging about in wine shops and bars, but his progress in debauchery soon outstripped his advancements in French. When Hervé literally stumbled over him early one morning in the doorway to the pension they shared on a street off the Boulevard Saint-Michel, he introduced himself with a hard kick, rousing Paul to a bleary consciousness.

"You look like shit," Hervé said, in French.

Paul peered through the slits beneath his swollen eyelids. "What did you say?" he mumbled.

"You smell like shit," Hervé said, in English.

And so it had begun.

❋   ❋   ❋

"Is it Jonnie?" Paul asked as soon as Antonio quit the room with an unnecessarily loud closing of the door.

Hervé sipped tea, then held up an index finger. "One. Mr. Jonathan Chandler of London is in Monte Carlo along with a friend, Clyde Hartfield, who is an assistant commissioner with the New Scotland Yard. They are residing at the Riviera Palace. The same Mr. Hartfield heads up the Yard's Anthropometric Bureau and is attending the International Police Conference Prince Albert convened. Were you ever enrolled in France's Anthropometric Bureau?"

"Once, as Leroy Israel."

"But yes, now I remember, but Mr. Israel died tragically. How did it happen?"

"Shot by a jealous husband, most likely."

Hervé nodded and held up a second finger. "The conference is to end Friday. Three. Jon and the estimable Mr. Hartfield will return to England aboard the *Rapide* the following day." Hervé gave a concerned look before asking, "What are you going to do about it?"

Paul's only answer was a couple of short shakes of his head.

"You cannot afford to delay. You have only until Saturday."

Paul shook his head again.

"You have only until Saturday."

"I heard that the first time you said it. You don't know what went on between Jonnie and me,"

"You never told me."

"It doesn't matter. It's too late, and I don't care."

When Hervé threw up his arms in exasperation, Paul abruptly set his empty cup on the table. "Ring that boy and tell him to bring some whiskey," he said. "The good stuff this time."

AFTER TAKING A HEALTHY SLUG OF THE LIQUOR AND LEANING BACK TO absorb its mellowing effect, Paul said, "I don't know that I'm not still angry."

"How does that change what happened?"

Paul took another large swallow, then spoke to the empty tumbler. "It was four years ago, 1910, the year luck finally ran us to ground. Marie-Odile had .... Well, I had lost her. A month later, and you .... Well, La Santé." He looked up. "Do you need me to remind you when that happened?"

"You may forgo the bother. I am unlikely to forget."

"Right. As I said, you and she were gone. Jonnie and I had been arguing through the post for the better part of a year before that. The letters, of course, had long delays."

"You were using the accommodation address in Sydney?"

"Yes."

"And still growing sheep somewhere in the great Outback?"

"Yes. I was about to get myself elected Governor of the Province or Police Commissioner or whatever it is they have down there. I was doing exceptionally well."

Hervé nodded.

"He wrote that he wanted to throw over his position in Muir's Chambers. That's what he opened the bidding with. Said he didn't find the work – I don't remember exactly how he worded it – but in essence, he didn't find the work congenial. I asked him what that had to do with the price of prunes in Jerusalem. I told him to name how many navvies or ironworkers or coal miners or, for that matter, rag-and-bone men he thought labored under taxing and dangerous circumstances because they remained in persistent enchantment of the labors they performed. It should have ended there, but it didn't. Each subsequent letter upped the ante. Next, it was that he had given it a deal of thought and believed he *might* like to work for a newspaper. Then it was, yes, he had definitely decided he wanted to undertake a career as a journalist. Naturally, I matched every raise with my unguarded opinion. We had a number of correspondences on the subject, but not long after I fetched up here, a letter arrived saying he had done it, thrown everything over, everything we had worked for, sacrificed for. He didn't say when, only that it was *fait accompli*."

Hervé picked up the decanter and poured a whiskey for himself before refilling Paul's glass.

"I read on. It only got worse. He wrote that he had thrown everything over, not so he could become an arbiter of taste, like Arnold, or a man with his foot on the throat of the prime minister, like Stead or Disraeli, not so he could be a name in the mouth of everyone of importance. No, he had thrown it all over so he could be a crime reporter. A crime reporter! He had the cheek to argue that he was particularly well qualified for this *profession* – his word, not mine. He was, he noted – as though I were ignorant of this feature of his character – an Oxbridge-educated man. In addition, he was well trained in the law, understood its requirements and procedures. Here's the priceless bit. Besides those sterling qualifications, Jonnie believed he was specially suited as a crime reporter because of his own 'long and intimate familiarity with the street-life of the lower classes.' I believe those are fairly close to his exact words."

Paul raised the glass to his lips but lowered it without drinking. "So that is, was, his unimpeachable argument. He had been pulled dripping from the sewers of Liverpool and handed the unheard of — for a boy like that — opportunity to take a degree at Cambridge and then had the great good fortune to land a position as articled clerk with Muir, only the most successful barrister in London, a secure, respectable position men of Jonnie's rank could only dream of – that is, if they ever managed to get their filthy heads far enough out of the gutter to see it. All of this, I was supposed to understand, led to the inescapable conclusion that he was destined to be a crime reporter."

Hervé said, "Perhaps he took a caution from Icarus. Am I to assume you did not put your imprimatur on this line of reasoning?"

"I don't know with whom I was more disgusted, with him for being such a scrupulous ingrate — he didn't have to tell me about it — or with myself for not letting Sophie give him to the baby farmer. I began my reply by pointing out the galaxy-sized difference between his version of 'long and intimate familiarity' and mine, of the difference between a day spent waiting to receive a paid-for supper – paid for by me, I might add, I was sending the money for his suppers – the difference between that and a day spent scrounging it by begging or picking pockets or stealing rotten turnips. I also pointed out those were the options on a good day, that on a bad day, a day when all four sides of a boy's stomach were stuck to each other, he would pray to be lucky enough to find a sodomite to lure him into an alley and pay a pence to bugger him, and that on a truly bad day, a day when he couldn't remember the last time he had feasted on a moldy morsel of bread, he hoped to be lucky enough to find a half-wit to lure into an alley so he could smash him over the head and try to sell his body to the dissectors. If all else failed, I counseled, as it often did, that self-same lad with whom Jonnie was exceedingly intimate would put rocks in his pocket and leap off a wharf. I went on in this heart-warming vein at some length." Paul drained his glass in one prolonged draught and waited for the burning in his throat to subside before he spoke again. "I concluded by saying it didn't matter what he did because, from that point onward, he was dead to me."

"And the rest has been silence?" Hervé said.

"Naturally, what was there left to say?"

"You will regret letting this opportunity slip through your fingers."

"As I said, it's too late. He was just a losing hand I decided to fold."

"It's a new game."

"As I said, I don't care."

Hervé regarded him pensively. "My friend, I know you. You always use anger and hatred to cauterize your wounds, thinking they will scar over with indifference. But permit me to tell you, whatever healing was accomplished thus far has been ripped open by Jon's appearance here. I repeat myself. You will regret letting this opportunity slip through your fingers."

Even as Paul sat locked in silence, his fury hammering at his unruffled façade, he had to acknowledge a degree of truth in Hervé's words. It had been so with Marie-Odile. During the final months of her life, he had hated her illness. For a long time after she died, he had hated her.

He saw her the first time in 1905 in Ostend. She had been twenty-four years old and slight enough to pass as an adolescent had she so chosen. Over the course of two days, he watched her flit from room to room, from crowd to crowd, from table to table. She never played herself, but she used a vague air of availability to draw the willing to a certain table or room and a pronounced air of indifference to rebuff any advances. She had been good, as difficult to pin down as the sparkle of light off a diamond. He knew she was working with someone because her seductive glances were aimed less at the patrons than at their opened wallets. Later, he learned her distance-vision was exceptional and that she could finagle a look at the other players' cards from greater distances than one would have supposed possible. At Ostend, Paul had never detected which sharper she was working with, but he extended them the professional courtesy of not giving their game away by drawing attention to her. However, when he happened upon her in an otherwise deserted corridor at the Club Prive of the Kursaal on the third day, he couldn't resist delivering a knowing wink that was as fast as a blink. No one else could possibly have seen it. Nevertheless, after that, he never saw her again in Ostend.

A couple of years later, when he and Hervé were between jobs on the Continent and were relaxing at an outdoor café on the Left Bank, Paul saw Hervé raise his eyes with a look of amused surprise at something beyond Paul's shoulder. Before Paul could turn around, Marie-Odile's cloth satchel was already swinging towards his head. Before long, she had been folded into their games. She traveled with them and acted as their scout, their spy, and their lookout even when she wasn't playing a full role in the current scam.

Paul had loved everything about her. He had loved her dark beauty and the way her body moved with the lightness of a feather. He loved the two moles on the nape of her neck and the little finger on her left hand, deformed by being broken and not properly set. He loved how she valued her independence above all the money in the world, how she gave but never sold herself, how, as an anarchist at heart, she recognized no law other than her own desires. He had loved her unyielding practicality in business affairs and her inexhaustible compassion towards the little street-Arabs. He loved her sharp tongue and brutal sagacity, even when they were turned on him.

When she came down with the galloping consumption, he had wagered everything on her recovery. There was no one he would not approach in seeking a cure, no remedy he wouldn't urge her to try at least once. He threw money at anything he heard recommended, including pellets of turpentine, tins of cod liver oil, and bottles of ass' milk. He bought every syrup every patent-medicine hawker had to offer, most of which she refused to take. Daily, he painted her back with iodine and carried her down four flights of stairs to escape the stifling atmosphere of the top-floor flat. He remained beside her in the open-air, and when she flagged, he carried her back up to rest. He brought fresh flowers each day to give her something beautiful to look at. He bought two birds, a canary for its color and a nightingale for its music, to lift her spirits. In spite of everything, she worsened. Her thin form shuddering on the mattress made his own bones ache. At the end, he completely abandoned Hervé so he could turn her hourly, in a futile effort to relieve the pain of the ulcerated sores on her back and buttocks. She had died in his arms, fully conscious, clinging to life, staring with fierce defiance into his eyes – as though he were willingly handing her over to death.

Setting his empty glass on the table, Paul got to his feet and crossed the room to stare outside, letting the darkness soothe the vestigial pain of that old amputation. It was a reminder that every grievous loss had a false bottom, that every time he thought he had struck its ultimate depth, another stratum always appeared.

Turning around, he said, "I need to know more about Joseph Murphy. The affair is turning into quite the dust-up, and I'm stuck in the middle of it."

Paul believed Hervé when he said Murphy had not attempted to unload any jewelry during his visit. He didn't bother asking about the disappeared wallet. Hervé could pick a man clean without touching his wallet. But it was obvious there was more than a necklace and some money at stake here.

Paul went on to outline the rest of the situation he hadn't disclosed the last time: the poison, the tickets to Ireland, the German dictionary. He ended with the news that he was to continue working with Wycliffe because the police had pulled out. As with Barousse, he omitted the presumed visits to Winzig Krenz. Nor was he ready just yet to bring up the ransacking of Mrs. Murphy's suite. He watched his friend reach for the ivory holder and the tall lighter.

"What do you make of the tickets to Belfast?" Paul said.

Hervé gave an uninterested shrug.

"He never mentioned Ireland?" Paul said.

"Not within my hearing. But the man was Irish."

"I'm well aware of that. And what do you make of the German dictionary?" Paul said.

Hervé didn't answer immediately. At length he said, "He wasn't speaking German when he was here."

"He specifically asked for a polyglot environment. It was the reason I sent him your way."

"As I told you before, perhaps, if we had had the opportunity to know one another better, he might have introduced his friends to me."

Paul didn't press the matter. It was clear Hervé wasn't going to divulge anything else.

"The relatives, the wife and the cousin, what about them?" Hervé said.

"She has a tongue like a timbersaw, and he has to be treated like unexploded ordnance."

"He is the one you are going to be working with?"

Paul nodded.

"So he is not congenial. Is he intelligent? Can he get to the bottom?"

"He loves to fan his feathers, but I doubt there's more to him than that." At this, Paul realized he was incapable of drawing an objective portrait of Wycliffe. The man was like a hair caught beneath his eyelid, irritating and obscuring his sight.

"If anything else should come to my attention, I will let you know," Hervé said.

Before Paul could mention how greatly he would appreciate being better informed this minute, the Victrola in the back of the house flared to life, blaring strains from *Swan Lake*. Hervé's fingers revealed a slight unsteadiness as they laid the holder against the ashtray.

Pointing toward the red samovar, Paul said, "I don't suppose that noise has anything to do with that beastly thing."

Hervé dropped his gaze. "Only everything," he said.

# Saturday, March 14, 1914
## VILLA ACHILLES

BY HIS OWN ACCOUNT, ALEXEI GORKY WAS BORN IN 1895 in the costume room of the St. Petersburg Imperial Ballet. His mother was so fearful of lowering her defenses against the perceived intrigues of her rivals she refused to quit the theater even to give birth. Despite such steadfastness, she failed to receive the coveted role of prima ballerina. Alexei's father was also a member of the troupe, but the parents' stage-careers came to an end after they participated in a poorly received strike in 1905. Alexei continued in the family's vocation but, like his mother, came to know the crushing disappointment of having his talent undervalued by the Imperial Ballet's administrators. Traveling to Paris with that company in 1912, he either became, as Hervé suspected, deeply despondent after a failed love affair with the choreographer Mikhail Fokine, or he actually had, as he claimed, grown tired of being hit over the head by the manager's walking stick. Whatever the impetus, Alexei had jumped the stage-lights and landed in Diaghilev's Russian Ballet.

"I tell you," Hervé said. "Nijinsky will soon be a name from the past. I have never seen Alexei perform on the stage, but even here, with the limitations imposed by my walls and ceilings, his vaults are magnificent. The spins, the leaps, head flung back in a triumph of power, his whole being pulsating with savage strength, it is ...." His shrug bemoaned the inadequacy of words.

His mouth gradually twisted into a grim smile. "What it is, when I think about it, is ironic. All that superhuman muscularity, and what is revealed most frequently? Nothing but the frailty of vanity. He also possesses the Slavs' endearing predisposition for temperamental *changements de pied*. He constantly alternates his landing between the heights of delight and the depths of despair. I tell you, everyone in Russia is half-mad. It is that damned Russian psyche, damned in the true sense of the word. They spend the whole of their miserable lives marinating in a toxic stew of superstition, mysticism, and artistic sensibility."

Hervé's shoulders expressed an acceptance that was more gnawed weariness than rational agreement. Paul hoped it was only the unstable dancer who was stretching his friend's nerves so tightly.

"Therefore, you understand, it is because of Alexei that I would appreciate your keeping me informed as to the manner in which these matters proceed."

Paul turned this thought over several times. "No," he said, bringing the word out slowly, "I don't understand. Nothing in what I said had anything to do with Russia, let alone Tchaikovsky or the ballet."

The music stopped. Paul avoided looking at Hervé as they waited for it to begin anew. It immediately obliged. The two friends sat in silence for several minutes.

"You wanted a name," Hervé said.

Paul had almost forgotten the second request he had left in Hervé's hands. He needed a verifiable name of one of Krenz's staff members to satisfy Cyril's most recent demand.

149

Hervé passed across a sheet of paper. "There are three names, but the most interesting is that of one of his chauffeurs. Krenz does not drive. He is said to be as wide as a mattress. I presume that would present some difficulty in fitting behind the steering mechanism. He has two chauffeurs. One limousine. Two chauffeurs. One of them is our old comrade from St. Petersburg, Friedrich Hoffmeister. That might even be his true name since he is still using it. You were Gerald Harper for that venture. I was Dmitri Kablukov, Kadnikov, something like that. He was the oaf who almost got us killed or what would have been worse, buried alive in a Russian prison."

Paul memorized the three names, then wadded the paper into a ball and tossed into the fire. He was about to let it go at that but was seized once more by his instinct for caution. Thus far, Murphy's known trail to Krenz's villa at Villefranche ran straight through Cap d'Ail, past Hervé's house without stopping. But Hervé wasn't coming straight with him. Who could say Murphy didn't stop here on the way back? Two chauffeurs. One motorcar. A one-in-two chance.

"Can you arrange for me to meet with Friedrich?" Paul said.

Hervé's eyes narrowed.

"As I told you, my colleague's nephew is looking for a position. I don't want to send him into a den of lions."

"You worry me," Hervé said.

Paul barked a laugh. "I? You?"

Hervé said, "If you are concerned about Mr. Murphy's interest in the German language, I doubt he was practicing it in order to converse with Herr Krenz. In fact, he expressed a distinct dislike of the Teutonic race."

"Can you set up the meeting?"

Hervé shrugged his resignation. "I will get a message to

your pension. Anything else? What about the names of Prince Albert's footmen? Might your colleague's nephew wish to seek employment there?"

"I can handle Prince Albert myself. But since you mention it, there is one more thing." He briefly described the hour or so he had spent amid the debris in Mrs. Murphy's suite. When finished, he inched his chair closer to the divan and leaned forward, his lips almost touching his friend's ear. "What were they looking for, Hervé?" he said.

# Sunday, March 15, 1914
## HÔTEL DE PARIS

PEERING THROUGH THE WARY TWO-INCH CRACK IN the opened door, Bridget Rose whispered, "Who is it?" as though she had never laid eyes on her visitor before.

Lily's annoyance showed in her voice. "I have instructions from Mrs. Murphy."

"Are you by yourself?"

Lily looked left and right down the empty corridor.

"The Barnum and Bailey circus was here, but now, I'm the only one. May I come in? I don't feel like communicating in this hallway."

Bridget Rose took a long time coming up with an answer. Lily's irritation increased. She had not asked whether the woman wanted death by hanging or death by drowning. The door inched open wider.

Lily immediately regretted having pushed her way into the windowless cell. There was barely enough space to stand beside the narrow bed and the undersized nightstand at its foot. It felt more like a casket than a room. Why should this be unexpected? Regardless of how much an employer paid for accommodations above, her maid was scarcely a person of distinction. But it did seem a harsh contradiction to the acres of luxury visible in the rest of the hotel. Then again, Lily had no illusions. The only reason she wasn't living next door to Bridget was the need for her quarters to accommodate a typewriter and files.

"What do you want?" Bridget Rose said.

Lily wanted to temper her response with understanding. Bridget was in the midst of a difficult, even dangerous, experience.

"*Mrs. Murphy,*" Lily said pointedly, "needs her things packed today. The hotel is handling the bulk of it, but she wants these items in her traveling valises." She held out the list, but the offer was ignored. Maybe Bridget didn't know that yesterday's inescapable objections had fallen short of their intended effect. "You are to go with her."

The maid's eyes remained half closed as she insolently regarded her visitor.

Lily raised her voice. "Bridget! Have you been drinking?"

That question drew a halfway legitimate response. "What do you think I am?"

Lily decided her sincere opinion would do nothing to further the rapport. "Here's the list," she said, again offering the sheet of paper.

Bridget Rose turned her head, like a child refusing bad-tasting medicine.

When Lily and Mr. Barousse's assistant returned to the hotel last night, she had been literally dragging her feet, exhausted from viewing the few far-flung villas available on the Côte d'Azur. They had found only one, west of Nice, with any potential, but she doubted the location would be acceptable.

When she reported the results to Mrs. Murphy, Lily's mood was temporarily lifted by hearing she was to remain at the hotel until the replies from the attorney and accountant were received. A message from Jonathan Chandler saying he was looking forward to the horticulture exhibition today had been left at the Front Desk. Even more important than the appointment with him was the desire to stay close to Sally Holmes and the prospect of more money. Lily was waiting for Ted to get permission for her to interview the chambermaids. And too, there was the next meeting with him tomorrow. Maybe he had learned something useful.

But none of that had anything to do with Bridget Rose and here and now. Determined to wait out the woman's obstinacy, Lily scanned the room's few contents. A necklace and a safety pin were about the only things that could be hidden in the tiny space. A coat and dress hung from a hook beside the door. A book with a dull-red cover lay upside down on the small table. As she tried to read the title, a frisson of *déjà vu* went down her spine. She had done the same with the dictionary in Mr. Murphy's room.

"I ain't going back to that death-chamber by myself," Bridget Rose said, "not for all the heat in hell."

"I'll be with you. I have the key. Let's get it over with, why don't we?"

Bridget said, "You know she wanted nothing better than to be shed of him, don't you? She probably would have gouged his eyes out a long time ago but what she keeps her fingernails bit down past the quick. And she was having men in, right under his nose. Young men. Young enough to be her grandsons. She even bathed with them." Her face was florid with indignation. "Served him right too. Him, never saying nothing, acting like he didn't know."

Decorum required Lily to tell the woman to stop, but this new perspective on her employer was not completely without its interest.

"He didn't care is more like it. She treated him like he was a hired mule. I wouldn't put it past her to be the one what done him in. A young buck in tow, needs to get rid of the old one. Happens all the time."

The idea that Mrs. Murphy fired the impotent bullet was scarcely a new one for Lily, but this assertion strengthened her reluctant suspicion. That someone could have scaled the outside wall in order to enter the suite seemed unlikely, so it was hard to see it as anything other than an inside-job. Then too, there was the question of where Mrs. Murphy stayed Wednesday night. Lily had been confident her employer could produce her ticket from Cannes because she never discarded a receipt, not even for a bag of sweets. While she obviously took pride in her possessions, she positively gloated over the evidence of their cost. In sorting the documents, however, Lily had not seen that train-ticket. Just as curious, or incriminating, the voucher from the Carlton Hôtel at Cannes did not include a charge for Wednesday night. Mrs. Murphy might have been invited to someone's yacht or villa, but would she have forgotten to brag about it? Even her decision to remain in the suite lent credence to the theory. If she were the would-be murderer, she would not have feared the murderer's return. It was only after a different intruder showed up that she felt driven to leave.

"Let's go to the suite," Lily said.

# Sunday, March 15, 1914
## HÔTEL DE PARIS

"Can I go now?" Bridget Rose asked, placing the last valise next to the door.

"Sit down a minute, if you please," Lily said.

The windows had been left open to air out the room, and she listened to the birds chatting outside while she considered where to begin. How much did Bridget Rose know about Mr. Murphy's death? Michael had seen the gunshot wound, and she was still talking as though he had been murdered. Apparently, no one had shared the police's report with the servants. Did they know about the poisoned whiskey?

Bridget was perched on the edge of a chair, her knees jerking vigorously beneath the folds of her skirt. They came to a standstill. Both were pointed towards the door. "Well?" she said. "Are we through or ain't we?"

Lily was having trouble constructing her questions. A good detective didn't start with a preconceived answer based on nothing more than stereotypes. She was counting too heavily on Sally's having the necklace. She needed to keep her mind open to other possibilities. Servants were usually the first-line of suspects when valuables went missing. But what would Bridget do with such a thing? Wear it to the next

Cakewalk? If she or Michael tried to pawn it, they would probably only draw attention to themselves. Lily didn't think Bridget Rose stole the necklace, but she should know a great deal more about it than Lily did.

"I'm curious," Lily said. "How did you and Michael come to work for the Murphys? What were you doing before then?"

Bridget looked like Lily had just invited her to take a trip to the moon. "You're wanting to hear my life's story?"

"Only the part that begins right before you boarded the train in San Francisco. As I said, I'm curious. You're a good lady's maid, but Michael's no valet."

Mrs. Murphy had turned out her other maid, Valerie, right before they departed. Valerie swore her mixed blood was the reason she was being left behind. To Lily's way of thinking, even if that were a consideration, why would Mrs. Murphy trade out that sweet, competent woman for this harridan? Furthermore, Mr. Murphy didn't have a man at home, so why had he felt the need to bring one to Monte Carlo? Time and again, when Lily arrived at the suite, she would find Mr. Murphy's shoes had been left outside for the hotel's bootblack, doubtlessly because Michael Gallagher had failed to do them. And listening to Mrs. Murphy reciting his sins of omission each morning, Lily suspected he failed to do just about everything else as well. On the other hand, while Bridget Rose lacked the disciplined indifference of a well trained servant, she functioned well as a lady's maid. Mrs. Murphy's coiffures were done with greater skill, even verve, than Lily would have suspected the woman was capable of, and while toiling at the desk in the Murphys' suite, she had observed Bridget Rose changing the linens, airing the mattress, cleaning the hairbrushes, and dusting the furniture as strenuously as a Calvinist evicting a lifetime of sins from the soul of a convert.

"So is that what you're saying? That Mikie and me ain't good enough for those two uppity pieces of trash?"

Lily hardened her voice to the same strength as Bridget's. "I'm *saying* nothing. I'm asking. How did you come to be hired by the Murphys?"

"Is Mrs. Murphy done with me here?"

"As soon as you answer my question."

Bridget folded her arms across her chest and turned her head in a perfect imitation of Mrs. Murphy's stubborn refusal to answer Chief Inspector Gautier's inquiry. Lily's determination flagged. She was realizing how onerous impassivity could be. She wanted to project the same unflappable air that Paul Newcastle consistently exhibited, but Bridget's grinding truculence didn't help. She lowered her eyes while she worked at keeping her face neutral.

Possibly taking this as an act of submission, Bridget Rose lifted her chin higher as she mechanically smoothed her skirt over her knees. She said, "I'll bet you can't tell me, can't even begin to guess, how much money those worthless scabs on the face of the earth waste in a day's time. Them, what're always scattering money to the four winds on trash the devil wouldn't let into hell and not never able to wring an ounce of satisfaction out of any of them fancies. Look at them, serving ten-course dinners to upwards of a hundred overfed jackasses while she, Her Eminence, counts every mouthful the help swallows. Just like the English, they are, getting fat off starving the Irish.

"They ain't the first of their kind whose butts I've had to wipe, and they're every one the same. Why, I've knowed knee-babies what could take better care of themselves. They spend years dragging around to spas like this here Monte Carlo, which ain't nothing but watering-holes for hogs dressed up in silks and feathers, always calling on someone else to wash their snotty handkerchiefs and put the bluing on white gloves gone black from counting chips in the casinos. They give fancy names to their houses and horses and dogs but can't figure out how to call the woman who stands over their bleeding hot stove all day anything but *Cook.*

"They're all just like this one here, chasing fashions the livelong day, buying expensive jewelry on the cuff in the morning just so they can hock it for ready cash in the afternoon, and yet they never have two cents to toss at a baby dying of the hunger."

Bridget drew a well earned breath before continuing. "And what about her not taking me with her this time? Didn't nobody notice that? Do you want to know why? Because she was back here Wednesday night. Not Thursday morning like she acted like. No sir, she was here Wednesday night all right."

Lily blinked hard, as though she had seen rather than heard something startling. "What makes you say that?"

"Just because she's the only one what can see a pinhead spot on the underside of a hem, she thinks everybody except her is blind. 'Cause of that, she thinks nobody notices she's wearing a good bracelet one day and a piece of garbage looking just like it the next."

"Why do you think she was here Wednesday, Bridget?"

"Wouldn't you like to know."

"Yes. Yes, I would."

When Bridget Rose turned away again, Lily held her silence. The woman obviously wanted to have her say; therefore, Lily saw no need to beg for it.

"I know," Bridget Rose said after several long seconds, "because I was up here Thursday morning way before the rest of you got here. That dogsbody of a cousin sent for me early on, first thing, to make sure everything was ready for Her Hind-End's arrival."

"He had the key?"

"Of course he had the key. Didn't you have the key?"

The heavy, bulky room-keys were left with the Front Desk when guests went out. Mr. Murphy would have had his with him when he died, which explained how Sally and her accomplice returned his body to the suite, but Mrs. Murphy would not have taken hers to Cannes. She could have left permission with the desk for Wycliffe to be given it, just as she had for Lily this morning.

"The two of you were here? You were here with Mr. Murphy in his bedroom?" It was *Mr. Murphy's body,* but Lily couldn't bring herself to say that.

"That lapdog, Wycliffe, said he must be asleep or out. You know as well as I do, he was never here longer than he could help."

Lily leaned forward to place her elbows on her knees and rub the bridge of her nose with her fingers. She felt as though she had plunged like an anchor to the bottom of the ocean and was fighting multiple currents in her effort to swim back to the surface. This detecting thing was going almost too well.

"What made you think Mrs. Murphy had been here?" she said.

"You think you're so smart, don't you, just because you can read and write fast. Well, I might come out of the hills of Pennsylvania, but I'm not so dumb. I've been around too."

Lily straightened to level a stern gaze.

"Her spare pair of false teeth were in a glass by the bed, weren't they? But she took them with her. I know because I packed them. And one of her hairbrushes had been used. I'd cleaned them all like I always did before she left. See what I mean by her thinking everyone else excepting her is blind?"

"And you tidied those things up before the rest of us arrived that morning?"

"You said I was a good lady's maid, didn't you?"

Lily decided not to ask if Bridget had pointed those things out to Wycliffe.

"And I'll tell you what else. She could've had a pistol. Why, her jewel box is so big, she could have a shotgun in there. There's things she don't never let me touch. Keeps them under lock and key, like I wanted to steal all them phony jewels."

Lily said nothing. There was nothing to say.

Bridget Rose stood. "If we're through here, I'm going back to my room. You ask Mikie how we ended up in this glorified outhouse. It sure wasn't my idea."

"Yes, I think –" But before Lily could finish the sentence, the room was reverberating from the sound of the slammed door.

# Sunday, March 15, 1914

BEGINNING A SECOND HOUR OF WAITING AT THE open-air café on the eastern flank of Villefranche's waterfront, Paul considered ordering a third glass of white wine. The establishment was empty except for himself and two men who were grousing about the state of the economy. Across the cobblestones, halyards clanked against the masts of the fishing boats returned from their morning run. Fish and other sea-creatures were spread across oil-cloths covering wooden tables. Besides the local shoppers, cooks from the yachts floating at anchor in the bay had come ashore with their market baskets. The ever optimistic seagulls circled overhead. There was nothing out-of-the-ordinary in the scene. Modern villas dappled the slopes above the village and across the bay at Cap Ferrat, but for the most part, the people around here fished for their livelihoods, harvested and cured their own olives, and drank the local swill.

Paul had wasted over an hour at Giorgio's this morning, twice as long as he normally would have waited for Cyril to appear. Since only he was required to be there every day, the journalist's absence was not unusual. Paul had never thought he would be disappointed when this occurred, but for once, he was as eager to use the leech as the leech was to use him. He was ready with one of the names Hervé provided, but not Friedrich Hoffmeister. In return, he would wring out of Cyril everything he knew or suspected or fantasized about Joseph Murphy's activities.

Hervé had thrown down the gauntlet when he tried to steer the inquiries away from Krenz. He wasn't usually so clumsy in misdirection, but he wasn't usually besotted with a nineteen-year-old Russian dancer either. What nettled the most was his admission of interest while refusing to divulge what that interest was, even when asked point-blank. Stubborn ass. Suicidal fool. Well, if he wouldn't volunteer the information, Paul would sleuth it out for himself. At the very least, he was going to find out whether those rides in Krenz's Daimler which Cyril claimed to have witnessed stopped at Cap d'Ail.

Across the way, Paul noticed a new arrival to the clutch of people gathered around a fishmonger in a tattered brown sweater and rubber apron. Wiping everything else from his mind, Paul left a handful of coins for the wine and casually worked his way over to the tables. He watched Friedrich Hoffmeister hand over a single banknote for a bagful of squid. Then he started the steep climb up one of the narrow cobblestone lanes into the heart of the village. He never so much as glanced in Paul's direction. Paul waited a full minute before following.

Hearing a low hiss coming from a path he had just crossed, he halted to check his watch and give it a slight tap; whereupon, he changed directions and followed the signal.

"Gerald! My old comrade!" Friedrich exclaimed in flagrant violation of the circumspection they had pantomimed up to this point. *Déjà vu* St. Petersburg. Some things never change. What had changed was that Friedrich had added about thirty flabby pounds and his heavy moustache had turned a wiry white. "I cannot believe it is you," he said. "Who could believe it? I almost didn't recognize you. You must have dropped a stone or two."

"Half of it was the beard," Paul said.

"I still cannot believe it is you, after all these years."

"Want to touch the hole in my sole?" Paul said.

"Is that why you are walking like you have a stone in your hoof?"

"What about you? You're as red as *blutwurst*. Too much sun?"

"As well off as God in France, that's what we used say. Now I am in France and I find it is true. I fish every chance I get. Whatever you do, be bold about it, isn't that what Dmitri said? I had to think hard after I got your message. It was the year of grace 1904 when we were together. How long have you been at the Côte d'Azur? I say to you, if the devil took a lease on heaven, this is what it would be like. What about Dmitri? Is he still drawing the longbow after you set up the targets?"

"What's with the Hide and Seek routine? I'm no trouble anymore. I haven't been trouble for a long time."

"I am begging your pardon, my old pal. It is not meant as a reflection upon you, but upon me. The people with whom I work suffer from what can only be described as – thank God, modern science has provided a word – paranoia."

"Afraid my science lessons aren't up to scratch."

"They are suspicious of everyone. We are required to be like Caesar's wife, above even a whiff of a whisper."

"Must put quite the crimp in your style."

Friedrich showed the palms of his hands. "It is not my style that has them worried. The politics these days, everyone is insane about the politics. Europe is nothing but a heap of swords, an armed camp. The French, they never stop provoking Germany, passing that three-year law, as if inferiority in numbers can be overcome by longer periods of conscription. Who can regard that as anything other than a deliberately hostile act? And the Russians, what short memories people have. Japan proved they have no officers capable of trailing their troops into battle let alone leading them. The Tsar sacked hundreds of generals after that debacle, which means they have only a few thousand of those incompetents left. Yet every night, German children are sent to sleep on stories of that *böggel-mann,* the Russian steamroller, the dreaded Slavic hoards."

Friedrich spoke as he led Paul down a series of shallow steps into a room where they were greeted by layers of smoke and stale beer-breath hovering over a foundation of spilled wine. Sawdust and dried tealeaves were scattered about the floor. Near the dead fireplace, two men lay stretched out motionless. Paul's cough, which had been in remission, sprang back to life.

They seated themselves at a much-bruised table, the package of squid contributing to the other nauseous odors. Friedrich took out a nickel-plated cigarette-case, with spots worn dull by his fingers, and studied the contents with enormous concentration, as if it contained a bewildering number of choices. He settled on one in the middle and tapped it three times against the closed cover while Paul ordered a pint from a man with an unshaven face and glass-eye. Friedrich added sardines, tomatoes, and cheese to the order. His lighter flared and acrid Turkish tobacco smoke mingled with the other vile smells.

The pair sat without speaking as they awaited their beers, Friedrich puffing his cigarette while Paul attempted to ignore the cacophony issuing forth from the raised platform, where an accordion and a mandolin were locked in a pitched battle within the strains of "When You Wore a Tulip and I Wore a big Red Rose." As the volume increased, several patrons joined by thumping their mugs on the tabletops.

"Who is your philosopher *de jour*?" Paul asked, raising his voice against the surrounding din. If he remembered correctly, there was no better way to oil this man's tongue. He had never stopped drooling over Hegel all the way to St. Petersburg.

Friedrich produced a satisfied smile. "Your compatriot Thomas Carlyle."

"I should have thought it would be Nietzsche, namesake and all that."

"Bah. Too ambiguous. At first, he was thought dangerous because he preached anarchism. Now, he is the darling of militarism. How can anyone trust a man whose ideas are open to such various interpretations?"

Paul stared at his mug as he moved it around in small circles. "What about those politics? Are they such a great threat?" he asked.

Friedrich's head bumped along with the racket for several beats before he answered, "Jealousy, fear, that is all politics are ever about. Take Great Britain. She is like a hysterical maiden, always screaming someone is threatening the purity of her defenses when in fact of the matter, she never feels in the least threatened. The British believe their navy is and always will be an impregnable bulwark to their safety." He leaned forward. "This is what they do not understand. It is not an invasion from the bases at Calais or Ostend they should fear. What they should fear is the ruin of their commerce. It is there they will be defeated, not on the high seas."

The sudden cessation of the music-cum-racket made Paul feel like he had landed in a deep mattress of pure eiderdown. Friedrich sat back as the crowd roared its appreciation. To Paul's indescribable relief, the two musicians declined to follow their first success with a second defilement of sound and made their way towards the bar instead.

Friedrich leaned forward once more. "Regardless, my old friend," he said, "war will soon come again because it must. Homer tells us Zeus instigated the Trojan War because he believed the earth to be overpopulated. It has been the same ever since. War is the salvation of the human race. It thins out the herd, so mankind can survive."

"I would have thought that in vast portions of the earth, starvation alone was doing an adequate job of saving the human race."

Friedrich beamed. "Precisely. The Malthusian catastrophe. But politicians cannot wait for that. Anyway, it would be too disorganized. How can one exact an indemnity from a famine?"

Paul was only half-listening. Friedrich's philosophizing always came across more like pontificating, but it must be suffered in order to put the man at his ease. His thoughts went to Lily. She was a curious girl, snarled in contradictions. Her gray dress was a confusion of sensuality in fit and severity in style. At times, she moved with the fluidity of a gazelle, and at others, she looked as awkward as a penguin. He wondered if she knew how intimidating she must be to a man like Wycliffe, whom she towered over in height, attractiveness, and intelligence. She caught Paul's silent teasing. He knew she did from the flash of irritation in her eyes. He also had sensed she was sitting on something, and it wasn't an egg. There was a subtle shift in her aspect each time the necklace was mentioned. Was she the thief?

Paul drained the dregs in his mug. It was time to get down to business. He said, "I got you here because I have a favor to ask. I would like to know something about your employer's guests."

"Herr Krenz's guests? There must be seven hundred a week. Everyone of importance has been through those doors at least once, with the possible exceptions of Moses and Pliny the Elder."

"This would be more recently than that, say, within the past two weeks."

"The last two weeks, you say?" Friedrich massaged the full crop of hair above his lip. "That would make it easier, for sure. Around Christmas and during Carnival, I am driving, driving, driving, day and night, night and day. Religion is very hard on a person, Gerald."

"This one would have been fetched from the Hôtel de Paris, an American, middle-aged with a lift to his right shoulder."

They were interrupted by the arrival of the food. While Friedrich exchanged friendly banter with the one-eyed man, Paul was growing increasingly certain he was going to choke to death in this smoke-filled hole before he could get Friedrich's meandering mind around to the answers he needed.

"Now," Friedrich said, blotting the remains of his lunch off his chin with his handkerchief. "That man you asked about, the one with the crooked shoulder." Not a minute too soon. "I remember him. He made himself easy to remember. *Zweifelhaft, louche,* crude, no gentleman, however you wish to insult him."

Paul almost smiled. His gamble on the one-in-two chance in chauffeurs had paid off. "Explain?" he said.

"You know the variety, blows his cigar smoke in your face and drops the ashes on the carpet, pours his drink on your jacket while he is standing on your foot, asks if your sister is for sale, and if not, what about your mother?"

Paul did know the type, but he had not put Murphy in this

category. Possibly, the more he drank, the cruder he became. Many men did fit into that category.

"In matter of fact," Friedrich said, "it was one of those who went so far last week as to spew his evening's repast all over the Daimler's silk curtains and velvet carpet. He could have told me to stop, but such a gold-leafed gentleman thinks nothing of sacrificing the upholstery to the relief of his stomach."

"Consider it an act of God," Paul said. "Was it the man I mentioned?"

Friedrich found it necessary to perform another close inspection of his shrinking selection of cigarettes. Only after completing the ritual of tapping and lighting did he confirm he had chauffeured Murphy two times in much the same circumstances Cyril had described. The revelation inevitably led to more digressions – on Monte Carlo as an *ex nihilo* creation, on the doubtful legitimacy of the Grimaldis, and on Charles Garnier's crime against taste in exhausting elegance not once but twice in the Operas at Paris and Monte Carlo.

Corralling the conversation once more, Paul said, "Is this right? You drove him from the hotel twice. Each time, you picked him up before midnight and returned him to the hotel around 3:00 a.m. What did he do during that time?"

"I did not accompany him inside. Prized as I am as a conversationalist, I am not invited to Herr Krenz's parties."

"They are the poorer for it."

A burst of laughter from the men at the next table made Paul snap his head in that direction. The word was there, *paranoia*. When he returned to Friedrich, his expression had hardened.

"You do not know my employer, Herr Krenz?"

"That is correct."

"You did not say how you know I work for Herr Krenz."

Paul said nothing.

"Forgive me. I must ask this. Do you and Dmitri have your sights on Herr Krenz?" It was impossible to mistake the menace in Friedrich's voice and face.

"It is as I said. I haven't been trouble for a long time. I am out of that life. Have been for years."

"And Dmitri?"

Paul shook his head. "I don't know where he is. We parted ways five years ago, in Paris."

"Where are you living? Nice?" Friedrich said.

"Cagnes. Auguste Renoir is giving me drawing lessons."

Frederick again mulled the selection of a cigarette and lit it after tapping it three times on the case. He took a deep drag and exhaled a long stream of smoke out the side of his mouth as his eyes read Paul's face. "You did not say why you want to know about this man, the hunchback."

Paul said nothing.

At length Friedrich said, "I owe you, you and Dmitri, an imperishable debt. We could have died at St. Petersburg, and I know the error was mine. I wish to repay the debt, but the payment must come from me, not from anyone else."

"If it will give you any reassurance, I know next to nothing about your employer – only that he's a nightclub entertainer and hosts lavish soirées."

"That proves you do not know anything at all about him."

Paul knew Friedrich could not allow this ignorance to endure.

He said, "There are talents which bloom only in the hospitable climate of the Côte d'Azur, but this is not Herr Krenz. There are men who live by applause and care not what they are applauded for, but this is not Herr Krenz. Those are among the things he is not. What is important is what he is. He is a famous comedian, of course. In addition, he played

Falstaff to great acclaim on the Berlin stage. But he is more than a performer. He is an artistic genius, a Universal Man. He writes plays and poetry. He composes operas, the lyrics and the scores. His latest interest is cinematography. That is a German invention, after all. Perhaps he will write plays for them too. There are many who do not take him seriously because of his size. Who takes a fat clown seriously? But his size is a merely a symbol of the enormity of his talents. He does his comedy with his left hand while his right hand is busy stirring many, many pots."

Paul nodded his acceptance of the lecture. "Sounds like you've landed an excellent situation, all that and fishing too."

Friedrich sopped the last piece of bread in the oil remaining on the tin plate. "There is one more thing about the hunchback," he said, not looking up. "However, without knowing what your purpose is, I find I am hesitant to mention it."

# Sunday, March 15, 1914
## PALAIS DES BEAUX ARTS

OUTSIDE THE ENTRANCE TO THE PALAIS DES BEAUX Arts, Lily paused to pull on her gloves and to enjoy the crisp, clear air after the fragrance-clogged, humidity-saturated atmosphere she had suffered inside. She was not, she told herself, dawdling to give Jonathan an opportunity to arrive with a credible excuse for his tardiness. If anything, it was to give herself the chance to cut him cold if he tried.

To her right, across the street at the corner of the Hôtel de Paris, a black-clad woman stood behind a cart brimming with colorful flowers. Like everything in this fantastic place, it was excess piled upon excess. A vast profusion of flowers lay within the central space encircled by the Café de Paris, the Casino, and the Hôtel de Paris. The exotic trees which commandeered the sprawling gardens on all sides of the buildings likewise swam among seas of flowers, everything in extravagant bloom. The horticulture exhibition she had just escaped swarmed with lilies, lilacs, orchids, tulips, and irises of every shade, with great clumps of yellow mimosa, and with roses, roses, and more roses.

Her gloves firmly set, Lily turned up her coat's collar against the mild breeze. Her focus landed on the terrace beyond the far edge of the Monte Carlo Opera, where people were scattering like pigeons around the man tearing through them at full pelt. She placed both hands on her hips and watched.

Jonathan twisted, turned, braked, pivoted, and dodged, barely missing a man in a wheeled chair, leaping over an outstretched dog's lead, ignoring shouts, raised fists, shrieks, laughter, and jeers. Clearing the length of the Hôtel de Paris, he caught sight of Lily and lifted an arm to wave. In the same moment, he blundered into the flower-vendor's cart, sending bursts of daffodils, lilies, gladiolas, primroses, and roses shooting into the air and skittering across the cobbles. He darted another look in Lily's direction before pulling the woman to her feet. Speaking constantly, he brushed her off, righted the cart, then scooped up armfuls of greenery and blossoms and tossed them back on the wagon. Finally, he removed a banknote from his pocketbook and handed it to her before gathering more crumpled stems and flowers from the ground.

Skidding to a stop beside Lily, he gulped air as some of the mangled plants clutched in the crook of his arm drifted to the ground. "You'll have to take my word for it," he panted. "Days on end can go by without my knocking a woman off her feet."

More flowers tumbled downward as he patted the corners of his face with a handkerchief. "Thank you for waiting. I am glad you didn't leave. But, you understand, it was Juarès."

"Juarès," Lily repeated blankly.

"Juarès. The great Juarès, sitting at the train station in Monte Carlo. I was gobsmacked." He took another deep intake of breath. "I apologize for being late. I am −" He stopped mid-sentence. "Jean Juarès. The man who brought together the feuding Socialists, made them a force to be reckoned with. The man who is going to keep us out of war."

Lily thought she had finally discerned the reason for this rambling excitement.

"You're a Socialist," she said. Wouldn't Effie have a time with that?

"A Socialist, a Tory, a Jacobite, a dancing horse, it doesn't matter what I am. What matters is who he is. I was racing alongside the car as it left the station shouting my last questions. I got his comments on the High Council of Labor set up last month at The Hague. What a day. What a story."

"Would you like to compose it now?"

"Why –" He seemed suddenly to discover the hard edge on her question. "It can wait. Still, that and now you."

Lily wanted to bring one of her severely polished boots down on his instep. Yes, now *her*. She had only been waiting for over an hour. Granted, it wasn't his fault she arrived half an hour early. Nevertheless, she had spent an hour enduring the furtive glances of that creepy little man with a complexion like undressed quarry-stone who had likewise lingered in the vestibule the entire time. The possibility that he mistook the purpose of her loitering had done nothing to make his company more agreeable. Besides the creepy man, she had had an hour to reflect on Bridget Rose's wild – or were they so wild – accusations; an hour to question whether Mrs. Murphy brought her insurance papers because she had known her necklace was going to go missing; an hour to contemplate the telegrams from Mr. Murphy's accountant and attorney that had arrived this morning and were to be delivered to Cap Ferrat tomorrow; an hour to ponder whether those telegrams would spell the end of her sojourn in Monte Carlo and the end of her role as *obersleuth* and the end of a chance to earn more money from Sally. It had also been an hour in which a great deal of time was lavished on hoping Fran would snag the wealthy client.

Jonathan gathered what remained of the broken stems and crushed blossoms and held them out. "For you, Milady, meticulously chosen and painstakingly arranged with your incomparable taste in mind." When she made no move to accept them, he said, "Don't trouble yourself. I shall carry them."

His face grew serious as he tilted his head to study her cheek. "The cut seems to be healing nicely."

"And I was afraid I was going to be scarred for life," she said.

Jonathan kept his eyes fixed on her cheek. "Has anyone ever told you that you have the most beguiling dimples?"

Lily rolled her eyes towards the sky and said nothing.

"Right," he said. "Flowers and flattery, not the things called for. Shall we?" He motioned towards the building behind them. When she made no move, he said, "But perhaps you've lost your enthusiasm for the horticulture exhibition. Perhaps you have heard we're too late to swoon over the royalty. His Serene Highness Albert paid a private visit the day before the opening, and the Austrian Archduke Franz Ferdinand and his wife graced the exhibition with their presence yesterday."

In spite of her resistance, his high spirits were lifting Lily's own. Fanning herself with her hand, she said, "It's just as well. Every time I get next to royalty, I grow faint."

To his question of where she would like to go, she said, "Anywhere, as long as it is far from here."

In a single movement, Jonathan forced the remnants of the bouquet into the arms of an uncomprehending passerby while he grasped Lily's hand and started pulling her briskly up the slope behind. At first, she had difficulty keeping up, but he would not slow. "Come on," he said, with a double-click of his tongue. "I know you can canter. I've seen it."

Soon she was matching her long strides with his. A block beyond the Boulevard de Moulins, they fell panting and laughing against the bulwark supporting the Boulevard du Midi above.

"You're mad, mad," she gasped.

His reply was drowned out by the whistle from the rack-railway's engine pulling into the station at the Gare de la Turbie.

"Quickly," Jonathan ordered, dragging her up the steps. "It's our getaway vehicle. Assault by flowers is a serious offense."

The second-class car attached to the small engine was soon filling with other Sunday sightseers. Sitting next to Jonathan, Lily gradually began to relax. She could smell sandalwood soap and witchhazel on his skin and a hint of coffee on his breath. The warmth of the sun lingered in the wool of their coats.

"It should take about twenty minutes to get to the top," he said. "There are terrific views along the way and at the summit." To Lily's question of how many times he had made the trip, he said, "Never. I am in Monaco as a camp-follower for an official meeting that's being held here. I interviewed some persons attending the conference and heard about La Turbie from one of them."

"You mentioned you were with a newspaper."

"You remembered. I am flattered. What about you? What are you doing here?"

"I don't think it would be an exaggeration to say I was kidnapped."

He handed two coins to the conductor. "Seriously," he said, "to what felicitous confluence of events do I owe the thanks for my good fortune?"

As with Sally, Lily had prepared for the question. She delivered a severely sanitized version of her life in Monaco, omitting such details as her employer's name and the recent excitements. It was a succinct, sufficient, and believable account.

After she finished, he waited a few seconds before he added, "And your employer is Joseph Murphy and your party has come all the way from San Francisco, California."

This addendum's effect on her mood was like a block of ice thrown into a pot of boiling water. When she found her voice, she said, "You made inquiries about me? How inexpressibly rude, not to mention indecent."

He had the grace to look chagrined. "Perhaps I should have said nothing, but not to let you know didn't seem sporting. It's an occupational hazard. I am unused to waiting for facts to come to me. I promise you, I indicated nothing that would have cast a reflection on your character or disgraced your honor."

It was not her honor that was offended. It was her privilege, her right, to invent herself as she went along. Not that she was given to outrageous distortions of reality, just a gentle bending here, a little shading there to disguise some of the more disfiguring facts.

As the little train pulled into the first stop, La Bordina, Lily affected a strenuous interest in the people getting on and off, refusing to look at Jonathan for even a second. A couple with a small boy took the seats directly in front of them. The pair spoke only clipped phrases to one another. The child never stopped sucking his thumb.

"That's where I'm lodging," Jonathan said, pointing towards the imposing structure to their right, "the Riviera Palace. Superb views, but those are commonplace here. And the light is magnificent. It brings one to life, nothing like what a man has to contend with in that black smear in the fog, London."

He was obviously trying to coax her back into friendliness. At the same time, she was delivering a small sermon to herself. As it was with Ted, as it was with Sally, so it must be with everyone. She must be ready to set aside her prejudices, her sensitivities, and her fears in order to open herself to facts, to clues, to experience, and to knowledge.

She said, "When you are not waiting for information to come to you, how exactly do you go about eliciting it?"

"It doesn't usually take any paralyzing originality, only a bit of baksheesh and an appearance that does not suggest an axe-murderer."

"That's it? Cross a palm with some cash, and I can learn anything I want to know?"

"Nothing is guaranteed. If an establishment has something it is dead-set on keeping under wraps, say, Rasputin and his entourage of female admirers have taken apartments on the third floor, a deal more than baksheesh would be required. That's when local influence or inside contacts come in useful."

Lily gave this some thought. It would seem Sally knew what she was about with her bribe. Mr. Murphy's demise was exactly the sort of thing the hotel would be dead-set on keeping under wraps. However his body had gotten to the undertaker, it certainly hadn't been carted through the lobby by the hotel's porters.

"I intended no affront by making inquiries although I might mention that you have turned a few heads among the lads there at the hotel. The sounds of breaking hearts, it was like a meteorite landing on the Crystal Palace."

Lily wasn't about to be bought off by blatant flattery. "Fine," she said. "You know you're not keeping company with an heiress."

"Since I'm not trying to auction a title, that's a matter of indifference to me."

"What are you selling?"

"You may keep your coins in your purse. I'll come clean at no charge. I am an investigative reporter. That's what I meant by 'occupational hazard.'"

She regarded him in wordless amazement. That was what happened when one sets aside her sensitivities. Immediately, her cup runneth over.

She unfurled the rest of her smile. "You're an investigative reporter. You investigate."

His face beamed. "Spot on! I have to say, not many people understand it so quickly and none so easily. At present, crime is my beat. That's why I cannot wait for information to come to me. A crime reporter has to wander the streets, visit jails and court proceedings, knock on the doors of barristers and politicians, and kick open the doors that don't yield to a knock. We don't try to steal the march on our competitors, we try to steal the whole parade. Reporters will stop just short of murder to be the first with the story. That's how we make money. That's how we keep our jobs."

He paused. "But you don't care about that. You want to know what I'm selling. Right now, it is myself to your countrymen in New York City. Listen to this."

He removed a sheet of paper from a pocket, unfolded it with elaborate gravity, and gave an extended mock throat-clearing before pretending to read, "*Brilliantly educated, indefatigably hard-working, devilishly clever gentleman of unimpeachable appearance and manners* – I will not give you as a reference – *seeks position as chief crime reporter for your newspaper. Available immediately to solve the next Crime of the Century* – as nearly as I can calculate, that singular phenomenon occurs, on average, once a month in New York City. *Responses should be addressed to Jonathan Chandler, in care of* ... and so on."

He lowered the paper. His eyes were smiling, yet questioning.

Lily said, "I wonder that you're not drowning in offers."

"I wanted to appear modest. I can only assume the replies from *The New York Sun* and *The World* were misdirected since they are among the few whose munificent proposals I have yet to receive. The difficult part is deciding which to accept."

Before she could respond, they and the other passengers were sent slamming forward as the engineer braked hard. After making sure Lily was all right, Jonathan leaned his head out the window and announced that a mother quail and five balls of feathers had completed their trek across the tracks. Following this interruption, he put away the sheet of paper, and they lapsed into a companionable silence as the little engine and its two cars labored through short tunnels and across bridges spanning ravines on their way up the mountain. At one point, Lily's ears popped, and with that clearing in her head, new doubts began to unfold. Realistically, she told herself, Jonathan Chandler was nothing more than a garden-variety Lothario, and his attentions to her sprang from the most prosaic of motives. But his revelation that he was a newspaper reporter interested in coming to New York City raised the specter of a more devious purpose. What if he were seeking a sensational story he could peddle to an American editor? What if he were pursuing her in order to insinuate himself into the circumstances around poor Mr. Murphy's death? He knew she worked for the Murphys. What other secrets had he purchased?

When the car gave another spasmodic lurch, he again put his head out the window. "This time, he's aiming for wild rabbits," he reported.

Lily could only stare. His words were marooned in a corner of her mind. It was there when he leaned forward. In profile, his nose looked short and blunt like a pugilist's, even though when viewed full-on, it appeared straight, regular. It was the same anomaly she had observed in Paul Newcastle. She lined up the other attributes. Same dark hair. Same dark eyes. Jonathan was taller, thinner, but essentially, their builds were the same. And there was that other, unmistakable similarity, the annoying glint of teasing each carried in his dark eyes, the way they had of mocking with silence, of laughing without laughter. The chief difference was that Jonathan's face projected good spirits; whereas, Paul's presented a bland, opaque façade. But there was no real distinction there either. In the world of drama, comedy and tragedy each wore masks. Her earlier curiosity about Paul's reaction to Jonathan at the elevator had since been superseded by matters of more consequence. Now it returned with redoubled force. Was the deceit worse than she had imagined? Was Paul the source of Jonathan's information about her and the Murphys?

"You are a visitor," she said. "Do you have family here? Where is your family?"

"Family?"

"Blood relatives, that's what we call them in the United States."

He looked at her, perplexed. "I thought you Americans were famously careless about the angles in society's posture. Did I not already confess a deficiency in aristocratic antecedents?"

"Then who are your relatives? Where are they?"

He drew back and regarded her down the length of his face. "It would appear my inquisitiveness is being repaid in kind."

The little engine released its wail. The cars were slowing for the approach to the terminus in La Turbie. The subject would have to be discontinued — temporarily.

# Sunday, March 15, 1914

STANDING ON THE TRAIN'S PLATFORM, LILY AND Jonathan took in the long, blue view stretching from far-away Bordighera, Italy, on their left, to Monaco below, to the far-away Esterel mountain range on the right. Then Jonathan put his hand under her elbow as they began making their way up the steep incline towards the Moorish-inspired Hôtel du Righi d'Hiver. Resuming her interrogation, Lily asked about his interest in America. For how long had he been thinking about immigrating? Why?

"In England," he explained, "one's so-called station in life exerts a harsh tyranny. The caste system there is no less rigorous than in India, and the practice of meritocracy is scarcely understood. After complaining incessantly to anyone who would listen that Great Britain was not devoting herself to making me happy, I finally realized that if circumstances were not to my liking, it was up to me to create circumstances which were. Ergo, I decided to go to America."

As they continued the climb, he demonstrated an impressive knowledge of the United States. She knew Americans who didn't know that Woodrow Wilson was president. He questioned why Roosevelt hadn't been reelected after his successes as a trust-buster. He seemed particularly interested in the more famous, too often deadly, labor disputes. He brought up the Pullman Strike, the Children's

Crusade, the '02 Anthracite Coal Strike, West Virginia's Paint Creek, and the troubles currently brewing in Colorado's coal mines. He wondered if the nation indeed was ravaged by predatory capital and whether the paramount villains in fact were Wall Street and the monopolies. Throughout, Lily listened hard for any hint of a sneer about the Suffragette Movement, but he emerged blameless in that regard.

At the hotel's restaurant, they were greeted by the maître d'hôtel. He apologized for not speaking English but assured them their waiter would. Many of the marble-topped tables and plush, red lounging-couches were occupied, some of them by persons Lily recalled seeing on the train, including the quarreling couple with the thumb-sucking kid.

Taking in the Turkish carpets, ceiling of punched-tin, and frescoed walls, Jonathan said, "I like this. At Monte Carlo, as odd as this may sound, the eye becomes fatigued by opulence."

The waiter, who had arrived in time to hear the comment, informed them that all these furnishings had come directly from Istanbul. He covered the small table with dishes filled with dates, figs, currants, and olive oil, along with a plate of unleavened bread.

After he carried away their request for a bottle of Bordeaux, Jonathan said, "I trust you have been awed by my vast knowledge of your country. Please tell me what else I should know."

She gave a half-shrug. "I'm sure you've heard the rest. We were all raised by wolves. We can all split a playing card at its side with a bullet from ninety feet. We drink firewater with the Indians and feel free to shoot any piano player we don't like."

He removed the piece of paper from his pocket and jotted on it in shorthand. He looked up. "Is it only pianists I can shoot, or does the freedom extend to violinists as well?"

"It depends on the state. Texas, yes. Massachusetts, no."

He made another notation.

Next, she answered several easy questions about San Francisco. Again, his knowledge was impressive. No, she hadn't experienced the big earthquake. That was 1906, and she had lived there less than a year. Yes, the beaches had glorious sunsets. No, she had not seen the Cliff House. It was too far out. Yes, she had seen Chinatown and Russian Hill and Telegraph Hill. As she responded, she was simultaneously attempting to grab hold of one of her contradictory feelings, so she could speak solely from its perspective. Should she take his interest at face-value, or should she continue to suspect him of double-dealing?

Suddenly her thoughts were truncated. Out of the corner of her eye, she saw the pockmarked man from the Palais des Beaux Arts following the maître d'hôtel to a table. The loathsome little creature was looking directly at her when she caught sight of him.

"Is something wrong?" Jonathan said.

"No. That is, I just remembered something. It isn't important." It was this murder business. It made her as nervous as a wild goose in a room full of mirrors. The interruption did serve to bring her to a decision. Whether Jonathan was or was not playing her, she could play him.

She said, "San Francisco is a potting shed for transplants from all over the world. That's why I asked about your relatives. I knew someone who looked a great deal like you, almost exactly, only older. I met him briefly. I don't remember his name."

He gave her a long, not altogether friendly look. "Hasn't it been said that everyone who goes missing is eventually seen in San Francisco? It must be a city full of *doppelgängers*."

She produced an innocent smile. "Well?" she said. "Might it have been a relative of yours?"

"I doubt seriously that you saw my uncle in San Francisco."

"Uncle." She tried not to gloat. "You have an uncle," she prompted when he failed to elaborate.

"Have, had, have. I don't know what the proper tense is."

"Let's pretend it is *have.* What of him?"

He looked down at his hands resting at the base of his wine glass, then took a great breath and released it. "I disappointed the man, and he refused to forgive me. That's the sum of it."

"Come now. I would expect a muckraker to tell a better story than that. Aren't you paid by the word?"

He drained the wine from his glass, then lifted his hands in a sign of surrender. "'But, yes, sweet Kate, my tongue will tell the anger of my heart, or else my heart concealing it will break.' I concede I owe him a great deal. He paid for my boarding school, which in turn greased the way for a scholarship at Cambridge. For me, it turned out a ripping success. For him, disappointed expectations. Employing some peculiar algorithm known only to himself, my uncle had calculated I would turn up as some toffee-nosed swell, succeed as London's leading barrister, be knighted for my service to the Crown, and finish off as Prime Minister of Great Britain or King of Portugal."

"Your becoming a journalist wasn't a part of that calculus?"

Jonathan's smile was sardonic. "You might say. For him, it wasn't even an apology for a proper career. He made it sound like I had had a chair broken over my head. No man in his right mind, no sane man would give up a brilliant future – that is to say, the future he had manufactured out of his own extravagant imagination – to pursue such a low form of existence. In fact of matter, I suspect that is what troubled him the most. Journalism's ranks are swelled by a considerable number of men who have decidedly less than genteel origins. I admit there is a definite rough-and-tumble to the penny-press trade, but it was never my plan to keep at that indefinitely. That's why I intend to become one of the 'lately landed' in your country. I believe my ambitions can be satisfied faster there – not that the United States has lower standards, only broader opportunities."

He speared one of the pitted dates with a toothpick, lifted it halfway to his mouth, then returned it to the dish. "In truth," he continued, "that is the principal reason I am at the Côte d'Azur. Even though *The World* and *The Sun* and a few thousand other New York editors managed the incredible feat of failing to appreciate my worthiness, I did take up a correspondence with Mr. James O'Flaherty of the *Home News*. It's a small publication, housed in a place called the Bronx, but it can be grown. You might think it leans too heavily towards boxing and murders and catfighting dance-hall girls, but let's face it. The yellows cater to the gross and savage in human nature, and that particular shade of yellow has turned to gold. But the money isn't in writing for a newspaper. The money is in owning one. That's why the *Home News* has potential. There's a possibility, a strong possibility, that I can become a partner." Jonathan waved a hand, like he was brushing away an objection she had not raised. "That's not as wild as it sounds. Joseph Pulitzer, Sam McClure, scores of others, started as virtual paupers. I'm a rung or two above that. I try not to get too far ahead of myself, but the negotiations with O'Flaherty look promising."

"Have you told your uncle of these plans? Where is he? What does he do?"

With his elbow on the table, Jonathan pressed his thumb and forefinger against his closed eyelids as he slowly shook his head. Then he raised his arm and announced, "I say there, one and all. This lass has the makings of a great investigative reporter. Move over, Ida Tarbell. Watch out, Nellie Bly. She's coming up the inside. Even you, Harriet Hubbard Ayer, yes, even you. Careful there. Move over. There's a dark horse in the competition."

Lily gave the humor a thin smile but refused to be deflected. "What is his name?"

"Who is he? Where is he? What does he do? You are persistent. I hope you don't find this disappointing. It's neither a state secret nor my secret shame, so there's no reason not to tell you. His name is George, George Chandler, my mother's brother. Uncle George is in Australia."

"Australia?"

"Australia. People do live there. He claims to spend his days raising sheep in the Outback. I suspect he's nothing more than an alcoholic layabout."

"He hasn't visited you, ever?"

"I haven't seen him since I was four years old."

"You're an investigator. Why don't you look him up?"

"I'm going to America, not Australia," he said with finality. He lifted the empty wine bottle, then took out his pocketwatch.

"Would you care to walk about? You may have noticed that pile of rocks behind the hotel when we arrived. It has historical interest."

THE PATH AGAIN LED UPWARD, AND JONATHAN TOOK HER HAND. As the ground became more uneven and rock-strewn, he put his arm around her waist. Even through the thicknesses of their coats, she felt the warmth of his touch. After working their way through several untidy piles of fallen limestone blocks, they came to a stop at the base of a towering, featureless, enormous dirt-gray clump of mortared rubble.

187

"What is it?" Lily asked.

"A product of *Pax Romana*, what today we would call 'Might Makes Right.' It's known as the Trophy of Augustus and was constructed somewhere around the 7th century B.C. to commemorate the Romans' victory over the local tribes. The original structure was much taller and far greater in circumference. Consider that La Turbie is 1,600 feet above the sea and add another 120 feet or so for the Trophy. Everyone must have been able to decipher its message: the intimidation of military strength, the reality of its power. Most of the huge stones were cannibalized for building the village during the Middle Ages. So what we're left with is another crumbling remnant of the grandeur that was Rome."

They stood in silent contemplation of the impermanence of all things, including the immense, the unmovable, and the irresistible. As the daylight began to leech away, the distant sea deepened to a sapphire blue.

When a solitary bell tolled in the church tower, it seemed to announce to Lily that the confines against which she had struggled all her life were releasing her from their limitations She sensed the miseries which had complicated her childhood and continued to haunt the corners of her life were sloughing away. The manacles of Chicago, the shackles of abandonment and shame, those too unlatched their grip. She was slipping free from her fears of the past and free from her fears of the future as well. She was floating in a timeless world with no horizons.

She turned towards Jonathan just as he turned towards her. He did not kiss her, not with his lips at any rate, yet he caressed her excessively with his eyes, letting them trace the outlines of her hair, her face, lingering on every soft and sensual place, below her earlobes, the center of her forehead, the tip of her nose, slowly, slowly circling her lips. She closed her eyes and lifted her head in open invitation of his kiss. She heard his sharp intake of breath.

The train's shrill whistle shattered the moment. They started but did not pull apart. Lily bit her lower lip hard, letting her dimples deepen, letting her eyes bore into his, wanting desperately to believe that he was not using her only as a means into the Murphy case, wanting desperately to believe, not in him, but in herself.

During the twenty-minute descent to Monte Carlo, neither spoke. Lily laid her head on Jonathan's shoulder. He responded by pulling her closer.

# Sunday, March 15, 1914
## HÔTEL DE PARIS

As Paul entered the Hôtel de Paris' basement kitchen, Olivier Broliquet signaled recognition by crinkling his eyes but without making the slightest break in his diatribe. "Is it not enough that the third Napoléon should hand them Alsace-Lorraine on a silver platter? No, exactly, it is not. They must have San Remo and half of the Italian coast. Still, it is not enough. Now, they take the Côte d'Azur."

Paul removed his overcoat and hat and considered backtracking to the cloakroom to hang them away from the kitchen's odors, then chose instead to luxuriate in an atmosphere of normalcy and more importantly, in a place that did not demand constant vigilance.

Olivier would have just finished decrying the incompetence of the kitchen's sous-chef, François de Clercq, and after he had finished with the current subject — the Germans with their pig-like eyes and picnic baskets filled with sauerkraut and deplorable bread — next to receive condemnation would be the perfidy of bankers and the evil machinations of the Bourse. If there was one thing Olivier liked to do with his voice more than gossip, it was to gripe, and his standard litany of complaints revolved with the regularity of a clock's ticking hand from the alarming indolence of today's youth to the bottomless ineptitude of the sous-chef, de Clercq, to the catastrophic degradations which befell Monaco with each fresh incursion of foreign barbarians to the contemptible corruptions of governments. Just for spice, every now and again he would remonstrate over the undeserved reputation of that "thief and Kaiser-lover," Auguste Escoffier, which was exactly the spur he was on now. "Everyone knows he and that criminal, César Ritz, stole wine and spirits worth thousands from the Savoy and avoided La Santé only by bribing their way out of the charges. And how do they employ their ill-gotten gains? They set up their own kitchen and have stolen all the Savoy's best customers."

Olivier paused in the routine long enough to lift his chin in Paul's direction. "Something to eat?" he asked.

When Paul declined the offer, Olivier returned to shaping the bread dough and his grievances.

Paul leaned against the wall situated between the clocking machine and a wash basin while his mind automatically tallied the number of cups of flour being added to the concoction on the table. Flour-dust covered everything from table to floor. Its bland powdery smell filled the air and blended with the savory scents of butter, olive oil, and rosemary. More than eleven kinds of bread were produced by this kitchen through the course of a day. To the uninitiated, Olivier Broliquet's imposing size, fit testimony to his skill as a *boulanger*, and his chronic complaining might cause him to appear formidable, but in truth, he was one of the gentlest souls Paul had ever known.

By conservative estimate, Broliquet was related either by blood or marriage to every true Monegasque still living or who have ever lived, including Paul's landlady, Madame Piggot. Not long after he took a room in her pension, Paul had devised a scheme to free her from her back-breaking labor at the nearby commercial laundry. Under his direction, she established a chalet-industry manufacturing good-luck charms. She specialized in the highly prized left-back-foot of rabbits, which she tied off with a piece of hemp from a hangman's rope. The latter was certified by a scrap of paper stating the criminal's name and date of execution along with a smudge of ink which was the hangman's mark. During the high season, she often had back-orders for these precious talismans, double-dyed as they were in good fortune – if one could overlook the fates of the rabbits and the hanged men.

Olivier had been delighted. "I tell you, Paul. If necessity is the mother of invention, laziness must be its father. Why should a man work all his life for something that can be taken in a single roll of the dice?" To cement his appreciation, Olivier offered his sister's lodger unlimited meals from the hotel's kitchen. Since January, Paul had taken advantage of this accommodation every Wednesday, right before his weekly flogging in the office overhead. Not only was the fare excellent, he particularly cherished the idea of feeding off the books of that glorified innkeeper, Barousse.

Raised voices on the opposite side of the enormous kitchen drew Paul's attention that way. A young man, built like a marling spike and dressed like a dandy, was being raked over the coals by an overseer. From the sounds of things, the boy was late to work. Paul cataloged the cheap suit, shiny with newness, the dark curls about a starched collar, and an Adam's apple that deserved to be surgically removed. The contrived attitude of insouciance was weakened by a slack-lipped mouth and receding chin.

Olivier used the crook of his elbow to nudge the tall chef's hat off his forehead. It was becoming increasingly difficult to distinguish the white hairs in his mutton-chop whiskers from the flour speckling his face. He said something to the assistant at his side, then came to rinse his hands in the basin beside Paul.

The young man who had received the dressing-down stormed past, his face expressing equal parts fury and amazement.

"You know that young scamp?" Olivier asked, drying his hands on a towel.

Paul said he did not.

"Include yourself among the fortunate. Thick as a roof beam. He thinks everyone is out to get him fired and with good reason – they are. He has been a floor-waiter all of a month and believes he is going to be promoted to maître d'hôtel next week. The way he slaps down the dishes, I am certain he is an anarchist. Who knows the number of plates he has broken? Even Jean has lost count. The first day, he arrived smirking like he had just made off with all of Prince Albert's old bones. It did not take Henri long to get that look off his face." Olivier removed a packet from his shirt pocket, shook out a cigarette, put it between his lips, and continued, "The management was deprived of his services recently. He went missing one whole afternoon last week and would have been fired if not for the fact he is the son of the sister of de Clercq's wife. But he is no different than any of those pups. All of them act like they have a hundred years to spare before they can be bothered to perform their duties. What will happen after us, Paul? Who will carry the load?"

He quit speaking in order to light the cigarette. At the far end of the kitchen, a parade of waiters passed through double doors, balancing on one arm loaded trays the size of a wagon wheel. Above them, Jean Reynaud sat in state in a raised glass-cage. Like a lighthouse on a promontory, his eyes swept the contents of each tray as it left or was returned to

193

the kitchen to ensure all the food had been charged and all the plate and silver accounted for.

"This isn't Wednesday," Olivier observed.

"I wanted to ask if I could borrow a hammer on Monday," Paul said.

They went through this charade every time Paul decided something at Madame Piggot's pension could bear neglect no longer. Olivier was many things besides a fine baker. A couple of years ago, he had taken up glass-blowing and spent his holidays at an island off Venice studying at the feet of the masters. Prior to that, he had taught himself to virtuoso level on the violin. Before the violin, he amused himself by developing his talent as a furniture designer and honing his skills as an expert woodcrafter. It was this skill Paul was soliciting. He always began by asking to borrow what he thought was the necessary tool, knowing full well that Olivier not only would accede to the request but would personally deliver the item and complete the repair.

Having agreed upon a time for Monday afternoon, Olivier said, "I hear Monsieur Barousse has you working with the Americans."

There it was, the opening to the bartering which was the true reason for Paul's visit. He pursed his lips and gave a short nod. Unlike most voluble people, who lost interest in a conversation the second they stopped talking, Olivier was an accomplished listener as well. He was the principal repository for all local news, from the most dramatic to the most trivial. His brother-in-law was on the police force and among those who kept the inventory of information current. Olivier would probably know who wanted to kill Murphy and who stole the necklace a full day before the police did. Fifteen minutes spent in the right conversation with him was worth a week's worth of shoe leather, and given the doubtful state of Paul's soles, this was a significant saving. His gossip, however, was usually a zero-sum game. For every crumb he dropped, he expected a morsel in return. Each time they swapped stories, Paul searched for the knowing glance, the subtle inflection, any indication that his affair with Céline Claudet was the topic *de jour*, but he never detected anything that suggested their wall of secrecy had been breached. When calling on her, he exercised the same excessive caution he used with Hervé. With Céline, however, the discretion was due to concern for her security, more so than for his own. No doubt, everyone in Monaco except Paul knew the name of her benefactor, but that was a subject he never raised. Having convinced himself he did not care to know, he lived in dread of someone's forcing the knowledge on him.

"What are you doing for them?" Olivier asked.

"As little as possible."

Across the room, the tardy waiter, now in uniform, was piling china on a cart, all the while staring with open suspicion in Paul's direction.

"Barousse is extraordinarily interested in it," he continued to Olivier. "He had me excused from the Casino, so I can give it all my time."

Olivier said, "An intriguing situation. The man not only was shot after he was dead from a bee-sting, but someone laced his nightcap with poison."

Paul delivered a wry grin. "What? Has no one has mentioned the pygmies with blowdarts?"

Olivier went on, "The police believe the body was moved. At the very least, he did not die in the position in which he was found. There is some suspicion, but no one knows for certain. Let me put it this way: he was a man who took dessert with his dinner. A quite delicious little dish, I am told. The big money is on her."

Well, well, Paul thought. The oldest story in the world. *Cherchez la femme.* Women were thought to be at the bottom of all of mankind's troubles. Pandora, the box to Epimetheus. Eve, the apple in the Garden. *It wasn't my fault,* Adam had whined. *It was the woman, Lord.*

In answer to Paul's question, Olivier said, "Mademoiselle Sally Holmes."

Paul said, "Any chance she's sporting an emerald necklace? That's what I'm supposed to locate."

"She was not wearing it when she left this hotel yesterday morning. She took the ferry to San Remo but carried only a small portmanteau with her."

That would have been large enough for transporting a necklace. San Remo would be a safer place to pawn it.

The tardy waiter was in line behind two other floor-waiters and their carts, awaiting Reynaud's inspection. To Paul's amusement, the lad had adopted avoidance as his tactic. His eyes seemed to be going everywhere except where Paul and Olivier stood. The lad has a lot to learn, Paul thought. He thinks we can't see him if he doesn't look at us.

"Your fine young friend over there," he said, indicating the weak-chinned waiter exiting the kitchen, "does he work the top floor?"

"Do you kid me? Not even de Clercq is stupid enough to let him near the richest guests. He works the second floor." Olivier interrupted himself to call an order to his assistant, then turned to run water over the stub of the cigarette before tossing it in the rubbish can.

Paul pulled out his pocketwatch. He wanted to stop by the Casino, let Maubert know the furlough was not his own doing, perhaps catch another sight of Jonnie. Not that the latter was important, but as long as Paul was there, he might as well look around, no harm in that. Besides, he had earned one more look at the young scapegrace. But it was more important to find out what else Olivier might divulge about Murphy, especially if there was a whisper of Hervé Andreas. Furthermore, even though Paul would have preferred to dismiss Cyril's suspicions about Basil Zaharoff, this morning's conversation with Friedrich Hoffmeister had only sharpened those allegations.

"What about the Americans?" Olivier asked. "What are they like?"

"The wife has left town, moved out to Cap Ferrat. Wycliffe, the wife's cousin, is doing the investigating. I rank him somewhere between a Tasmanian devil and a rabid weasel. Puffs himself up as the reincarnated soul of Allan Pinkerton, but I doubt he has a clue as to what's really gone on."

"What about the tall young woman?"

Paul felt an inexplicable impulse to be protective of Lily. "Basically, she's an amanuenses. She's been thrown into it just as I have, and she does what Wycliffe tells her to do, which isn't much beyond taking notes."

Olivier fished a toothpick out of his apron's pocket and rolled it between his lips while his eyes studied the scene in the kitchen before him. "Keep this under your hat," he said, adjusting his own as he did so. "I am curious to know if the American will say anything about it. There was a German dictionary with markings in it. Chief Inspector Gautier went through it page by page. What do you think he was looking for? Invisible ink? Perhaps it was a code book?"

Paul came close to groaning aloud. If Cyril caught wind of this, Paul might just have to kill that man.

"I'll let you know if Wycliffe mentions the markings," he promised. At the same time, he recalled there was none in the book The Hyena had shown him.

# Sunday, March 15, 1914
## HÔTEL DE PARIS

LILY SANK DEEPER INTO THE CHAIR'S CUSHION, clutching the man's handkerchief she had intentionally forgotten to return, refusing to relinquish the afterglow of the day, choosing to linger in a Never Never Land shorn of empty bank accounts, dunning landlords, obnoxious male masters, tyrannical employers, dead husbands, and ungracious suspicions of a charming suitor's duplicity. It felt ever so much better to soak in the memory of his warmth, his touch, his smile. It wasn't merely that she found him physically attractive. What woman wouldn't? He was personally attractive as well: witty, intelligent, educated, diffident and confident in balanced measure. Too perfect by half and too dangerous by twice for her good sense. And to top it off, he intended to come to the United States, to New York City no less. She had not, could not, say anything about her ambitions there, not yet.

On the ride down from La Turbie, with her eyes closed and her head on his shoulder, she was certain their kiss would have been consummated if it had not been a public conveyance. She would have insisted. Next time, she would make sure. Day after tomorrow, Tuesday, they had agreed to meet at the Oceanographic Museum. It was foolish for her to make rash promises to him or to herself. Her time was not her own. The telegrams would be delivered to Cap Ferrat tomorrow. Quite possibly, she would not remain in Monte Carlo long after that. Right now, that didn't matter. Such a dismal contingency didn't belong in her dream.

The rap on her door was so light it might well have been the brush of a feather duster. Lily wasn't even sure she had heard it.

A soft voice said, "Miss Turner? Lily? It's Sally Holmes."

Before the door was completely opened, Sally squeezed past and pasted herself against the inside wall. "Shut it. Quickly, please."

Lily did as she was told.

"Someone's been in my room," Sally whispered. "Someone tore up my room."

Lily wordlessly led her guest to the sofa and took a seat on a footstool directly in front of her.

Sally essayed a smile but immediately abandoned the effort. "I'm sorry to bother you," she said. "I needed to pull myself together. I need to catch my breath."

"I'll pour a brandy," Lily said. "Then you can tell me what happened."

Taking a seat on the footstool again, Lily waited for Sally to bring herself around. At the same time, Lily's mind was fully engaged fitting this latest development into her existing store of knowledge. It was as though she had set aside all the straight-edges prior to constructing a jigsaw puzzle, then found another large piece lying on the floor. Someone else knew about Sally Holmes and Mr. Murphy, and that someone knew, or suspected, more about Sally Holmes than Lily did.

Sally took a sip, lowered the glass, returned it to her mouth, and drained it. Both hands gripping the tumbler, she pressed it to her chest. "I was away all day yesterday, last night too. I returned about five, ten minutes ago. I opened the door and switched on the electric light. It was like a tornado had gone through. I didn't go in. I shut the door and came here.

"I was thinking – I don't know what I was thinking. I was hoping you would go with me. It's not that I'm afraid. No, that's not true. I am afraid. But it would be plain foolish for me to go in alone. Stay in the hallway if you prefer. I don't want to go there alone. I'll pay –"

"Be quiet," Lily said.

# Sunday, March 15, 1914
## HÔTEL DE PARIS

IN THE CORRIDOR, LILY LIFTED THE PRIVACY PLACARD and held it towards Sally. She shook her head. Lily placed her hand on the knob and turned it. It was unlocked. She looked at Sally again. She nodded. Lily pushed the door open. The electric light was on. The chaos had a familiar feel. As in Mrs. Murphy's suite, the smaller items on the tabletops were undisturbed, while the cushions of the sofa and upholstered chairs had been sliced. Stuffing protruded from the tears. The desk wasn't splintered, but the drawers had been removed, thrown aside, and their contents scattered. Magazines were fanned across the floor. The draperies were drawn open, so rather than risk being seen by someone outside, Lily worked her way along the wall to the bedroom. Sally followed close behind.

In that room, exactly as in Mrs. Murphy's, the dresses and gowns were turned inside out and tossed in heaps on the floor. The ripped mattress leaned against the side of the bedframe. The pillows likewise were slashed. Most unnerving, the dressmaker's manikin had been eviscerated. Lily hoped this sprang from the same impulse that had gutted the cushions and wasn't intended as a threat.

Satisfied that no one was lurking in the bedroom, Lily told

Sally to switch off the lights in both rooms and close the door to the corridor to shut out that light as well. Navigating by the bright moonlight pouring through the windows, Lily closed the curtains but left the shutters latched open so she could peek out, perchance to catch someone gazing upward from below. Offshore, running-lights on boats threaded their way across the inky sea. No one suspicious was revealed by the string of gas-lamps forming a secular rosary around Monte Carlo's grand basilica, the Casino.

After the room's lights were switched on, Lily drew the first full breath she had drawn since leaving her room. That one felt so good, she took another. Positioned next to the buttons for the lights, Sally was literally wringing her hands. The expression on her face was more pensive than fearful.

Lily said, "You're sure you didn't leave the privacy notice on the door?"

"That was the first signal that something was out of sorts. I was certain I removed it. The room needed cleaning."

"It definitely needs cleaning now." Lily held out one of the shredded cushions. "What were they looking for inside your cushions and mattress?"

"I don't know. Valuables, I guess. But the most valuable things I have are those bolts of fabric, which they didn't take."

At last, the opening Lily had been waiting for. But she needed to tread lightly. She couldn't afford to alienate Sally. "I didn't mention it before," she said. "I didn't mention it because I couldn't see how it had anything to do with you, but Mrs. Murphy is missing a valuable emerald and diamond necklace. Would you happen to know anything about it?"

The look on Sally's face said she clearly knew something about it. However, in the same instant Lily's hopes started to soar, they were dashed to earth by Sally's bitter laugh. "That damned necklace, will I never hear the end of it?"

Lily said nothing. She wasn't about to be the one to bring an end to the subject.

"No, I don't know anything about Madeline's emerald necklace. I never wanted to know anything about Madeline's emerald necklace. What I do know is that Joe had a paste copy with him. He thought I might like to wear it. I wouldn't wear the real thing, so why would I want to wear a gewgaw like that? He had known me over a year and still couldn't get it into his head that not every woman has a jackdaw's love of shiny objects, that we're not all entranced by a *miroir aux alouettes*."

Lily thought that denial might or might not be true. At any rate, Sally was changing keys; her anger was dissolving into tears. "You see," she said, her voice breaking. "It still infuriates me. I hate that. The last time we were together, we had words over it. That is, I had a few choice words to say about that damned necklace. I was vicious, merciless. I wish I hadn't been so harsh. He was only trying to please me, but he just wouldn't listen. I told him a thousand times, diamonds are nothing but chains in disguise, so what does he do? He brings along that paste one. Through some convoluted logic, he thought I would like to wear it because it was pretty but not valuable. Madeline or someone must have instilled in him the idea there isn't a woman on the planet who wouldn't trade her soul for a big diamond or pearl. I didn't understand. He confused me so. At times, he was –" She broke off. "Do you think someone ripped this place to shreds looking for a necklace?"

Instead of answering, Lily returned to the bedroom door and studied the destroyed manikin. "Why are you here?" she said. "You could be in danger. Why did you leave and then come back?"

Sally looked down at her fingers, which were twining

and untwining themselves at her waist. "I told you. I want to know about the arrangements for Joe, for his, for his body."

Lily intercepted her grimace before it could attach itself to her mouth. Was this going to be a case for Edgar Allen Poe? She said, "His body was embalmed and placed in cold storage. He will return to San Francisco with the rest of the party in two weeks or so."

"He's here in Monaco? Where, exactly?"

Lily could see no reason to discuss this particular matter amid the distressing debris. She said, "Let's get out of here. Take what you need for overnight and leave the privacy placard on the door. I agree with the intruders. The hotel doesn't need to know about this just yet."

# Sunday, March 15, 1914
## HÔTEL DE PARIS

AN HOUR LATER, SALLY HAD CHANGED INTO HER PINK dressing-gown and was on a third glass of brandy. Lily had relaxed only to the extent of removing her boots and loosening the top two buttons on her shirtwaist blouse. She again sat on the footstool facing Sally, who was picking through her embroidery basket for a skein of thread.

While Sally was changing clothes in the next room, Lily had wrestled with her new perspectives. She would have preferred not to believe Sally's story about the necklace. She liked the other, more straightforward answer to the missing piece and the prospective reward. But she couldn't cling to an erroneous theory simply because it was convenient. Where was the profit in that? Furthermore, if what Sally said was true, the paste necklace found in Mr. Murphy's pocket would be explained. And if what Sally said was true, it was unlikely he had ever had the genuine one. Therefore Lily had to abandon her preconceptions and begin anew. She also had to acknowledge that something was afoot besides one or two aborted murders and a missing necklace. Those were past. This "something" was quite alive. Sally had offered to pay a handsome sum to learn who wanted to kill Mr. Murphy. But why would anyone kill him and later go around turning apartments inside out? And Mrs. Murphy was offering a reward for her necklace, but why tear up her apartment after it was stolen? For that matter, if the intruders were after jewelry, every room in the hotel should be lying in tatters. Even Lily owned an expensive pair of diamond earrings. These, she kept in her handbag and never wore because, she told herself, she was too conscious of their value, and that was true. But it was also true that she was too conscious of the emotional freight weighing them down. Effie had sent the earrings instead of attending Lily's graduation from Bryn Mawr. If she had made the journey from Chicago to Pennsylvania, Lily knew full well she would have been mortally embarrassed by Effie's unschooled grammar, flamboyant manner, and unapologetic attitude. At the same time, it had cut to the bone that she had elected not to share Lily's achievement.

Realizing that Sally's hands had fallen still, Lily jerked herself back to the present. She said, "I thought I was the only person of significance who was privy to your friendship with Mr. Murphy. Obviously, I was mistaken. I need you to tell me everything. I'm playing Blind Man's Bluff, and I don't like it. It feels dangerous."

"I know," Sally said.

Lily waited but nothing more was forthcoming. "All right," she sighed, "let's begin at the beginning. Tell me about you and Mr. Murphy."

Sally leaned closer to her needlework. "What do you want to know?"

"Everything."

The little hands stitched faster, but again, Sally said nothing more.

"Tell me, if you will, when you met, where you met, what you've been doing since you've been here. Most importantly, tell me what you know about Mr. Murphy that might shed light on these incidents." Lily didn't know what "incidents" she meant, but that left the door wide open.

Sally put down the embroidery and pressed her palms together, intertwining her fingers so tightly her knuckles turned white. She focused on the ceiling, her eyes welling with tears. "It's not easy to talk about." Her eyelids lowered slowly, gracefully forcing the tears onto her cheeks. "It's not easy because I am so embarrassed. I am so very ashamed."

Lily could see she was about to be treated to another top-notch dramatic performance.

"First of all, please believe me when I say I fought it. I did. I fought him. I did."

Perfect, Lily thought, the standard lamentation over the unwilling surrender of virtue. No question about it. Sally was good. She could out-Bernhardt Sarah. Lily pulled Jonathan's handkerchief from her pocket and passed it over.

"Everything I had put my life into for seven years was swept away as if they had no more substance than dandelion seeds being scattered by the wind. In fact, that's what my principles turned out to be, as flighty, as insubstantial, as dandelion seeds. I was worse than insincere. I was worse than a hypocrite. I was a traitor, a traitor to myself, a traitor to my sisters. Don't you think I knew it then? Don't you think I know it now?"

What Lily was thinking was that the anger-piece in Sally's repertoire — the flushed cheeks, the tears of temper — was as finely developed as the broken-hearted weeping. Maybe it would do to revisit the tantrum over the paste necklace.

"When I met Joe last year, thirteen months ago to be precise, I was twenty-six years old, scarcely in my first youth, one foot already on the shelf, but that didn't matter to me. That was something else Joe couldn't get into his head. He said his marriage to Madeline had been nothing but a slag heap for years, so he wanted to get an annulment from the Church, so we could marry. I told him over and over, I would never submit to the immurement of marriage. You know as well as I do, for a woman, marriage is nothing but institutionalized, legalized self-immolation. All that gush about hearth and home. A woman can't be a wife and have a career or make a difference. That's what I set out to do, to make a difference. Most of the women who have made a dent in the status quo were divorced or widowed or never married, ever. I mean, look at Jane Addams. I met her, you know. I visited the Hull House. And look at Susan Anthony, Florence Nightingale, Clara Barton, even Carey Thomas. They never married, and they didn't marry for a reason."

Lily knew of a reason Carey Thomas never married which was broadly hinted around Bryn Mawr, but now didn't seem the right time to inject that complication into the conversation.

Sally went on, "I was helping the women garment-workers organize. We had a terrific strike in '09, but we have miles to go before the pay is anything near decent and the working conditions anything less than appalling. Years ago, I put myself in their place. I started out doing slopwork, the lowest paid of all. After that, I spent seven months sewing men's underdrawers for thirty cents a dozen. That way, when I talked about joining the union, I wasn't some dilettante, bored with afternoon teas and tired of listening to mind-enriching lectures on deathless topics such as the demise of the S-corset and when gloves must be worn above the elbows.

"Over and over, Joe promised he wouldn't interfere. He promised he wouldn't get in the way of my causes, but look at me now. Do you know what I think every time I look out the window here? I remember that line about being able to see the way to hell even from the gates of heaven. It's true. Traitor that I am, I'm sitting in this tinsel palace while they go on slaving in deathtraps like that Triangle Shirtwaist Factory for three dollars a week.

"Lily, you can have no idea how lucky you are. For someone like you or me, life offers so much, but for a woman working seventy hours a week, existence is nothing more than work, sleep, and eat. That, and praying that she doesn't get too sick to work. I'm not making any sense, I know. It makes no sense to me either. Why would I throw over everything I worked for, believed in? Why would I throw over all that for this gilded hell, this gilded hell which killed Joe?"

She snatched up the cloth and resumed stitching, working the needle with considerably more force than was necessary. Bright red spots had appeared on her cheeks. "But that's my question, not yours," she said without looking up. "Yours were *when* and *where*, not *why*."

Lily would have expressed her agreement, but she was too astonished to speak. Even though she had never taken her eyes off Sally, it was as though one woman had laid aside the embroidery-hoop and silently left the room while a different person stole in and took the same place on the sofa.

When Sally resumed speaking, her voice was soft but clear. "Since you work for Madeline, you probably don't know this. Joe Murphy had a monstrously large heart. Unlike many people who suddenly become violently rich, he was never careless with his wealth. He believed he had a responsibility to it beyond mindless extravagance. He always carried a substantial amount of cash, in case he met someone in dire need. Most of the time, he dispensed his charity anonymously. He said if he did it openly, it would draw charlatans and phony pleas he didn't want to have to sort out. Nevertheless, sometimes he appeared personally to do his bit. That's where we met, at the Salvation Army's hall on Mission Street. He didn't follow their brand of religion, but he remained grateful for what they had done for San Francisco after the earthquake. I'm not wild about their sermons either, but they're one of the few groups who haven't given up on the so-called fallen women, and I'm grateful for that. I had seen him there once or twice before, but we had never been introduced." A slight smile touched the corners of Sally's lips.

"He didn't look like a man who could sweep a girl off her feet. Maybe that's why I let myself get close. I never dreamed I would be taken unawares. I discovered I enjoyed talking with him. He was extremely intelligent and well read. He could expound on history, art, philosophy, politics, but he could also make me laugh. When I brought up the garment workers, without missing a beat, he said, 'The wages of prostitution are stitched into your buttonholes and into your blouses, pasted into your matchboxes and your boxes of pins.'"

Her smile widened. "I melted on the spot. 'You will not cheat the Recording Angel into putting down your debts to the wrong account,' I answered. The way we were gazing into each other's eyes, you would have thought we were quoting *Romeo and Juliet* instead of Bernard Shaw.

"That same night, I let him give me a ride home. We talked. He convinced me he hadn't simply pulled those words out of his amazingly retentive memory. He convinced me he sincerely believed prostitution was an economic evil, not a moral one. He convinced me of that and a great deal more. And then?"

Sally brought the linen to her mouth and bit off the thread next to the cloth. "Well, and then," she said.

# Sunday, March 15, 1914
## HÔTEL DE PARIS

LILY STOOD AND CROSSED TO HER WRITING DESK. SHE straightened some folders that didn't need straightening, then picked up a pencil and rolled it between her thumb and index finger. Whatever propelled Sally's fingers into perpetual motion apparently was contagious. She stared at the drawn draperies and listened to the dull thump-thump of a loose shutter outside. Her smug stereotype of Sally was tumbling head over heels. Significant revisions needed to be made to the assumptions about her age, background, and character. But even if she were Mother Jones, Emmeline Pankhurst, and Joan of Arc all bundled into one beautiful package and even if every word she had uttered was the God's truth, there remained lake-sized lacunae in her account. For instance, why did she come to Lily to report the incursion into her room? Why not go to the hotel's management? Possibly she was reluctant to draw attention to herself considering the circumstances of Mr. Murphy's death and didn't want to invite an encounter with the police. Lily's instincts, however, said it was more than that. Earlier, when Sally surveyed the damage to her room, she looked thoughtful, not bewildered or mystified. And where had she been for the past two days? If the intruders and the would-be murderers were the same and if Sally knew what they were looking for, why would she engage Lily to learn their identities? More importantly, while the answers to those questions might be interesting, Lily couldn't see how they would lead to more money for her. This thought led to the next question. How much cash did Mr. Murphy have on him? Was it enough to pay all the checks Sally's mouth was writing? During the first visit Lily made to Sally's apartment, when she asked whether Mr. Murphy might have been looking for a way to raise cash, there had been an undefinable but definite response in Sally's expression. Just because she didn't want to wear the necklace, that didn't mean she or Mr. Murphy didn't pawn it or sell it.

Lily snapped the pencil in half and dropped the pieces in the waste-bin. Sally was regarding her with widened eyes and looking as innocent as a newborn lamb. That was something else to keep in mind. Sally might appear to be as sweet and pliable as honey in the comb when in fact, she was as hard and strong as a crowbar.

Lily produced a sheepish grin and waved a hand towards the waste-bin. "It's been a long day," she said. After stopping to pour a brandy for herself and another for Sally, she resumed her place on the footstool. She began with the ransacking of Mrs. Murphy's suite, noting that the method employed there was identical to that used in Sally's rooms. "I would say they didn't find whatever they wanted in Mr. Murphy's suite, so they came searching for it in yours. Now that you've had time to think about it, what do you suppose they were looking for?"

"I don't know, but they didn't find it in my room."

Lily could have asked how Sally knew they didn't find it if she didn't know what they were looking for, but there was nothing to be gained by driving that point home.

Sally said, "Joe wasn't always with me. When Madeline

was in town, he spent a significant amount of time elsewhere. I don't know what he might have been getting up to."

"The intruders obviously knew about you and Mr. Murphy. How did they know?"

"We never went out together in Monte Carlo. When Madeline took herself off to Cannes or Grasse or wherever, Joe and I went to San Remo, so we could move about freely. We didn't flaunt ourselves. We traveled separately and stayed in something less than top-drawer establishments under a different name. He presented me as his wife. We didn't hide, but it was an altogether different crowd in the places we frequented."

"Were you in San Remo the last couple of days?"

A shadow passed behind Sally's eyes, like a dark form swimming beneath the water's surface.

Lily took that as confirmation. She said, "Did you always stay at the same hotel, see the same people? The persons who destroyed your room knew you were away."

Sally put her glass down. Her right hand crept to the top button on her dressing-gown. She rubbed her thumb across the button over and over. "It makes no sense. Even if the people in San Remo knew my real name and where I was staying, why would they come here?"

Lily pulled herself upright before delivering the *coup de grâce*. "Last Wednesday, Mr. Murphy was stung by a bee in your apartment and died there. Who helped you move him upstairs?"

Sally's perfect little mouth formed a perfect little "O."

Lily went on, "So far, I haven't heard Mr. Wycliffe or anyone else say Mr. Murphy died anywhere other than in his room. I put it together myself."

A smile slowly stretched across Sally's lips. "Well done," she said.

Last Wednesday, Sally said, she and Mr. Murphy had left San Remo before noon. She took the ferry while Mr. Murphy rode in the carriage which transported daytrippers between the two towns. At the Hôtel de Paris, by unspoken agreement, she disappeared into her bedroom to unpack her valises and to examine the suitability of the recently arrived new fabric.

"I spend a great deal of time alone in my room when Madeline is in residence," Sally explained. "I occupy myself with designing dresses and developing patterns for them. Someday, who knows? Someday, I may have a roomful of women to whom I am paying a living wage for turning out my creations."

Returning to her story, Sally said that while she was in the bedroom, Mr. Murphy was in the salon with the French windows open, smoking a cigar and having a whiskey. "We were always a bit withdrawn from one another on the eve of Madeline's return. It was nothing to me if she found us out, but Joe believed the secrecy was necessary."

At some point, Sally said, she thought she heard a commotion coming from the other room, but when she called out, he didn't reply. She returned to her preoccupations, laying out the fabric, envisioning the finished product. By the time she returned to the sitting room, it was too late.

"I knew almost immediately what had happened. My parents have a country cottage outside St. Louis. One of my mother's friends, a young man, died there after being stung by a bee. I heard how painful his death was: the swelling, the burning, the inability to breathe. Joe tried to call for me. I know he tried but couldn't. He couldn't, and me, not twenty feet away."

Lily could barely understand the last few sentences. Sally's face was buried in her hands, and her shoulders were shaking violently. Lily retrieved Jonathan's handkerchief and placed it on Sally's lap. She allowed Sally a decent interval to dry her face and to clear her nose before asking how she had managed to return Mr. Murphy to his suite.

"It was Dominique, the floor-waiter. You saw him the first time you called. I've always thought he was a bit taken with me. At any rate, I rang for a meal. Taken with me or not, he was more than happy to take the large sum of money I gave him. He brought a wheeled chair and put Joe in it. It was his idea to remove the shirt." At the next onset of the tears, Sally bit down on the back of her balled fist. She seemed as eager to get to the end of this story as Lily was. "Joe had torn at his shirt, ripped it, trying to relieve his distress. Dominique covered his shoulders with a blanket."

Lily waited for the silence to settle again before asking, "You kept his money?"

"Yes, I used some of it to pay Dominique."

When Lily questioned whether he might think Sally or Mr. Murphy was keeping a pile of money hidden in their apartments, Sally said, "I removed the wallet and moneyclip before I called him. Besides, Dominique wouldn't tear up our rooms looking for cash, would he? I mean, if that's what he was after, why wouldn't he tear up every room in the hotel?"

Lily allowed she could not answer that question. It was time to bring up the tickets to Belfast and the dictionary.

"Those tickets," Sally said, "they were for Michael Gallagher and his wife. It was the arrangement Joe made with him. I told you he was generous. He particularly liked helping out Irishmen. He was only too familiar with the insults thrown their way. 'White but not quite,' 'No Irish need apply,' that sort of rubbish. I don't remember the whole story, something about Michael was a ship's carpenter and Joe was helping them get back to Ireland. He told Madeline he would pay the couple's wages if she would let Mrs. Gallagher act as her lady's maid. Madeline leapt on it. This abominable trip was her idea, so most of the cost was coming out of her funds. They kept their money separate, you know. Joe had also promised – I doubt Madeline knew this – to pay the Gallaghers' passage to Belfast when their work here was concluded. There's a shipyard or some such there. Again, I don't remember all the details."

That explained the tickets to Belfast. But nothing Sally had said accounted for the dictionary with the mysterious markings. Chief Inspector Gautier apparently considered it significant since he substituted a different one when he returned Mr. Murphy's belongings.

Sally interrupted these thoughts. "Do you think Madeline tried to kill Joe? She has all the makings of a Clytemnestra. That's why Joe insisted on keeping our friendship secret. He said her rationality could not be relied upon. He was genuinely afraid she would become violent."

"We shouldn't pick our conclusions before they're ripe, but just for the sake of argument, let us say it was her. Regardless of her motive, wouldn't it be a good idea for you to leave Monte Carlo before she finds out about you?"

"I asked about Joe's remains. You talked to the undertaker, correct?"

Lily concurred.

"That means the undertaker doesn't know what Madeline looks like, correct?"

Lily again concurred, but she was beginning to get a bad feeling about where this line of questions was going.

"The White Star liner is due in port within three days," Sally said. "When it sails, Joe and I will be on it. He made me promise, almost like he had a premonition of what was going to happen. He made me promise that if he could not be buried next to me, I would make sure he was returned to

Wiggins Patch, Pennsylvania. Weedless Patch, he called it, because the coal-dust choked out everything, including the weeds. He wanted to be buried next to his mother. He said if he couldn't be laid to rest with his greatest joy, he would settle for being next to his greatest sorrow. Madeline's not leaving for another two weeks. By the time she misses him, he'll be home — his home, not hers."

Her voice cracked again at the end, but Lily wasn't thinking about Mr. Murphy's wishes for the disposition of his remains. She was unraveling the implications of what she had just heard. She had always understood that being a private detective would be to traverse a moral landscape carpeted with bear-traps. Ethical compromises were inevitable if she wore disguises, lied about her identify, and befriended persons she intended to betray. She had not, however, anticipated that she would be confronted with so many ethical dilemmas in her first case. Satisfying her duty to her employer while maintaining her silence about Sally's existence and selling her services as a detective had seemed quite enough in the way of questionable choices. But now, if she let Sally's plan go through, she was also going to be an accomplice in a body-snatching.

# Monday March 16, 1914
## GIORGIO'S CAFÉ

THERE BEING NO BABY SEALS AT HAND TO CLUB OR anything else on which he could lavish his distemper, Paul scowled at his teacup. In the branches of the olive trees, the birds were having such a ferocious conversation, they had to be discussing politics. How typical of Cyril, Paul fumed. He hadn't been here at Giorgio's yesterday or the day before and now again today. Most of the time, he was like a hair in the soup, but when he was wanted .... Paul was ready with the name from Krenz's staff he had been ordered to provide. On any other morning, he would have been resenting the insistence on a verifiable name. There could be only a couple of reasons for that criterion, neither of which he liked. But this morning there were plenty of other things to mull. For one thing, after talking with Friedrich, Paul wanted to hear more of Cyril's theories about Basil Zaharoff, credible and incredible. Conspiracy theories came flying out of Cyril's mouth like skeet from a trap, but even lunatics got it right once in a while.

Paul was also pondering when and what to report to that small-time Torquemada, Barousse. A schedule hadn't been specified; therefore, Paul intended to run the "when" to the limit. If challenged, he would say he had been waiting for the meeting at Wycliffe's this afternoon. As for the "what," he couldn't know how he was going to sail through those straits until he knew what was and wasn't relevant to Hervé.

That thought brought on the next major annoyance: Hervé's stubborn refusal to take Paul into his confidence. He even had the cheek to send a signal to Paul's pension this morning indicating he wanted a meeting this afternoon at their prearranged place below Cap d'Ail. This had further disturbed Paul's plans for the day. He wanted to be present when Olivier showed up to replace the rotten step. Although he didn't need tutelage, it seemed the decent thing to be standing by.

All that should have been enough for a man to awake to, but there was also the matter of Jonnie. After leaving Olivier and the kitchen yesterday afternoon, Paul stopped by the Casino to speak to his boss, Maubert, then to make a circuit of the Rooms. Afterwards, he spent a couple of hours drinking coffee outside the Café de Paris, watching the pedestrians and the new arrivals at the Casino across the square. When dusk dissolved into darkness, he considered returning to the Rooms. However, for no reason he wanted to admit, he preferred to avoid Céline, so he called it an early evening and returned to Madame Piggot's pension.

The way his thoughts kept circling back to Jonnie was especially irritating. Paul had sauntered past the Police Conference a few times but turned up nothing. He didn't want to speak to the young scoundrel. He wanted a better look, that was all, preferably in a public place where the scrutiny would pass unnoticed. He wanted a chance for a leisurely observation, an opportunity to take the measure of the man.

He had visualized several scenarios in which he

encountered the boy. In one, he approached Jonnie on a pretext. He would be who he was now, Paul Newcastle, not George Chandler. Or – Paul let this scenario play out as well – he acknowledged himself as George Chandler and concocted a story about operating incognito for the British Secret Service. If the Service would use the likes of Cyril Phelps, they would use George Chandler. It was not an uncommon name, and most of this sanitized George Chandler's life would have to remain cast in impenetrable shadows. That was true of the unsanitized George's life as well. Otherwise, there would be a capital-sized Gordian Knot of lies and misrepresentations to be cut through. All the scenarios were ultimately deemed irrelevant. Paul would never speak to Jonnie, not even if the chance presented itself.

He was so preoccupied by these nagging questions he didn't notice Chief Inspector Gautier threading his way through the closely spaced tables until he heard, "Good day, Mr. Newcastle. May I have a word with you?"

Paul hastily arranged his features into a medley of surprise, curiosity, and openness. Even if he had wanted to delude himself that Gautier might be here socially, the somber face would have punctured the delusion.

"Certainly, what will you have to drink?" Paul said, lifting his hand in the direction of the amazed Giorgio.

Gautier offered Paul a cigarette, then lit one for himself, breaking the burnt match in half before tossing it to the ground. He abstractedly studied the end of the cigarette as it burned between his fingers, then took two short puffs and tossed it into the ashtray without stubbing it out. The smoke drifting across Paul's face brought forth a cough as Giorgio placed the coffee cup on the table.

"I believe," Gautier began, ignoring the effect his smoldering refuse produced, "you are a friend of Cyril Phelps."

Paul froze, by necessity, not by design. He had always recognized his vulnerability in working with the leech. Cyril claimed he burned the guest lists after reviewing them, but Paul couldn't know if that were true or if it had ever been true. In fact, it would have been more in keeping with Cyril's character if he kept them to use later for blackmail.

"I know him, yes."

"When was the last time you saw him?"

Paul didn't answer immediately. He wanted to appear to be retrieving the memory. "It would have been a few days ago. Yes, Friday. Morning, it was."

"Where did you see him?"

"Here, at Giorgio's."

Paul let his eyes interrogate Gautier's. "Why are you asking? Is there a problem?"

"We believe Monsieur Phelps is dead."

Paul didn't have to feign his astonishment or his concern. If Cyril hadn't finished with this week's lists, they would be in his room. Fortunately, he hadn't followed the instructions and written the name of Krenz's staff person on a slip of paper and inserted it inside the newspaper on the table. The less written, the less intercepted. If a man couldn't remember two words, that was his lookout.

"I would like for you to accompany me to the Hôtel Dieu," Gautier said. "I would like you to identify him."

Once more, Paul's reaction was genuine. "Me? Identify him? Get Giorgio to do that. He saw more of Cyril Phelps than I ever did."

Even as his mouth was forming these words, Paul's mind was weighing the relative advantages of Morocco and Algeria. It didn't matter. The first ship setting sail from Marseilles would determine his destination.

Gautier looked over his shoulder as if uncertain what

person Paul was talking about. "I must have a British subject," he said.

"Let the Vice-Consul, Mr. Sim, do it."

"He is away."

"Find his Chargé d'affaires."

Gautier's face said he was disappointed that Paul did not realize he had already tried this. "Your standing as one of the Casino's subdirectors for the Commissariat of Surveillance gives you a semi-official standing. I believe you have spoken with Monsieur Phelps quite often, yes?"

Paul at last trusted himself to lift the cup to his mouth. There was no point in overdoing the objections. He should appear cooperative. The last thing he needed was another knee in the middle of his back.

He gave a small gesture of compliance. "Just so. When would you like this done?"

# Monday, March 16, 1914
## HÔTEL DIEU

IF PAUL HAD THOUGHT CYRIL'S APPEARANCE IN LIFE was grotesque, it was only because he had never been able to foresee this scene. Certainly, he never could have imagined the stench.

Two thin boards held the head in place on the narrow, metal cot. The body had been thoroughly washed. No blood was visible in the uncombed hair or the wild, wiry beard. A coarse sheet was drawn to the bare shoulders, and a rectangle of cloth, brashly white against the blue-gray skin, covered the forehead. A white towel lay draped across the throat. The gaping mouth revealed the three gold teeth, their useless ostentation another forlorn feature in this surreal tableau.

Gautier took out a meerschaum pipe and tobacco pouch. His cheeks turned cavernous as he drew the fire into life. "The wind is blowing from a bad quarter this morning," he observed.

"How?" Paul asked.

"He jumped or accidentally fell or was pushed off a cliff."

When Paul remained silent, Gautier said, "You will sign a statement to the effect that this is the English journalist Cyril Phelps?"

Nausea was threatening to unman Paul's stiff upper-lip. "Somewhere else?" he said.

"This is Cyril Phelps?"

"Yes."

IN THE GLOOMY ANTEROOM, PAUL SAT UPRIGHT ON THE EDGE OF HIS chair, as if expecting to be called out at any time. Beginning with his escape from Liverpool decades before, at the first sign of danger his instinct had always been to scurry off like a crab. He had never understood the encomiums heaped on the Roman soldier found guarding his post at Pompeii even in death. Anyone with an ounce of sense would have decamped as soon as the sparks started flying. Since leaving Giorgio's with Gautier, Paul hadn't stopped reviewing his options. Probably too late to hitch up with Shackleton's Antarctic Expedition. Pity. That would have been ideal. Egypt, perhaps. No, Egypt was all the rage these days. It would be crawling with Englishmen. Bora Bora. He should be able to hide forever in Bora Bora. There was nothing to slow him down. In anticipation of a rapid departure in May, he had already purchased two new passports from the Spaniard, the expensive ones with the embossed stamps. They were secured behind a piece of the carved molding in Madame Piggot's downstairs parlor.

When Gautier took the chair next to him, Paul had to marshal his self-discipline not to make a break for the door. The small room filled with smoke from the pipe as the inspector took an inordinate amount of time reviewing the pages in the notebook he produced. Occasionally, he would return to a previous section before finally arriving at a blank page. Not a muscle of his face revealed what was going through his mind.

"How well did you know Monsieur Phelps?" he asked.

"We talked over coffee from time to time. His language was a bit salty for my taste."

"Who were his acquaintances in Monaco?"

"Phelps knew everyone. That was his job."

"Whom did he spend time with when he was not on the job?"

"What happened to his neck?"

Gautier's apathetic eyes flashed interest. He scratched a note before answering, "The throat was cut."

"Presumably," Paul said, "that was before he accidentally fell or jumped or was pushed off the cliff?"

"Whom did he spend time with when he was not on the job?" Gautier repeated.

"I saw him only at Giorgio's."

"You never saw him at the Casino?"

"Certainly, he was in the Casino from time to time. Usually looked like he was there to appraise the livestock. Can't say I ever saw him on the wheels. He wasn't a person I needed to keep an eye on, so I didn't pay much attention to him." In fact, every time Cyril set foot in the Casino, Paul felt like acid was dripping on the back of his neck, but that didn't seem the sort of confidence he needed to impart to Gautier.

"You came here from London, it is true?"

Paul disliked this question intensely. "Not directly. Most recently, I spent a number of years in Africa."

Three years ago, after Pierre Vioget's cousin recommended Paul to the Casino's management, his letters of reference had equipped him with an impeccable character and history, much of which was spent on the African continent. The letters were signed by estimable individuals selected because they never frequented the Riviera. Three years ago, it would have been a matter of little consequence if the Casino's managers failed to believe Paul's trumped-up history. It would be a matter of significant consequence, however, if Chief Inspector Gautier failed to believe it now.

"Where were you last night?" Gautier said, his eyes on his notebook.

Paul said he had been in his room all evening. Yes, he had been alone.

"Did you know Monsieur Phelps to be a gambler?" Gautier said.

The question, coming out of nowhere, put Paul off-stride. Gautier's pencil scratched on.

"Outside the casino?" Gautier added, his pencil poised above the paper. "Did he gamble outside the casino? Cards?"

"I play cards around town myself, Chief Inspector," Paul said, as though this fact might come as a surprise to the detective. "But I've never played cards with Phelps. Whether he sat down with anyone else, you'll have to ask them."

"You never heard him speak of losing money at cards?"

Too late, too late, Paul understood where this was going. So that was how the police intended to scrape Cyril's murder off their shoes. He used an indignant tone. "Are you saying this was a suicide? Are you saying Cyril Phelps cut his own throat, then threw himself off the cliff clutching a handful of pawn tickets? Or has someone pressed a bundle of IOUs on you?"

When Gautier lowered his eyes to his notebook, Paul glimpsed the truth he had struck upon.

Fifteen minutes later, standing on the stoop outside the sidedoor from which he had exited the Hôtel Dieu, Paul gulped the fresh air and wished the wind sweeping in from the sea could carry away the image of Cyril's head. The notion of suicide was preposterous. Paul had known suicides, and Cyril Phelps was no suicide. When Paul questioned why a man would cut his own throat *and* jump off a cliff, the chief inspector had responded, "To ensure the deed was accomplished," as though this were the way it was always done.

Paul checked his pocketwatch. He would walk down to La Condamine and take the tram to meet Hervé at Cap d'Ail. His knee wouldn't let him contemplate walking the full distance again. He was glad after all that a meeting had been prearranged. Whatever Hervé intended to discuss, Paul's topics were going to take precedence. First, there was Joseph Murphy, dead three times over, and now Cyril, dead two times over. Cyril could have been involved in any number of things that had nothing whatsoever to do with Joseph Murphy, but only an idiot would sing himself to sleep with that as consolation. Furthermore, whoever was at the bottom of this clearly liked variety. There were plenty of other ways to kill a man: drowning, bombing, stabbing, beating, boiled alive, fed to lions, even a nice, clean hanging. Which method did they have in mind for himself and Hervé?

Paul brushed his fingertips along the scar on his cheek and stepped off the stoop.

# Monday, March 16, 1914
## VILLA ILE DE FRANCE

As the automobile pulled up at the front of the grizzly pink Italian palazzo villa, Lily had the door open and her foot on the running-board before they came to a full stop. Stepping to the ground, she yearned to shake out her whole body, like a dog emerging from a pond.

The hour-long drive from Monte Carlo to Cap Ferrat had been, in a word, insufferable. Ted had found it necessary to give voice to everything his eyes fell upon as though he were a tour-guide for the blind. To their left, there was the rest of the winding road, which hugged the railway and the sea. To their right, were the encroaching granite hills, which could spare only a thin edge of land next to the water. There was the sun and the way it struck the cobalt-blue sea. There were the villas mottling the slopes, the outcroppings of scrubby pine and marquis among the rocks. The car's seat offered little enough physical distance between her and Ted to start with, and he proceeded to further minimize it by edging microscopically closer when he leaned across to point out the villa Charles Schwab inhabited the year he broke the bank at Monte Carlo or the trail above Eze sur mer Nietzsche climbed while composing *Thus Spake Zarathustra* or where Pierpont Morgan's first wife died or along what street in Beaulieu sur mer Lord Salisbury had wintered or the Bay of Villefranche, a deep-water port which had held military significance for hundreds of years.

Most of these "facts" Lily didn't embarrass herself by believing. But even worse than the guided tour were the platters of platitudes, often ladled out with a "My dear Lily," along with a vulpine smile. He even had the gall twice to pat her hand.

Much of the time, she succeeded at distancing him from her mind, if not from her person, by returning to thoughts of Sally. The first thing this morning, she put her sewing skills to work letting out or taking in seams to accommodate her newly padded torso and flattened bosoms. Meanwhile, Lily had gone out to purchase Henna coloring for her client-cum-guest's newly shorn and ironed-straight hair. She had also provided a different hat and shaded glasses. The *pièce de résistance* was the cane Lily convinced the owner to part with by using the ever reliable persuasion of Sally's pocketbook. Lily also gave instructions for imitating a limp which was serious enough to justify the cane but not so severe as to be memorable. When Sally perfected the technique after only one lesson, Lily again questioned how much of her client's story could be believed. She obviously was a natural actress.

From behind, she heard the car's door being opened, and the driver say something to Ted. Ignoring them, she took in the commanding view of the harbor at Beaulieu to the east and the one at Villefranche to the west. It was a characteristic Mediterranean day, fantastically beautiful, with a refreshingly mild wind, radiant sunshine, and a sea like rich blue silk. She made her way towards a marble-well styled after the Corinthian-order with curious wrought-iron. Since the villa was surrounded by ground denuded by recent construction or by native olive trees, the well represented the front's only exterior decoration. Three bicycles leaned against it. She studied the collage as though it were a masterpiece by Michelangelo.

This morning, Sally had given no explanation of where she was going or why she was leaving after returning only last night. Lily could only presume that the information concerning the whereabouts of Mr. Murphy's remains had made a difference—that and the fact that someone had destroyed her rooms. Lily believed Sally knew what was being sought. Lily also believed Sally had a good idea of who was doing the looking. Lily also would be unsurprised to learn the same persons were redecorating her quarters in the same mode this very moment. A small comfort could be found in the thought that if physical violence were intended, the intruders would not have waited to search the rooms until after Sally and Mrs. Murphy were away.

The slamming car-door and the sounds of Ted's footsteps crunching the white gravel made Lily turn towards the house. To the left of the entrance was a staircase tower with an open design, to its right, a porticoed wing. Overall, the architectural concoction looked like a monstrous pink-and-white gingerbread house gone to seed atop a rocky isthmus. It overwhelmed neither by the elegance of its design nor by the elegance of its proportions. It merely overwhelmed.

As she waited for Ted to join her under the filigreed white-stone baldachin protecting the porch, she heard voices within, all male. When Ted drew up beside her, he did not immediately pull the doorbells. Instead, he chose to further unburden himself of his vast knowledge.

"The baroness, Madame Ephrussi, pinched this ground, about ten acres it was, out of the grasp of that personification of wickedness, Leopold of Belgium. In keeping with his habit of unbridled avarice, he wanted to grab this land and attach it to his estate behind here. But while he was thinking about it, she bought it. Took her years to bring the house into being, so he didn't live to see it. She's not only a Hebe; she's scandalously rich. Millions of francs were laid out just for flattening the rock and hauling in top-soil, and there's no telling how many architects she hired and then harassed and nagged into extinction because they couldn't please her. She had a full-scale mock-up constructed in canvas before it was built. Couldn't trust the drawings or her own imagination. The house was finished only last year. Next, she'll be embarking on landscaping, more rock-leveling, more top-soil, another fortune or two."

"And you just happen to know all this about the baroness and her villa," Lily said. She kept her eyes fixed on the door but was unable to keep the skepticism out of her voice.

"Remember I told you I was a top operative for Pinkertons?" he said, reaching for the bell-pull.

"Hardly a minute goes by that I don't think about it."

"Well then, my dear Lily, let me say that in the fullness of time, you will come to understand that research is one of my specialties." He jerked the pull.

As the door swung open, raucous sounds, loud enough to terrify the dead, flared. The rigidly sober demeanor of the liveried and powdered footman who answered the door contrasted dramatically with the scene behind. There, Mrs. Murphy, attired in plum-colored pantaloons and a blouse consisting of layers of scarves, spun at the center of a circle of young men, who floated in the opposite direction. All the men were handsome-looking and handsomely built. All were outfitted with embroidered, sequined jackets of green and gold with wide crimson sashes and pants that looked suspiciously like the bloomers worn by female bicyclists. After Bridget Rose's allegations, or revelations, of Mrs.

Murphy's appetite for younger men, Lily regarded the scene with heightened appreciation, maybe a splash of admiration. She looked at Ted. His nose was wrinkled tightly, as though he smelled a polecat instead of the incense and coriander which thickened the air.

If one could set aside the dissonance, Lily thought, it was possible to imagine she had stepped into the central courtyard of a Renaissance palace. A colonnade comprised of vaulted pink-marble arches lined the four sides of the space and supported an overhead gallery. There, white arches and fretwork reinforced that on the exterior. Red-tiled eaves fringed the gallery's arches. Stretching from corner-to-corner above everything, a *trompe-l'œi* recreated the Empire of the Sky, giving the occupants a sense of being in the open-air, surrounded by buildings.

The footman waded into the noise blaring from the eccentric grouping of a lute, a piccolo, an oboe, a harp, two sets of cymbals, and several tambourines. They were wielded by musicians wearing long white robes and white turbans. The spectacle came to a halt. Mrs. Murphy said something to her coterie and approached her visitors. Besides the outlandish garb, since leaving Monte Carlo she had acquired a peculiar mincing step. It gave off the paradoxical impression of simultaneously floating and lumbering. Waving a mauve scarf like an aspergillum, she floated and lumbered across the mosaic-tiled floor, her feet protected by felt slippers. A dozen or so charm-bracelets spanned her wrists, and her ears were decorated with hoops of Oriental filigree, set with bosses of harlequin opals. Long strings of the same stone cascaded over her bosoms.

As familiar as Lily was with her employer's transmutations, she couldn't begin to fathom what alien form of life now inhabited that body. Perhaps this avatar had always existed, and today was merely the first time Lily had walked in on it. After all, she was never included in the social side of her employer's life. Regardless, Loie Fuller and Isadora Duncan could rest easy one more night. As of now, they were in no danger of being overtaken by Madeline Murphy and her Dance of the Seven Veils.

Coming to a stop, Mrs. Murphy stretched her right arm to its full length in front while her left arm did the same behind. Then she brought her fingertips together, touching them in front of her abdomen before lifting both hands over her head and snapping her fingers three times, the bracelets jangling agreement.

"What do you think?" she said, her smile broadening.

That she could be making a fortune in vaudeville?

"Exotic," Ted said.

He must have likewise decided it wasn't the right time for wanton candor.

"You're learning to dance," he added.

"No," Mrs. Murphy said, "I meant, what do you think about this villa? Can you believe it? For a small country place, I mean. Eight bathrooms *and* an elevator. See that?" She pointed to a painting of a woman in white drapery with a partially bared breast. "Titian painted that with his own hands."

Besides wondering whose hands besides his own Titian could possibly have painted with, Lily wondered if Mrs. Murphy had any idea who he was.

She went on, "I know people say nasty things about the baroness' Jewishness and all that, but I don't see why that should matter to anyone other than herself." She flung her arm towards the ceiling, sending the scarf fluttering aloft and setting off a gale of heavy perfume and a riot of clattering bangles. "Certainly, I don't care," she finished.

233

To Lily, this abrupt break from Mrs. Murphy's past attitudes about Jews was understandable, but Ted looked nonplussed. He apparently was not accustomed to his cousin's radical metamorphoses. In the space of the next several seconds, Lily sensed the alien-creature taking its leave. Mrs. Murphy's eyes lost their dreamy cast, and her face put on its business-mask.

"Good, the replies from Joe's attorney and accountant," she said, reaching to take them from Lily's hand. "It's about time. I thought I was going to have to go down to the telegraph office in Beaulieu and send them again myself. I've been down there once, to send others. You weren't here to do it." She sounded like she had been forced to scrub all eight toilets by herself. "Lily's going to stay with me, Teddy. I'm going to need her to follow up on this business in San Francisco." She looked at Lily. "You can send for your things."

The emotions gripping Lily were so contradictory it was impossible for her to distinguish how she felt. Even though a part of her had understood that remaining with Mrs. Murphy was a distinct possibility, the reality nonetheless required an adjustment. On the one hand, she was relieved beyond all expression at the thought of no longer having to answer to that revolting blend of toadying hypocrite, unabashed egoist, and incipient lecher. On the other hand, what about Fran, what if the rich client materialized? Her communications would be delayed, maybe lost. And what about the plan to pursue the necklace in Monte Carlo's shops, possibly those in San Remo as well? And what about the rendezvous with Jonathan Chandler tomorrow? And what about Sally? Setting aside bonuses for murderer suspects and pay for sleuthing work, there was a clear moral-imperative not to put Sally in danger. What if Ted took it upon himself to supervise the packing of Lily's belongings and Sally blundered in? What if he were one of the would-be assassins? He hadn't been eliminated from the list of candidates for that honorific.

"Maddie." Ted's hand made tight circles in the air, like he was winding himself up for the rest of what he had to say.

"Don't argue with me. I have enough life left to divine my own desires. Lily stays. I'm getting together a *bal masque*." To Lily, she said, "You'll need to address the invitations. The boys have many friends, but it won't be a large affair, no more than fifty people, and I won't need a huge dinner, not more than ten courses. I want your best calligraphy, and you'll have to go to Nice for the printer. I want menus like Mrs. Green had, each guest's name in gold on the cover. Maybe I'll have lamb with mint sauce, caviar d'Astrakan, lobster Thermidor. I need you to get with Cook about what's fresh. I was thinking about some Vouvrays, but I'm told they don't travel well."

Ted looked like he was about to pop the pin on his collar. "But, Maddie," he said, "Joe's murder."

Her attention swirled back to center stage. "Wait, wait," she yelled, rushing towards the small herd of Adonises. The balls of her feet struck the floor first, in a wretched imitation of a ballerina. Her left hand was bent back above her wrist, like a broken twig. Her right hand gripped the unopened telegrams. "What do you think this is?" she screamed. "A bawdy house? This is art. This is grace. This is beauty. This is *life!* Treat it with respect!"

No longer able to bear silent witness to this freak-show, Lily turned around to watch two footmen emerge from a stairway leading below, lugging between them a massive silver epergne filled with calla lilies, white roses, and cords of ivy. The thing must have weighed as much as the men hauling it. She kept her eyes on them until they disappeared by turning at the end of the short corridor to the right. They were followed by another footman carrying an immense gold-basket heaped with fruit and two more men balancing a soup tureen the size of a small bathtub.

Having counseled and corrected her *corps de ballet*, Mrs. Murphy rejoined Lily and Ted. While she ripped open one of the envelopes, her eyes continued to dart towards the troupe. "As for Joe's murder," she said, "I don't give a pin who killed him or tried to kill him and who ever once thought about killing him. You can stop looking into that right now. You have more important things to be taking care of, don't you? Only get this straight. I am not going on any more wild-goose chases."

"Maddie, don't let your judgment desert you now. We can't stop. There's too much at stake. You know that."

"My judgment already deserted me, and I know precisely what's at stake, down to the last dime because those are my dimes. For your information, I can stop now. I can stop paying. I'm not throwing away any more money on you. This girl works for me. After you've produced everything you promised, you can go back to looking for footprints in the dirt and killers behind every curtain. That's up to you, but I'm no longer financing it."

Her eyes swerved to the dancers. "Stop! Stop!" This time, she omitted the hideous footwork.

Ted's eyes were dark, narrow slits. "Stubborn as a piebald mule," he muttered under his breath. "Come on."

Lily followed him to the room's center.

"Maddie," he said, "would you please settle down and say everything you have to say?"

"Are you deaf? I already said it."

She seemed suddenly to remember the telegrams in her hand. She unfolded the first. As she read, her jaw slackened and the muscles of her face froze. The hand grasping the string of opals jerked downward, sending a slurry of small stones scattering over the floor. She ignored them and continued reading. Her eyes returned to the top of the page. She read it again, then again. Opening the second envelope, her hands trembled. That one, she read only once, rapidly.

She looked at Ted, her eyes full of astonishment and pain. "A woman scorned," she rasped, then turned on her heels and bolted out the door behind them.

Lily hesitated through several ear-throbbing crashes of the cymbals before following Ted after her.

# Monday, March 16, 1914
## VILLA ILE DE FRANCE

EXITING THE BACK OF THE HOUSE, LILY TURNED right towards a flagstone terrace which had been hewn out of the native landscape. Marble benches framed a fountain, and a pergola ran along one side. Mrs. Murphy was seated at one corner beneath a latticed bower. Ted's fingers were massaging the back of her neck. Lily approached slowly, expecting to be ordered away, but Mrs. Murphy's eyes remained closed, and Ted gave no sign of noticing her. Through the arched windows of the dining room to their side, she could see a footman presiding over the setting of the table.

"Your shoulders are as hard as a board, Maddie," Ted said.

She dabbed at her face with a corner from one of the scarves and groaned in response.

Lily took a place behind the pair and shaded her eyes with her hand as she watched a steam-powered yacht, sails lowered, plowing the water beneath them, headed in the direction of the armored cruiser lying at anchor in the Bay of Villefranche. Her anxiety had decided to focus primarily on Sally. She hadn't said when she would return to Monte Carlo. Her exact words were, "In a day or two." She took a room-key with her, the one Lily told the Front Desk she had misplaced. A privacy sign was now on Lily's door, but she wouldn't put it past Ted to insist the hotel let him in. She didn't dare urge him not to. That would only make him suspicious. Oh, Jesus. All because that madwoman had been soaking her head in absinthe or opium and had her heart set on a masquerade ball. If only, if only, if only Fran would land that client. All these miseries could come to an end. As for Jonathan Chandler and the Oceanographic Museum tomorrow, it would be polite to get a message to him canceling the appointment. Polite, but not urgent, not even necessary, not as it was with Sally. He was nothing but the gloss on the shine. Their acquaintance would have come to an end soon enough as it were.

Mrs. Murphy's hand came up and covered Ted's. "Everyone in San Francisco, in the whole state of California, must be laughing at me," she said.

And they haven't even seen you in that get-up, Lily thought.

"Do you know how long it took me to be accepted by the Garden Club? I mean, really accepted, accepted in spite of people like Caroline Spitzer and her sharp-toothed back-biting ways. You know perfectly well, Teddy, father's family, our family, was the *crème de la crème* in Chicago, and my mother was a New York Elling. But I had to go and marry an Irish nobody who wanted to live in that outpost of civilization. All of it for nothing. I must be the laughingstock of the city."

"Maddie, don't upset yourself. It can't be as bad as all that."

She smacked his hand away. "Not as bad as all that? Before you tell me it's not as bad as all that, do you want to know what that attorney said?"

"Yes, if you want to tell me."

"And the comptroller, that mealy mouthed little man with the rat-eyes? I wouldn't trust him with my coin purse. I told Joe that too."

Lily didn't have to be a detective of any class to know what was coming wasn't good. Maybe the accountant and attorney thought they could hold up the widow for exorbitant fees. If so, that only showed they did not know the first thing about Joseph Murphy's wife. She always did business out of her coin purse.

Ted eased around the side of the bench to lower himself onto it. He lifted his cousin's hand and cradled it between his own. "Come, it can't be the end of the world. Joe had excellent holdings, and his businesses must have been doing well. Wasn't that why he consented to making this trip?"

"I don't know why he consented. I only know why I did."

"It'll work out. It will. But the telegrams, what did they say?"

"The first one was from the rat-faced Mick bookkeeper. I can see him, slime oozing down his rodent chin, gloating over every word. Here." She pulled the crumpled transcription out of a deep pocket in the baggy pants and thrust it at Ted.

He smoothed it flat. As Mrs. Murphy had done, he read it once, then once more. Lily peered in vain over his shoulder. "I'm not sure I understand," he said.

"Don't you? Some detective you are." She jabbed a gloved finger at the paper. "He asked me, *asked* me, did I know that over the past nine months, that hairball of a man had liquidated almost all his assets? Everything he did not sell outright, he mortgaged to the hilt. He also drained every dollar out of his bank accounts. It's a wonder the ship didn't sink with all the money he was carrying."

"Are you saying he brought it with him?"

"Joe would never leave that much cash lying around while he was thousands of miles away, not even in a bank. He always lived his life like he was on the run."

"Maybe he had to redeem a foolish investment, or he was being blackmailed, or he had gambling debts. He couldn't

240

have, wouldn't have converted everything to cash simply to carry it away."

"Joe Murphy never let a bad investment ride, and he would murder a man before he would pay him blackmail. He never, ever bet large on games of chance. He said he had rather bet on a business venture."

"But if he brought it, how? Where did he put it? It must have been a great deal of money."

"Upwards of a million dollars I should think."

"In cash?" Ted asked in a dulled voice.

"Or something close to it. Joe used banks only because he was forced to. As far as he was concerned, Pierpont Morgan and his ilk are all confidence tricksters, practicing voodoo or black magic. He would have put it in bearer bonds or a letter of credit, something as close to cash as he could get."

Ted looked toward the dining room, a contemplative expression on his face. He might have been observing the activity there, but Lily knew she must be in his peripheral vision. She took a step forward, making eye-contact certain. He gave a couple of barely perceptible nods in her direction before returning to his cousin.

"I've been thinking about this a great deal since Saturday," he said. "Now, it's starting to make sense. That's the reason someone tore up your apartment. They were looking for cash, a lot of it. Maddie, you must come back to Monte Carlo. We have no reason to think the attempted murder of Joe was a fluke. We have no reason to think that was the end of it, and it won't be hard for someone to find you at this place."

"So what? I have fifty servants around me here."

"What about the thieves who destroyed your suite? Do you think they found the money, a million dollars? They sure looked hard enough."

She waved the second sheet of paper in his face. "What

difference would it make to me? It wasn't mine. That's what the attorney, that tool of the devil, wrote. He told me not to hurry back on account of the probate. He said he thought it only right – that was the exact word he used, *right*. He dares to tell me what's right! It was only right, he said, to let me know without disclosing the details – *details*, he calls them– without disclosing the details before the formal reading of the will, that none of Joe's estate was left to me, not one penny to his wife. He said he was telling me this only, according to him, so I wouldn't cut my trip short unnecessarily. Made it sound like he was doing me a favor. Don't think I don't know what joy it gave him, telling me that. I'm sure he and Rat-Face were popping champagne corks and counting their fees together after they sent those wires. A bunch a Mick crooks, that's all they are."

"If you're not the beneficiary, who is?" Ted said.

"How should I know? That jackass, Joe, had the spine of a soap-bubble. He couldn't screw up the courage to tell me himself. Don't think I'm going to ask who the beneficiary is either. I'm not giving that Mick lawyer the pleasure of telling me."

"You can fight it. You must have rights as a wife."

"What am I going to get for my trouble? Some insolvent shipping and timber companies? A mortgaged interest in a consortium of mines? An emptied-out brokerage account? Legal bills that will bankrupt me? Another Jarndyce v. Jarndyce? Enough people are laughing at me without putting it on every front page and dragging it through the courts for years."

"But the bonds, the letter of credit, they have to be somewhere."

"Do you expect me to scour the Rivera looking for them? How would I go about doing that? How much would it cost?

How long would it take? If I did find them, how would I get them transferred to me without the will?"

Behind the cousins, Lily was performing elementary exercises in mathematics. Two and two equaled four. Mr. Murphy and Sally made two. Add two torn-up rooms, and that was four. Divide four by one fortune, and there was still four. Lily supposed that if she had been in Sally's shoes last night, she too would have kept quiet about the money. They had met only once before, and she worked for Madeline Murphy. People had been known to turn coats for considerably less than a million dollars. Lily also believed the intruders had not found the money in Sally's room just as they had not found it in the Murphys' suite. Sally's excursion today probably had everything to do with Mr. Murphy's money. Chances were, he and Sally visited San Remo for more than an opportunity to smile at one another in public. That left the question of who else knew about the fortune Mr. Murphy brought to the Riviera. Possibly there was a bank clerk in San Remo who would fit that bill or, for that matter, several bank clerks in San Francisco. From the sound of things, Mr. Murphy had not only burned his bridges, he had burned the boats and docks as well. The flames should have been visible to any number of people.

"Lily," Ted said.

It took her a couple of beats to react.

"Go find Bridget Rose and tell her to draw a bath for Mrs. Murphy. Tell her to make it plenty warm with lots of salts. Have the brandy ready too."

Lily expected Mrs. Murphy to countermand the order, but she sat with her lips pinched and her eyes closed.

When Lily had gone ten or so paces, Ted added, "And stay there until I return."

# Monday, March 16, 1914
## EDEN HÔTEL

THE EDEN HÔTEL HAD BEEN BUILT ON A GRAND scale, but in defiance of recent conventions, it was not overly wrought. When Paul arrived there, he went around the side in order to take a shortcut across the rear terrace, where a fountain burbled in blissful oblivion of its insignificance next to its audacious cousin, the sea below. At the top of the balustraded stone-stairway, he gazed around one last time.

At Monaco, Paul had made a point of being the last to jump aboard the tram as it left the station. After getting off at Cap d'Ail, he lingered until all the other disembarking passengers disappeared from view. His habitual caution never knowingly left a hole anything larger than an ant could crawl through. Today, however, his movements needed to be hermetically sealed. He was in Gautier's sights. Additional care must be taken to ensure the chief inspector was not literally keeping his object in sight. Satisfied, Paul descended towards the sea.

As he rounded a bend in the trail, he came upon Hervé, who was gazing at a ship in the far distance as though he wished he were on it. Paul took in the sagging shoulders, the dark circles surrounding the eyes, the rumpled shirt, and grimy cuffs and had no trouble identifying the wellspring of the haggard appearance.

After the exchange of salutatory kisses, Paul raised his hand to silence Hervé before he had a chance to speak. "I know you wanted to talk to me," Paul said. "But I have something I want to say first." Glancing at the bend in the path behind them, he motioned they should resume walking. "I just came from a sobering visit with Banquo's cousin at the Hôtel Dieu. This chap, a newspaper correspondent for *The Times*, had also expressed an interest in Joseph Murphy. Now he is dead, his throat sliced. Unlike Murphy, this one was murdered while he was alive." When Hervé made no response, Paul bit back his frustration and plowed on. "I spoke with Friedrich Hoffmeister yesterday."

"How pleasant for you. Is he willing to assist your young friend in securing a position with Herr Krenz?"

Paul ignored the sarcasm. He hadn't expected Hervé to believe that story. "He says he ferried Joseph Murphy to Winzig Krenz's villa, not once but twice. What's more, Friedrich is certain he drove Basil Zaharoff there the same nights."

Something rustled behind Hervé's eyes. Yet he said nothing.

"Zaharoff, of course, is the world's most notorious munitions salesman," Paul continued. "However, he has spent every winter for the past twenty years in Monaco, and he always dosses on the top floor of the Hôtel de Paris. Until yesterday, I saw nothing out of the ordinary in the fact that he and Joseph Murphy each had suites there."

"Perhaps you should make nothing of his visits to Winzig Krenz either. Everyone goes to Krenz's."

"True. But Friedrich drew a straight line between the appearance there of our friend, Joseph Murphy, and every belligerent's friend, Basil Zaharoff. He didn't explain what caused him to associate them. Perhaps he was instructed to pick them up back-to-back, or perhaps it was only instinct." Even if Friedrich had not made that connection, Paul would have insisted on it. He had been winged many times but never brought to ground in part because he chose never to mistake a suspicious occurrence for an elfin coincidence.

"Friedrich did not say what the American was doing there?" Hervé asked.

"Other than the company he was keeping, I don't think he knew, but I have a nagging suspicion the friendship was more commercial than social."

"Why jump to the conclusion it had to do with Zaharoff's arms-business? He has friends besides Vickers and Maxim. He also set himself up in Paris by buying L'Union Parisienne des Banques and the *Excelsior* newspaper."

"Those enterprises merely support his thriving trade in demolition, mutilation, and murder. The bank helps his customers finance their purchases. Back in the '90s, he was selling submarines to the Turks and Greeks and Russians. After a time, only a drunken crew would sign on because once those vessels submerged, they remained submerged. Financing their purchase must have become something of a problem. That's where the newspaper comes in. It mops up after the bad reviews, and at the same time, it gins up demand for his wares. If a government happens to forget it has mortal enemies, *Excelsior* will gleefully provide irrefutable evidence of sabotages, conspiracies, unholy alliances, and imminent attacks."

The two men stopped walking when silence again separated them. Paul looked out towards the sun-sequined sea, where a squadron of seagulls was skimming the surface a couple of hundred yards offshore. Hervé stared into the far-distance as though he could still see the ship that had disappeared beyond the horizon.

Continuing to stare straight ahead, Hervé said, "I doubt there is anything in the circumstances Friedrich described which points to me."

"Perhaps, but I didn't take the time to stop off at the murderer's place and find out what he has on you. Here's the point. You refuse to tell me what your game with Joseph Murphy was. Have it that way, but let your mind pasture on this for a while. This is a high-stakes game, the highest. You knew Joseph Murphy, and I knew the journalist."

Below, just to the right of where they stood, what had been minor bickering erupted into a shrieking ruckus. Peering over the edge, Paul saw a nest set in an outcropping of rock, guarded by one adult gull against the forays of another. A third bird dived from the sky, adding its squawks and shrieks to the objections coming from the nest and at the same time drawing off the interloper. Dipping, swooping, circling, darting, screaming at the tops of their lungs, the two made their way out over the sea, the rescuer in relentless pursuit of the invader. Paul returned his attention to his friend, who was stroking the light stubble on his cheeks.

Hervé said, "I put out some inquiries about that necklace. Once you took a perch on the ladder of uprightness, your reputation was destroyed. The local thieves would never come clean with you. At any rate, no one has seen the piece. No one has been approached about it."

The intelligence was not unwelcome. It would lend substance to Paul's next reports to The Hyena and Barousse about his fruitless searches. However, Hervé was telling him this for one of two reasons. Either Paul erred when he trusted his friend's claim that Joseph Murphy had not tried to peddle the necklace, or a *quid pro quo* was about to be exacted. He decided to go with the latter. "I owe you," he said and waited to hear what the cost would be.

The shrug indicated there was no obligation; it was a gift. "But," Hervé said, giving his mouth a wry twist, "since you insist, there is a woman associated with Joseph Murphy, not his wife."

The tasty dish on the side Olivier Broliquet mentioned. After that, Paul had inspected the hotel's register and confirmed that Miss Sally Holmes took up residence at the Hôtel de Paris the same day the Murphy party arrived. A number of new guests registered the day the *Olympic* docked, but only one woman from San Francisco had checked into the Hôtel de Paris alone. How many others knew about her? Did The Hyena? Since she and Murphy shared the same establishment, surely Barousse and Gautier knew of her. Secrets were impossible to keep for long in a hotel.

"Her name is Sally Holmes," Hervé said. "She is at the Hôtel de Paris, room 240. I wish to be introduced to her."

Paul let the words echo in his mind, wanting not to have heard what he knew he had heard. "No," he said, "I'm not shilling for you unless I know what the game is. And if you want to play Hide and Seek with the same people who slap Basil Zaharoff's back, leave me out of it."

"If you will inveigle an introduction to Miss Holmes for me, I pledge to tell you everything. If I am unable to speak with her, the whole matter will become moot. There will be no need to burden you with the knowledge."

"Perfect. In the meantime, if I am picked up by the felons, I can be tortured to death because I will be unable to provide the right answer."

"I am confident you will be able to invent something equally interesting."

Paul didn't bother hiding his bafflement. The only things he knew to be missing were a wallet full of cash and a relatively modest piece of jewelry. That wasn't enough to justify a dalliance with the devil.

"You have contacts at the hotel and legitimacy in Monte Carlo," Hervé pressed. "You also have a presentable appearance, one which should not frighten her off."

Paul removed his hat and ran his fingers through his hair. "After such fulsome flattery, how can I refuse? I'll drop everything and get started on it right away." Settling the homburg back on his head, he traced the brim with his fingertips, confirming it was positioned correctly. "Can it be possibly be worth that much," he said, "whatever it is you're after?"

"This much I can promise you: Mr. Murphy was not looking for the object of my interest at Herr Krenz's. In fact, I believe you are trying to tie too many things together with one piece of string. They do not all fit with one another."

Paul decided to let the debate rest. He had said what he had come to say, and he wanted to get back to meet Olivier. Hervé was under no obligation to tell Paul his business even as Paul had revealed next to nothing to Hervé about the fake medieval manuscript he was on the verge of unloading at Antibes. That was just as well. Paul's thoughts hadn't fully coalesced, yet he could feel the pull of an imminent sea-change.

His ruminating stare took in a solitary bird gliding along the shoreline. He watched it smooth the pleats in the air with no visible effort. How he envied those creatures' agility in taking on nature's forces. Sometimes they rode within the force of the wind. Sometimes they found a protected space, a church tower or the bower of a tree, and stoically waited for a storm to pass.

"Where will you go if you get run up a pole here?" Paul asked. "Algeria?"

Hervé snorted a laugh. "Most likely to Siberia, with Alexei."

They slowly made their way to the point along the trail where the waves, scraping across beds of small rocks during the withdrawal into the sea, sounded like hundreds of chattering castanets.

Hervé stopped walking. "About Miss Holmes," he said.

"I'll think about it."

Hervé dipped his head in humble acknowledgment. "Everyone goes to Krenz's," he said.

"We already established that."

"Jon has been at Krenz's."

Paul kept his face averted as he leaned down to pick up a stone. He warmed it between his hands before hurling it with all his strength out to the sea. His shoulder retaliated by rocketing a sharp stab of pain.

"Pardon me," Hervé continued. "As a friend, I must say this. You persist in claiming indifference, but methinks the uncle doth protest too much."

"And?" Paul let the one word convey the full strength of his displeasure with Hervé's continuing to pound on this subject.

"I suspect the reason you are reluctant to approach him, but I urge you not to let it stop you. We know your life has not been a model of the irreproachable respectability and dazzling social distinction you hoped he would attain, but who is not guilty of a little hypocrisy at some point? If Balzac was correct when he said a great crime lies behind every great fortune, does it not stand to reason that a few petty crimes must lie behind the petty fortunes?"

Paul couldn't hear the grinding of the waves over the rocks for the grinding of his own teeth. There was no use in trying to explain it. Besides being mired in sentimentality, Hervé had been born into a social order which officially exalted equality and fraternity. Whereas, even as a child,

Paul had accepted the uncompromising truth that he would have to shift for himself in the world and that if he ever got the worst of it, no one else would notice, let alone care. In its way, he had found running confidence tricks to be no different from the other forms of menial labor. One survived only if he performed. One ate only what he had killed. Paul had done everything he possibly could to lift Jonnie above that harsh reality. He had been positioned, at least professionally, where people could notice him and would care. As a part of this careful placement, Paul had made sure Jonnie never made a connection or formed an alliance with the uncle who made his living by swindling people.

Hervé heaved a heavy sigh and put his hand on Paul's arm to indicate they should retrace their steps to the Eden Hôtel. "A couple more things concerning your nephew," he said. "Don't stiffen; I am finished with the other subject. As I said, he was seen at Winzig Krenz's villa. I know this because I took it upon myself as your friend to learn more. Tall, handsome man, easy to spot. I shall spare you the tedious details, but he has been seen in the company of James O'Flaherty of New York City. Among that gentleman's holdings is a fledgling newspaper. He is also a partner in the Independent Moving Pictures Company in New Jersey. That is an American state. Winzig Krenz is mad about moving pictures. It is unclear whether he envisions himself as a director or an actor or merely sees the potential for profit. Everyone goes to Krenz's. But yes, and everyone in the entertainment world goes there ten times over. Mr. O'Flaherty has been at Krenz's the past two nights. Jon accompanied him."

Keeping his eyes on his feet, Paul gave the information a dismissive wave of the hand.

"It seems that Mr. Chandler also has been seen with an

attractive young lady, American. Rather tall for a woman, I was told."

Paul felt himself slipping downward even as he clung desperately to the useless hope that this was not going where it was going.

"Rather tall and with beautiful eyes, I was told."

It not only was going there. It was traveling fast and straight as an arrow.

"The young woman, we have discovered, is a companion to Mrs. Joseph Murphy of San Francisco, California. No doubt, you know her."

# Monday, March 16, 1914
## VILLA ÎLE DE FRANCE

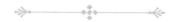

LILY LEANED HER HEAD AGAINST THE PATIO'S WALL, her eyes focused on the painted firmament overhead. The only thought she could muster was to question why anyone would pay good money for such a silly fraud. Its verisimilitude might deceive upon initial acquaintance, but the immutability revealed by repetition converted it and, by extension, the rest of the patio into a stage-set. In the present instance, it would be for a farce. From beyond the corner to her left, she heard the revelers buzzing around their luncheon. The musical instruments, reprieved from abuse, lay on the floor.

Upon leaving the cousins on the outside terrace, Lily had raced around the side of the house to locate the chauffeur. She wanted to hand him two hastily scrawled notes to leave at the hotel's Front Desk after Ted was seen safely away. The first was addressed to Sally in her old room, telling her not to return to Lily's until further notice. Now that she knew her erstwhile guest had something in the neighborhood of a million dollars at her disposal, Lily was confident the cost of a separate hotel room would not be an insurmountable problem. Furthermore, she was confident Sally would not be lugging around valises filled with the bearer-bonds or cash Mrs. Murphy was certain her husband had brought. Sally would have exchanged those for something incontrovertibly hers. The second message Lily wanted the chauffeur to deliver expressed her regrets to Jonathan without further explanation. She considered giving him the address of their office in New York City, but too many things about him remained unexplained. She could not leave that part of herself exposed. The notes were a good plan. However, when she arrived at the front of the villa, there was no chauffeur, and there was no motorcar either.

From the dining room, shouts of laughter shot up along with the champagne corks. Lily's disappointment settled into resignation. It was just as well the driver hadn't been there. She might have been overcome by the temptation to kidnap him at gunpoint and force him to drive her back to Monte Carlo.

She addressed a maid scurrying across the patio's tessellated floor. "Excuse me, Miss." The woman slowed, then accelerated. Lily got to her feet. "Excuse me," she repeated, still in French.

This time, the woman turned. To the question regarding Bridget Rose's whereabouts, she said Mrs. Murphy's maid was out at the laundry, which was located in a different building on the grounds. Her face took on a knowing smirk. "If you want to see her, you will have to go there. She will be hours. She is very meticulous, that English woman. She needs hours to wash a few laces."

In answer to the request for directions, the woman gave a meaningless motion with her hand and hurried away. Lily decided to find a footman, but by the time she did, her question had changed.

AT THE BOTTOM OF THE SAME STAIRS THE MEN WITH THE EPERGNE HAD ascended earlier, Lily stood enveloped in shadows. From this point within the basement, there were cupboards, doors, and corridors leading in every direction. In the brightly lighted area at the far-end, she heard the clattering and banging of pots and pans, the smacking and scraping of knives on boards and tabletops, the clinking of dishware, and the rising and falling of voices. The smells were undefinable but utterly enticing. She heard someone being instructed to deliver another dish upstairs. Her hand sought the doorknob behind her and turned it.

The long hallway was punctuated every seven feet by a door on each side. The floor was concrete, and the lighting came from an electric bulb at each end and three spaced along the middle. This foundation of toil and deprivation upon which the luxury overhead rested was as bleak as a prison and as quiet as a crypt; even the smell was hard and cold. She felt undeniably jittery and afraid, but there was nothing for it. As Jonathan said, a good investigator didn't wait for facts to come to him. Yesterday, Bridget Rose had twice intimated that Mrs. Murphy was given to hocking her jewelry. Possibly, the intention had not been to spill the truth but to deflect suspicion. With the sympathy draining away, Lily's vision was clearing. The unilateral alliance she wanted to establish between Bridget Rose and herself had resulted in a false sense of solidarity. This in turn blinded Lily to reality. Most people believed Mr. Murphy was responsible for the disappearance of the necklace. However, Sally's disclosures had come close to absolving him of guilt in Lily's mind. Consequently, Mrs. Murphy, Ted Wycliffe, and the Gallaghers were back in the spotlight, and it would be shortsighted to overlook the most obvious suspect among those. There were ways around any lock, and even though Mrs. Murphy was the last thing from careless, especially about her possessions, there might have been an unexpected interruption, a brief absence, a seized opportunity. The idea that Bridget Rose was innocent because disposing of the necklace seemed impossible was merely logical thinking. Emotions lacked rational organization, and they seldom adhered to logic's course. She may have wanted the necklace so she could feel good wearing it beneath her high-necked blouse while she scrubbed Mrs. Murphy's dainties. Besides, if the Gallaghers were on their way to Belfast and a bevy of relatives, the opportunities for disposing of the piece multiplied exponentially. Most important, when viewing it dispassionately Lily recognized the scorched reality which lay beneath Bridget's ranting. Her hatred was undeniably raw and personal, despite Lily's desire to dilute and generalize it.

Hearing the distant, muffled sounds of footsteps going up the stairs, Lily took her first step forward. Her instinct was to sidle down the corridor with her back and palms pressed against the wall, ridiculous as that would appear if someone happened upon her. She gritted her teeth and took a second step, glad she didn't have to worry about floorboards creaking beneath her feet.

The knob on the first door was, as expected, unlocked. Privacy was another luxury the poor could seldom afford. The faint light seeping into the room from the hallway was insufficient for making out the room's contents, so she felt along the wall for the button to switch on the light. The framed photograph on the chest immediately told her this was not Bridget Rose's room. The light was pressed off and the door shut in a matter of seconds. She moved to the next door. Before long, she developed an efficient rhythm. It took precisely four steps to cover the distance between each door. The buttons for the electric-lights were in precisely the same place in each room, on the left and about chest-high. She was usually able to instantly identify something that seemed out of character with Bridget Rose, an embroidered handkerchief, a pair of slippers for tiny feet, a small mirror freckled black with age, or most often, another photograph. Occasionally, there was no sign of the inhabitant's personality. Lily would return to these if the first inspection turned up nothing.

Captivated by the rhythms of her progress and her concentration in listening for sounds other than the ones she was making, she had automatically closed the door before her mind registered the red book, the only thing on the small chest next to the bed. She stepped inside, closed the door behind her, and remained perfectly still, feeling each shallow breath enter and leave her lungs. She inched the door open to peek out. Of course the hallway was empty. She had just come from there. She decided to leave the door ajar, so she could hear if the outer door were opened. She quickly saw that wouldn't do. She might become absorbed in her task and not hear it, leaving her exposed to a passerby. She shut it again. It wouldn't take long to search every speck of this space.

She began with the small deal-chest. The top drawer held several pieces of string, a comb with only five teeth, two hair pins, one safety pin, an eyedropper, a couple of inches of green lace, and a single pair of grayed underwear. The bottom drawer housed a thin flannel nightdress, a faded black skirt, a once-white blouse, and a crushed hat. Nothing in the way of emeralds and diamonds.

With the coat hanging on a hook on the back of the door, she spread the cloth at the hem, revealing a deep pocket on each side. She slid her hand into one pocket and immediately jerked it out. The pocket was empty, but the coarse cloth had delivered a fierce, painful shock, not from electricity but from the acute memory sparked by the fabric's feel. She had once known well the despair which inhabited that coarseness. She stared at the coat, half-afraid of it.

❊   ❊   ❊

SHE HAD BEEN FIVE YEARS OLD. IT WAS ONE OF THOSE DISMAL WINTER days when the sun never once cast off its gloomy mantle of clouds. The steely Chicago wind sliced through her third-hand coat, bought two sizes too large so she could grow into it. A pair of pigeons pecked anxiously across the bare ground of the small, square city-park, outlined by a black wrought-iron fence. That fence was the only thing in the neighborhood without peeling paint. She didn't want to share the path with the pigeons, especially with night not far away. Darkness descended early in December, and she hated feeling defenseless and exposed. Covering her face with her arms, she squirmed between the branches of the yew hedge to hide within their shelter. She managed to stifle most of her shriek when a squirrel thrashed out the other side. After achieving a fixed position in the hedge, she shoved her hands up the coat's coarse sleeves to warm her fingers in her underarms. The day was on the cusp of crossing over to night when she heard her name being called. She crawled from beneath the hedge and got to her feet but didn't return to the path. She just stood beside the yews. She didn't answer the call. She just stood there.

Effie squatted, her face close to Lily's. Effie didn't kiss or hug her. Lily would have liked Effie to kiss or hug her. The mist of their breath mingled for a fraction of a second before the callous wind swept it away. Effie would have been about nineteen, two years younger than Lily was now, but not one one-hundredth as wise to the world as Lily was now.

"Time to come home," Effie had said. "I'm going to bake you a cake tomorrow. I have money for an egg and flour. Sugar, too."

✻   ✻   ✻

THE DOOR SLAMMING AT THE END OF THE HALL SNAPPED LILY OUT OF her trance. Footsteps were approaching. She couldn't hear Ted if he were looking for her above. The footsteps continued past the door. After confirming the coat's other pocket was empty, she reached for the red book.

Most of the pages were uncut, but more interesting than the lives of the saints was the thin, square-folded piece of waxed-paper inserted between the cover and the front end-paper. She unfolded it to reveal a gray-colored powder. Sleeping draughts? She refolded it and dropped it in her handbag. Another packet of the same was at the center of the book and another at the back. She returned the book to the chest.

The footsteps again, returning. Their echoes seemed to be coming from a long way off. She repeatedly pushed her stomach back out of her throat as she waited for the sound of the closing door at the end of the corridor. She was frantic to escape unobserved, to be upstairs before Ted came looking for her. She would say she searched the grounds for Bridget Rose but was unable to locate her. What did it matter what lie she told? He would never know the difference. He was going back to Monte Carlo without her.

She eased open the door and listened hard. All she could hear was her own fear pounding in her ears. She gently closed the door behind her before remembering the electric light. When she opened the door again, her focus went to the bed. The bed. She hadn't looked there. Kneeling beside it, she ran her hand inside the pillowcase and found nothing but

259

a pillow. The bed's cover was stretched so tautly even the proverbial pea would have been evident, so she didn't pull it back, but she did peel the thin mattress away from the frame.

She sat back on her heels. There it was, something. There something was. Lying dead-center on the wooden slats was a package, about four inches by six inches, wrapped in brown butcher's paper and tied by sturdy string. She fumbled briefly at the knot but gave it up. It wasn't necessary to open it. She could tell from the weight and the feel beneath the stiff paper.

Her hand was trembling as she switched off the light.

# Monday, March 16, 1914
## PENSION PIGGOT

WHEN PAUL PUSHED OPEN THE DOOR TO MADAME Piggot's pension, Olivier looked up. The rotten board had been pried off the riser, and he was removing the square nails that had come up with it.

"She has some other ones that should be replaced," Olivier said. "But this is the worst."

Paul removed his overcoat and suit coat, detached his collar and rolled up his sleeves. For the second time today, he was glad for a previously arranged meeting. Yesterday, he had used the repair only as a pretext for calling at the kitchen in order to solicit information. He and Madame Piggot had long since trained themselves to step over that tread.

Olivier placed the old board on the floor and unfolded a measuring stick to take its length. "You had an unpleasant duty this morning," he said around the nail gripped between his front teeth.

"True."

"Who did it?"

"I was hoping you could tell me."

"Hold that while I measure it."

Olivier wrote the figures on the piece of freshly planed oak at his feet, then sat studying it like a sculptor contemplating a block of marble.

"Monsieur Phelps had many unusual friends, including you," he said without looking up.

Paul could not allow that designation to pass uncontested. "Cyril Phelps was not a friend. He was an acquaintance."

"But yes, you are a man who has only himself for a friend. Tell me, was he working for the British Secret Service? The Principality is small, but its turnover is large. It is not as easy as one might think, keeping an eye on the spies and the spies who are spying on the spies. It is like living in a House of Mirrors. So, was Monsieur Phelps with the British Secret Service? Everyone believed it. *Newspaper correspondent*, it is synonymous with *spy*, is it not?"

"He may have exaggerated his importance," Paul said.

"But you concede he claimed it?"

Paul nodded, making it his turn to extract information. "What about the Murphy incident?" he said. "Are the police in truth finished with it?"

Olivier apparently had found the figure in the wood. He was drawing lines with a pencil between the markings. "Chief Inspector Gautier is keeping his own counsel in the matter. He also is keeping the codebook I told you about before, or what everyone thinks is a codebook."

Interesting, Paul thought. The Hyena showed him a dictionary and claimed it was the one found in Murphy's room. What did Gautier keep?

Clutching the new board beneath his arm, Olivier took the hand-saw and disappeared out the front door. Paul sat on the bottom step while he contemplated the day's accumulation of fresh complications: first, Cyril's murder; then, Gautier's pulling him in to identify the body; next, Hervé's interest in Sally Holmes. And when did Jonnie take up with Lily? Had they parlayed that innocuous encounter at the lift into an affair? He would prefer, far prefer, the boy not be within shouting distance of the colossal heap of entanglements surrounding the Murphys, especially not with a fresh murder on hand.

A blast of cool air announced Olivier's return. "Hold this steady against the riser," he directed, pulling a hand-drill out of the burlap sack at his feet. He leaned his head parallel to the board, lining up the place where the nail would go. "Jacques Barousse is rabid with nervousness," he said, turning the drill's handle. "Even before this business with the journalist, there was a noticeable increase in the number of men with military-bearing coming and going from the manager's office."

Paul judiciously pulled his hand away as the hammer hovered over the first nail. "What's Barousse got to do with the military?" he said.

Olivier sank the nail with two sure blows, then leaned to visually line up the board before drilling the second hole. "You do not know? There has been a rumor since he arrived in Monaco that he is, or was, with the Deuxième Bureau. Impossible to verify. Since that appalling Dreyfus affair, the department overseeing France's military espionage activities has changed beds more often than a whore. But Barousse, some whisper he was cashiered out of the Bureau. Others say he still works for them and his job at the hotel is an excuse to be in the middle of all these foreigners and their spies."

He proceeded with drilling the holes for the third and fourth nails without inspecting the horizontal alignment.

Paul filled his cheeks with air and exhaled a long breath. Why should he be knocked back by learning Jacques Barousse was not what he seemed? No one was ever entirely the person he appeared to be. The tidbit did go far in explaining why Barousse wanted someone on the inside of the Murphy affair. It also explained the insistence on detailed reports.

Olivier continued over the hammer's blows, "It is the coded dictionary that has everyone's hearts humming. I tell you, a man cannot swing a cat around here without hitting two or three spies. If all the foreign agents were chased out, the Principality would have to tear down the villas and return to cultivating oranges for neroli oil."

He stood, eyed the new step with satisfaction, then removed a rasp from the canvas bag to smooth the edges. Last, he pulled a rag from his back-pocket and wiped the wood shavings off the surfaces. "Rumor has it there is serious discord between him and his lady-friend as well."

Paul got to his feet to help gather the scattered tools. He was about as interested in Barousse's love-life as he was that of the duchess' borzoi, less interested if it came to that. He wanted to have time to clean up before going for another round in the cage with The Hyena this afternoon. "Yes, well, thank you," he began.

"You know her. She goes to the Casino regularly. Madame Claudet, Céline Claudet, a most attractive woman."

Paul stared at the rasp in his hand, wondering why it was there. He stifled the first disbelieving laugh but didn't repress the next.

"You find that funny?" Olivier said.

Smiling broadly, Paul dropped the rasp into the burlap bag. He had, so to speak, cuckolded his archenemy. It would have been a thousand times more satisfying if he had done so intentionally.

"I suppose I do," Paul said. "Barousse is the last person I would have guessed."

"You did not know? It was no secret."

His smile fading, Paul slowly shook his head. "I never cared to know," he said. Only he understood the depth of his honesty.

# Monday, March 16, 1914
## HÔTEL DE PARIS

LILY WAS BARELY LISTENING TO PAUL AS HE DETAILED the steps he had taken in his search for the necklace. He concluded by assuring Ted it wasn't being fenced locally or through any of the known sources. Of course it wasn't. It was what made the handbag on her lap feel like it held an anvil.

Ted shot a finger towards Paul like Zeus hurling a thunderbolt. "That necklace is as much mine as it is my cousin's. I expect you to look harder. I expect you to find it." Without waiting for a reply, he turned to Lily. "My dear, it's time for me to see that journal of yours again."

Lily bit her tongue and passed it across. When she had returned from villa-hunting last Saturday, he had left a message for her to send her journal up to his room then. As far as she knew, he had never seen Paul's. But that was nothing more than a prick of injured pride. Soon, all of this would be the unlamented past.

On the return from Cap Ferrat, Ted had given no explanation of why Mrs. Murphy changed her mind and allowed Lily to return to Monaco, but she wouldn't have heard him if he had. Her apprehension over her purse's cargo and her relief over not having to worry about Sally would have prevented any other thought from taking hold. Since then, her mind had been absorbed by the news which had been waiting for her at the hotel. Fran had wired. The rich client was theirs. Lily was to be in Paris by Saturday. The cur of a husband and his mistress were to arrive Sunday. Lily would observe them registering at the Hôtel Bristol, then shadow them, documenting their movements, confirming everything with piles of photographs. Fran would wire money tomorrow. There was enough to pacify their most strident creditors. There was enough to cover Lily's expenses, enough for bribes to maids and porters, enough for train and taxi fares, enough for rolls and rolls of film for the Brownie, enough obviously for a long telegram at twenty-five cents a word.

"We need to bring this to a close," Ted said. "We're leaving in a couple of weeks, and we're leaving with this resolved. The facts continue to change. That is to say, they look like they're changing, but they're narrowing to the truth. It is the revealed facts, not the true facts, that have changed. Remember, we have been looking only at the means, not the end. The end has never changed. In the end, like I've said all along, justice will be served."

Lily's fingers tightened on her handbag. She had taken the necklace reflexively, aware only of the need to get out of the basement before Bridget Rose or Ted found her there. Now she was coming to realize that collecting the reward was going to be more problematic than originally foreseen. The difficulty lay in discovering a way to present the stolen jewelry without implicating herself as the thief. Furthermore, even if she accomplished that much, she most likely would hear that as an employee, finding the necklace was part of her job. Therefore there would be no reward, no additional compensation, probably not so much as a pat on the back.

Ted said, "It's a complicated situation, Paul. Pay attention because this is going to be hard for you to follow. My cousin learned this morning that her husband had cashed out all his holdings in the United States before coming here. Everything. But why? What was he going to do with the money?"

Start a new life with Sally, Lily silently answered. She cut another sideways glance at Paul. There was nothing she could put her finger on, but she sensed an unaccustomed coolness in him this afternoon. It was more than the lack of the taunting twinkle in his eyes. He seemed to avoid looking at her altogether. He wasn't coughing anymore. Maybe this was how he behaved when he wasn't sick.

She had arrived at the meeting determined not to make more of the similarities between him and Jonathan. She wasn't going to let doubt taint their final meeting at the Oceanographic Museum tomorrow. The business with the nose? It was like learning a new word. It immediately starts popping up in every book and magazine article. Thousands of men must have that same anomaly. She had simply never noticed it before. As for Paul's reaction at the elevator? He had suddenly remembered he had forgotten to wind the clock or feed the dog. That was all.

Ted went on, "Think about it. What was Joe's most prominent characteristic?" His audience's silence required him to answer the question. "He was Irish, staunch Irish. It's the key to everything. We cannot overlook the fact that they have a long tradition of violence. As an Englishman, Paul, you must be familiar with their centuries of rebellions and bloodthirsty clan-feuds. Now listen carefully. I had to spend considerable time piecing this together myself. First, let me tell you I would give anything in this world not to have my cousin's name besmirched, but I can see no way around it. You may not know this, but there are plenty of Irishmen in the United States who are actively supporting their brethren's cause back home. As they say, blood is thicker than water. Here, here in Monaco, Joe was going to make his most significant contribution ever. He was working with some Germans to use his money to buy weapons – guns, ammunition, bombs – for Irish rebels. And after that? Have we forgotten the tickets to Belfast? Remember? One-way passage. There you have it. He cashed out of the United States and was going to Ireland. He was going to Ireland and not planning to return."

Lily crammed her handbag firmly in the corner of the chair and stood. "I'm ready for a whiskey. Would anyone else like one?" She ignored Ted, acknowledged Paul's nod, and headed for the decanters.

Paul said, "Not to put too fine a point on it, Ted, but where do the Germans come in? After the shooting-match you Americans had in the '60s, seems to me there are a number of manufacturers of weapons in the United States. Why not buy them off the shelf there and get it over with?"

"Like I said, I had to think hard about that myself. But once I understood it, I could see it was perfectly obvious. Joe couldn't buy that quantity of weapons in the States. It would look like the Rough Riders were planning another invasion of Cuba.

"This is where the Germans come in. You must be aware of Germany's military build-up over the past few years, not least in their navy. Everyone knows they're itching for a fight. Now consider this: according to the agreements in place, if Germany declares war on France, Russia will declare war on Germany. If Germany declares war on Russia, France will be at war with them too. Germany and its allies would have their hands full fighting France and Russia. What they wouldn't need is for Great Britain to jump into the fray alongside France and Russia.

"But what if Great Britain were busy fighting the Irish

while Germany and France and Russia are thrashing it out across the Channel? Would the British voluntarily open a second front? Joe saw a weak spot he could exploit, and he approached the Germans with his proposal. He told them if they would find a supplier and help with the European logistics, he would purchase a whole arsenal to import into Ireland, maybe even big guns which could be used by Germany's army if they landed there. After all, Britain's enemies have been using Ireland as a bolt-hole since the days of the Spanish Armada.

"Here is, as they say, the icing on the cake. Joe had a fleet of merchant ships. He was going to buy the equipment and land it. I spoke with Michael Gallagher. He tells me Joe always put him out of the way when Mrs. Murphy left town. I didn't understand this before, but now I know he did that to keep Gallagher from seeing the kind of visitors he was receiving."

Ted leaned back, his arms crossed over his chest, allowing his audience the time needed to recover from their stunned amazement of his brilliance.

He continued, "I want you to appreciate how perfectly all this ties together. It explains what happened in my cousin's apartments. Someone knew about Joe's money and was looking for it. I think we can safely say it was the same people he was hatching his scheme with. They knew he had cash on hand to pay for arms and tore up the place looking for it. Whether or not they found it, I cannot say. Be that as it may. The important thing now is to limit the damage to my cousin's reputation. What if word of her husband's nefarious conspiracy got back to San Francisco? For me, it would be, as they say, sticks and stones, but she doesn't see it that way."

Paul said, "Why would Murphy keep that much cash sewn up in his furniture? Didn't he know about banks?"

"Never mind why. Just know that's the way it was. There's something else I regret to say must be addressed." He heaved himself off the sofa, taking time to straighten his back with the ball of his fist and secure his balance on the walking stick. Lily checked the clock on the mantle, almost five o'clock. It had been one long day. Ted gimped his way to the writing desk. His eyes ranged across the top before he pulled out one of the drawers. Lily noticed the box of blotting papers had been opened and was down inches from the top. He must have been writing up a storm, probably composing his memoirs to stand next to Allan Pinkerton's.

He waved a packet of papers aloft. "These are the tickets to Belfast. They are for two people. I've given these a lot more thought too. Again, for my cousin's sake it pains me to say it, but Joe Murphy had a mistress." The long, hard look he gave Lily almost stopped her heart. It was as if he knew she was in league with Sally. "You will recall there was a glass of poisoned whiskey in Joe's room. Poison suggests a woman. It is impossible that my cousin would have poisoned her husband, but his paramour could have."

Lily kept her eyes steadily on Ted. She was having a hard time following his reasoning. While it might appear logical to him, significant elements disagreed with the facts as she knew them, starting with what Mr. Murphy was getting up to when Mrs. Murphy was out of town. Also, Sally said the tickets were for the Gallaghers. Even if they hadn't been, it was silly to think Mr. Murphy and his lover would travel third-class. Also, the accountant said Mr. Murphy liquidated all his holdings. He no longer owned ships which could be used for transporting guns or Teddy bears or anything else.

When they left Cap Ferrat earlier, something had seemed to be at war in Ted's countenance. Possibly, he too suspected his cousin of trying to kill her husband, so he concocted this fantastic tale to deflect suspicion from her. Certainly, her reaction to her disinheritance would have calcified any such suspicion. She had demonstrated significantly more grief over that than she had over her husband's death. The book Chief Inspector Gautier confiscated remained unexplained, but there might be a benign explanation for it too. Last night, Lily had become distracted by Sally's plan for abducting Mr. Murphy's body and not gotten around to asking about it.

Ted was probably right about a female poisoner, wrong about the paramour. Lily needed to have the powder analyzed. If it were arsenic, she could collect one of the bonuses. But why would Bridget want to poison poor Mr. Murphy? To hurt Mrs. Murphy? Hardly. Yet there must be a reason. Lily wanted to talk to Michael Gallagher. That would have to be done without Ted's knowing, at least until after she left for Paris.

"It's time to move to the next stage of our investigation," Ted said. "Chief Inspector Gautier informed me that Joe Murphy was hobnobbing with a certain well known German here at the Riviera. What do you think about that, Paul?"

Paul canted his head and studied Ted for several seconds before answering, "I think that's a rather quaint locution for a Frenchman."

"Don't be flippant," Ted said. He again bestowed that hideous smile on her. "Lily, your hour has come. You are going to pay a visit to that same person Wednesday night."

The statement caught her in mid-gulp. Her hand flew to her mouth as she choked and gagged, trying not to spew out the whiskey. "Wh - what?" she managed.

"The man's name is Winzig Krenz. He's an actor or comedian or some such. It doesn't matter to you. He regularly hosts large entertainments. Wednesday, night after next, you're going to one."

"No, I'm not."

"I've found a gown for you. A seamstress will come to your room tomorrow morning to see that it is properly fitted."

"You can save yourself the trouble. I won't allow her into my room."

"I believe that room belongs to my cousin."

"Fine. Let her come pin up my dress. I'm not letting your seamstress in." By Wednesday, the money from Fran should have arrived. By then, Lily may have figured out a way to collect on the necklace and the hundred-dollar bonus. By then, she might be on her way to Paris with the extra money she had earned in the meantime.

Paul was looking at her like a hanging-judge about to hand down a sentence. He said, "Actually, my dear Lily, that sounds like an excellent idea. It's my understanding Herr Krenz does like the ladies, and I've heard he is particularly inclined to the taller ones."

She was momentarily taken aback. Not only was the hint of conspiratorial humor missing, his tone was anything but friendly. "What about hair color and complexion?" she retorted. "And figure, what is his preference there?"

"I'm afraid I don't collect orders from him."

"Are you sure?"

Ted cut in, "Lily, it's time you quit, as they say, hiding your light under a bushel. People should see you as you are. You should be remembered as a beauty. Don't worry. I know you're a respectable girl, and I'll make sure your escort knows as well."

Escort? Who said anything about an escort? No reason to pursue it. She wasn't going, full stop. "What would be the point of such a venture?" she said. "Do either of you really think that all I would have to do is waltz in there, and he — Wilfred or Winfred or whatever his name is — will say,

'Oh, by the way, Miss Turner, one of us shot Joseph Murphy because we wanted his money.' Or will he say, 'Did I mention my villa is a honeycomb of saboteurs? May I show you the guns stacked out back waiting to go to Ireland?' Is that what you expect?"

"That would be a good start," Paul agreed.

She shot him a murderous glare, slammed her empty glass on the table, and didn't bother closing the door behind her.

# Monday, March 16, 1914
## LA CAVE DU RENARD

PAUL STARED AT THE CARDS FANNED FACE-UP ON THE scarred, wobbly table. He had been mechanically sluicing them from hand to hand, then spreading them in no particular order since arriving here. Seated at the rear of Pierre's den, his back to the wall, he was shielded from the rest of the room by the three men in front of him. The trio, all in donkey coats and one with a large gold hoop on one ear, had tanned skin corroded by years of harsh weather and salty winds, topped up by a poor diet. One of them kept giving Paul an oblique look. Deducing the sailor either wanted to pick up a game or to pick a fight, Paul resolutely refused to make eye contact in return.

Pierre's dark, bushy eyebrows pinched in consternation when Paul entered the bar a couple of hours ago. Word of Cyril's death would have gotten around. Perhaps Paul's role in identifying the body had been bruited about as well. What an absurd exercise that had been. No one else on earth could possibly look like Cyril Phelps. Regardless, Paul's presence alone was unusual enough to elicit this response from Pierre. Paul never came here solely to drink, let alone to get drunk, as he was set on doing tonight.

He slid the tips of his fingers under the last card and

glided them once more into a tidy stack in the palm of his hand. Until five days ago, his future had been roseate. His plans for Antibes had been meticulously conceived, precisely scheduled, and flawlessly executed. But dark clouds pushed in by a wind from the north had cast a long shadow over his Eden. Although he believed he had every right to be disappointed by the recent turn of events, he knew he had no right to be surprised. Fate always dealt last, and it frequently pulled a card off the bottom of the deck to queer a deal at the last minute. This wouldn't be the first time he had had to scuttle a plan with barely enough time to toss a collar-stud and a toothbrush into a grip. The difference was, before Monaco he had lived in perpetual expectation of a signal to abandon ship, sometimes sleeping with his boots on. But three years of draying in a respectable job had softened him to the point of laxness. This time, he had been caught unawares, and for that, he had only himself to blame.

He smacked each side of the deck against the table, shuffled three times, cut the cards, and turned over the King of Diamonds. There was nothing for it. Even though he was loathe to admit it, Antibes would have to be jettisoned. For days now, he had been rowing against the tide, and the harder he worked at moving forward, the stronger the force sucking him backward became. Not only prudence but common sense decreed he should cut free, even if he ended up having to navigate cross-sea in an open boat. He couldn't sit waiting for the police to arrive to arrest him for the stolen guest-lists and for God-only-knew-what-else. Nor could he crawl away under the cover of night, hide in the brambles, then reappear two months later down the coast, not even in disguise. To attempt that in the midst of this escalating chaos and diminishing control would be too risky for his cautious nature. Naturally, his disappearance from the Principality would be trumpeted as *prima facie* evidence of his guilt in Cyril's death and the theft of the necklace, along with the sinking of Atlantis, the sacking of Rome, the Great Pearl Heist, and all of Jack the Ripper's murders. Hervé might try it. He didn't mind running a scheme with a hole the size of a tramcar in it because his plans always worked perfectly, brilliantly – as long as no trams came along.

Paul fanned the deck to locate the Queen of Hearts and the Two of Spades. He reassembled the stack, shuffled four times before discarding the top-card face down, then turned up the Queen of Hearts. Flicking the card's edge with his thumbnail, he stared hard at the face, recalling a painting he had seen in the Low Countries of an impish Cupid with a playing card dangling from one hand. It was a reminder that, like everything else, love was governed by chance. This was scarcely the first time his affections had miscarried, only the most recent. He was glad he had never flaunted his prospects of future wealth before Céline. To be discounted because he had no money was one thing. To be basely used was something altogether different. At last, he apprehended Barousse's relentless hostility and attempts at humiliation. The man would not know the full extent of his mistress' duplicity. She would never be so foolish or bumbling as to tell all. However, she would have known how to incite jealousy without implicating herself. A hint that her eye had innocently strayed, an offhanded compliment, a casual inquiry, and the green-headed monster would be fully mobilized, all the ramparts manned against an invasion by the Mongol, or mongrel, hordes. The heightened vigilance would be accompanied by increased consideration, an expensive bauble or two, perhaps a profession of undying love. Paul saw himself as doubly used. She had used him as an instrument for her carnal pleasure, no doubt stoking her vanity in the process, while at the same time he had served as a device for magnifying the attentions of her benefactor.

He returned the cards to the stack to repeat the ritual of shuffling and cutting. He had never before flaunted his dexterity here. Too dangerous to his winning. Too dangerous to his health. But what difference did it make tonight? His vessel was going down with all hands. Besides, except for a worried glance from Pierre every now and again, no one was paying attention to him. Even the three sodden sailors were fully absorbed by a game of dice and oblivious to his presence.

There being no jokers in the deck, the King of Clubs was the best he could conjure. The thought of abandoning Hervé was no less depressing than the thought of abandoning Antibes. Leaving his friend to founder unaided was unthinkable, but no one could rocket a towline to him if he insisted on remaining shrouded by fog. Paul had been as discreet as ever in meeting this afternoon, but three calls in four days was pushing the odds in every direction. Olivier's bringing in the Deuxième Bureau was deeply troubling. It was bad enough to have drawn the police's notice after Cyril's misfortune in catching his throat on the stropped edge of a blade. But to have the French Military Intelligence sniffing around one's latrines was entirely outside the realm of the tolerable.

Since learning about the fortune Joseph Murphy brought with him from America, Paul better understood Hervé's keenness for catching up with Miss Holmes, but if money were all he was after, why didn't he come out and say so? And did Hervé actually believe Joseph Murphy would have sewn piles of cash into the cushions in his apartment? That and a few other questions might have gotten sorted this afternoon if the atmosphere hadn't turned testy at the end.

He flipped the face-card so it could no longer stare back, drained off the rest of the beer, and studied the empty jar.

The atmosphere had turned worse than testy this afternoon. In point of fact, it had turned bitterly personal. Hervé was on edge because his affair with Alexei was crumbling. Anyone could see that. But Paul had been a bit on edge himself. After all, there was nothing quite as cheer-killing as the contemplation of a man laid out in the morgue with a sliced throat.

"Find Jon," Hervé had insisted. "You need him even if you don't know it."

"I don't need him," Paul said. "I don't need anyone. I've proved that." And he had. Until four years ago, he had believed he needed Hervé in order to develop a good game and bring it to completion. Then Hervé disappeared into that hell-hole of a prison. Until then, Paul thought he needed Jonnie to provide for, to plan a future for. Then Jonnie rebelled and removed himself. Until then, Paul knew that without Marie-Odile the sun would never rise. But she deserted him too. What Hervé could not comprehend and what Paul himself could only vaguely articulate was that on some inaccessible level of his being, Jonnie and Marie-Odile were the same loss, the same grief. He had put everything he had into saving each of them, and with both he had failed.

The silence that had descended between the two friends this afternoon could have been carved with a chisel. Hervé put the end to it. "Why do I argue?" he said. "Go ahead. Let this opportunity slip away. That is you, is it not? Always alone. Always afraid."

It wasn't the argument that was disturbing Paul tonight. He and Hervé had argued before, said unforgivable things to one another before. But when Olivier observed this afternoon, "You are a man who has only himself for a friend," Paul had heard an echo of Hervé's unjust indictment.

Again, the ritual of slapping the cards against the table,

shuffling, cutting. Behold, the Jack of Spades. Despite the useless protestations to Hervé, Paul knew he would find leaving Monaco without laying eyes on Jonnie again particularly galling. It wasn't that he needed to kindle a friendship or even a nodding acquaintance. It was that fifteen years of scrimping in order to provide for the boy should have earned him one good, long look at the man his nephew had become.

Leaving the deck of cards on the table, he made his way to the bar. Slowly pushing the coin across the stout plank, he listened to its tiny scraping sound instead of meeting Pierre's inquiring eyes.

Staring at the shivering surface-tension on the fresh beer, Paul muttered, "Poor bastard." No one was paying attention to him, so he said it again, "Poor bastard."

Over the past two hours, as he had surveyed the scorched earth of his existence, another image lingered to the side, like a ghost's reflection in a mirror. Oddly enough, that which haunted Paul's thoughts was not the blue-gray face fastened between the boards nor the towel draped across the butchered neck. It was the pile of muddy clothing on the shelf overhead. That vision of Vanitas lacked a skull and hourglass, but the fruit had been there. He had seen it. Peel away the fine clothes, and the only thing left was the black, rotted fruit of a Liverpool guttersnipe.

Paul could picture a child, his nose pressed against a plate-glass, physically pained by the sight of the men on the other side, men outfitted in morning coats, swamped in money, smothered by security. He remembered the wrenching grip of longing and understood the boy who promised himself that the misfortunes into which he had been born would not be the ones in which he would choose to live. Against all the odds, that ugly, pathetic, little guttersnipe had been reincarnated in Monaco, where he had masqueraded in bespoke Saville Row coats and High Street top-hats. For a time, he must have felt well dressed, well fed, perhaps secure. Yet the mud-drenched clothing on the shelf at the Hôtel Dieu had given the lie to those pretensions. They said Cyril Phelps had breached eternity clad in old mufti.

A layer of cold slapped the back of Paul's neck. The door was being held ajar. He hadn't realized how badly he needed fresh air. His head was clearing as though someone were slapping him awake.

"Sylvie?" the voice at the door said.

Paul's interest came on point at the sound of the heavy German accent. He didn't move a muscle.

"Sylvie?" the man repeated.

"Not here," Pierre said.

The man either said "I need her" or "I am a flagpole." His French not only was abysmal, he was squiffed to the gills.

Paul casually looked over his shoulder to observe the newcomer's entrance. He had the swaying walk of a man used to the rolling and tossing of the waves. Another sailor, possibly off a yacht, a notch or two up from the three at the back table.

"Don't we all," Pierre said, winking theatrically at Paul.

The sailor made a lunge at Pierre over the plank separating them. Paul jumped out of the way, knocking over a stool in the process. Bruno the Oak, who had been lounging in another corner all evening, no doubt waiting for Sylvie as well, bulled his way across the room in three strides, knocking the other patrons out of his path. He wrapped his arms around the newcomer with the strength of a vise and lifted him off the floor. Paul headed for his recently vacated table. The three sailors were on their feet, ready for a brawl.

"Get the fuck out of here," Pierre ordered in German. He knew that phrase in no fewer than twenty-seven languages.

Bruno didn't wait for the sailor to apologize and make a gentlemanly exit. He carried the man to the doorway, forced it open with his gigantic foot, and dropped the man just outside the threshold, where he landed in a sputtering heap. The only words Paul picked up before the door was slammed shut, besides the alluring Sylvie's name, were "danger" followed by something about "cliff" and "Sunday."

Fishing another coin from his pocket, Paul returned to the counter, where Pierre was toweling away the spilled beer. Bruno remained uncomfortably close.

"So," Paul asked, after taking a sip and wiping the corner of his mouth with his thumb. "Where is Sylvie?"

Pierre scratched the back of his neck and kept his gaze fixed on the towel. "She must have forgotten to stop by and give me her reservation book."

"That sailor said something about danger," Paul said.

"Bah. He was in here with her only last night. It is too soon for the clap."

Paul obligingly smiled and carried the beer to his table. The three sailors, still on their feet, parted to let him through. The same one who had studied him earlier now eyed Paul like a boxer sizing up an opponent. Paul kept his stare fixed straight ahead. He was feeling enlivened by the fresh air and the rude awakening. He even felt a sliver of optimism wedging itself into his dark mood. What was the point in sitting around moaning over his plight? Self-pity was nothing more than a perversion of self-recrimination, and he had never known either to be useful.

He fanned the cards face-up on the table, gathered them, shuffled once, and dealt five cards. Turning them over, he revealed four Jacks and an Ace of Spades. Always alone, always afraid? Hervé wasn't always right either. Always alone? Always afraid? Not always, not this time.

An opportunity for catching another look at Jonnie had presented itself earlier today. Paul had toyed briefly with the idea of putting in an appearance at Krenz's, then tortured Lily about her going just for the spite of it. He had dismissed the thought of going himself because a day or two would be needed, and he had determined he should make his way out of town posthaste. Viewed in a different light, however, a minor delay could work to his advantage. There would be time to organize a tactical retreat instead of settling for the usual rout. He could quietly remove his few belongings to Hervé's, so he could be driven to Marseilles at a moment's notice. If he chose not to panic, he could acknowledge that in their eagerness to deny a murder occurred on their shores, the police were calling Cyril's death a suicide. Furthermore, if they intended to immediately charge Paul with the misuse of the guest-lists, it would have happened by now.

Leaving the beer unfinished, Paul pocketed the cards and got to his feet. His mind was set. He might be deeply drafted and loaded to the gunwales, but in the time he had left here, he was going to stand on the deck with a glass of whiskey in his hand while the band plays on.

# Tuesday, March 17, 1914

❖

"GOOD MORNING, MISS TURNER," PAUL SAID, LEANING across the back seat of the motorcab to open the door. "May I offer you a ride?" When she did not reply, he said "I've been watching you stand at the entrance to the Oceanographic Museum for over an hour. I admit that temple to science is an imposing construct, but Prince Albert has made some twenty ocean-research voyages and returned with shiploads of mummified sea creatures. The displays, however, are inside. One gets a deal more out of them there."

Lily turned expectantly towards the motorcab drawing up across the street. The elderly man who emerged offered his hand to the woman behind him.

Paul extended his arm. "Climb in," he said. "Let's take a ride."

She looked down the street one last time before taking a seat. Paul rapped on the glass separating the back seat from the driver. "We're going to take the Grande Corniche up to Roquebrune," Paul said. "You'll like it. Wonderful views, but then the Côte d'Azur is brimming over with wonderful views, isn't it? Do you have spots like this in America? I understand it's a huge country."

Staring straight ahead, Lily said, "I want to go to the hotel."

"Did you come up only for the air? You stand for an hour, then return to the hotel?"

"How did you know I was here?"

"You're not hard to follow, especially when you take a motorcab to your destination."

Lily's hands gripped her handbag as tightly as a clamshell while the driver downshifted to descend the Avenue de la Porte Neuve, passed through the Place d'Armes, and coasted to the right to take the Boulevard d'Ouest. Paul prattled on about the local brewery, founded on the Bavarian model. Far superior, he said, to the arsenic consumed by those Manchester beer drinkers. The sound of the car's engine again deepened as it summoned the energy for the climb to the high road above Monaco.

Paul put his lips next to Lily's ear and said, "We need to talk." Lily's lower lip dropped. She slowly closed it, never taking her eyes off the road ahead as it was consumed by the hood of the car.

# Tuesday, March 17, 1914

HAVING DIRECTED THE DRIVER TO WAIT, PAUL TOOK Lily's elbow to guide her along a narrow path leading away from the road. It was an afternoon of wind and cloud, and both her hands were occupied, one holding onto the handbag, the other pressing her hat against her head to keep the wind from tearing it off. While they remained within the driver's eyesight, Paul made a show of smiling broadly and pointing left, right, up, down, straight ahead, but as soon as they rounded a knoll, he came to a standstill. He reached over, deftly removed the long pins, and handed Lily her hat. Then he stood squinting at a sailboat tacking its way across the choppy gray water. Having left his hat in the taxi, he occasionally combed his fingers through his hair in a futile attempt to keep it off his face.

He said, "I believe it is time we got to know one another better."

'I would prefer to know you less."

"I will try to take that in a manly manner."

"You can take care of that while we're on the way back to the hotel. I have work to do."

"Do we always have to be at daggers drawn? I don't know who stood you up, but it wasn't me."

"Why did you pressure me about going to Krenz's?"

"Before we get to that, why don't we talk about what's in your handbag?"

This time, when Lily's mouth fell open, she did not close it.

"Since yesterday, you've been carrying it like it was a reliquary. What's in it? Mary Magdalene's molar? The Baptist's toenail?"

"Did Ted notice?"

"Can't say. He's generally too busy overawing himself to pay attention to anyone else."

A strong gust almost ripped the hat from Lily's hand. Taking her elbow once more, Paul guided her down a natural run of rock-steps. They halted in the lee of an immense bolder with broaches of small bushes clinging to its indentations. With a grand flourish, he pulled a handkerchief from his pocket and dusted off a place, then indicated she should sit. Surges of wind continued to lick at the edges of her long skirt. Farther down the trail, a lizard scuttled out of sight between two rocks.

Perched next to her, Paul said, "What do you suppose Ted does with his time when he's not regaling us with his exploits?"

"How should I know? Maybe he combs through that junk in his room. Maybe he grooms that appalling toupee. Maybe he polishes his becoming modesty."

Paul appeared to give these ideas serious consideration. "We now know Joseph Murphy cashed out his holdings in America," he said. "Ted's theory about arming the Irish revolutionaries has a certain believability to it. A man doesn't have to attend Sandhurst to know no commander wants to divide his forces between two fronts. It's probably there in the Army manual right after 'Don't march on Moscow in the winter.' Have you come across anything else that would lend credence to his postulations?"

Lily shook her head. "Ted's in charge of theories."

Paul said, "If Murphy died before the deal was completed, could be there's a good deal of loose change floating around. Have you ever considered that Mrs. Murphy might have been the one who shot him?"

"The idea never crossed my mind."

Paul arched an eyebrow. "People are odd like that, aren't they? A husband catching his final rest in the next room didn't spook her but someone trolling through her knickers did."

"It was more violent than trolling," Lily said.

"But less violent than shooting."

"Why do you care?" Lily said. "You're only supposed to find a necklace."

"Let's just say the sooner this matter is concluded, the happier Jacques Barousse will be, and the sooner Jacques Barousse is happy, the happier I will be. Why do you think Wycliffe wants you to go to Winzig Krenz's?"

"It doesn't matter. I'm not going. And I repeat, why were you pushing me to go?" Another gust made a grab at Lily's hat. She crushed it against her thigh.

"Before you go laying your ears back, consider this. Wycliffe may possess epic ineptitude, but I suspect there are other, less benign aspects to his character. In other words, I don't trust him. You don't trust him. Let us use that as a foundation for an *entente cordiale* between you and me." He gave her a long, penetrating look. "I want you to agree to go to Krenz's."

"I told you —"

"I want you to tell Wycliffe you will go to Krenz's but only on the condition that I accompany you."

"If you and Ted are so enthusiastic about this Krenz, why don't you go together? In fact, you can both go to hell as far as I'm concerned."

As she started to her feet, a blast of wind stripped the hat from her hand. When she instinctively reached after it, Paul slid the handbag from her other arm. He was opening it as he turned away. The blow of Lily's fist against his back sent him pitching forward.

He faced her again, holding the purse behind his back. "That's quite a wallop you pack. You might want to think about repeating that year in charm school you did. You also might want to explain why you have your employer's emerald necklace in your handbag."

Lily looked like she was going to say something, but no words came. She sank heavily onto the rock and crossed her arms over her chest, drawing the black coat tighter against her body. Paul sat beside her and handed over the handbag.

She said, "I didn't steal the necklace."

"I never said you did."

"But you're going to blackmail me anyway."

They watched the wind harrowing the sea for several minutes. At last, Lily released a sigh which expressed resignation, exasperation, and capitulation. "Fine. I'll go to Krenz's, but only if you do something for me. I want to talk to Michael Gallagher. Today, if at all possible. I want you to arrange the meeting and come along."

"Gallagher," Paul said.

"Mr. Murphy's valet, Bridget Rose's husband."

Paul's eyebrows shot up. He looked at the handbag, then at Lily. "The maid?" he said.

Lily nodded.

"It's not that I don't desire to satisfy your every whim, but what do you need me for? I don't even know him."

"He's old-school. I expect he will answer better to a man."

"I cannot tell you how good it feels to be needed, especially by you."

"It's a trade, that's all. *Quid pro quo.* I go to Krenz's. You bring Michael Gallagher to me."

Grinning, Paul ran his hand through his wind-tussled hair once more. "I'm not above bending an elbow with an Irishman. They're a perfectly decent race. I mean, if one can overlook the fact that they're all indolent, poverty-ridden drunkards and insanely violent criminals, not to mention idol-worshiping Papists."

Lily regarded him incredulously. "Is that what you think?"

"No, that's what most people who aren't Irish think. Myself, I think Guinness is a fine beer."

"Then you'll do it?

Paul nodded.

"There's something else," she said. "Do you know what arsenic looks or tastes like?"

Paul gave her a blank look.

"I think Bridget Rose was the one who tried to poison Mr. Murphy. Besides the necklace, I took some powder from her room."

Paul released a low, slow whistle, then remained quiet for several long seconds. "Before I answer that question, I have a business proposition for you, Miss Turner. I propose we, you and I, divide equally anything either of us clears from this situation." He put his palm up to forestall her objection. "Wait, hear me out. I don't know what your game is, but trust me, I can spot one at a hundred paces. I'll work with you on this, but I want a share in the take. What do you say, fifty/fifty?"

Lily pressed her handbag to her chest. "What do you expect to gain that you can share with me?"

"Why don't we start with the necklace? The reward is a tidy sum."

"Did you have a stroke? Your job is to find it. How can you claim the reward?"

"Why don't you let me work that out? How were you planning to divest yourself of it? Were you going to pawn it locally? That would be risky." When Lily said nothing, he went on, "Are you afraid of being conscience-stricken if we claim the reward? Allow me to alleviate that worry. Taking money from the rich is like taking a cup of water from the ocean. It's that inconsequential."

Her face remained expressionless.

He extended his hand. "Deal?"

She didn't move.

"It's a good one for you," he said. "According to my arithmetic, you have three things you need help with: Gallagher, the necklace, and the powder. I've asked for only one. I can get to Krenz's without you. Can you take care of the others without me?"

Staring fiercely into Paul's eyes, Lily placed her gloved hand in his outstretched one.

# Tuesday, March 17, 1914
## HÔTEL DE PARIS

ALTHOUGH TED HAD IMMEDIATELY ACCEPTED THE request for an impromptu meeting, he looked like they had found him asleep or hung over. Bleary-eyed, he sagged, not sat, on the sofa. It was difficult for Lily to keep her eyes on him. She had thought he couldn't possibly look any worse.

Paul was providing the embellishments needed to make the feat of locating the necklace sound as intricate as it should have been. The thief was demanding 12,500 francs in exchange, Paul said, and no, he did not think that was too much, considering the value, but that decision was up to Mrs. Murphy.

Lily's mind registered the increase from 10,000 francs. Her putative half of the reward had increased by 1,250 francs, but there were six ways from Sunday for Paul to doublecross her, ranging from the most dastardly, exposing her role in finding the necklace, to the most banal, refusing to hand over her share. There was no way of knowing when Bridget Rose would discover the necklace and packet of powder were missing, but what kind of alarm could she raise when she did? Even if she wanted to ask questions, she didn't speak French, and the chances were that few of the other servants spoke English.

In that case, Ted was saying, why was the thief willing to part with it for a relative pittance? Because, Paul explained, his motivations were as strong as his options were limited. He had coincidentally been seized by a desire to see more of the world in the same hour in which he had made a mortal enemy of a local thug. No, the man couldn't simply be arrested. He was not so stupid as to carry it in his pocket.

If Paul went through with the interview with Michael Gallagher, Lily thought, and if that session panned out and if Sally returned, she could collect the hundred dollars for the name of one of the would-be murderers. Half of that would belong to Paul, but half of what? Half of her money belonged to Fran. So, what if she gave him half of her half, half of fifty dollars, twenty-five dollars? That felt right. That would be fair enough. And to think, he had thought she needed to be schooled about the benefits of a latitudinarian approach to ethics.

Yes, Paul was saying, he must have the money in hand before the thief would release the ill-gotten goods. No, Paul would not turn over the money to the thief until the necklace was certified as genuine. A sort of escrow, he said.

Lily listened to him with renewed admiration. What marvelous insincerity. Few men could prevaricate in such a convincing manner and with such an honest expression. It was too bad she found him to be so irritating because she definitely could learn a thing or two from him.

Neither man seemed to notice when she went to the table that held the whiskey bottles and poured two fingers for herself. The money from Fran should have arrived by now, but it hadn't. This only made Lily more aware of how intensely eager she was for her manumission. She and Fran had thoroughly prepared themselves for cases involving missing daughters, unfaithful spouses, and insurance frauds.

Working for a murderer had never once made their list of preferred professional engagements. She was virtually positive that Mrs. Murphy acting alone or the two cousins working in collusion had shot poor Mr. Murphy. Everything pointed to it: the expectation of a large inheritance, Bridget Rose's assertion that Mrs. Murphy had been in Monte Carlo the night Mr. Murphy was shot, the lack of proof that Mrs. Murphy spent that night in Cannes, even Ted's delusions — or red-herrings — of smuggled armaments, which Lily was certain was not where Mr. Murphy's fortune had been destined.

Yes, Paul was saying, he would bring the necklace to Mrs. Murphy, so it could be examined by a reputable jeweler to ensure the jewels were the originals. No, Paul could not give it to Ted to take to his cousin. Yes, tomorrow morning would be agreeable, but he would have to have the money in hand before they left Monte Carlo.

Lily returned for another whiskey. If she didn't have so many other things to worry about she would have been sharpening the remarks with which she would harpoon Jonathan Chandler should she ever lay eyes on him again. Not only had he stood her up, she had been entrapped by Paul in the process. Maybe that was no accident. Maybe he and Paul were working together. Maybe her earlier suspicion about his using her for access to the Murphys was correct. Maybe Jonathan had lied and lied.

No, Paul was saying, he did not personally know the thief, but the man trusted Paul's probity. No, Paul would not be taking a commission on the transaction. He was merely fulfilling his duty as an employee of the SBM. Did Mrs. Murphy want a receipt?

Lily tossed back the fresh drink. At the rate she was going, she thought, her first action upon landing in New York City should be to take the Cure.

Ted looked at her for the first time since the exchange with Paul had begun. He seemed to have shed most of the fuzziness. "Have you been listening? We're going to see Maddie tomorrow, all three of us. Now let's go back to Winzig Krenz. I don't think you understood me yesterday."

"I understood you perfectly." She waited to see what tack he would take. Threaten her? With what? Ask courteously? That would be a change. Plead? That would be laughable. She was going to agree to go, but she wasn't going to give up too easily. Then again, she was more than ready to get out of this room, away from these two. She said, "You never explained why you want me to go to Krenz's. What am I supposed to do there?"

She could practically see Ted swelling with indignation at having to explain himself to her. When he spoke, his voice was as tight as a piano-wire. "Chief Inspector Gautier said Joe Murphy was seen at that man's house."

Lily said, "And you think I'm going to find out what Mr. Murphy was doing simply by eating canapés at the same place?"

"My cousin's reputation must not be tarnished by her husband's activities. I want to know what goes on there. What kind of people are there, that sort of thing. I don't expect you to be introduced to Krenz. I've heard he's like the Pope. One must be invited for an audience."

Lily looked at Paul like she had just discovered his existence, then back at Ted, then back at Paul. Keeping her eyes on him, she said, "Fine. I'll go. But only if Paul escorts me."

"Never mind that. I have arranged an escort for you."

"Someone I don't know?"

"Someone I do know," Ted snapped.

She laced her fingers above her waist and stiffened her

back, precisely like the nuns at Mount Saint Joseph Academy. "Fine. Then I won't go. I go with Paul, or I do not go at all."

Ted looked at Paul. "When did you two become inseparable?"

Paul said, "This is news to me. Lily, if you want someone you know, why not let Ted be your escort?"

She speared him with a look. Of all the men on God's green earth, why had she been so stupid as to trust this one? At least she hadn't been such a dunce as to hand over the necklace before Ted agreed to the arrangement.

Ted said, "I've gone to a great deal of trouble to make the acquaintance of Nicholas Breedlove. Ask Lily, Paul, I am an expert at research. Breedlove is an American and not only knows Krenz, he's played cards there every Wednesday night since he's been on the Riviera. That amounts to some two months now. His father made a fortune feeding the Union troops during the war, and Nicholas is determined to better himself as a financier. Lily, your father made a fortune mining in Colorado. Nicholas would like to help you invest your money. I have everything set up. How can I explain another man at this point?"

"I don't care what you say. Paul can be my grandfather or my great-grandfather. I'm not leaving with a man I've never met before. It wouldn't be proper, and you know it. "

Ted's eyes shifted back and forth between Lily and Paul. "Maybe it wouldn't be such a bad idea if Paul went along. As they say, two heads are better than one, so four eyes will be better than two."

Paul coughed lightly against the back of his hand. "Awfully glad we got that bit straightened out. Miss Lily, I shall be pleased to be your escort and to ensure that your honor is honored. Just let me know what time I should hove into view. Ted, I regret to have to say this, you understand, but there is one small difficulty with the plan. At the moment, I am slightly embarrassed — financially, that is. I'm afraid I must ask you for a small advance for the occasion."

Lily almost laughed aloud at the look on Ted's face.

"What? I'm not your banker. If you need money, get it from Mr. Barousse."

"Be assured, I will submit an accounting to him once this is all said and done. In the meantime, you may put my advance of 5,000 francs along with the 12,500 francs against your hotel bill. That's how we do things here."

"That doesn't tell me what you need 5,000 francs for."

"Miss Lily, you understand, must be free to move about with Mr. Breedlove and keep her two eyes open. My presence will also have to be justified. I must show myself as available for something other than the defense of Schopenhauer. There are card games at Krenz's. My participation in a few of those would overcome any prejudice that might be aroused by my lack of reputation. All in the interest of keeping my two eyes open, you understand."

Before Ted could raise another objection, Lily said, "Take it or leave it, Ted. If you want me to go to Krenz's, give Paul his advance and tell your seamstress to be in my room first thing tomorrow morning. That is, before we leave for Cap Ferrat with the necklace."

# Tuesday, March 17, 1914
## HÔTEL DE PARIS

PAUL SNAPPED A SHARP SALUTE AT A PORTER IN THE hotel's lobby. He felt oddly buoyed after the meeting with Wycliffe, odd because there had been no significant improvements to his circumstances. In a couple of days, he was going to be leaving his future behind at Antibes. He had to admit Jonnie's involvement with Lily was going to add a touch of piquancy to Wednesday night. He hoped he would be able to observe Jonnie's reaction to her being with another man. What a slick little liar she was proving to be. Watching her play Wycliffe like a trout had been pure pleasure, but it also made Paul question whether he had been played by her too. Did she know Jonnie frequented Krenz's? Is that why she agreed to go? Regardless, he would call at Wycliffe's room the first thing tomorrow morning and collect the payment for the necklace and the five-thousand-franc advance, a minuscule gain in this monumental saga of defeat, but better than none at all.

Observing Paul's approach, the doorman pushed open the door. Paul stopped to check his pocketwatch, gave the man a nod, and reversed directions. Hervé and Paul had both known Hervé's request for an approach to Miss Holmes would be granted in spite of his protestations. If he hadn't had the breath knocked out of him yesterday by the revelation about Céline and Barousse, he would have contrived a way to bring up Sally Homes with Olivier then. Might as well give it a go now. The inquiry would have to be made with delicacy. When it came to sniffing out juicy gossip, Olivier had the olfactory senses of a bloodhound.

In the kitchen, a shift-change was taking place. At the far end of the corridor, Paul saw the floor-waiter who had caught his notice the last time. He watched the boy's back disappear into the changing room. Olivier said he worked the second floor. Sally Holmes occupied rooms on the second floor. Olivier also said the boy missed an afternoon of work last week. He hadn't specified which day. However, Paul wasn't going to waste money backing coincidence on that one either.

# Tuesday, March 17, 1914
## HÔTEL DE PARIS

DOMINIQUE LEBRAUN WAS PLACING A WORN SLOUCH hat over his black curls as he came out the postern door used by the employees. The starched collar gripped his neck like a garrote, and his freshly barbered hair had left a narrow line of white skin at the neck. The jacket's poorly fitted sleeves exposed long, bony wrists.

When Paul spoke his name, Dominique jolted to a stop. Confusion, then recognition, then fear, then defiance rang the changes across his face.

"Just got off work, did you?" Paul said.

The surpassing inanity of the remark should have drawn a sarcasm, but speaking to a spot on the wall behind Paul's left shoulder, Dominique answered, "Yes, I get off work every day at this time."

"You deliver to the second-floor guests," Paul said.

Dominique looked like a strenuous effort was required to determine whether this were true. Tapping his foot, he cast a questioning look at the sky, then at the cobblestones while the prominent Adam's apple pumped vigorously and red blotches broke out on his pasty skin.

"Let me help," Paul said. "It was not a question. You do work the second floor and have for the past month."

Dominique apparently was constitutionally incapable of looking directly at the person to whom he was speaking. His eyes darted everywhere except in Paul's direction. Paul hated this kind. It was more difficult to separate the wheat from the chaff with them than with the consummate liars. At last, Dominique said, "And you are the Englishman who works at the Casino."

Another nail in the coffin of anonymity. As a Monégasque, Dominique wasn't permitted inside the Rooms, so he hadn't seen Paul there.

Paul said, "I've been detailed by Monsieur Barousse to ask for more information about one of the guests on the second floor."

Dominique tried unsuccessfully to insert an index finger in the space between his collar and neck. His lower lip was drawn back like a horse with a bit in its mouth. "I cannot talk to you about the guests."

"I'm sure you're the very soul of discretion. But Monsieur Barousse does not want to hear about all the guests, only one: Mademoiselle Holmes, in room 240."

Dominique suddenly squared off like a guttersnipe who has vanquished every challenger to his territory save the one in front of him. He then broke the mood by swiping at the thin stream running from his nose with the back of his hand.

Behind them, a car's horn hooted peevishly. Paul put out his arm and moved the boy to the side. "Do you know the person of whom I speak?" he said.

"Ask Monsieur Renault," Dominique told the sky. "He keeps the books."

Paul regarded the boy sadly. What was it about people in a hole that made them go on digging? Could they see nothing except the earth beneath their feet? "Room 240,"

Paul said. "Mademoiselle Holmes. She's been there about a month. Pretty lady."

An admixture of hatred and fear flared in Dominique's eyes. "I deliver coffee to that room. Food, too."

"When was the last time you made a delivery?"

Jumpy as a flea, Dominique slipped into a small frenzy of agitated movements. The rapidly blinking eyes searched the edges of the rooftops while he smacked his lips and rubbed his palms along the sides of his thighs. He was hiding something and hiding that something not well.

"Is Mademoiselle Holmes always alone?" Paul said.

"No," Dominique answered with unmistakable bitterness. "No, she is not always alone."

"Mademoiselle Holmes' friend, Joseph Murphy. You know he died, yes?"

"Of course I know. Everyone who works in the hotel knows. We cannot have police at the hotel without everyone knowing."

Paul shifted his weight. It was becoming increasingly difficult to hide the pain when it decided to shoot through his knee. He reached out and plucked an imaginary piece of lint off the shoulder of Dominique's coat. "That is a fine-looking suit," he said. "Is it new?"

"I doubt Monsieur Barousse is interested in my clothing."

"On the contrary. When Joseph Murphy died, his wallet went missing. I will not learn you purchased that suit since he died, will I?"

"You think I would rob a dead man?"

"Am I going to learn you have been spending money on other new things as well?"

Dominique's face was all the answer that was needed. "Monsieur Jean Renault will tell you, there have been no orders from Room 240 in more than four days. There is a

*No-Disturbance* sign on the door. There is nothing more I can tell you."

Dominique began to walk away, then turned back. "They are all alike, those rich ones. We are only something to scrape their shoes on, something to use and throw away like rubbish." He twisted his head to the right to spit at the ground. "If you want to know more, talk to that woman in Room 203."

Paul stared at him uncomprehendingly.

"Room 203, the tall woman, Miss Turner. Talk to her if you can. The *No-Disturbance* sign is on her door too. Those Americans, they are like all the others. They want to use people, but they do not want to keep them."

He looked like he wanted to say something else. Instead, he touched his hand to the slouch hat and walked away, moving with rapid, long strides, and leaving Paul dumbstruck.

# Tuesday, March 17, 1914
## LE PERROQUET ROUGE

PAUL STOOD TO ACKNOWLEDGE LILY'S ARRIVAL AT the restaurant in Beausoleil. It was an unremarkable place with a simple menu and only eight tables arrayed in close order within a dimly lit room.

Michael Gallagher was grousing about the glass of whiskey in front of him, "I told you, I don't want nothing."

"What's this world coming to when a man can't buy an Irishman a drink?" Paul said. "It's the good stuff they have here, none of that tourist swill."

Michael pushed the glass towards Paul. "Drink it yourself then."

Somewhat awkwardly, Lily sat with her umbrella on her lap. The waiter was standing too close to easily place it next to the identical one on the table. She ordered a cup of coffee for herself and another for Michael and watched the waiter retreat.

"You are acquainted with Miss Turner, I believe," Paul said.

"Her, I'm acquainted with. You, I'm not."

"I explained that below. I'm with the hotel's security. I'm looking into what went on around Joseph Murphy's death."

"That's what you told me, all right, but like I said, the

police done talked to me. They even searched my room. Mr. Wycliffe talked to me. I've told everything I know again and again. Mr. Murphy was on the bed. The bullet hole was in his back. How many ways can a man say that? What'd you bring me up here at night for?"

Lily unobtrusively laid the umbrella on the table beside the other one, then removed her notebook from her bag.

"What's she doing?" Michael said.

Paul said, "Mrs. Murphy wanted one of her staff to hear what you had to say. I'm thinking it was so the hotel can't cook up a case against her own people. The hotel's not wanting to take on any blame in this matter. That's why I'm talking to you. I want to know more about Mr. Murphy, who he was when he was at home with himself, that sort of thing."

Lily futilely surveyed the room once more. She had established Jonathan wasn't present when she entered and hung her coat. Not that she expected him to be. This place, Paul had said, was frequented by and large by locals who did not speak English. Nevertheless, the possibility of a chance encounter had not been entirely absent from her mind since she received the note telling her where they would meet. This was the same mind she was longing to give Jonathan Chandler a piece of.

"Mrs. Murphy wants the hotel to look again at what went on," Paul said. "So I'm thinking — tell me if I'm wrong here — no one knows a man better than his own man. No man's a hero to his valet. You've heard that before, haven't you?"

"Can't say that I have."

"What say we start at the beginning?" Paul said. "What's your full name? How long have you worked for the Murphys?"

Lily noted the folksy quality in Paul's diction, obviously meant to put Michael more at ease. A broad tessitura was something else she and Fran would want to add to their professional bag-of-tricks.

"Michael Francis Gallagher and we've been working for them since they left San Francisco." He jerked a thumb in Lily's direction. "She knows that. So does Mrs. Murphy. What'd you have to ask me for?"

Lily had told Paul everything she knew about the couple, which was only that they had joined the party immediately before it left San Francisco and that, while Bridget Rose was competent in her role, Michael was not. It hadn't been Lily's place to question where the couple came from or how, but in the midst of a lengthy complaint about the lack of ability in the one and of agreeableness in the other, Mrs. Murphy blamed Mr. Murphy for engaging them. This squared with what Sally said Sunday night. Lily had also given Paul the questions she wanted asked. She didn't have to prove Bridget's culpability in a court of law. She needed only enough evidence to justify the bonus.

"San Francisco," Paul said, "how long have you lived there?"

"How does that matter?"

"Just getting the background. You see, I'm paid by the hour. How long?"

"Most all my life."

"Most? Where was the rest of it?"

Michael's body straightened with an infusion of pride. "Belfast. Me and my folks, we left there in '79, the last famine. Landed in New York. Made our way out west there afterwards."

"You were how old?" Paul asked.

"Eight or nine, near as I can tell." His head swung from left to right as though looking for a way out. But he was hemmed in by Lily on one side and Paul on the other, with a wall behind.

"Your wife's full name is what?" Paul said.

"Bridget Rose Gallagher."

"Maiden name?"

"O'Donnell."

Lily felt a buried memory stir, but she couldn't delve for it just now. She was again doubting the wisdom of handing over the necklace tonight. It wasn't too late. The umbrella was still on the table. Listening to Paul soothe this man into comfort and confidentiality, she couldn't help looking back on their conversation outside Roquebrune this afternoon. Had he persuaded her in the same guileless-sounding manner? It didn't matter, she reminded herself. It wasn't as if she had figured out a way to collect the entire reward by herself. The only way she could see to do it was anonymously through the post, and there wasn't enough time for the back and forth of that, let alone enough time to develop a disguise whereby she could not be identified as the sender. Despite her distrust of Paul, he was the only hope she had of reaping any of the reward she had earned.

"What kind of work were you doing before?" Paul said.

"Ship's carpenter."

Paul flashed a smile. "Thought you had the look of the noble seafaring profession about you. Ship's carpenter to valet, not a turn seen every day. How'd you come to make that leap?"

"You take what you get, or you take want."

"That's not a heap of help," Paul said, his voice chilling a couple of degrees.

Michael's gaze did a sweep of the entire café as if searching for a weapon or a friend. Finding neither, he settled for a shrug and a sip of coffee. "Word got around Mr. Murphy was looking for help, so I went up to him. Isn't that how a man always gets a job? They don't come looking for you."

Lily knew there was more to it than that. For one thing, Sally said the tickets to Belfast were for the Gallaghers. That inducement surely hadn't been in the word going around. She said, "Mr. Murphy needed a man and Mrs. Murphy a lady's maid. What about after Monte Carlo? Was he thinking of keeping you on after you got back to San Francisco?"

"I'm supposed to know what he was thinking, am I?"

Paul said, "Word was going around, and you went up to him. Where did you go up to him?"

"At his offices. They're down by the docks. That's it. We showed up at the train, and we're here. Like I said, I done told Mr. Wycliffe all this. Why don't you ask him?"

"I work for the hotel," Paul said. "They pay me to ask you and not bother their guests. I'll tell you something else besides. I had in mind to bring up a few things you didn't discuss with Mr. Wycliffe. For openers, why did your wife want to poison Joseph Murphy?"

Michael's face passed through several distinct stages of dawning comprehension. First, he looked confused. Then, he blanched as understanding darkened his eyes. Next, he pinched his lips as his features turned bright pink before blooming into a red rage. When the last stage passed, his aspect settled into a grayish pallor.

Lily was only slightly less shocked than he was. She had given Paul a sample of the powder. She had no idea if his accusation was based on certainty or a hunch. She looked down at her notebook and wrote something nonsensical. There was a memory connected to Bridget Rose's name, O'Donnell, but it was like a dark shape in a dream that refused to resolve into an identifiable person.

Michael's eyes darted back and forth between his two interlocutors. Previously, she thought, he had found the whole scene so fantastic, he literally had not known how to act. Now he was cornered. He should find his footing soon and come out fighting. The only question was whether it was going to be fisticuffs or a shillelagh.

Paul took a long pull of whiskey and smacked his lips with satisfaction. "This kind of business does raise the thirst. You may as well go and get yourself comfortable." He indicated the other, untouched glass. "And sure, go ahead and give that a think before you answer because we're going to be here until we get to the bottom of it."

Michael looked at him with undisguised loathing.

"No?" Paul said. He clasped his hands behind his neck. "Suit yourself. Here's the thing. I'm not usually one to complain about how a person may choose to murder his fellow man, but arsenic? Inheritance powder, that's what we used to call it. Definitely shows a poverty of imagination." He lowered his arms and leaned forward. "Here's another question I ought to raise while we're about it. Sir, do you own a pistol?"

"Mother of God, you are insane. Shoot a man who owes me full wages? You think I'm stupid as all that?"

Paul regarded him for several long seconds. "That takes us back to the first question. Why did your wife want to poison a man who owed you full wages?"

"God as my judge, I don't know what you're talking about."

"You knew about the gunshot. Did you also know the cause of death was not the gunshot? That it was accidental?" Paul asked.

Michael nodded.

"But you didn't know someone left poison in his whiskey glass," Paul said. It was not a question.

Michael pressed his back against his chair, his muscles tensed like he was ready to let fly at Paul. He appeared to be grinding rocks in his mind. Then he shook his head like a horse shaking off pestering flies. "I can tell you what. If you're right about somebody wanting to poison Mr. Murphy, if you're right about that, so be it. But if you're thinking my Rosie was the one, you're mad. Why would she? I know a little something about how the law works. You can't make bricks without straw. You got to have a reason to kill a man. What'd she want him dead for? There was plenty of other people must've wanted him dead. I don't know who. When Mrs. Murphy was gone, he always shooed me off, so I don't know who else he knew, but it must have been them. Look to them." He slid his palms to edge of the table, preparing to push it away. "So I reckon I'm ready to go unless you're wanting to tell me I shot Joseph Murphy so as to steal his cufflinks."

While listening, Lily's mind had been working out the stirred memory, the possible, the probable fatal connection.

"Michael," she said, "where in Pennsylvania did Bridget Rose hail from?"

He swung his head in her direction. "How'd you know she come from there?"

"You better listen to our young lady," Paul said. "She knows a whole lot more than you would ever guess."

Lily kept her eyes on Michael. There was an unmistakably mean edge in Paul's tone, but she couldn't worry about that. She believed she had all the pieces. She had to make sure they fit.

Michael said, "I'm wanting to go back to the hotel. I done told you what I know, and I don't know nothing about Rosie and no poison. I don't know nothing about nothing and no poison." The veins on the back of his rough hands were distended by the pressure he was exerting on the table.

"It goes back to Wiggins Patch doesn't it?" Lily said. "Back to Wiggins Patch and the Molly Maguires."

Beads of sweat blossomed on Michael's brow. "I'm telling you, I don't know what you're talking about, and you leave her alone. You need to talk, you talk to me." He swiped his hand across his brow. "You leave her alone, you hear me? She's had the hard time of it. You leave her alone."

The restaurant's other patrons might not understand English, but his tone needed no translation. His clinched fists trembled. The violence he was suppressing might spring from fear and protectiveness, but its motive made it feel no less threatening to Lily.

He said, "This here place ain't no different from every place else. Long as a man lays quiet-like under the lash, nobody says a word. Lift your head up once and what? You'd stand a better chance being hunted down by rabid wolves."

It had been more than ten years since Lily researched the history of the Molly Maguires and their fellow workers in Pennsylvania's anthracite coal mines. The miners' bloody confrontations with Philadelphia and Reading Coal and Iron and its army of private police and murderous vigilantes had on occasion been turned back on some of the miners' neighbors. Certain of these events had proved indelibly horrific.

She said, "There was a family massacred in Wiggins Patch in 1877, name of O'Donnell, the same as Bridget Rose's maiden name. Back then, it was an open secret who did it. Maybe Mr. Murphy wasn't directly involved, Maybe it was only a relative, just as it was with Bridget. But the O'Donnells were a large family, and families have long memories, especially when it comes to revenge. Those kinds of motives get passed down to the children. We're not out to hurt Bridget Rose. She didn't cause Mr. Murphy's death. All we want is the complete truth about your arrangement with Mr. Murphy. Why don't you tell Mr. Newcastle about it?"

"You didn't know about the poison," Paul said. "If you had, you would have got rid of it before setting up the alarm. And you didn't know Mr. Murphy came from Wiggins Patch before you hired on, else you wouldn't have put your wife into the situation. Somehow or other, she figured it out after you got here. Where'd she get the poison? You two don't usually travel with a load of arsenic, do you?"

Michael took a sharp intake of breath. Paul continued, "Attempted murder is a serious charge. I regret to say I know what the jail in Monaco is like, and I don't think Mrs. Gallagher will find it to her liking. So here's the thing, Michael. Joseph Murphy had you up to something besides polishing his buttons. I'll tell you what else. If you fill me in about Murphy's intentions, I'll forget about your wife's mistake. Miss Turner will too. Isn't that right, Miss Turner?"

"That sounds right, Mr. Newcastle," Lily said. "Michael would never deliberately place his wife in service with a mortal enemy. She must have found out about it after they arrived here, very recently in fact. Anybody could understand her mistake, and it came to nothing." Lily also was thinking this history might explain why Bridget Rose stole that necklace, thereby incurring the enormous risk such a theft entailed. She wasn't after something valuable. She was wreaking more vengeance on Joseph Murphy and his clan.

"It ain't her fault. She's had the hard life, growing up in that Schuylkill County. Something about them mines, sucks the souls right out of them people, all of them nothing but black shells of what a man oughta be. Anyhow, they're all crazy as bedbugs. She come away to get shed of them. Gentle and sweet and pretty, she was. And seven times, seven babies she couldn't carry all the way to birthing. It weakened her, all that did. She didn't mean no harm."

Lily had to wonder what whiskey laced with poison meant,

if not harm. She said, "Bridget Rose never mentioned the babies, but I could tell beneath all that kindness, she bore a great sorrow. It wouldn't be right if this business with Mr. Murphy brought more grief onto her. Mr. Newcastle only needs you to tell him what else Mr. Murphy wanted you to do. After that, I'm sure he'll forget he ever heard of Bridget Rose. Isn't that right, Mr. Newcastle?" Once more, Paul was giving her an indecipherable look. Once more, she didn't have time to sort it out.

"That's right, Miss Turner. I'd just as soon get out of here before midnight myself, so let's see if Michael can't tell me what I need to hear so I can be on my way."

"Do you swear nothing will come back on Rosie?" Michael said. After Paul and Lily gave their assurances, he said, "I didn't know Joe Murphy from shoe leather when we got hired on, and I don't know how she come to find out who he was, but she did. She told me she did, but I didn't know she would try to do something about it. She told me she had a rat in her room. By all the saints, I didn't know what she was going to do with the stuff."

Paul gave Michael a look of open skepticism. "I'm waiting for you to say how it was a ship's carpenter came to be Joseph Murphy's valet. And don't give me that bit about the word going around."

"Thing is, last three, four years, I couldn't ship out no more. Got to where I couldn't hardly climb aboard a vessel at anchor without being laid out by the seasickness. The trip over here, I like to of died. So anyhow, back in San Francisco, I'd been doing what I could, working as a stevedore when I could, down at the docks. That's how I come to know about Joe Murphy. He had merchant ships and a name for helping the Irish out. I wanted to take my Rosie back there, back to Ireland. She's had the black dog on her back a long time. If

I could get her back to Ireland, away from the thoughts, the rest of it, clean away from that crazy family, back with my kin, who didn't have to know nothing about nothing. If I could get her back there, everything would be all right again."

He looked down, no doubt conscious of the moisture in his eyes. He placed one of his work-scarred hands on top of his head and left it there as though it could keep his emotions tamped down. "I didn't go looking for no handout. I ain't that kind. Don't think for a minute I went crawling to Joe Murphy begging for alms. Like I said, I ain't that kind. I had something to trade. I won't go into how I got ahold of them. Let's just say I got my hands on some papers what looked like they might be worth something to somebody besides me. I say somebody besides me because I couldn't read them and that ain't because I can't read writing. I can. I just can't read that kind of writing. Somebody else told me it was German. They was all bundled up in a leather case with a tie around it and a big red seal on it. They was military in nature. I won't tell you how I know that, but I know it. So I went to Joe Murphy. Don't think I don't mark that day as the sorriest day of my life. Anyhow, I went to Joe Murphy, and I showed him those papers. I was thinking maybe he could make something of them, make himself important by giving them to the right people, sell them, I didn't care, not so long as he helped me get my wife to Belfast. I told him she worked as a lady's maid, which she had, maybe not for a woman of Mrs. Murphy's standing, but she had. Mr. Murphy made up his mind on the spot. Said he was leaving in three days to go to Monte Carlo. Said he would take us with them and when we was finished there, he would pay us for our work and see to it that we got to Belfast. It wasn't no hand-out. We was to earn our money and our passage to Belfast. There's a shipbuilding trade in Belfast. My cousin was going to get me on with Harland and Wolff, the same yard what built the ship we come over on. Now look at us. We can't leave until Mrs. Murphy settles up with us, and she won't pay us until we get back to San Francisco. We come all this way, and we're no closer than ever we was to Belfast."

Michael's statement came as a sharp reminder to Lily of her own vulnerability. Until the money from Fran arrived, she too was dependent upon Mrs. Murphy. She felt Paul's gaze on her. He was telegraphing his perception of the meaning behind the tickets to Belfast. At the same time, he was reeling her back into the conversation.

"You told Mr. Wycliffe none of this?" she said.

"If you want to know what I told Mr. Wycliffe, why don't you ask him? The hotel ain't paying you not to bother him, is it?"

She saw Paul open his mouth to intercede, but she got there first. "That's true. But you're paying me not to tell Mr. Wycliffe about Bridget Rose and the poison."

Michael's howl, half fury, half pain, had the people at the other tables turning to openly stare. "Jesus wept! Don't you people got no souls? Here I am, halfway around the world, and you're holding me up? I done told you, I ain't got no money. Don't you know, if I had money, Rosie and me would already be in Belfast?"

# Tuesday, March 17, 1914
## VILLA ACHILLES

ACROSS THE THRESHOLD, THE TWO MEN REGARDED one another with mutual curiosity. Despite the hour, almost midnight, and the darkened house, Hervé was fully dressed in white linen trousers, pink silk shirt and wide leather belt. Even though his aspect was softened by the thin glow from the single gas-jet in the foyer, he appeared more despondent than the day before.

He spoke first. "Good evening, my friend. I must say, you look rather blown. Would you care to come in and take a rest?"

"Where's Antonio?" Paul said, placing his overcoat and hat on the hall-stand and positioning the umbrella against the wall behind it. The necklace was weighing down his left pocket.

"He is away."

"Where's Alexei? We must have complete privacy."

Hervé motioned towards the sitting room. "What is on your mind? Have more corpses washed up on the shores of Monaco?" He drew the heavy velvet curtains across all the windows, then turned up the flame in the paraffin table-lamp. "We will know when the boys return. It is impossible to enter other than by ringing the front bells."

Despite the assurances, when Hervé took his place on the divan, Paul placed a chair directly beside him. "I owe you an apology," he said, plunging straight into it. "Until this evening, I was convinced you must be after something as pedestrian as money. I confess I was disappointed when you refused to own up to it. It wasn't as though I were going to horn in on your game. Then yesterday, I learned that upwards of a million dollars of Joseph Murphy's money had come unmoored, and for several delightful hours, I thought I understood why you insisted on playing it close to the chest. A million dollars, no room for folly there. But that was before this evening, before the scales had fallen from my eyes."

"In that case, you have the advantage of me," Hervé said. "To this minute, I have no idea what you are after or why you persist with wild stories about murdered journalists and nonsensical theories about Basil Zaharoff."

"I'll get to that later." Paul paused to catch up with himself. Since depositing Michael at the hotel, he had been wrestling with his anger, unable to determine where it should be directed, how it should be expressed. "On second thought, I'll get to that right away. When you showed up here nine months ago, after leaving La Santé, I mentioned I had been working for some time on a complicated trick. I gave few details because there was nothing you could do to help. You were freshly out of prison and known to the local authorities. The risk was too great."

Hervé nodded his agreement.

"That deal was close. I was less than two months away from tying it up. When I learned that Joseph Murphy's death was being investigated by the police, I was keen to ensure that the connection between him and me through you, no matter how faint, could not come back on me and scupper the years I had invested in my project. In other words, I wanted to protect myself from your entanglement in the matter. As events marched on, I came to believe I should also protect you from yourself. That is, I wanted to make you aware of the dangers that continued to swirl around Murphy and his activities. Because the police professed to have lost interest, I believed we were dealing only with such trifles as money and murder. The more fool I. Now I see I should have been worrying about every espionage and counterespionage agency in Europe coming down on us."

He paused once more. Berating Hervé wasn't going to accomplish a thing. It didn't even make Paul feel better. In the silence, he heard a lorry rumbling along the road above. Not quite the hour for an exemplary Christian to be abroad. Hervé rose and stood first by the door to the foyer, then went to the one that led to the back of the house. Taking the lamp from the table, he went out one of the French windows and slowly traced the perimeter of the terrace. Paul realized he had never seen Hervé's Vauxhall on the road above and wondered where he kept it. That would be important to know since he was depending on it to make good his impending escape to Marseilles. He wondered if "the boys" were in it and felt a stab of sympathy for his friend. Romantic love had to be the most ruinous force in nature, far more destructive than lust. A man in love can only ever imagine his beloved as tragic or afflicted. It is impossible for him to see the adored one as greedily manipulative or contemptibly squalid.

Hervé closed the curtains and returned to the divan. "Precisely," he said, as if the interruption had not occurred, "it was dangerous knowledge. That is why I did not want you to know."

There was a pinch of truth in the statement, but Paul suspected the overriding reason was that Hervé didn't want to be discouraged from pursuing his course of action. "It might have helped to know I was in danger," Paul said.

"What difference would it have made? You always consider yourself to be in danger."

"Regardless, I am now in possession of part of that dangerous knowledge. I know it has to do with German military documents. Perhaps you could brighten the dark corners in my understanding."

Hervé's hand moved towards the cigarette holder, stalled in midair, and returned to rest on his thigh. He gave an exaggerated shrug of concession. "You know Murphy stressed the importance of linguistic abilities. When he contacted me, he said I had to be able not only to speak but to read every major language. Yet he arrived alone. After a few cursory inquiries into my credentials, he apparently found me sound. He said, 'I'm going to have to trust you.'"

"Obviously, a shrewd judge of character," Paul said.

"He had documents he wanted translated from the German into English. He believed they might contain important military information. When he refused to say how he came by them, I told him if I could not know their source, I could not have anything to do with them."

"Nice touch," Paul said.

"One must demonstrate a consistent core of principle. He objected, but I was firm. The tale he related might have contained elements of the truth. He said he owned a shipping concern and that a man, unnamed by Murphy, had made a round of the freighters docked at Hamburg looking for a captain who would let him hitch a ride. This same man proceeded to die aboard one of Murphy's vessels and was buried at sea. The ship's captain turned the man's possessions over to be returned to the relatives, but there were no addresses for him. As for his identity papers, those were not mentioned. Murphy said he brought the documents to Monte Carlo to be translated in order to determine how best to dispose of them.

"I gave every indication of believing this Homeric narrative and took him to the privacy of my study. The papers ran to some fifty pages and in short contained a plan for the German Army to conquer France. A general named Von Schlieffen was named as the progenitor. The operations were outlined in minute detail. They included mobilization timetables; troop strengths and objectives; artillery placements; rolling-stock dispositions; precise logistics for men, materiel, and horses; and day-by-day deployments. They stated not only where the Germans were supposed to be, but where the French and the Russians were expected to be as well.

"In its essence, the plan was nothing more than a variation on a familiar strain. Every great general — the unstoppable Alexander with the Uxians, the magnificent Hannibal and his elephants, the insatiable Napoléon — they all employed surprise as their most effective weapon. The surprise here is to be Belgium. Its neutrality is guaranteed by every major country, including Germany. Who in his right mind could envision Belgium's flower beds being crushed beneath an invading army's hobnailed boots on their march to Paris? The German High Command, that is who. The timelines have their troops sipping wine on the Left Bank before the French have finished wringing their hands and shitting their scarlet trousers."

As Paul listened, a part of his mind was considering Wycliffe's wild theory about Joseph Murphy's buying guns for the Irish with the aid of certain Germans. He said, "Why would they go through Belgium and risk bringing in England? Why not use the frontier at Alsace and Lorraine?"

"If you thought of that, would not everyone else think of

it too? France has fortresses all along that common border. The element of surprise would be lacking."

"As a guarantor of Belgium's neutrality, Great Britain would have to respond to an invasion. Therefore, I repeat, why risk bringing in England? It goes against plain common sense to add a powerful enemy."

"The papers did not expend unnecessary ink defending the rationale. It is a matter of military necessity, and to the German mind, there is no higher need nor right. France and Russia are committed to defending each other against the enemy of either. That is to say, if France is forced to defend itself against Germany, Russia must fight Germany as well. No sane general wants to wage war on two fronts simultaneously. It will take Germany two weeks to mobilize, the same for France. With Russia's vast spaces and meager railroads, it will be physically impossible to fully mobilize its army and move it to the front in less than six weeks. Germany expects to defeat France before the Russians have finished lacing up their boots. Therefore, there will be no need to divide their forces."

There would be no time either for England to pull troops away from its campaign in Ireland and make a difference on the continent. Paul's mind was grasping the logic, but he hated badly for Wycliffe to be right.

Hervé continued, "The American, Murphy, seemed far from dull-witted. However, he never once asked how much the French or any other government might be willing to pay for this intelligence. I thought he was playing coy, so I attempted to draw him out by acting as the Devil's Advocate. I told him that even if those plans had once been valid, they were surely superseded. I explained the German High Command does nothing day in and day out except devise schemes for invading every known continent, including

Antarctica. In other words, I told him, the plans were worthless. He said that was irrelevant because he had no intention of risking his life for a few francs. Now that he understood the content, he claimed, he was interested only in getting the documents into the right hands. He asserted this in a believable manner, and I assured him that as a French citizen such an aim was my consuming desire as well. I told him that, given a couple of days, I was certain I could be of concrete assistance in making sure the documents were correctly placed. I exaggerated only slightly the degree of my consanguinity with Joseph Noulens, the Minister of War, and the strength of my influence over General Joffre. Perhaps I did go overboard by mentioning my monthly visits to Quai d'Orsay, but who knows? Circumstances prevented Mr. Murphy from making use of my valuable connections."

Paul regarded Hervé with open amazement. "Did you tell anyone else about those papers?"

"Do you think I have been stricken with the brain fever?"

"Not even Alexei?"

"Especially not Alexei."

"And you're still after them? Can they be worth stretching your neck across the guillotine's block? Around here, spies are thicker than lice in a doss house. If you try to peddle those papers, the news will be all the way across France and halfway across the rest of Europe before you finish the sentence."

This time, Hervé got as far as picking up the cigarette holder. He dropped it back on the table and stood. At the window, he parted the drapes and stared gloomily at the moonlit terrace. "My motives have nothing to do with anything, as you so adroitly put it, as pedestrian as money although, had I known the amount that was in play, I might have been tempted. Alas, Joseph Murphy made me neither his confidant nor his banker." He closed the draperies but remained with his back to Paul.

"You will recall," Hervé said, "during our youthful days in Paris, there were many with living memories of the siege during the Franco-Prussian War. It was intensely cold that winter, and there was no fuel. The supply of bread failed, and the people were reduced to eating unspeakable things, dogs, rats, the zoo's animals, even the much loved elephants. The wounded died for want of a little soup. Old people and children perished by the hundreds."

Of course Paul had heard these accounts. Some who had experienced it could not bear to speak of it. Others seemed unable to go a day without recounting it.

Hervé abruptly turned around as if deflecting the memory. "There is a parallel between those hellish but passing days in Paris and the permanent state of existence in Russia. Everyone in that country, everyone except those bloated, self-absorbed aristocrats, spends the entirety of their short, miserable lives besieged by crushing oppression and unimaginable deprivation. Diseased and starving, they shiver permanently within the frigid shadow of that devouring double-headed eagle which mendaciously claims to protect them."

Paul suddenly felt very tired. It had been a long day, and tomorrow would be even longer, starting with the trip to Cap Ferrat to collect on the necklace and ending at Krenz's.

Hervé went on, "No one inside or outside of Russia wants to acknowledge that their rulers are dining and waltzing on the rim of an active volcano. Consider how many times the anarchists and the revolutionaries dynamited Tsar Alexander II before they finally succeeded in killing him in the '80s. More decades of disasters, famines, uprisings, and massacres came to a head with the Bloody Sunday. That was ten years ago. Since then, matters have only become worse. A week cannot go by without an assassination attempt on some grand duke or prince or his wife. There are continual strikes, riots, attacks on property. It is impossible to say who is doing the greater damage, the terrorists or the Tsar's secret police acting as *agents provocateurs*."

Paul said, "I can understand you would be worried about Alexei, but –"

Hervé cut him off. "Alexei is of military age. He is forbidden to leave Russia without a permit. He deserted the Imperial Ballet, so he no longer is under its protection. He no longer is exempt from conscription. In the Tsar's army, he would be only another scrap of flesh to be fed to the cannons. With or without war, such a fate would be tantamount to a death sentence. Even if he were to survive physically intact, the mechanical drudgery and demeaning hardships would be devastating to his undisciplined nerves. His parents add to his peril. They have been in bad odor with the Okhrana since they participated in a strike at the ballet in '05. Here or anywhere, he lives in constant danger of being arrested for evading compulsory conscription and being deported, probably never to be seen again."

"What's the difficulty?" Paul said. "Buy him a new identity and passport. Have him grow a moustache."

"He wants to keep his name. He is fond of the reputation he has made for himself. It is for this reason that I must have those documents. Many persons, Alexei included, believe passion is the fountainhead of great art. That is false. Great art can be achieved only when a great passion is controlled, when it is dominated by a hard, cool head. Alexei possesses passion, but his mind must be disciplined. He needs time for this to be brought about, but first he must come to understand it is required. I have made inquiries, very discreet inquiries, naturally. I have reason to believe it will be possible to trade those papers for a ukase from Tsar Nicholas. Alexei will be granted amnesty and freedom of movement inside and outside Russia. He will be given the freedom to develop his art."

Paul closed his eyelids and massaged them with his fingers. Hervé's expectation did not strain credulity. It had been his rhizomatous network of confederates who smuggled them out of St. Petersburg along with Friedrich Hoffmeister. "One question," Paul said, lowering his arm. "Those plans concern Germany and France. Why would the Russians give two pence for them?"

Hervé held up a delaying hand. "I am sorry, Old Friend. I did not anticipate the pleasure of this conversation would run so long. May I offer you a restorative? You look like you could use one."

It was the sleep he was forgoing Paul could use, but it was he who had inaugurated the meeting. He dismissed the offer with a shake of his head.

Hervé said, "You ask why someone in Russia would place a high value on those plans. I could tell you it is because the fate of their army is tied to the fate of the French. I could tell you that after France is defeated, the full might of the German army would be turned against Russia. That dolt, Nicholas, cares no more if one man is spared a war than if a million should perish in it. But there might be two, even three, men who have his ear and who also possess the acumen to understand the implications to the welfare of the Tsar's army. However, that is not the reason they would want to get their hands on those documents."

Hervé's mouth stretched briefly into a humorless smile. "If this were not so serious, it would be laughable. On the official level, most nations prefer to conduct their espionage activities like gentlemen. Their local attachés cultivate social contacts with officers and politicians, hoping the table conversation can be turned to naval or military matters. A liaison with the proper wife is not considered out-of-bounds either. On the surface, these nations pretend to rely upon what can be learned over soup or a cigar or on a pillow. The Russians have neither the patience nor the delicacy for that kind of finesse. For them, spying is great game. They want to break into offices, photograph blueprints of fortresses, ferret out the identities of secret agents, and gather the tactical plans not only of their enemies but also of their allies. They are unabashed about reading another man's mail or snooping through a lady's lingerie drawer. They want these papers because they love stealing secrets — anyone's secrets." Hervé's shrug signaled the end of this line of thought.

Paul closed his eyes once more, trying to separate the elements in the puzzle. There were the military plans held by Murphy which Hervé lusted after. But Cyril's suspicions had centered on visits to Krenz's villa and the notorious Zaharoff, who peddled armaments, not paper. Wycliffe believed the people who ransacked Murphy's suite were looking for his gun-money, but it was Hervé's crew looking for the documents.

As if reading Paul's thoughts, Hervé said, "That is why I told you Joseph Murphy did not go to Herr Krenz's to share there what he had shared with me. What need would the German Government have for a copy of those papers? They have Schlieffen's original. I doubt they would have cast a benevolent eye upon Murphy's possession of them either."

Paul said, "Yesterday, I told you Friedrich said he had driven Joseph Murphy and Basil Zaharoff to Krenz's on the same night. This afternoon, the cousin, Wycliffe, said Chief Inspector Gautier also reported Murphy's presence at Krenz's. Wycliffe had this whipped into a frothy conspiracy involving the purchase of arms from Zaharoff for Irish revolutionaries. He managed to fold the Teutonic race into the concoction by noting that an actively rebellious Ireland would serve Germany's interests by distracting the British from what might be happening on the Continent. Based on Schlieffen's plan, what might be happening on the continent is starting to come into focus. But you're right. The documents and the weapons don't dovetail."

Staring past Paul, Hervé sat tapping the tips of his fingers together. He said, "I told you before, everything could not be of one piece. Allow me to play the woodsplitter. Basil Zaharoff's skill in playing both ends, or all four sides, against the middle is spectacular. Yet dozens of double-agents are doing the same everyday although on an immensely less profitable scale. There is nothing to say Joseph Murphy wasn't up to the same. He had two games going. He was betraying the German Army with the one hand while helping them out with the other."

Paul felt his resentment growing. How much wasted worry could have been saved if he had had all the facts sooner. The resentment spread to Lily. Every time he turned around, he uncovered another layer she had kept concealed. Judging from her leading question to Michael Gallagher this evening, she knew in advance that the tickets to Belfast were meant for the valet and his wife. And that tidbit paled in comparison with her familiarity with Sally Holmes.

"I believe I have a line on Miss Holmes," he said.

"You know where she is?"

"Perhaps. Tell me, did those bumbling fools tear up her room the same way they did Murphy's?" He caught the flicker in Hervé's eyes. "No wonder she went to ground," he said.

"We can find no trace of her. Only one person was available to watch. He couldn't be everywhere all the time."

"You don't think she's clever enough to disguise herself?"

"She is a true beauty. I do not know how clever she is."

"A couple of warts on her nose and chin should do it." And Lily was clever enough if Miss Holmes were not.

Hervé kept his eyes locked on Paul's. "Regardless of what anyone was getting up to at Krenz's, my interest lies only in those documents. Joseph Murphy had them. The woman, Sally Holmes, must know where they are. I ask once more, will you help me with her?"

# Wednesday, March 18, 1914
## GIORGIO'S CAFÉ

PAUL'S TIRED, DULLED EYES WERE INCAPABLE OF exercising their usual vigilance as he regarded the other patrons at Giorgio's. Despite the late night at Hervé's, he had awakened early this morning. Consequently, he propelled himself to the café. He might as well pretend for one more day that he came here voluntarily, not to meet with Cyril Phelps. He was also in need of massive quantities of coffee to fortify himself for the journey to Cap Ferrat with The Hyena and Lily. He toyed with the idea of arriving very late, just to panic her. She deserved more than a few ounces of torment. If he didn't need her to get into Krenz's or to unlatch Sally Holmes, he would have been sorely tempted to fail to show at all.

Still nothing about any hotel-guest lists found among Cyril's possessions. Possibly they hadn't been there. Possibly Gautier was keeping that as an ace up his sleeve. If the latter, all the more reason for Paul to maintain this act as his normal routine. There might be a presumption that the lists had come from him, but proof should be lacking. As with everything, he had dusted his tracks. He copied the lists in a hand not his own, using a pen and ink reserved only for that task. Nor did he duplicate the mimeographed pages he was given verbatim.

Rather, he rearranged the order and sometimes omitted middle initials or Christian names. So why blame him? Why not blame Barousse? Not only did he have the lists, he and Cyril were brothers in the confraternity of secret agents.

The sun had risen this morning over a new perspective on Joseph Murphy. Even in the clear light of day, Paul could find no reason not to agree with Hervé's belief that the American was playing both sides of the chessboard. He was dabbling with Zaharoff and possibly the German government while simultaneously intending to sell or give away its military secrets. The Hyena had spun his elaborate theory-of-everything, including the ransacking of Mrs. Murphy's suite, out of the tickets to Belfast, the German dictionary, and the visits to Krenz's villa mentioned by Chief Inspector Gautier. Gallagher explained the tickets last night. According to Olivier, Gautier believed the dictionary to be a codebook. Possibly, but Hervé said Murphy had a general idea of what the documents represented. More likely, he tried to decipher them with the use of the dictionary. That left the visits to the villa at Villefranche.

Paul was having difficulty putting aside thoughts of the million or so Murphy had set loose. If he wanted to lend a hand or a stick of dynamite to the revolutionaries back home, why hadn't he been a donor, a financier? Nothing easier, nothing less risky. Why would he leave a safe harbor to come to France and put himself and his cash into the thick of it? All the more reason to locate Sally Holmes. She would scarcely be the first young vixen who persuaded a love-stricken old fool to part with a generous slice of his money. She was probably already in Paris, tricked out in a new Worth gown, scanning the horizon for the next millionaire she could bag.

The cup Paul lifted to his lips was empty. One more and he might feel vaguely human. He raised his head in search of Giorgio, who was across the terrace, bobbing his head in Paul's direction. Beside him stood a tall, thin, dark-haired man. Too late for Paul to let his eyes slide indifferently past. Too late to guard against a sign of recognition. Damn the boy. Damn the boy to hell. Blindsided again. He managed to smooth his features into their normal placidity as he watched Jonnie approach.

"Mr. Newcastle?"

The second surprise was the depth of Jonnie's voice. He sounded like a man, a fully grown man.

"Yes."

"My name is Jonathan Chandler. Do you mind if I join you?"

Paul half-stood to reach for the proffered hand. The handshake was confident in its firmness and appropriate in duration. "Pleased, I'm sure," he said.

He had to force himself to keep his eyes on Jonnie while he gave Giorgio the order for tea. After all the years spent anticipating this moment, now that it had arrived, it came as a light too bright, a sound too loud for comprehension. Paul tried to translate the sensations into rational terms. Jonnie had filled out in the face and shoulders since graduating Cambridge. He was well dressed, well spoken, and not chewing on a soggy cigar. The mouth, Paul was glad to see, was pleasantly shaped and smiled easily. The downward pull at the edges of the eyes, not Sophie's, not his. Paul didn't like the eyes. He couldn't. He was relieved he had lost that rib-rattling cough somewhere over the past couple of days. He wished he had put the better silk handkerchief in his breast-pocket this morning. He watched Giorgio's retreating back with something like dismay.

"I apologize for intruding," Jonnie said. "But I understand you were an associate of Cyril Phelps."

Reeling from the lack of sleep and the unexpected appearance, Paul needed every ounce and inch and sinew of his self-control not to leap up, flip the table, and bolt off. His mind fumbled desperately to sort out the words. It was like a palsied hand attempting to insert a key into a keyhole.

"Using the term loosely," he managed.

"I don't want to take up more of your time than I must," Jonnie said. "So I'll get straight to it. I am taking his place."

Paul felt the full impact of the statement, but his mind pushed back with a feeble hope. Cyril after all had been an actual reporter. "Congratulations," he said. "*The Times* is a prestigious newspaper. I read it myself every now and again."

"*The Times*. The other as well." Jonnie lowered his voice. "We would like you to continue working with us."

"Us," Paul repeated stupidly.

"The terms will be the same," Jonnie said. This was accompanied by a look which mingled friendliness with solemn earnestness. Somewhere within that barely restrained eagerness and open-heartedness, Paul glimpsed the child who used to come flying across the cobblestones in Liverpool, flinging himself into the air, all shrieks and giggles, believing, knowing, trusting his uncle would catch him, would never let him fall, would never let him injure himself. The terror of seeing a flicker of recognition in Jonnie's eyes suddenly transformed itself into a severe stab of disappointment.

"That is to say." Jonnie's smile was wavering in the face of Paul's on-going stupefaction. "Your compensation. Three pounds a week for the registries and twenty pounds for news of, shall we say, an especially sensational nature."

As these words soaked into Paul's paralyzed brain, they gradually stimulated it back into life. Cyril the dandy, Cyril with the Saville Row bespoke frock coats, the Lock's of St. James's hats. The underlying fact was no surprise. He had long suspected that Cyril insisted on verifiable names so he could pad out an expense sheet. No, the fact was not surprising, but the amounts were. Paul's three pounds a week over two years must have made a tidy contribution towards a gentleman's wardrobe. And there was no guessing how many pieces of trumped-up rubbish, at twenty pounds per, he had to his credit. For the second time recently, Paul had to stop himself from bursting out laughing at the part of the fool he had played, the fool he had played consciously, willingly, and above all, consummately.

He packed his laughter into a congenial smile. "Please, Mr. – Forgive me, what did you say your name is?"

"Chandler. Jonathan Chandler."

Paul limited his hailstorm of questions to, "Is this a permanent position for you? Will you be living in Monaco?"

Jonnie hesitated before answering, "At least until the matter of Phelps' death is resolved. Can you tell me what he might have been looking into when he died?"

Paul decided he might as well say it. No telling what Cyril had passed along to his superiors. "Phelps was always peering under more rocks than I knew anything about. But there were some questions surrounding the death of an American at the Hôtel de Paris, Joseph Murphy by name, from San Francisco." How refreshingly quaint, to be speaking the unblemished truth at such a time. He supposed the two creases that appeared between Jonnie's eyes had everything to do with Lily Turner.

"What kinds of questions?"

"Let's just say I believe I should have some news of the twenty-pound variety soon enough."

Paul pushed his chair back and laid a few coins on the table as he spoke. He knew where he had to go, and he had to get there before meeting up with Wycliffe and Lily.

The "matter of Phelps' death" must be resolved quickly, so Jonnie could be on his way back to England. Whatever had gotten Cyril killed wasn't going to kill Jonnie. The drunken sailor Bruno tossed out of Pierre's a couple of nights ago had sounded like he had a clue. After following that lead, Paul would buy a gun and put it to Lily's head if she didn't tell him everything she knew about Joseph Murphy, about Sally Holmes, about the Gallaghers, about Wycliffe, about Mrs. Murphy, about every person on the planet. That baboon, Wycliffe, was undoubtedly withholding information as well. There could be no gun to his head. It would be too hard not to pull the trigger.

"Where are you lodging?" Paul said.

"The Hôtel de Paris."

"Just so. One o'clock tomorrow. I'll meet you in the lobby."

# Wednesday, March 18, 1914
## LA CAVE DU RENARD

"THAT SAILOR WILL NEVER FIND HER," BRUNO SAID, refusing to adopt Paul's subdued tone. "He is too stupid to find his own toes."

"It is not about him. It is more serious than that." Beneath the table, Paul tapped his fist against his thigh. He had arrived at Pierre's with no time to spare. Having to coax this love-sick fool into cooperating was putting a severe strain on his patience.

"You tell me," Bruno insisted. "I will tell her." A menacing scowl backed up the demand.

From the corner of his eye, Paul could see Pierre's attention fixed on the conversation. Unfortunately, the gormless Bruno was the only person who would admit to knowing where Sylvie lived.

Paul shook his head and ominously lowered his voice. "This involves powerful people, people from the hotels and the villas. You should not put yourself in danger. If you were injured or God forbid worse, who would watch out for her then?"

Apparently unable to visualize himself injured, let alone dead, Bruno remained unmoved.

Paul said, "Blindfold me. Stay while I'm there. I must

make sure she understands the danger she is in."

"I will tell her."

Paul threw up his hands. "Good, you tell her."

He pressed his palms against the tabletop and leaned in. The big man's breath was a toxic medley of plentiful garlic, infected gums, and spoiled cheese, with a soupçon of stale beer.

"Will she believe you?" Paul hissed.

# Wednesday, March 18, 1914

PAUL DIVIDED HIS STRIDES BETWEEN SKIPPING AND limping as he labored to keep up with Bruno through the warren of narrow lanes, ascending and descending shallow steps, past plastered and stone houses with shutters that hadn't felt paint for years. To his immense relief, after only ten minutes, they stopped outside a low doorway covered by a dingy brown oilcloth. The pathway ran between three-story buildings on each side, so natural light was at best discouraged. An old, fat mongrel lay in the doorway, oblivious or wise to the black cat rubbing its back against the wall and strenuously meowing. After motioning at Paul to park himself on the opposite side, Bruno stepped over the dog and pushed aside the makeshift portière. The shrieking of an angry woman followed. Shortly later, the big man put his arm outside the doorway and beckoned.

"*Sacré bleu*," Paul mumbled as the sickening odor assaulted his nose. A marginal amount of light crept through the solitary soiled window-pane. A dead oil-lantern, its glass broken, hung from a beam overhead. A spent candle was the only thing on the table. Much of the space was absorbed by the straw cot on which Sylvie lay beneath a cloth of indeterminate lineage and color. Long tangles of oily black hair fell to her shoulders as she raised herself on one elbow. Her face and neck were extremely dirty or badly bruised or both.

While Bruno performed his version of a formal introduction, Paul peered into the gloom, searching for somewhere to sit and relieve his leg. This impulse was squelched immediately by an instinct for self-preservation. He didn't want his trousers to touch anything in the revolting filth. He didn't even like having the soles of his boots against the dirt floor. He had not expected a Turkish mattress covered with white cashmere and scented petals, but he definitely could have done without the smashed chair and broken pottery littering the floor, not to mention the heap of rotting cabbages, potatoes, and onions in one corner.

Bruno apparently had received his marching orders before Paul entered. Following the introduction, he stepped out the doorway without further comment or instruction. Paul disliked standing over the supine woman with his hat in his hands like a supplicant. However, he didn't want to place it on the table. It would be better off tossed out the door. He hitched up the fabric of his trousers and squatted beside the cot. His right knee howled with pain, forcing him to reach down to secure his balance. He was certain he felt lice racing up his arm as he studied Sylvie's blackened eyes, bruised neck, swollen jaw, and cut lip. Even though she looked like she was well into her thirties, Paul estimated she was in her early twenties. Like anyone who worked in conditions which demanded exceptional physical and mental endurance, the stresses on her body told early.

"You look like you were in a fight with a panther," he said. Her sullen eyes grew more resentful. "Did your protector do that to you?" What depth of stupidity did it take to incapacitate one's own work animal? "Or was it a customer?"

Her lips drew back to reveal the rotten teeth. "Did you come to get your ashes hauled, Englishman? It is my time of month. Come back next week."

"Irresistible as are your charms, I am not here because of them. If you please, I wish to talk to you about last Sunday night, when you were with the sailor."

The room's temperature instantly dropped about twenty degrees as Sylvie's sullenness turned to artic coldness. It was as good as anything a British blueblood could have mustered.

"Three nights ago," Paul said. "German sailor, off a yacht."

"Do you have a cigarette?"

"I will get you one after we talk."

"I want it now."

"It will not take long to tell me." Paul's knee was insisting on that.

"My sister is coming this afternoon. She has three sons, going on four. She said she would come yesterday and the day before. She always says she will come. She goes to Monique every day. Every day she goes to Monique. The four-year-old, he eats too much oranges."

Fighting back his revulsion of the grime invading his pores, Paul placed his knuckles against the floor to push himself into a standing position. He wiped the back of his hand with his handkerchief while Sylvie rambled about her father, about the other whores, about a song, about a dog, about the fruit-saturated nephew, and Yves, who was, Paul assumed, her pimp. Perhaps her monthlies made her crazy. Or perhaps nicotine was not the only poison her system was running low on. She resurrected memories of the rum-fits his father would have when he was too sick to go out for gin and Paul heartlessly refused to do it for him. That was always good for another beating. The word "cliff" put a stop to the reminiscences.

"Did you hear me, Englishman?"

He had been gazing in the direction of the window, wanting to spare his eyes and more importantly his sympathy

339

from the sight of the pathetic creature on the straw. His father was not the only ghost Sylvie evoked. If Paul had been a man given to spitting in the wind, he would have counseled Bruno about the uselessness of trying to rescue Sylvie. Look at what trying to help Sophie had gotten him: charged with a murder he could never prove he didn't commit.

He turned. "Yes, Mademoiselle."

"You want to know about the men, don't you? Those goddamned German men and the cliff."

If forced to confess only the most stringent truth, Paul would have to say he did *not* want to know. The "goddamned" Germans was right. Why couldn't they stick to roulette like everyone else? "Yes," he answered stiffly. "The Germans. And the cliff."

Her expression twisted into a grotesque mime of seduction. She delivered a long, slow wink, then extended her opened palm towards him, curling one finger back at a time. Where had she picked up that gesture? Perhaps she had seen it used by the plastered girls of the boulevard, the ones who were refused entrance to the Casino but were admitted to a barely respectable *table d'hôte*, where men played baccarat after dinner on a wine-stained tablecloth. For a prostitute of Sylvie's class, who plied their trade on their feet against a wall in dark alleyways, a move into that world would have been a long step up the professional ladder.

"You are going to get me some cigarettes?" she said in a high, wheedling voice.

"After we talk."

Her eyes narrowed, then her eyelids lowered. Paul thought he was going to lose her to unconsciousness.

"I am listening, Mademoiselle."

She literally lifted herself into awareness. Opening her eyes, she struggled into a fully upright position, grunting with pain throughout the maneuver. Her dark eyes were like those of the feral cats which roamed the streets and hills around Monaco.

"This sailor," she began, "he was going to rent a room. Then he says, 'But no. It is a beautiful night. The sky and the sea call for us. Let us love under the shining stars.'"

Paul wanted to ask what language the sailor used to utter these poetic flights of seduction but decided it didn't matter.

"Beautiful night, my ass. It is freezing at night, even when you do not take off your clothes. You try it sometime, Monsieur."

"Maybe next week."

She produced a wide smile, once more revealing the missing and darkened teeth. "Certainly, next week," she said, disconcerting Paul with the thought that she believed her prospects for the immediate future to be settled.

"Continue," he prompted.

"You are rich, Englishman?"

Paul's sense of urgency was welling again. He forced himself to keep his voice level. "Continue with the story about the night with the sailor."

Sylvie's eyes shifted to calculating. "But yes, the sailor. He has not only the money, but the bottle of wine—two bottles of wine—and he has the cigarettes and a lighter, one of those that works on the deck of a ship, in the wind, on the top of a bluff, anywhere. It is what the sailors use. But this sailor, he had all this, and he wanted us to pretend we are blind. Not that I have trouble with that. You live in Monaco among these thieves and brigands, you are blind and deaf, mute too, from birth. So it is not me who has the trouble. It is him. Trembling scared, he is. Cannot finish what we go for. I was amazed he did not piss all over me."

She looked squarely at Paul. "I need that cigarette."

341

He had to hand it to her for the timing, perfect. He looked at his feet, slowly shaking his head. "After you finish, I will be pleased to provide you with a whole pouch of tobacco with papers."

"Send Bruno," she commanded.

After The Oak had departed with an order for bread, hard-boiled eggs, a tin of soup, an *ordinaire* of wine, and candles, in addition to the tobacco, Paul said, "Continue."

On Sunday night, Sylvie said, she and the sailor, whose name she had forgotten or never known, sat on a bluff overlooking a sliver of land at the water's edge, taking turns at a bottle of wine. The much vaunted lighter failed to ignite and the man had, with a show of disgust, walked to the edge and tossed it away, muttering oaths in German. Sylvie resolved to return the next day to look for it. That had proved impossible.

After draining the first bottle of wine, the sailor decided it was time for affection and leaned against a boulder. Sylvie, feeling the wine and frustrated for want of a cigarette, was proceeding to get on with business when they heard low voices, approaching on the same trail she and her customer had followed. The pair froze in the shadow of the boulder. The moonlight was repeatedly broken by the coming and going of clouds, but she could see four men standing where the sailor had stood to dispose of his lighter. One of the men was bound and gagged. All except the prisoner wore gray military uniforms. She had enough custom among different nationalities to distinguish the more common languages. When the others spoke to the prisoner, she was sure it was in English. She thought they spoke German among themselves. She was very sure her companion understood them because, from time to time, he would be gripped by tension after something was said. There were two guns and a knife, which they waved in front of the man's face as they said things to him in English. They would talk to him for a while and then confer among themselves for a while. She was glad the lighter hadn't worked. Smoking might have given her and the sailor away.

Sylvie knew what to do in this kind of situation, but she had nothing but disdain for her companion. She longed for something to stifle his sounds. Each time one of the uniformed men stuffed a cloth in their prisoner's mouth and proceeded to nick his throat with the knife, she was sure the sailor was going to scream. Had he never seen a bar-fight? Had he never seen a man cut? Eventually, the bound man let loose with a long rift. His words obviously didn't please his captors because they were cut short by a choking, gurgling sound. With the swift movements of the well practiced, the men cut the cords and pushed the man off the cliff.

After Sylvie stopped speaking, Paul regarded her in silence, letting his mind absorb and slowly dispel the vision she had conjured. He leaned out the doorway and saw Bruno, clutching a basket with his enormous fist, approaching from the far-end of the pathway.

When Paul turned back, his voice was creased by honest curiosity. "Sylvie, you are deaf. You are blind. You are mute. As you said, you come by these qualities naturally. You must know the danger you are in because of what you saw. So why did you tell me all this?"

# Wednesday, March 18, 1914
## VILLA ILE DE FRANCE

LILY LOOKED BACK AND SAW TED STANDING BESIDE the driver's door, rolling his fist across the small of his back. Paul grimaced as his right foot landed on the ground. Looking up at her, he said, "When you get to be our ages, you'll find the hinges get a little rusty."

She wanted to soak them both in boiling brine. The arrival of the wired funds from Fran this morning had blown the lid off her sufferance of these two fools. The one week she had spent with them had given her a far better understanding of an eternity in hell than the nuns had managed to browbeat into her in seven years. She was leaving for Paris tomorrow. If Sally didn't return before then, Lily would mail the information about Bridget Rose's responsibility for the attempted poisoning along with a bill for one-hundred dollars and hope for the best. If Paul didn't hand over her half of the reward plus half the advance he extracted from Ted, she would kill him. The thought of what she should receive from Paul temporarily mollified her feelings towards him. Half of 12,500 and half of another 5,000 would total almost as much as she would have reaped from collecting the stated reward for the necklace alone. Her doubts returned. She had no means of enforcing the debt should he renege.

No mitigation was available for her ill-will towards Ted. She had scraped her nerves raw by forcing herself to be civil, if not pleasant, to him during the ride out. She was determined he would never know how appalled she had been by the gown the seamstress brought to her room that morning. The garish red-velvet abomination was designed to cling so tightly it would have needed to be sewn onto her. The fitted sleeves, which came to a sharp point just above her fingers, only emphasized the *décolleté* neckline. While the woman unpacked her basket, Lily disappeared into the bedroom to boil over. Eventually, she persuaded herself that she was on trial in this, her first paying job as a detective, not for Ted, but for herself. She would prove she was capable of submerging her pride, her stubbornness, her — Effie's word — contrariness and see the job through. The fact that she felt nothing but disdain for Ted Wycliffe made the situation all the more suitable as a crucible.

She stepped under the filigreed baldachin at the villa's front before she realized she had left the old men and their troublesome joints behind. She saw Paul had removed the necklace from the chamois bag and was dangling it before Ted's face. They looked like children, dazzled only by the sparkle.

Adding to Lily's bad mood was another memory which had broken the surface this morning. Maybe it was the additional distance she had put between herself and Effie by coming to Monaco, which had only reinforced the barrier of stubborn silence erected last year. Maybe that was what was unearthing these old thoughts and feelings. At any rate, after convincing herself to don the costume, she had stood perfectly still, allowing the woman to take her measurements. While in this position, she found herself transported back to Chicago, back half a lifetime.

345

It was after they moved to the big house and Effie had gone downstairs for the night. Listening to the vague sounds of music and conversations and laughter coming from the front of the house, a ten-year-old Lily sneaked into Effie's room to rummage through the magnificent wardrobe. She had felt inexpressibly grand lying on the thick feather-mattress of the four-poster bed, smothering in a fur-lined opera cloak. Next, she slipped one of the creamy silk gowns over her head. Because Effie was a petite woman and Lily was tall for her age, the gown wasn't overly large. She had curtsied and flirted outrageously with herself in the full-length mirror.

Unfortunately, she failed to foresee the awful price she would have to pay for the impertinence. Within a month, she was exiled to Pennsylvania, condemned to live under the thumbs of those freakish nuns, condemned never to see Piedmont again. Effie always denied that the one event led to the other. She steadfastly maintained that Lily's enrollment at Mount Saint Joseph's Academy had been put in motion long before, that it was what was best for Lily, that it was not to get her out of Effie's hair. As a child, Lily had been unable to believe this. A part of her still could not.

When Ted rang the bells, a different liveried footman opened the door. The two men were escorted to a room at the opposite side of the patio while Lily seated herself on the same cushioned bench beneath the vaulted arches where she had sat before searching Bridget's room.

It was all Paul's fault, she brooded. She could be on her way to Paris and her new life instead of cooling her heels in this monument to conspicuous consumption, waiting to be accosted either by Murderess No. 1, Mrs. Murphy, or by Murderess No. 2, Bridget Rose. It was all Paul's fault, and she still had no idea what crime she was helping him commit by securing an entrance to Krenz's. She could only hope he didn't assassinate the Great Man before he had handed over her money. As for Jonathan Chandler, after setting her up for entrapment by Paul, he should count himself as the luckiest man who ever drew a breath if she never laid eyes on him again.

Her brooding stopped when Paul emerged from the room. He slowed as he passed a tapestry, running a finger along its bottom edge. When he took a place on the bench beside her, Lily did not look at him.

He said, "It would appear the baroness is another one of those who is unembarrassed by her riches."

Lily made no reply.

He said, "I have been dismissed. I assume to allow the man to make his appraisal without the intimidation of my presence. Splendid woman, your employer. Once she deigns to shine the light of her countenance upon a person, she is extraordinarily generous in giving him the benefit of her prejudices. She treated the jeweler like he was there to pocket the spoons and me like I was going to smash up the china. But that's neither here nor there, is it? What do you say we take a turn out of doors?"

This time, Lily did look at him.

"That's right," he said. "We need to talk."

# Wednesday, March 18, 1914
## VILLA ILE DE FRANCE,
## CAP FERRAT, FRANCE

THE WHITE GRAVEL CRUNCHED CRISPLY BENEATH their boots as they crossed the wide space carved out of the olive trees for the motorcars. As at Roquebrune, Paul took Lily's elbow to steer her towards a trail leading along the edge of the property away from the villa. After traveling about ten yards, they stopped. To their left, red-tiled roofs flecked the trees below on Cap Ferrat. To their right, lay another area cleared of trees. The space smelled of freshly turned earth and contained a vast accumulation of ancient stone-works. Haphazardly spread around were marble busts, full-length statues, large urns, bare plinths, a Gallo-Roman bench, an artificial grotto, several ephebes, and at least one sarcophagus. Scattered among those were amphorae, sun-dials, and bas-relief disks. At the back, a pile of marble columns looked like someone had exploded a pound or two of dynamite among them.

Paul studied the artifacts. "I've always wondered what became of the Parthenon's missing parts," he said, then turned to look towards Villefranche Bay. His thoughtful gaze seemed to focus on nothing in particular.

Lily stepped in front of him, blocking his view and whatever he was contemplating. "When do I get my money?" she said.

"Must you always be so mercenary?"

"That's certainly the cauldron calling the kettle black. When do I get my money?"

"I assume neither you nor Mrs. Gallagher made substitutions in the stones, so it can be pronounced whole?"

"Of course not. But what if they make a substitution or cut a deal with the jeweler? Maybe that's why they wanted you out of the way."

"You must learn to trust people."

She glowered at him.

He said, "I told them I had my own man verify the principal stones using the insurance papers Wycliffe gave me."

"Did you?"

"Have someone look at it? No. It's only important they think I did. Either way, I got the money from Ted this morning, and they're not getting it back."

"Do you think I won't keep my end of the bargain if you give me the money before tonight? You must learn to trust people."

"Tell me, were you more surprised or relieved when I fetched up at the hotel today with the necklace?" he countered.

"Did Ted give you the 5,000 francs? I have no doubt you're intending to keep it."

"Tonight. I'll give you all your money after Krenz's."

"If you get caught picking pockets there, I'm not going to bail you out."

"You underestimate me. But that's not what I wanted to talk to you about."

"What now? We made a deal. What else do you want?"

"I want your roommate, Sally Holmes."

349

Lily mouthed the name silently, then spun on her heel and started away. Paul grabbed her arm, none too gently. She glared over her shoulder at his face, then down at his hand gripping just above her elbow, then back at his face.

Releasing her arm, he said, "Michael Gallagher told us last night about some documents Joseph Murphy had with him. That's what I must speak with Miss Holmes about."

"Why ask me? I never said anything about her."

He put his hands on her shoulders and seemed about to shake her. "You didn't have to. And stop lying to me. I've got Time's Winged Chariot doing a flamenco on my back, and I don't have the luxury of waiting for you to spool out your secrets one a day."

When she said nothing, he loosened his grip but did not remove his hands.

He said, "Her room was torn up the same as Mrs. Murphy's, and she's no longer there. She's with you."

He dropped his arms to his sides. "Look, I still don't know whether Joseph Murphy was running with the hares or hunting with the hounds, but this much I do know. There was another man interested in Joseph Murphy who was murdered recently. That girl could be in serious danger, and so could you."

"How did you know her room was searched?"

Paul said nothing.

Lily said, "The people who tore up the rooms, they were looking for those documents, not money like Ted thinks."

Paul nodded. "They pose no threat to you or to her. However, she must get rid of those papers and get rid of them in the right place."

Lily gave a derisive chuff. "And the right place is into your unrighteous hands? Why should she trust you?"

"You have me there. Why don't we let her decide for herself? I want only —"

He was interrupted by the sound of the motorcar's engine sputtering to life on the other side of the trees. He looked hard at Lily. Her look of defiance had been replaced by uncertainty.

"I don't know where Sally is," she said. "She left Monte Carlo Monday. I don't know when she'll return. I don't know if she'll return."

# Wednesday, March 18, 1914
## HÔTEL DE PARIS

LILY'S FOOT BEAT AGAINST THE FLOOR AS SHE WAITED for the American couple to suspend their arguing long enough to conclude their business with the hotel's desk-clerk. She had tried in vain to catch his eye. All she needed was her room key. He could pass it to her with scarcely a break in his concentration on the couple.

"I don't see why we have to go rushing off to Nice just because there's a new hotel. I don't like the name," the woman said. Her face was barely visible over the collar of a white-ermine coat. "It sounds too foreign, too African. When I send letters home, I want the stationary to sound French."

Few words had been spoken among the three passengers during the ride back from Cap Ferrat. For once, the throttle-valve on Ted's luxuriant vanity and supernatural ability to bore was shut tight. Paul's face had looked like it was set in marble, his eyes as blank as those on an ancient Roman bust. But he had continued to simmer in the bad humor he had exhibited back at the Acropolis. Lily could sense his tension in the hands that never moved, in the eyes that barely blinked.

"But, my dear," the man said as he read the statement the clerk presented, "it was designed by the same architect who decorated this place. It is very, very French."

This afternoon, Paul had overturned yet another of Lily's assumptions. She had believed the vandals were seeking Mr. Murphy's money. When it came down to it, so did Ted. However, according to Paul, it was a bunch of papers they were after. That truth might interest Ted, but it didn't matter to her whether they were looking for documents or the Crown Jewels of Ireland. It was all the same to her, nothing.

She watched as the American signed a Cook's traveler-check with the solemnity of a signatory to the Declaration of Independence. He blotted the ink repeatedly, as though the future of Western Civilization depended upon its remaining crisp through the ages.

The clerk looked at her expectantly. Unless he had received a hard blow to the head since yesterday, he knew her and her room number perfectly well. He usually handed over the key along with a pleasantry without her having to ask. Jonathan said she had turned a few heads at the hotel. If this clerk were one, there was no flattery there.

As the pair gathered themselves for their disputatious departure, she opened her mouth to speak. Before she could utter the first syllable, a man on the other side of the couple blurted, "Excuse me. Excuse me. I'm in a terrible hurry."

The clerk flashed Lily an apologetic smile and addressed the usurper. "If you please, Monsieur," he said, "Mademoiselle —"

From behind, she heard, "Miss Turner. Lily." The weakness in her knees identified the speaker before her brain did. She signaled to the clerk to take care of Mr. Etiquette.

"Mr. Chandler, I thought you must have ...." She searched for the words, then decided to leave it at full-stop. Let him figure out what she thought he *must have.*

"I was hoping to see you," he said. "I didn't want merely to leave a note although I would have if it had come to that."

353

He looked like she was supposed to provide the cue for the next line. She said nothing. He was going to have to make his way to the finish unassisted.

He shot a look towards the front door, then back to her. "I wanted very much to speak to you."

She said, "Unless I'm hallucinating, you are speaking to me." Mr. Etiquette crossed her line of vision behind Jonathan. She held up a finger. "Excuse me."

To the desk-clerk she said, as if he didn't know, "Room 203, Turner. My key, if you please."

Jonathan glanced again at the front door. "I apologize. I was called away suddenly. It was inexcusable not to give you notice when I couldn't meet you at the Oceanographic Museum. Inexcusable but unavoidable. I would like to go into it now, but I have an appointment."

"Indeed, I know how punctilious you are about your appointments."

Jonathan's hands were rotating his hat by the brim like it was a steering wheel. "I deserve that and more. Meet me this evening. I'll bring the molten iron, cat o' nines, whatever you want to use for punishing me. As much as I would like, I cannot explain now. Someone is waiting outside, but I swear to you, this evening I'll be wherever you say, whatever time you say."

Not in her most fantastic hallucination could Lily have imagined herself as profoundly grateful as she was in this moment to Paul Newcastle for forcing her to accompany him to Winzig Krenz's villa. "No," she said without the slightest tinge of regret. "Tonight will not be possible."

"Tomorrow?"

Only if he intended to be on the train to Paris. "Leave your address here at the desk," she said. "I'll let you know." It wasn't the first lie she had ever told.

The privacy placard was on the knob of Room 203, but the warmth spilling out as Lily pushed open the door said Sally had a fire going. She lowered the embroidery hoop in her hand and smiled. The shorter, dyed hair was all that remained of the disguise. The shaded glasses rested on the table next to door, and the cane leaned against the wall. Her body was reasserting its natural curves beneath the pink dressing-gown.

Lily turned the lock, crossed her arms over her chest, and leaned against the door, willing her internal agitation to quieten, unable to decide whether she was more angry with Jonathan for disappearing or for returning.

After pouring a generous measure of whiskey, she sat to remove her boots. Then she undid the top two buttons on her gray dress and sat back to sip the drink and watch Sally at work with her needle. There was a comforting air of domesticity in the scene. Lily felt herself slipping into the same soft, soothing feelings she used to have when she would sit and watch Piedmont rolling pie-dough on a pastry cloth. When finished, she always shook the flour remaining on the cloth back into the bin.

Sally looked up when Lily lowered herself onto the footstool. The small fingers continued pushing the needle and thread along the stenciled pattern.

"I'm leaving Monte Carlo tomorrow," Lily said, "for good."

"And Madeline?" Sally asked, her eyes on her needlework.

"I'm leaving on my own. My partner and I, our agency, we have a job in Paris. As far as I know, Mrs. Murphy and her entourage will stay another two weeks as planned. I've not heard anything different."

Sally's hand patted along the sofa's cushion until it landed on a pair of scissors. She snipped the thread. "Congratulations — for you and your partner, I mean. The White Star liner should be docking any day now. Joe and I will be gone by the end of the week too. May I stay here until tomorrow morning? I'll make other arrangements after that."

"As you like, but a few other things came up while you were away which we might want to discuss."

"Yes?" Sally said.

"First, Mr. Newcastle has asked that you agree to meet with him. He is interested in some military documents Mr. Murphy had. Those documents are the reason the rooms were searched, yours and Mr. Murphy's suite. Mr. Newcastle either wants the papers for himself or he's helping another person find them. I don't know which."

Sally displayed no sign that the subject held any interest for her. She leaned over the thread-box and sorted through the various packets before selecting a deep violet.

"Another thing," Lily said, "Chief Inspector Gautier told Mr. Wycliffe that Mr. Murphy attended parties at the villa of a German named Winzig Krenz. Does that name mean anything to you?"

Sally shook her head.

Lily said, "I suspect there's a connection between the papers and Krenz because Paul Newcastle has insisted that I go with him to that man's house tonight."

Sally held the needle towards the window, backlighting the narrow aperture so she could insert the thread. "Tonight?" she said.

"Tonight. Don't tell me you had something special planned for us."

Sally decoupled the hoops in order to reposition the cloth. "If I had but known it was to be our last night, I would have."

Lily got to her feet and paced the length of the room twice before returning to stand in front of the sofa. "Until this afternoon, when Mr. Newcastle told me otherwise, I thought the people who tore up the rooms were looking for money, for cash or bearer bonds or something like that."

Sally was staring at her in the same way Balaam must have stared at his ass. "Why on earth would I have sewn money into my mattress and dressmaker's manikin? Or the better question is, why on earth would you think someone believed I had sewn money into my mattress and manikin?"

Lily lowered herself onto the stool once more and related the story of the telegrams and Mrs. Murphy's comments on their meaning. She omitted the hysterics and histrionics.

Sally hooked the needle through the linen twice to park it and placed the needlework on the cushion. "May I join you?" she said, indicating the empty glass in Lily's hand.

After they were equipped with two whiskies, Sally said, "If you went looking, if you raked the four corners of the earth, you would never find a less reliable witness to Joe Murphy's character than Madeline Wycliffe Murphy. She is on far more intimate terms with Cerberus than she ever was with her husband. Joe was not so stupid nor so naïve as to convert his holdings into cash and haul it around in trunks. That's absurd. It's true that he liquidated his assets. But when each transaction was completed, he immediately transferred the funds to Baring Brothers in London. He had also spent considerable time looking for suitable investments in Europe." Her eyes drifted away from Lily's as her finger edged over the rim of the glass as though she were going to stir the drink with it.

She brought herself back with a sigh. "Joe wasn't going to return to San Francisco with Madeline. He was going to board the liner in Monte Carlo as if he were, but he would have disembarked along with the rest of the visitors before it sailed. They had separate staterooms and could barely abide the sight of one another. Madeline wouldn't have discovered

357

his absence until well past the coast of Portugal, possibly not until New York City. He thought it best for the health and safety of them both if she learned of his defection from afar. He in no way trusted her violent temper." Sally again fell silent, possibly to contemplate the might-have-been.

She canted her head and frowned. "How did Mr. Newcastle know I was with you?"

"Some way or other, he figured it out. Maybe someone saw you leaving this room. Maybe that floor-waiter, Dominique, told him about my visiting you. Maybe he's been window-peeping. I don't know."

"Did you tell him I would meet him?" Sally said.

"I told him I would ask you."

The knock on the door startled Lily and pasted fear on Sally's face.

"Is that him?" Sally whispered.

"Not by my invitation," Lily said.

# Wednesday, March 18, 1914
## HÔTEL DE PARIS

SALLY SLOWLY CIRCLED THE CHAIR OVER WHICH THE red-velvet monstrosity lay draped. She stopped to let her index finger trace the silk-piping on the edge of the scooped neckline.

"I told you I was going to Winzig Krenz's this evening," Lily said.

Sally gave a sly wink. "In style, no less."

Lily took the gown to the bedroom, out of sight. When she returned, Sally was rearranging a burning log with the poker.

"So you will know, I asked for my luggage to be sent up," Lily said. "In case it comes after I leave this evening, you may answer the door if you like. That's up to you. It's nothing to me now if the hotel finds you here."

Sally nodded her agreement and returned the poker to its stand.

Lily said, "I would prefer to have a better idea of what I'm getting myself into tonight. Mr. Newcastle didn't say why he wanted to go there, but I know he wants those documents. There's something else. He told me another man interested in Mr. Murphy has been killed. He didn't elaborate on the circumstances, and I didn't have time to ask. He said he wanted me to stress the potential of danger to you, to us.

What should I know before I go there tonight? Was Mr. Murphy trying to sell the papers? Is that why he went to see Winzig Krenz?"

Sally intertwined her fingers and tapped her thumbs lightly against her lips. Lily could practically hear what was going on in Sally's head: *Once upon a time, in a land far, far away* ....

Sally said, "I have no idea why the chief inspector said what he did, but I can tell you Joe had nothing to do with that man, Krenz. I've never heard of him before. I don't know exactly what the documents contained. Joe bought a German dictionary and made an attempt at deciphering them. No one can deconstruct a complex text in an unknown tongue using only a dictionary. However, we were able to discern that they were military in character and contained immensely detailed logistical data. They looked official. Joe was determined to understand them in order to know what should be done with them. It gave him a challenge to tackle, a problem to solve, when Madeline was in town and he couldn't be with me. He put out some inquiries, got some names, and vetted these as well as he could, which, given the circumstances, was not very well. No one was perfect, but he visited three candidates before identifying the one he thought would suit best. I won't say his efforts were desultory, but this wasn't his life's mission either.

"This is what I keep telling you. Joe was a good man. I don't mean that he walked on water and cured cripples, but he was a highly ethical man. He had possession of those papers by chance, and they aroused his curiosity. He wanted to see that they were properly handled. He wouldn't have sold them. Why should he? He didn't need the money."

Maybe, Lily thought, but for some people, and often it was the very rich, the word *enough* never applied to money.

"Joe settled on Hervé Andreas. You might think it odd that he would select a man released not long ago from prison, but Joe had his own ideas about things. He said he would never completely trust a man with the kind of friends who could see to it his record was kept spotless. After meeting with Andreas, he told me it was imperative the documents be turned over to the proper authorities. He wanted to discover a way to approach the right official with them. Andreas offered to help, but Joe was skeptical of his motives. I'm sure it was Andreas who turned over the rooms. No one else knew about the documents."

Lily smiled inwardly, once at Chief Inspector Gautier's subterfuge with the dictionary and again as she pictured herself whispering the name *Andreas* into Paul's ear.

Sally went on, "It was essential, Joe said, that they not fall into the wrong hands. The right hands were one thing. The wrong hands, another." As if to emphasize her choice of words, Sally massaged one hand with the other. "The wrong hands would be German hands. So you see, Joe would never have tried to sell those documents to Winzig Krenz or to any of his compatriots."

"All right," Lily conceded. "Mr. Murphy wasn't there to market papers. Mr. Wycliffe has put forward the thesis that he visited Krenz because he was seeking help in arming Irish rebels."

Sally's look of amazement appeared to be perfectly genuine, but Lily had come to appreciate how perfectly genuine Sally was capable of appearing while she was lying through her perfectly white teeth.

"That's also absurd. Joe would never do that. And I told you I never heard of this Krenz."

Lily decided to call Sally on the illogical stance she liked to adopt. "If you didn't know what Mr. Murphy was doing when he wasn't with you, how do you know he wasn't out buying guns for Irish rebels?"

"Because Joe would never put a single gun in anyone's hand. He and I agreed completely with Miss Addams, Bernard Shaw, Tolstoy, a host of other right-thinking people. No society can lay claim to advancement until it has fully incorporated a commitment to nonviolence. It's an unpopular principle, and it was one of the things that united Joe and me. He said, 'The meek shall inherit the earth, all right, but only after the powerful have finished plundering and blowing it up.' He believed it was up to the rest of us to bring violence to heel. 'You don't do that by feeding it,' he said. I think his philosophy had a lot to do with his upbringing in Pennsylvania. He never said much about it, but we know from what's gone on with all the coal strikes, those are rough places.

"Even if he hadn't been a pacifist, Joe would never have given his hard-earned money to those murderers. He liked helping his fellow Irishmen because he understood only too well they oftentimes don't get a fair shake. But he wasn't filiopietistic. He was third-generation American. He marveled at those expatriates who speak of Ireland as though she were a living, breathing sweetheart or mother. In other words, he simply was not enamored with the calls for Irish freedom."

Sally's fingers drummed against the sides of her crossed arms. Red spots had blossomed on her cheeks, but when she spoke her voice was matter-of-fact. "Joe told Madeline he would make this trip only after I agreed to stay in Europe with him, not forever, but for one or two years. Before we left the States, Joe visited his attorney and made me his beneficiary in a new will."

At last, Lily thought, an assumption that hadn't been turned on its head.

"Madeline will learn that as soon as she gets back to

San Francisco. But that's the other reason I'm certain Joe wasn't buying weapons. The funds, all of them, were put in my name, another remove from Madeline. We established a relationship with a bank in San Remo that was working with us and Barings for the interim. I confirmed this morning that all of Joe's money that was supposed to be at Barings was there."

Lily reflected that Ted's theory of an arms-conspiracy rested on three things: the tickets to Belfast, the German dictionary, and the visits to Krenz's villa. The tickets were for the Gallaghers, and Sally had just explained the dictionary. The ransacking of the rooms had not been, as Ted asserted, Germans looking for Mr. Murphy's cash-hoard. Maybe the visits to Krenz's villa were only for playing cards or flirting with other women. If so, Mr. Murphy certainly wouldn't have told Sally about it.

Sally said, "I'm not disputing Mr. Newcastle's warning of dire danger. We have ample evidence of that. Have you turned up anything on the potential assassins?"

Lily bit down on her lower lip. This was it, the one-hundred-dollar opportunity. It wouldn't last long, and it wouldn't come again. There had been a promise to Michael Gallagher. She and Paul had assured him nothing he told them would go any further. That promise was a part of her hesitation, but it was more, much more, than that. It was because against all their desires, against all their best interests, the Gallaghers remained in bondage to Mrs. Murphy. It was because Piedmont said her sister had opened her veins in an outbuilding, so she wouldn't make a mess in the house for someone else to clean up. It was because Effie would never say where Piedmont had gone after Lily was sent away, where she had gone or when. It was because of a coarse black coat.

"No," Lily said. She might have passed along Bridget's assertion that Mrs. Murphy was in Monte Carlo the night Mr. Murphy was shot, but she decided to file that under "Sleeping Dogs" also.

Looking at the watch pinned to her bodice, she said, "I must get ready for tonight. What shall I tell Mr. Newcastle?"

"You may tell him that if it's those documents he's interested in, he need not bother. They were Joe's hobbyhorse, not mine. I burned them."

# Wednesday, March 18, 1914
## VILLA MERCURII

AT THE BOTTOM OF THE STEPS LEADING TO THE entrance of Villa Mercurii, Paul offered his arm to Lily. She gave him a searing glare that would have melted a bronze and set off for the top unassisted. After checking to see that Nicholas Breedlove was paying the driver, Paul followed. Pausing at the top, he looked back at the next two cars waiting to disgorge their passengers. Neither was a Daimler, nor did he recognize Friedrich Hoffmeister through the windscreens.

The villa's vestibule would have been a paradise for frolicking chimpanzees. A riot of exotic plants climbed brass trellises, accentuated by china jardinières filled with flowering bushes. Marble statuary floated among masses of potted ferns. There was not one inch of the stairs' gilt-railing that was not festooned, banked, or showered with roses, lilies of the valley, and elaborate orchids. On the mezzanine overhead, three members of a string quartet rested in silent sympathy while a violin grieved itself to death.

Beyond the vestibule, a room of dazzling white and gold, lined by soaring windows, gave onto a view of a terrace lighted by torches embedded in the ground in the South Seas style. The scene sparkled with all the satisfaction self-conscious artificiality could muster. Murmurs of the crowd's conversations, trapped beneath an elaborately plastered ceiling and three mammoth crystal chandeliers, thickened the air like a fog. Most of the men were in tails and boiled shirts. The women were woven into the scene as a medley of colors, fabrics, feathers, and jewels. There must have been more gold-spangles per square inch than a Danzig cordial. Here and there, groups of men in gray uniforms appeared like smears of mud in an Impressionist painting.

*Why, this is hell, nor am I out of it,* Paul quoted to himself. It was the same sordid collection of humanity that could be found in the Casino. He should have outfitted himself with a vial of strychnine, like an African explorer.

He watched a footman help Lily remove her cloak. Paul had always known she was meant to be a presence. Tonight, she had accomplished it with magnificence. Her hair was arranged in a becoming coiffure. Her eyebrows had been shaped and her lips and cheeks touched with rouge. The red-velvet evening dress was too provocative to be severely elegant. Yet on that long figure with its finishing-school posture, it was too elegant to be vulgarly provocative. Her only jewelry was a pair of respectably sized diamond-solitaire earrings. The settings' gold was the older color, predating the California gold rush, not seen so often among the *nouveau riche* Americans. Was this the woman Jonnie knew?

"That's an enchanting gown," Paul said. "It becomes you."

"Really? I think it makes me look like the Whore of Babylon."

"Which is exactly what I admire."

Her retort was cut off by Breedlove's arrival.

Ted had introduced the three in the lobby at the Hôtel de Paris. Paul had seen their escort countless times in the Casino. Tonight, he was kitted out in striped trousers, black tails, and a top hat that looked like it could double as a drainpipe for a swale. Each hand bore a diamond ring, and the cufflinks were diamond horseshoes. About thirty years of age, he was too young for the rolls of fat squeezing out of a collar that looked like painted plate-armor. Paul too had hoisted full *costume de rigueur* for the occasion. Even Lily had regarded him with something like respect before she remembered she disliked him. Breedlove had frowned when he saw the three of them coming off the lift. As soon as Paul was introduced as Lily's uncle, Breedlove's attitude grew friendlier. The friendliness registered as delight when Uncle Paul said he liked nothing better than a good game of cards, provided he could play high.

"Well now, Paul," Breedlove was saying. "I'm guessing you're going to like this place just fine. There's a number of Baccarat tables in the rooms at the back and Trente et Quartante. What do you usually play, Paul?"

What was it about these Americans that had them always "guessing"? Moreover, the excessive familiarity and overuse of the Christian name made Breedlove sound like a patent-medicine salesman. Paul braced himself for the slap on the back that was sure to come.

"Well now, Nick," Paul said, pulling a semblance of an American accent out of his grab-bag. "I guess I usually pick Trente et Quartante, but anything will do. Lily here, she knows. Don't you, Girl? Nick, why don't you two youngsters go on and enjoy yourselves. I'll catch up with you later."

Plucking a champagne coupe from a passing tray, Paul set off towards a portal that promised food. Much had changed since Monday night's *volte face*. No longer expecting to see Jonnie or hoping to spite Lily, his reason for this evening's visit had shifted from whim to urgent necessity. Nevertheless, he must spend a decent amount of time inside before reappearing out front.

In the dining room, long tables gleamed with platoons of silver utensils, battalions of crystal glassware, and wagonloads of porcelain plate. The baronial table at the center held fillets of fish, partridges with truffles, numerous aspics, platters of langoustine, and a roast the size of a small cow. Fitting enough, a fat man should never serve thin soup. The four corners of the globe must have been raided to supply one of the sideboards. There, gold baskets overflowed with pulpy summer fruits: fat strawberries, chubby peaches, unblemished pears, plump casaba melons, papayas, and many Paul could not identify. He stabbed a piece of pork with a fork. Moist. Flavorful. He chewed another piece while eavesdropping on the two women nearest him. One, a pudgy woman with auburn corkscrew curls, was recommending a specialist in carbohydrates and extolling the virtues of jalap. The other countered with a seven-day regimen comprised exclusively of milk. To their left, a short, stout man with a long face, large nose, and Scottish accent licked pastry crumbs off his fingers while decrying his workers' feckless demands. "Cut them to eight hours a day and double their wages like that fool Ford did, and I can tell you what will happen. They'll drink themselves into an early grave, that's what," he declared.

Paul remained beside the table, filling his plate with samples from various dishes while listening to conversations, many in English. From the standard streams of mindless dribble he panned a few grams of interesting subjects, ranging from the depraved, unnatural demands of the Suffragettes to the ineluctable connection between Free Love and Utopian Socialism to Reginald Engelbach's finds in his excavations at Haraga to someone named Carl Jung and the wild theories about dreams he was spreading in talks all over London to the craven concessions Smuts had made to an Indian in South Africa.

Leaving the dining room, Paul passed two superb drawing rooms where clusters of people were engaged in talking and drinking, then by an impressive picture gallery before coming to a second, smaller ballroom. There, he took in the dipping, slithering dancers as they pranced through the Tango, accompanied by an invisible set of musicians hidden within another jungle of potted palms.

Hervé was right. Joseph Murphy never would have brought Von Schlieffen's design for shattering the peace here. Therefore, something other had gotten Cyril killed. Something other posed a threat to Jonnie. And what precisely did the British Secret Service or the Foreign Office or whoever-the-hell-sent-Jonnie want? Only an answer to Cyril's murder, or was his death to be avenged? It was well and good that someone of importance thought enough of Jonnie to send him on this errand. He might even feel flattered. Above all, however, he needed to get back to England, where he belonged.

Paul slipped his hand into his pocket to touch the rouleau of 500-franc notes Wycliffe handed him this morning. The look on The Hyena's face alone would have made the transaction worthwhile. At least, Paul reflected, he may have succeeded in getting Sylvie out of Monaco. He gave her the hundred francs she demanded and told her she must leave. Go to Marseilles, he had said, plenty of sailors there. Of course, that money would last no longer than it took the next pimp to beat it out of her, so he gave Bruno another 400 francs and told him to take Sylvie to Marseilles. Handing over an additional hundred-franc note, Paul said, "Perhaps get those teeth looked at." The rest was up to them. He was through with it.

While pondering these matters, he had gravitated to the rear of the villa, where the games of chance were played. Upon seeing a chair being freed at a table occupied exclusively by men in gray uniforms, he ambled over to it. Nodding agreeably at the august group, he replied to their salutations in German by grinning idiotically and shaking his head. He signaled he also was hard of hearing and let his money speak for itself as he joined the scrum. It was human nature to erase from one's consciousness a person who can neither speak nor hear, but Paul didn't expect these men to be so negligent as to chat openly about clifftop murders. This was regrettable. Nothing brightened discourse like a debate around the best way to cut a man's throat. Regardless, Cyril had been murdered by Germans of the military caste who were probably known in this house, so this group looked as good as any place to start.

The talk flowed freely as Paul repeatedly squinted at the money in the center of the table as if flummoxed by the amounts. He proceeded to neither win nor lose in a spectacular manner and folded with an apologetic smile in the middle of many games. From time to time, he palmed his cash in order to make his winnings look less than they were.

Over the course of an hour, other players, often uniformed officers, came and went. It wasn't difficult to appear uninterested in their prattle, most of which centered on gossip about persons and events unknown to him. A pang of nostalgia was incited when an officer with snow-white hair and a thin, tanned face expressed his admiration for the United States' use of gunboat diplomacy in securing a canal at Panama. It aroused memories of Paul's early years in Paris, when the scandal of the "Panama Affair" and the losses to enormous number of investors had preoccupied the newspapers.

When the talk turned to the race for the Schneider Trophy next month, he felt another minor pang of regret over having to leave the Côte d'Azur prematurely. Derision for last year's winner was passed around the card-table like a plate of bon-bons. Granted, it had not been France's finest hour in its miniscule aviation history. Prévost and his craft were awarded the trophy only after the other three aeroplanes, all French, developed waterlogged engines or sank. Nonetheless, Paul had been looking forward to this year's event. Its novelty multiplied its excitement.

At one point, his act was sorely tried. After another player announced that a large wart on Rasputin's John Thomas accounted for his extraordinary popularity with the ladies, the ensuing ribald humor had Paul posing as thoughtful, using his palm to hide any errant twitches of his lips. Still working at giving the appearance of not understanding, he openly gazed around, as if bored. For a heart-thumping moment, he thought he saw Céline. The dress was the same green as the one she often wore; however, the woman was younger, not nearly as beautiful. It wasn't her, but it would not have mattered if it had been. Céline Claudet, he repeated to himself, was just another losing hand he had decided to fold.

Suddenly, he realized the talk around the table had ceased and that the other men were staring at him. Laying his cards face down, he got to his feet, bobbing like an Oriental at each man. He flashed his idiot's grin and raked off his remaining cash into his hand.

It was time for fresh air and a clearer head. And even if he had to hold a knife to someone's throat, he was going to get an answer.

# Wednesday, March 18, 1914
## VILLA MERCURII

LILY STOOD OUTSIDE THE BALLROOM, HER HEAD swaying along with the dancers gliding with magically synchronized movements to the "Emperor Waltz." The plush music blanketed the room like cashmere, from beneath which came the low hum of voices and rustle of women's undergarments as they swept past. She had arrived at Krenz's villa feeling like the damsel tied to the railroad tracks in *Oldfield's Race for a Life*. In this version, Paul Newcastle had her roped to Nicholas Breedlove. Even though she seldom spoke to him, he gamely or gallantly or obtusely stayed close to her side, attending to her comfort and taking obvious pride in having her as an ornament. Now, she told herself, she had only to endure the lonyueurs of waiting, so Paul would pay up when they parted.

She wished she had some idea why he had insisted she bring him to this gala. For that matter, Ted's reason for sending her was about as clear as ditchwater. He must have rented, not bought her clothing. Even then, it was amusing to picture the scene in which he tried to justify that cost to his magnanimous cousin in addition to the 5,000 francs Lily was certain he would never see again. If she listened hard, she would probably hear Mrs. Murphy's reaction all the way from Paris.

After a second glass of champagne and an hour of proud attention from Breedlove, she found herself no longer proof against an assault of vanity. The gown was undeniably eye-catching. In addition, Sally had tweezed Lily's eyebrows, applied cosmetics, and arranged her hair in curls on top of her head, with flattering tendrils framing her face. Not for the first time, Lily wished it were Jonathan Chandler, not Breedlove, who was tracking her like a pilot fish. The thought cracked open her smile. On her way to the train tomorrow, she would leave her New York address at the desk. If he came to America, well, as Sally put it, "And then ...."

"Ah, there's our host," Breedlove said.

Lily's eyes followed his to the commotion taking place at the other end of the wide corridor. Winzig Krenz was even more massive than she had imagined. He was eccentrically clad in a maroon-velvet smoking jacket over dark formal trousers. A white silk scarf was draped around his shoulders, and he wore a yellow velvet cravat. His procession was like a conscientious pontiff's. He slowed to speak to, or bless, virtually everyone along the way. At the same time, his gaze continuously swept the area around him, like the beam from a lighthouse. His focus slid past Lily, braked, and returned. Her face retained remnants of the smile intended for Jonathan. Krenz let his stare linger boldly on her bosoms and hips before returning to her face. He waved the empty cigarette holder in inquiry. She gave a tiny dip of her chin and turned to Breedlove. "How long did you say you've known him?" she asked.

"Welcome," a voice proclaimed from several feet away. "Please allow me to introduce myself. I am Winzig Krenz." The words were directed at Lily, but as he drew nearer, he said, "So good to see you again, Nicholas, and so gorgeously accompanied this time."

"Winzig," Breedlove said, "may I present my fellow countryman, Miss Lily Turner?"

Krenz lifted Lily's hand and kissed it. Then covering her hand with his other, he retained hers softly yet firmly. "Never. Never before have I seen such convincing evidence of the futility of gilding a lily," he said. And never, never before had she heard that worn-out phrase so convincingly applied as a compliment. "Is that champagne, Miss Turner?" he asked.

Without waiting for an answer, he raised his arm and inaudibly snapped his fingers. Before the arm could be lowered, a servant sailed up beside them. Lily made this her opportunity to slip her hand free. Placing her half-filled glass on the tray and taking a fresh one, she became increasingly disconcerted by their host's steady gaze. It was audacious, but at the same time, more appreciative than predatory. It was difficult not to feel flattered, especially since it came from the man everyone around was fawning over.

"Are you from Cleveland too?" he asked.

Krenz not only remembered Breedlove's name but where he was from. He must meet dozens, if not hundreds, of people every week. Should she have accorded her escort more importance? "No," she said, "I live in California, San Francisco."

"California." Krenz's tone swooned the word. "Paradise. Paradise on earth. Have you been to Los Angeles?"

"No," she said unapologetically.

"Your friends, are any of them in the moving-picture business?" A clear note of hope rang in his voice.

"No."

"A pity. You have a face, a presence, any camera would love. You could easily eclipse Dorothy Gibson without having to sink another *Titanic* to do so. These days, many of the companies are moving from New Jersey and New York to

California. The better weather, the longer days, these are
good things for making moving pictures. You are nearby. You
should be introduced. You must be introduced."

When Krenz's next question abruptly went to Breedlove
to inquire after his opinion of the opera that he had
mentioned he was planning to attend, Lily abhorred the
pang of disappointment, or jealousy, that struck her. Good
grief, was she fated to be a sucker for any man who kissed her
hand? If so, she would dip them in acid. As Krenz continued
conversing with Breedlove, she could tell their host was
simultaneously surveying everything around him, like he
was deciding which was the juiciest peach in the orchard. At
the same time, he appeared to give Breedlove his undivided
attention, nodding, smiling, asking the exactly right question
at the exactly right time. No doubt, he had done the same
with her, taking advantage of the seconds in which she had
exchanged champagne glasses or blinked.

She relaxed. She had regained her equilibrium after being
briefly swayed by his celebrity. She sipped the champagne
and returned to observing the tribal customs of the rich and
the connected. A shift in Krenz's tone brought her attention
back to the two men.

"Would you mind, Nicholas," Krenz said, "if I borrowed
Miss Turner for a few minutes? Miss Turner, may I show you
my picture-gallery? I pride myself as an enlightened amateur.
While we are at it, I would like to exchange a few more words
about California."

# Wednesday, March 18, 1914
## VILLA MERCURII

FROM HIS POSITION BESIDE ONE OF THE HEAVY columns supporting the portico, Paul regarded the line of parked motorcars and their drivers, some in conversation, some standing alone, one or two sitting in the driver's seat. The strong smell of burning wood indicated every fireplace in the villa was in use. It didn't take long for the warmth Paul had carried outside to be dispelled by the cold night. He hadn't asked for his overcoat because that would have suggested he was leaving, not merely stepping out for a breath of fresh air. Behind him, the door opened and two men, civilians, came out. One stood at the edge of the landing and lifted his chin in the direction of the waiting cars. A chauffeur ran over to light the acetylene gas-lamps on the front of the vehicle while a boy jumped in front of the machine to crank the engine into life. At once, a footman appeared at the bottom of the stairs to assist the pair into their automobile.

After they departed, Paul said to the footman, "I need Herr Krenz's automobile. Is it available?" He hoped he had mustered the appropriate tone of authority. The man turned and raised his arm.

The Daimler approached from the darkness on the other side. With relief, Paul recognized Friedrich as the driver in the open-air front seat. When he climbed into the rear-seat and the footman shut the door, Friedrich did not look back, nor did he lower his driving-goggles. Ignoring the speaking tube, Paul slid aside the pane that divided the passenger from the driver. "I would like for you to take me to buy cigarettes," he said, watching the footman climb the steps to tend to a couple at the door.

"You do not smoke," Friedrich said, without looking back.

"Seemed like a good time to start."

"There are cigars in the humidor."

"Drive out to the road," Paul directed. When Friedrich did not move, he said, "Would you prefer to sit here and talk?"

As the car descended the sloped drive, Paul fixed his eyes on the beams from the headlamps bouncing in sympathy with the rough, rutted road. At the first crossroad, Friedrich stopped. After some movements Paul could not see, he put a cigarette to his mouth and lit it. He smoked with short, jerky movements before tossing the smoldering stub away and easing the car forward once more. At the next intersection, where the road led either left to Monaco or right to Nice, he braked to a hard, swaying stop. "Where do you want to go?" he yelled through the glass.

Paul opened the pane. "Find a place to pull over," he instructed.

Inside of five minutes, the car crunched to a halt on a cart-track off the main road. Friedrich kept the headlamps burning and the engine running as Paul climbed into the front alongside him. Beneath them, the car throbbed nervously, like a spirited horse behind the starting gate.

"What are you doing here?" Friedrich demanded, pushing the goggles onto his forehead. "You told me you and Dmitri had no designs on Herr Krenz."

Paul told Friedrich the truth, or the truth as it had evolved.

He said he did not know and did not want to know Krenz, that he had engineered an invitation specifically to have this opportunity for asking Friedrich a few questions.

"Ask them," Friedrich said. "So I can get back to the villa."

"Winzig Krenz is a comedian, isn't he?"

"You wanted to ask stupid questions?"

"How well do you know him?" Paul said.

"I am a driver. He does not speak to me as an intimate."

Paul nodded thoughtfully. "Do you not know what he is up to?"

"There is a vast difference between knowing as an abstract and knowing as a concrete certainty."

"I don't have time for a lecture on nominalism. Is Herr Krenz aware of some of the more hilarious antics his guests get up to while staying under his roof and using his limousine?"

Friedrich looked like he had discovered for the first time that he possessed hands and had no earthly idea what he was supposed to do with them. He squeezed the steering wheel, then released it to rub his gloved palms on his thighs, then returned them to the steering wheel, then adjusted the goggles on his forehead.

"For example," Paul said, "when they go star-gazing on a cliff outside Monaco?"

Friedrich's whole body seemed to deflate. "Why are you doing this to me?" he rasped. "The weight of my own existence is enough to bear. I do not wish to carry yours."

"I'm not asking you to."

"You are wrong. The questions you ask are wrong."

Friedrich gripped the gear-stick and disengaged the clutch. Paul touched him on the shoulder. "We're not ready to leave," he said.

Sylvie's disclosures had not pointed directly to this moment, but they had pushed the odds in its direction. An automobile large enough to carry four passengers suggested something as large as a Daimler limousine. There was no shortage of limousines around Monte Carlo, and the fact the men spoke German weighted the odds only slightly more because there was no shortage of Germans, military and otherwise, at the Riviera. What had sealed it was Cyril's obsession with the connection he had made between Murphy and Krenz, the two times he had seen Murphy climbing into Krenz's limousine behind the hotel.

"An uncertain past has a kind of yeast to it," Paul said. "It tends to go on rising. Does the incomparable Herr Krenz know you were brought to book for fraud in Paris? Does he know about Ostend?"

Friedrich's considerable moustache vibrated as his hand gripped the gear-stick. "Are you blackmailing me, Gerald?"

Paul kept his eyes on Friedrich's hands. He wasn't perfectly certain — in fact he was nowhere close to certain — the situation wasn't going to turn violent. Friedrich was threatened, and threatened men often turned to violence.

"That's as good a word as any," Paul said. "We all fear those blots on our escutcheons to some degree, don't we? I swear to you, Friedrich, tell me what I need to know, and you'll never hear from me again, you or your employer or any of his friends. I only want an answer. It will go no further than me. I only want to know why the journalist was killed. I knew him. He wasn't a friend, but the police asked me about him. The police put me together with him. Who else has put me with him? I need to know if I am in trouble. I need to know if I should get out of here, leave. You told me about the American and Zaharoff. Is there a connection there with the journalist? Am I going to be killed for knowing that?" He was on the verge of saying Friedrich owed him as much, but it was better that the man should come to that conclusion for himself.

In the half-light of the waning moon, Paul saw Friedrich pull the tarnished case from the pocket of his white driving-coat, withdraw a cigarette from it, close the case, and tap the cigarette on it three times before putting it to his mouth. His hands were shaking. In the crisp night air, the bitter smell of the Turkish tobacco stung Paul's nostrils.

Paul said, "I'm confident you weren't directly involved. I want to know why he was murdered, that's all. I need to know if I'm in trouble."

When Friedrich spoke, his voice sounded like it was coming through an olive press. "He was like you are right now, prowling around the wrong place. He was where he should not have been. He was snooping in the man's room at the Hôtel de Paris, not the hunchback, the other man, Zaharoff. He was in that man's room. They found him there. They saw him there. I do not know which. They knew he was there. That is all I heard before they left the Daimler. I do not know what he found. I do not know what he was looking for. That is all I know."

And that was all Paul needed to know: who killed Cyril and why. Jonnie could take the information and go home.

Friedrich said, "To answer your other question, yes. If I were you, I would be making plans to leave this place soon, very soon."

Paul barely had time to shut the door to the back seat before Friedrich jammed the gear-stick into position and rocks exploded against the rear fenders.

# Wednesday, March 18, 1914
## VILLA MERCURII

INSIDE THE VESTIBULE ONCE MORE, PAUL LOOKED AT his palms, somewhat surprised to find they weren't bloody from clinging to the Daimler's hanging strap in order to keep from being hurled against the doors during the death-defying ride back to the villa. Friedrich had let speed and recklessness say everything else he wanted to say.

Paul vowed to avoid getting close to any more Germans in uniform. He wasn't certain he would be able to stifle his revulsion. As he wandered aimlessly through the vast expanse of the house, he contemplated how he could make sure Jonnie would leave the Côte d'Azur. There was nothing that could be done for Cyril now. He had been a Holy Fool at a Witches' Sabbath. The only remaining question was whether the men who sent Jonnie were going to be satisfied with that answer.

Although Paul thought he would not be betrayed by Friedrich, he couldn't put perfect faith in the idea. Friedrich didn't know Paul's current *nom de guerre* or location, but those things could be discovered. The vital question was whether he would be willing to show his own hand by taking the initiative tonight or whether he would rely on Paul's assurances. One more reason to decamp as soon as Paul was sure Jonnie had left.

At one point in his wandering, Paul caught a glimpse of Breedlove in a group of boisterous revelers. Nowhere did he spot Lily. The young hussy was probably snorkeling around the Great Coral Reef. How might he drop a hint to Jonnie that she didn't deserve his regard?

Eventually, Paul entered the small drawing room closest to the front of the villa, where three other guests were listening to a pianist play selections from Beethoven on a grand piano. Paul took a chair which commanded a view of anyone moving to or from the entrance and waited.

The first few bars of the "Moonlight" sonata had sounded when Lily made her appearance. Paul had expected her to make an impressive entrance, but he hadn't expected that particular impression. Trailed by an anxious servant, she was more stumbling than walking in the direction of the vestibule. Paul was immediately on his feet.

He gripped her arm as remorselessly as a shark. "If I'd known you were going to get staggering drunk, I never would have brought you to the dance."

It seemed to take her several long seconds to focus on his face and yet more time for recognition to register.

"I'm not drunk."

"You could have fooled me."

He maneuvered her to the piano. Propped there, she clung to its edge like Odysseus denying the Sirens' song. "Don't you dare move," he hissed in her ear. "I'm going to find Breedlove."

The pianist's fingers continued producing notes while he followed the scene with his eyes. "She's an embarrassment at family reunions too," Paul told him.

# Thursday, March 19, 1914
## HÔTEL DE PARIS

⟶ ◆◆◆ ⟵

AT THE HÔTEL DE PARIS, PAUL STEPPED OUT OF THE motorcar and waited for Lily to summon the consciousness needed to negotiate her way across the seat and take his hand. He had to strongly resist the urge to slap her sober. She had slept with her head on his shoulder the entire way from Villefranche. Breedlove, filled to the gills as well, either didn't notice or didn't care that she had effectively taken her leave. He had rattled on about how much he enjoyed the evening, how much he was looking forward to seeing Lily and her uncle again, and how pleased he was Krenz had taken to her. The last comment further fueled Paul's anger.

With Lily finally extricated from the vehicle, Paul assured Breedlove for the fifteenth time that he did not need to accompany them inside and slapped the side of the motorcar like he was sending a horse on its way. Turning to the swaying figure beside him, he said, "That was quite a coda you performed. Come on. I'll see you to your room."

"I need to talk to you," she slurred.

"Tomorrow, when you're able to speak."

"Tonight. I need to talk to you tonight." She blinked hard several times and shook her head as if trying to clear it. "Not here," she said, "we need to go somewhere else."

"It's three o'clock in the morning. Where do you suggest?"

"My head's buzzing. I have a terrible headache." She clutched his arm as her feet started sliding in separate directions. Gradually, she got them under control and back beneath her body.

Paul said, "I'm sorry about the pumpkin, Cinderella, but we have to go in. It's cold out here."

"No," she pleaded. "We have to go somewhere private. Some place perfectly private. The Hermitage, it's close by, isn't it?"

"That hotel's lobby is no more private than this place," Paul pointed out.

"Take a room if you have to."

Paul placed his hands against her shoulders and pushed her away to look fully at her face. He frowned deeply. "Has Miss Holmes taken to snoring?" he said.

# Thursday, March 19, 1914
## HÔTEL HERMITAGE

LILY FLUNG OPEN THE DOOR BETWEEN THE BEDROOM and sitting room. Her face was shiny with water and bare toes peeked from beneath a soft-flannel dressing-gown. Paul looked up from the morning newspaper. Freshly shaven and collarless, he sat with his legs stretched before him, one ankle over the other.

"Coffee or tea," he said, indicating the china pots with a movement of his head, "and there's toast in the rack."

"Do I need to slap you first?"

"Why would you want to do that?"

"To recover my dignity. You undressed me."

"Why don't you take that notion off the boil until after you've had a cup of coffee? Besides, don't think it was easy. I've carried logs with more life in them." He returned to the newspaper.

Lily leaned over the service-tray but stopped suddenly, an anguished expression covering her face. She gripped the back of the chair next to her. "My eyes feel like you emptied a bag of sand into them. What time is it?"

Paul peered over the top of the newspaper. "I'm not the Sandman, and it's almost ten-thirty."

Holding the chair with one hand, she pressed her free

hand against her forehead as she rocked back and forth. Without looking up, she said, "Where's my money?"

"There, on the table, along with your earrings. I removed them, lest they disappear among the bedclothes."

"Do you mean you don't want to sell them back to me?"

"Are they Wycliffe's? Were they provided with the gown?"

"They're mine. They were a gift."

Paul arched an eyebrow.

"Not that kind."

"No call for biting off my head. It's nothing to me if someone wants to give you a gift. The money's all there, 6,250 for the necklace, half of what Wycliffe advanced me, and half of what I won at the tables. As far as he will know, I had a run of bad luck and lost it all. I deducted our expenses, this room, your dressing-gown, and that." He wagged a finger towards a blue day-frock lying across one of the chairs. "The raiment you showed to such spectacular effect last night is not the thing for morning-wear. In spite of what you may think, Miss Lily, I am quite anxious about your reputation. A lady should never be seen leaving hired accommodations wearing the same evening-gown in which she arrived the night before."

She snatched a napkin from the service-tray and held it against her mouth, her eyes no longer focused on him.

"What about Miss Holmes?" Paul said. "Does she have the documents? Will she speak with me?"

Bent at the waist, Lily made her way to the sofa by transferring her hold from one piece of furniture to the next. She sank onto the cushion like a ship going down without a trace. "I'm leaving Monte Carlo this afternoon," she said. "If I get any more money, I'll leave it for you at the Front Desk."

"I'm not inquiring after your take. I want to meet her, to talk to her."

Lily leaned forward and vomited a thin stream of yellowish-green bile onto the napkin. Paul snapped the edges of the newspaper twice before folding and smoothing it until it appeared untouched.

"I would have thought you got all that out last night," he said, removing the napkin from her hand and replacing it with a damp hand-towel. "Look, I know you don't take advice, but just because the champagne is free –"

"Mr. Murphy was never at Krenz's villa," she blurted.

Still pinching the edges of the soiled napkin, Paul looked down at her. "Regardless of who makes the claims to the contrary, Joseph Murphy was seen there."

Lily shook her head. "Mr. Murphy was never at Krenz's villa," she repeated, enunciating each word slowly and distinctly.

# Wednesday, March 18, 1914
## VILLA MERCURII

By the time Winzig Krenz and Lily arrived at the door to the majestic library, the effects of the additional champagne she had drunk along the way had begun to register. Upon taking her in tow, Krenz had plowed through the crowd like a ship at full sail while manifesting no sign of being in any particular hurry. Without slowing his pace, he tossed out inquiries like confetti, asking about wives, children, businesses, hobbies, dogs, horses, meting out what sounded like genuine concern and sincere compliments to old and young, male and female. He transitioned effortlessly from French to English to German to, less assuredly, Italian and back again, making a joke here, a good-humored taunt there, a measured observation somewhere else. Every now and again, they came across someone too important to dispatch with a quick remark. Lily was introduced to Comte de Bussy, Grand Duke Ivan Something-or-other, and Herr Jagow. Each time they stalled, a servant arrived with a tray. And each time, Lily, viciously torn between her unearned pride in her escort and her instincts' shrill warnings, helped herself to another drought of Dutch courage.

"Do you mind if we talk in here?" Krenz asked, ushering

her through the double-doorway. "This is the best place for conversation."

The room, about thirty-five feet wide and equally long, smelled of musty books, Morocco leather, and the scent of cedar from the burning logs. Eight tall mullioned windows and an enormous fireplace were the only things allotted space on the walls besides books. The carved mahogany shelves teemed with volumes, many bound in gilt and calf. Bronze busts, flanked by potted aspidistras, were strategically placed about the room and appeared to be cogitating upon the tomes at their bases. An exceptionally wide sofa and three brass-studded leather chairs were situated near the fireplace.

The servant who had followed them into the room slipped away after opening the magnum of champagne which had been waiting, iced, in a standing bucket. Nothing, Lily was willing to bet, not even a need to announce the chimney was on fire, would induce the man to return until ordered to do so.

Krenz piloted her to the sofa and extended an invitation to sit. She ignored this suggestion in favor of a maroon-leather chair next to one whose width proclaimed its suitability for its owner.

"I see you wanted to be closer to the fire," he said. "I apologize. I did not ask if you were cold. Here, let me replace your drink." He held out a coupe fizzing with fresh champagne.

She gripped the glass she held as if he had threatened to rip it from her hand. She had drunk enough. "No, thank you. I'm fine with this."

He set the new coupe on the table beside her and lowered himself onto the other chair. There was nothing lascivious in his smile. If anything, it was shy, embarrassed.

"Have you read all those books?" she asked, more by way of making idle conversation than out of true curiosity. The *nouveau riche* were notorious for ordering books for their

389

libraries the same way they ordered sod, by the color and by the yard.

"Only the ones on those two walls," Krenz answered. "This wall." He indicated the one behind him. "Is my holding pen. The things in the cases around the windows are collector's items. I have some remarkable folios, treatises, incunabula, a few illuminated manuscripts — Carolingian and Ottoman — account books from medieval abbeys, holograph scores by Mozart, Verdi, and Wagner, holograph manuscripts by Goethe, Schopenhauer, the great Hugo, even Rider Haggard. With those treasures, however, I have difficulty digesting their content even when I can interpret them. I become preoccupied with worry, afraid I may soil a page. They have taught me that I dislike owning something I have to treat with greater respect than I do my own mind. There should never be a gulf between the beautiful and the useful, would you not agree?"

He opened the lid on the humidor at his left and remained silent while removing the small band from a cigar with minute care. "I know I promised my picture-gallery, but I decided to forgo it in favor of my library. It is immeasurably more meaningful. Ideas, ideals, philosophies, histories, in short, knowledge and wisdom reside here. That is why I brought you. I could see you are a woman of – how shall I say it – of substantial mental capacity."

*Substantial gullibility* would probably be closer to his true estimation. No longer outnumbered by the groveling guests, Lily's practical sense was regaining control. She knew where this fulsome flattery was intended to lead, and she had no interest in arriving at that destination. She looked at the doors the servant had silently closed behind him. She wanted to leave but felt rooted in place, restrained not by some moustache-twirling villain, but by the thoroughly prosaic clutches of good manners, mild inebriation, and simple inertia.

"I am intensely desirous of making a good impression on you, Miss Turner. You are a striking woman." He clipped off the tip the cigar with practiced precision and held a flaming match near the end without drawing on it. "But you know that," he added quietly.

Lily lowered her head. She hated to admit it. In spite of having taken up arms against her vanity, a part of her wanted to be praised by him. A part of her was attracted to his vaunted brilliance, his abundant talent, his acknowledged fame, and apparent wealth. Enough, she silently scolded. She might not be entirely sick of him, but she was entirely sick of falling for his honeyed hogwash. The servant ready with chilled champagne, the softly glowing Tiffany lamps, the splashes of firelight, the over-sized sofa, these traps of seduction, these stage-props, were laid before she even left Monte Carlo.

"That champagne has gone flat," Krenz said. "Let me get you another."

She paid scant attention to his removing the untouched glass and replacing it with a fresh one. Another thought was scratching itself to the surface of her mind. Krenz had a phenomenal memory. Why not deflect him from where he expected his compliments to take him, or them? Why not get her own mind onto something else also? As long as she was here, why not try to settle the matter before returning to Sally?

"You know, I just thought of something," she said. "You wanted to talk about California. You may have met some acquaintances of mine from San Francisco."

"It is likely," Winzig said. "I am happy to say I have entertained many persons from your foggy city."

"I'm thinking of Joe Murphy, Joe and his wife, Madeline."
She meant the inclusion of Mrs. Murphy to be misleading.

"Murphy. San Francisco." Winzig appeared to be thumbing
through a card-catalog in his mind. He apparently found the
one he was looking for. "Of course. Murphy. Of course. Bad
back. Shipping is his line, is it not? How is he? How is that
bad back?"

"Bad back? No. I mean, yes. He carries his right shoulder
higher than the left because it was injured years ago." She
deliberately kept Mr. Murphy in the present tense.

"Sure, sure. Right shoulder higher, but he has a bad back
too. He doesn't mention it, but he has a habit of pressing his
hand against the small of his back. I noticed because I have
the same pain although I cannot reach it so easily." Smiling,
Krenz leaned forward to demonstrate the impossibility of his
reaching his own back.

A peculiar sensation had filled Lily's ears and was
pinching the corners of her mind. He was mistaken. He
meant something else. But she knew he was not and did not.

Krenz must have spoken or asked a question. He appeared
to be waiting for an answer.

"Pardon?" she said.

"You look like you do not feel good. Would you prefer a
brandy?" He was on his feet.

"Would you please ring your servant for ice-water?" She
wanted the doors opened. She wanted fresh air. She wanted
time to think. She wanted to leave.

Instead, she watched Krenz slide a removable shelf from
a rosewood console, revealing a cut-glass pitcher of water
and a bucket of ice. He did not bring it directly to her but
disappeared behind her chair. From there, she heard him say,
"How is Joe? He was here two or three weeks ago as I recall.
Or it could have been a year ago. Time melts and blends on

the Riviera. It is these monotonous days of endless sunshine. Has he had gone back to San Francisco?"

She took the tumbler with both hands. She wanted to down the water in one gulp, but the years spent at Mount St. Joseph Academy and Bryn Mawr asserted themselves. She took a ladylike sip off the top, then another, larger sip. Her stomach shot back a wave of mild nausea. In a matter of seconds, however, it was not her stomach but her vision that had gone awry. Krenz remained in the chair beside her, but she was having difficulty finding him within the wavering light. Not only was her will enervated, but her arms, her legs, her mind, her whole body as well. A sheen of perspiration covered her forehead, and she was growing short of breath.

She knew precisely what had happened. The bastard had drugged her. No wonder he was so keen about fresh drinks. Effie had warned her about this. Effie had said that Stanford White was scarcely the only debaucher with that trick up his sleeve.

A voice came from within the shimmering light. "Drink that water, my dear. You look like you need it."

Lily fought to keep her eyelids from drooping lower and her jaw from slackening further. She must get away from this monster. She had to get out now, while she still could. She would never be able to defend herself, not in this state. It was a good thing she hadn't drunk as deeply as she wanted to, as deeply as he intended her to. With an enormous exertion of will, she secured her feet against the carpet, then carefully set the glass on the table and placed her hands on the arms of the chair to assist in leveraging herself to a standing position. If she didn't make it with the first try, she would be lost.

She came close. She managed to get upright but immediately swayed backwards, landing on an arm of the chair. She sat, listening to the throbbing of her pulse, summoning her strength and will for the final push.

She gave Krenz a wan smile. "I need to find the powder room," she said, hoping he didn't have one of those stashed in a nearby rosewood cabinet. "Then...I believe...I will...have a brandy."

# Thursday, March 19, 1914
## HÔTEL HERMITAGE

LILY EMERGED FROM THE BEDROOM THE SECOND TIME in her stocking feet. Her damp hair was loosely pinned in a chignon. Straightening the sleeves of the blue frock, she said, "I hate to ask, but how?"

"I had to call in a favor or two," Paul said. "And I handed over that red concoction as a guide." His eyes took in the hem. "It's too short."

"I'm not going far in it."

"Do you feel better?"

She nodded. A faint blush crept up her neck and spread to her cheeks. "Thank you," she said, a firm gaze underscoring her sincerity. "Thank you for taking care of me."

Paul's eyes widened in mock surprise. "And I thought the Age of Miracles had passed. That must have hurt."

"You will never know how much."

She crossed to the table to put on her earrings.

"Sit down, if you please," he said. "We have some things to talk over."

"I did mention you to Sally. She admitted the plans were what you said. She also said they no longer exist. She burned them."

"That's not what I care about. We need to decide what we're going to do."

"Not I. I know what I'm going to do."

"Tell me," he persisted. "Why would Wycliffe masquerade as Joseph Murphy and go to Krenz's?"

"Because he's barking mad. Anyone who's not locked up in an insane asylum can see that."

"Even the crazy have their reasons."

"Where are my shoes? Sally must be wondering what happened to me last night."

Paul reached over the arm of the chair to hoist them aloft. Motioning towards the sofa, he said, "I know you're in a hurry, but give me a few more minutes."

She sat to pull on the shoes. "You want reasons," she said. "Maybe Ted got tired of being left out. Maybe he couldn't get an invitation to Krenz's for himself, so he accepted one for Mr. Murphy."

"How did he pull off the disguise?"

"He spent years with Pinkertons. Haven't you read Sherlock Holmes? Disguises are basic tools for a detective. They were close to the same height. Mr. Murphy was stouter, but padding would have taken care of that. Mr. Murphy wore a full beard. For a false one to pass as real would have taken more finesse than padding, but he apparently pulled it off."

"That brings us back to *why*."

"He's disgruntled, vindictive. You've seen how Mrs. Murphy treats him, how she treats everyone. He claims to be rich, but next to her, he's the poor relation. She's paying for his room at the hotel. Maybe resentment and envy have eaten his heart out. Maybe he sold his soul to the devil."

"In that case, the devil got short-changed." Paul looked past Lily. "The best lies are based on truth. Wycliffe spun the

396

story that Joseph Murphy was working with the Germans to arm Irish revolutionaries."

"That's what he claimed, but his evidence — the tickets and the dictionary — have different explanations. As for Chief Inspector Gautier's intelligence about Mr. Murphy's being seen at Krenz's, we know the truth about that too. What's more, Mr. Murphy no longer owned a merchant fleet. He couldn't have transported arms or anything else."

Paul said, "Wycliffe didn't know about Murphy's selling up until a couple of days ago, when Mrs. Murphy heard from the people in San Francisco. My money says Ted invented that story about the chief inspector in order to explain how he knew Murphy had been to Krenz's."

"If Ted, disguised as Mr. Murphy, was cooking up a conspiracy in Winzig Krenz's house, why would he have insisted I go there? He must have known Krenz would remember Mr. Murphy. He remembers everyone."

"He didn't expect you to meet Krenz, or certainly, he didn't expect you to become, dare I say it, as intimate as you did. Or even so, what of it? Ted's not aware of his tell-tale habit. He would have been confident the impersonation would hold."

"Even so, why would he insist I go there?"

Paul moved his head slowly back and forth. "The more I think about it, the more I believe Wycliffe was behind the bullet in Joseph Murphy's back. As long as Murphy was alive, he might have exonerated himself from whatever it was Wycliffe had him involved in. He might have been able to provide a watertight alibi, say, in the form of Sally Holmes, for his whereabouts on a key date."

"That's a plausible theory," Lily said. "Feel free to do whatever you wish with the great god Hypothesis. I won't be around. I'm going to the hotel, pack my bags, bid Sally good-bye, and take the next conveyance out of here. I don't care if it's a haywagon. Thank you again, Paul. It's been a rare pleasure."

"You can't leave."

"Why on earth not? Mr. Murphy is dead. Ted is a lunatic. Mrs. Murphy isn't far behind him. The necklace has been returned, the attempted murders explained. You have your money. I have my money. It's a really, really good time to leave. If fact, I know you don't take advice, but you might want to give that idea some consideration yourself."

"Are those glass slippers pinching your toes? There is more at stake here than money."

"Don't you think I know that? I would just as soon be alive when I leave here too."

"Shouldn't you tell Mrs. Murphy what her cousin' has been getting up to?"

"You can take care of that for both of us."

"It's larger than that. We have a responsibility to the weal of the State."

"Pardon me, but at what point in our acquaintance did you become civic-minded?"

"We have to stop him."

"Stop him from what?"

"We have to expose him."

"Expose him to whom? Who is going to take your word or my word over that of Mr. Edward R. Wycliffe the Third of Chicago? What has he done anyway? He made up like Mr. Murphy and went to a party. Is that a crime?"

She got to her feet, studied the heap of red velvet on the sofa, and wrinkled her nose.

"Lily, please, I have never sought a favor from you before."

"Now is not a good time to start."

"I'm not asking you to go over Niagara Falls in a barrel. Just go back to the Hôtel de Paris, brush your teeth, pack your bags, learn to knit, write an opera, do whatever you do to beguile away your time, but meet me at two o'clock in the restaurant there. That's over two hours from now. You can catch the eight o'clock *Rapide*. I need time to figure out what to do next."

With Lily gradually advancing and Paul gradually retreating, they had made their way to the door that opened onto the corridor.

"I hate knitting," she said, putting out her arm to indicate he should step aside.

"I will have Jonathan Chandler with me," Paul said.

# Thursday, March 19, 1914

THE SPARKLING SEA, THE CLOUDLESS SKY, SEABIRDS
floating overhead, yachts dozing in the distance, the endless
procession of well groomed people along the promenade, the
rainbows of flowers fringing the walks, the polka thumping
enthusiastically in the bandstand behind the Casino, nothing
in these matchless surroundings impressed itself on Lily's
mind as her feet automatically made their way from the Hôtel
Hermitage towards the Hôtel de Paris. She was concentrating
on keeping her thoughts contained within the boundaries
that would deliver her to the only sensible destination. In
spite of her efforts, these thoughts continually spilled over
their banks in great waves of rationalization or eddied in
small pools of indecision or were sucked into an immense
vortex of longing.

Paul had meant his parting enticement to surprise her,
but it had fallen short in that respect. That man was never
without a trick up his sleeve. Yet he had explained nothing.
Did that validate her earlier fear that Jonathan was only using
her to get a story he could sell in America? Was Paul feeding
him information about Mr. Murphy, the thefts, Sally? What
had he told Jonathan about her?

A pair of women posing for a photograph with Doré's
statue *Dance* in front of the Opera snapped her attention
back to its proper focus. Purchase the Brownie and film

in Monaco or wait until Paris? The question was quickly settled. Here, if time permitted after packing. There would be numerous, more challenging orientations to manage in Paris.

As she rounded the corner of the Hôtel de Paris, her mind went truant once more. She hadn't promised Paul she would delay her departure. She had said only that she would think about it. He had the good sense not to show it, but she knew he was confident she would turn up. She hated him all over again. She could fix that. She wouldn't be at the restaurant. She would be at the train station. On her way out, she would dispatch a letter of resignation to Mrs. Murphy along with the address where her final paycheck could be sent. No holding her breath waiting for that.

At least the unknown dangers to Sally had been substantially reduced. Paul's friends had invaded her apartment, and Lily had told him the plans were destroyed. There was nothing for them to pursue. She had uncovered Bridget Rose as the poisoner even though she was forfeiting the bonus. There should be no further threat coming from that direction. She would give Sally Paul's theory about Ted's shooting Mr. Murphy. After Bridget's revelations and what Lily had seen at Cap Ferrat, she still favored Mrs. Murphy as the culprit, but there wasn't time to prove it and collect that bonus.

Lily slowed as she neared the entrance to the hotel, only a few paces away. All right, if she put off leaving until the later train tonight, she could meet with Jonathan and Paul in the restaurant at two o'clock. It would delay her departure only a few hours, give her extra time for buying a camera. She would hear what Jonathan had to say. He had a great deal to answer for, not least his acquaintance with Paul Newcastle, but nothing, not Jonathan, not anyone was going to eclipse her plans for the future.

With a start, she realized she was staring into the eyes of the doorman holding open the door to the Hôtel de Paris.

# Thursday, March 19, 1914
## HÔTEL DE PARIS

INSIDE HER ROOM, LILY'S FIRST ACTIONS WERE TO kick off her shoes and remove the earrings. She noted the luggage and hatbox in the center of room and was relieved Sally had the bedroom door closed. After last night's upheavals, Lily wanted a few minutes to savor her satisfactions. She had done it. She had escaped from a monster who would have callously raped an unconscious woman. She had freed herself from the brainless, demoralizing work as Mrs. Murphy's secretary. She had removed herself from the dictates of that insanely duplicitous cousin. She and Fran had landed their first substantial client. In a few short hours, Lily would be on her way to proving that she was capable of hacking her own way through the tangled jungle of life.

The hairs on the back of her neck were the first to shriek the alarm. Next, her breathing stopped. Then her thoughts stopped. It had been a small sound, a slight sound, a barely audible sound. It had come from the bedroom, from behind the closed door. Like a thunderclap in a mountain valley, it had split the silence, then refused to give back the quiet after it faded away. It notified Lily that, since arriving, she had been surrounded by a preternatural stillness. If Sally were there, by now she should have made a sign. If Sally were there, she would never have been so utterly quiet.

Lily swirled and grasped the doorknob. At the same time, the bedroom door opened. From behind, she heard Ted say in a low, unfamiliar voice, "Turn that, and I will shoot you."

His words hit the back of her mind and slid to the bottom, like mud hurled against a wall. She kept her eyes fixed on the painted plank of wood which barred her from safety.

"Is that you, Ted?" She twisted to look at him. He indeed held a pistol. It was pointed at her chest. "I thought a burglar was in my bedroom. What is the gun for?"

His lips curled back in a snarl. "I'm sure you thought it was a burglar. Or maybe you thought it was your little roommate." His voice quivered. She wanted to think it was fear but knew it was rage. Her face went cold as the blood drained from it. The bluffing was over as soon as it had begun.

He indicated the luggage with a motion of his head. "How convenient you had your bags brought up. I was going to have that done, but it was considerate of you to put in the request personally. I made good use of them in your long absence. I packed your belongings."

Lily had noticed the bags were strapped but barely gave it a second thought. Maybe this hotel didn't store the straps inside the empty cases the way most did.

Ted's strangely low voice ran on, "When they come to search your room, the police are going to discover that you were about to run away. Where will not matter. What will matter, my dear Lily, is that you knew certain incriminating evidence was about to be brought to bear against you and Joe Murphy, and you were about to bolt." He let loose a cackle that would have done high honor to a witch. "Turns out, you actually were preparing to leave. What a pity, only I will be able to enjoy that irony."

Lily wanted to say something, needed to say something,

but at present, her supreme difficulty was breathing. The room's air had become thick and heavy, the way it was when a storm was brewing.

"Ted," she began.

"Shut up!" He wiped at the sweat beads that had formed above his mouth. "You were got out of the way last night to make sure incriminating evidence would be found here when the police search your room. As they say, heaven helps those who help themselves. You were got out of the way exactly so certain facts could be established.

"*Exactly so*," he sneered. "Nothing in the last week has gone *exactly so*. Time after time, I have had to, as they say, snatch victory from the jaws of defeat. First, those bumbling, incompetents wouldn't investigate, then the necklace goes missing and that fop Newcastle got involved and started mucking things up, then those tickets to Belfast, then Madeline moved to that Hebrew's house, then Joe leaves her nothing. Time after time, I had to recover, had to keep in front of the changes, but I caught and redirected every twist. Then, what do I find when I get here last night? Something else unexpected that had to be worked into the story, something else to stretch my powers of ingenuity. But, you see, I am equal to every task."

He waved the gun. Lily pressed her back against the door.

"Put your shoes on."

"What?"

"You heard me. Put your shoes on. We're going to my room."

"Where?"

Ted exhaled a long, theatrical sigh. "That's been your problem all along. You don't listen. We're going to my room, and we're going to wait for Maddie."

So, Mrs. Murphy was in collusion with this maniac. Lily

had entertained that theory off and on but had never grown fond of it.

"I have a blister," she said. "I want to get my boots." In the bedroom or between there and here, somewhere, she would find a weapon, Sally's scissors, a lamp, an ashtray, a teaspoon, anything.

He looked like a schoolmaster who, after hundreds of efforts at correction, was finally conceding the intransigence of his pupil's stupidity. "Put your goddamn shoes on!" His voice, shrill, metallic, vibrated like a cymbal.

After she complied, he said again, "We're going to my room."

Lily was swamped by hope. She could raise a riot in the elevator. He wouldn't shoot her *and* the operator. There might be other people in the hallway. She would knock him aside and run screaming for help.

"If you think you're going to pull another one of your underhanded tricks, Sally Holmes is in my apartment. I'm sorry to tell you, she's suicidal. It is in her best interest that you return with me."

"What do you mean, suicidal?"

"I mean, if I don't return, she will die. If you do not return with me, she will die."

His words only singed the edges of Lily's mind. She was trying, unsuccessfully, to picture how he could have left Sally that she would die without him. Was she hanging by a thread off the balcony? Was the fuse to a stick of dynamite burning away? The threat felt incredible, but Lily couldn't ignore the murderous shine in his eyes. She could not ignore the threat either.

# Thursday, March 19, 1914
## HÔTEL DE PARIS

LILY'S LAST HOPE EVAPORATED WHEN TED GAVE HER the key to unlock the door to his apartment. Her plan of raising a ruckus in the elevator was squashed when he diverted her to the stairwell, the cold steel of the gun's muzzle pressed against the small of her back. There, the only sounds she heard were their shoes hitting the stone steps, Ted's breathing, and her heart beating like Vulcan's hammer against her chest. The empty corridor on his floor eliminated the next possibility of rescue. Therefore, her last chance had been to catch him off-guard while he was distracted by fitting the key into the lock.

She shoved open the door. No sign of Sally. "Have you gone out of your mind?" she said. "What is this about?"

A muffled sound came from the left, from behind the opened door. "Get inside," he said, pressing the pistol harder against her spine. "Now."

She did as she was told. Sally was gagged and tied to a ladder-backed chair placed against the wall abutting the corridor. Her arms were strapped to her sides and secured to the chair's back by several turns of rope. Each of her legs was lashed to one of the chair's. Why had she allowed him to do that? Did she sit on command and bleat like a lamb? An identical chair stood beside Sally's, a length of rope coiled at its feet. Lily processed the implications. He would have to put down the gun to tie her. As soon as he did, she would tear his eyes out, rip his throat to shreds.

"Take a seat," he said, indicating the second chair.

"What if I don't? You can't shoot two women in your sitting room and expect to get away with it, not even in Monaco."

"Pick up the handkerchief that's on the chair and sit, or Miss Holmes will shoot you and then turn the pistol on herself. That's not the story I prefer, but in the event it has to happen, that will be the story I give the police. I have a sound-suppressor on this gun. No one has to hear it until I'm ready for them to."

The rope on the floor was curled into a circle and knotted near the center. One end extended out several feet. He instructed Lily to tie the gag on herself. "Tighter. Tighter," he ordered. She obliged, pulling the cloth so hard it cut into the corners of her mouth.

"We have a few things to discuss," he said. "I'll remove it in a minute."

Next, he told Lily to place her feet within the circle of the rope, then lean down and hold that rope around her ankles. She did so only after removing her shoes, so her feet could rest flat against the floor. She was relieved when he made no objection.

Keeping the gun aimed at her, he took the end of the rope and jerked it hard, closing the slip-knot. She realized she had been rendered incapable of running or even of walking. All very dramatic, she thought, but it would be impossible to tie her arms to the chair like Sally's, and she saw no rope prepared for that purpose. Once more, he dashed her hopes by leaning over the sofa and bringing up a second rope, also circled and knotted.

"Hold your arms out in front of you, palms together," he said. Just like that, he lassoed her wrists from two feet away, again tightening the slip-knot with a swift tug. And just like that, Lily was bound and gagged. She searched for any benefit in the arrangement. She could stand, but she could not walk. She could move her arms and her fingers, but so what? Even though she easily believed Ted capable of being this crazy, she never would have given him credit for being half this clever.

"Well done," he congratulated himself as he pushed an armchair to a position in front of his captives. "I'm going to put this gun down and remove your gag. It's still handy, so don't do anything that might upset me."

Watching him place the gun on a nearby table, Lily had to fight back a fresh wave of disorientation. The number on the door was Ted's, but the room was not. It was as though a stage crew had swept in and rearranged the set. It was an ordinary hotel sitting room. Every speck of the clutter had vanished. Where had all those props gone?

After the handkerchief was removed, she worked up saliva to replenish her dry mouth. She twisted to look at Sally. Above the gag, her eyes were bloodshot and wild with fear.

"That was the hard way to go about tying you down," Ted said, settling himself in the chair with the pistol on his lap. "But I couldn't wait for you to come around from the chloroform. I need answers before four o'clock. That's when the final act is going to take place. Let's begin with why you didn't come home last night. Breedlove offered you money, didn't he? You couldn't turn it down, could you? That wasn't why you were sent there, but that didn't matter to you."

There was nothing in that string of questions and accusations Lily cared to dignify with an answer.

He rose to stand beside Sally and lift her chin with his

thumb. She turned her face away from him. "I don't know what to make of this one. Her passport gives San Francisco as her home. Has she been a stowaway all this time? Was your friend taking a free ride on my cousin's account?"

Some investigator. He didn't even know about Mr. Murphy and Sally.

"She hasn't had a chance to say much. I was caught off-guard when she answered your door. Not knowing what she knew, I had to come back here to get the chloroform and put her down immediately. Don't think it was easy, dragging a half-conscious body up those stairs. But, as they say, all in a day's work."

He returned to the chair and regarded Lily with hateful eyes. "Last night should have been easy. Days and days of putting together evidence — the diary, the letters. All I needed to do was plant a few inescapable, unmistakable clues while you were miles away. But you, you treacherous Amazon, you had to see to it that I was forced to adjust again. Do you have any idea how many hours you set me back? It will be the last time, I swear."

This was like having a nightmare in hell. Why hadn't she made a run for it when she had the chance? Hadn't she acknowledged to Paul how utterly mad and evil he was?

"The story, you see, is going to go like this: you were a naughty girl, and you paid a heavy price for your misdeeds. You desperately hoped to keep your lover's dealings with certain foreign powers hidden. I fought hard to keep the truth from coming out because I didn't want my cousin, Madeline, to be further humiliated, not when her mind was already unhinged by jealousy and grief. Everyone will know my motive was not to protect Joe, but to protect my dear relative. In the end, there was no help for it. This time, those prize-incompetents, the Monaco police, will not be able to sidestep their duty. This time, they will have to investigate. In your room, they will find a diary. In spite of the strongest possible objections, I shall be forced to hand over the journals you prepared for me, to be compared with the handwriting in that diary. From the entries there and from the torrid love letters that passed between Joe and you – the things he said, they made me blush – from those, everything will be revealed: his infidelity, his treasonous plans.

"I wasn't sure what I might do with your handwriting when I had you keep those journals. But that shows what happens when a man can think ahead. I should note that Joe's handwriting, lacking your privileged education, took more work to reproduce. But that was merely one more difficulty I successfully overcame."

His voice trailed off as his attention turned once more to Sally. He studied her, his lips pursed, a crease between his eyebrows. "Maybe it will turn out this woman was also involved with Joe. Maybe she was. Were you, my dear? Were you Joe's whore? I know he had plenty. Unfortunately, in the months before this trip, I was distracted by other pressing matters and wasn't able to develop the background I like to do. But that will be moot. This woman's involvement with Joe will be something else I heard from my cousin which I will repeat to Chief Inspector Gautier. It doesn't matter what is true or what I believe. It's what Madeline believed before she shot you two that matters.

"You came to my room this afternoon as you are known to do. You brought this woman with you. Madeline was here. What could be more natural? She was my cousin, your employer. I stepped out for a few minutes. Better yet, she ordered me to leave. Everyone knows how slavishly I obey her. While I was gone, she shot you both. I came back. I tried to talk her out of killing herself. Poor, wretched woman. I tried to stop her. I did. But she never would listen to me. The chief inspector himself can attest to that."

He patted the butt of the revolver with his left hand in what looked like silent applause and lapsed into some sort of interior reflection. The clock on the mantle chimed one o'clock. Why hadn't she promised Paul she would be at the restaurant at two o'clock? Would he conclude he had failed to convince her to join them? Would Jonathan try to contact her anyway? What good would that do? No one knew she was here. Pride was a deadly sin, all right.

"Maddie shot Joe, you know, but that will never be proved. She never produced a railway ticket, did she? That's because she didn't return from Cannes on Thursday like she claimed. She was here Wednesday night and shot her husband in the back. That wretched Gallagher woman could have told the police, but they didn't care. They were supposed to care, but they didn't."

Lily was having no difficulty reading between those lines. Without knowing how he had done it, she knew he had set up Mrs. Murphy to take the blame for her husband's murder. Paul was right. Ted had shot Mr. Murphy.

"So ladies, make yourselves comfortable. We're going to have to wait until the guest of honor gets here in a few hours."

Matters were slowly, painfully sorting themselves in Lily's mind. Ted's accusations, actions, machinations, were all part of a larger game. She and now Sally were nothing but incidental pawns in that game. "Why, Ted?" she said. "Why do you want to do this to Mrs. Murphy?"

In one fluid motion, he leapt to his feet and smacked her across the face with his open hand. He hadn't been in a position for delivering a hard blow, so she was more stunned than hurt. She heard Sally moan.

"Why?" he growled. "That's the part I hate. That's the part

you ruined by staying out all night. She was supposed to be in jail, waiting for trial, waiting to be hanged, while the damning truth unfolded. Now, everything's going to have to happen too fast. I won't have time to rub her nose in it. She'll die without knowing that I have, at long last, taken my revenge, our revenge. Her father, he was the Jacob to my father, the Esau. He stole the family's inheritance. By the time my father came of age, nothing was left. Her father got richer and richer, and we got poorer and poorer. As they say, charity begins at home, but he never threw more than a few crumbs our way."

He wiped at his nose with the back of his coat-sleeve. "Maybe I should thank you because in the end you made me enlarge the scandal and the crime. Maddie will be guilty of not one but two murders. It will come out that Joseph Murphy was involved in treasonous plots against his own and other governments. It wasn't enough for him to be arming Irish rebels. That would bring little obloquy in America. So I had to find out he was conspiring with Germany against his own nation. The evidence is in the documents and letters I placed in your room, rock-solid evidence. The police cannot avoid coming to the right conclusions this time. Joe had been empowered to offer the Mexican government Germany's help in retaking territories in Texas and New Mexico if Mexico agreed to take up arms against America in the event of a European war.

"The Monaco police won't care about Joe's involvement with espionage, but the people in San Francisco will; the people in California and Washington, D.C., will. It's a pity dear Maddie won't live to feel the shame that will be heaped on their heads, hers and her husband's."

He rubbed the butt of the gun against his forehead, a pained expression on his face. "I'm not sure who shot Joe. Maybe it wasn't Maddie after all." It sounded like he was

413

adjusting his plot one more time. "Maybe it was the German spies he was working with. I know they were the ones who ransacked her rooms and ran her out of town. Damn them to hell! Everything would have been so much easier if she had stayed in Monte Carlo."

The strands of Lily's logic were becoming tangled. Reality had torn loose from its moorings; it had gone sideways, upside-down. She struggled to keep her facts upright in the midst of his lies and erroneous assumptions. Apparently, he genuinely believed the people he worked with while pretending to be Mr. Murphy were the same people who had searched Mrs. Murphy's suite. Why shouldn't he? Ted knew nothing about the military plans or Hervé Andreas. How could he? Regardless, she needed to get a toehold in his thinking before she could possibly negotiate with him.

"Why would Mr. Murphy spy for Germany?" she asked.

"Money, what else? Spies are well paid, especially the traitors and collaborators who can turn the tide of war."

"Is that what you want, Ted? Money? Sally and I, we can come up with money."

"That's all you bitches ever think about, isn't it? You're just like Maddie, no idea of what matters to a man." He abruptly stopped and stared as if seeing her for the first time. "That's not the slatternly gown I got you."

It was such an absurd non sequitur, Lily half-laughed. "Nothing gets past Pinkerton's greatest detective, does it?"

He rose slowly, glared at her for several long seconds, then half turned, as though he were going to leave. Instead, he whirled and slammed his fist into her face. She heard the crack of her head against the wall. Her eyes filled with tears of pain. With nothing to bank them, they spilled onto her cheeks. She tasted blood. Her tongue hurt as much as her jaw. More blood oozed from her nose, and her ears wouldn't stop ringing.

"You slept with him, didn't you?" Ted hissed. "Breedlove paid you, and you slept with him."

There was no correct answer. "What." She coughed in an effort to clear her throat of blood and phlegm. "Possible ... difference ... could ...that ... make ... to ... you?" She measured each word with precisely the same emphasis as though the slightest imbalance would ignite an explosion.

He snorted and straightened, pressing his palm against the small of his back, and approached the decanters. Lily could sense Sally looking at her, but she kept her eyes leveled on their persecutor.

Drink in one hand, pistol in the other, Ted paced the length of the room, back and forth, back and forth, like a caged coyote. He had lost his limping gait. Another act, something else to put everyone off-stride. Her eyes took in the clock each time he approached the fireplace. Eighteen minutes past one.

Ted returned to the decanter to pour a second drink. The left side of Lily's face was swelling and throbbing cruelly. Her mouth had run out of space for her tongue. Surely that blow hadn't been part of the plan. If either Sally or Mrs. Murphy shot Lily before killing herself, how would a bruised and swollen jaw be explained? Ted might say they got into a catfight. It seemed far-fetched, but would Monaco's police trouble themselves about such an inconvenient assessment? Damned clever, all of it: the halting gait; the sycophancy; the bumbling, bombastic personality; the chaotic environment, nary a hint of the devilishly cunning mind.

She drew in a deep breath, savoring the pain because it sharpened her mind and will. She needed a plan. She closed her eyes, willing herself to step back mentally, away from him, away from her fury and her fear.

After a minute, which felt like an hour, ticked by on the

mantle clock, she looked up. She had one-half of a plan. She hadn't heard him turn the key after they entered. The door must be unlocked. She could stand. It would difficult, but she should be able to hop. Her hands and fingers were free. She should be able to turn the knob or pull the cord for the floor-waiter or both. But Ted had to be got out of the way. If she could invent a reason for him go to the bedroom for a few minutes, only a few minutes should suffice.

Ted tossed back the rest of the drink and turned his venomous glare on her again. She needed something to keep him at bay until she finished working out her plan. She couldn't trust him to keep his brittle temper intact until four o'clock. He could chloroform her and Sally, smother them while they were unconscious, and shoot them after Mrs. Murphy arrived.

"I have to say," she began, then checked herself. The flattery could not sound phony or condescending. She could not make the mistake of underestimating him again.

"It pains me to say it," she started again, "but in spite of the setbacks, you executed everything to perfection."

Ted pulled at the corners of his mouth, his eyes bright with suspicion. Poor Sally, she had spent the night with this crazed hound.

"There were a lot of moving parts that had to work together," Lily said.

"You cannot imagine how many."

"Like the gears in a watch," she said, striking a minor note of awe, "all the parts had to work together. But you're right. There's much I don't understand."

"You're not capable of appreciating it even if you knew everything."

"I certainly didn't fully appreciate you." A calamitous truth.

He straightened his posture, again pressing his palm against his back. At least that hadn't been part of his act. "But I fully appreciated you," he said. "You, parading around like somebody respectable. I knew who you were all along. You're nothing but a buttoned-up tart, nothing but the daughter of a whore."

A tsunami of emotion rolled through Lily's head, washed past her throat, undulated down her chest and abdomen until it reached her feet. Her mind constricted to the point of paralysis. That was not part of her plan. That was never supposed to be a part of any conversation.

"Maddie had me investigate you before she took you on. It was easy and not so easy. You had been in school back east since you were ten years old. That was simple enough to verify." His lips peeled back in a wicked rictus. "She did a good job, your mother, erasing the trail back to her. Told the school you were an orphan. Her attorney drew the bank drafts against a trust. But remember? I told you I excel at research. I kept digging. I found your mother, Effie Turner, and I found out she was quite alive in Chicago. I didn't pass along that choice piece of information to Maddie. I thought I might want to use it myself someday."

Lily's mind was unseizing. She could practically hear the hinges creaking and the joints unsnapping. This was her opportunity. His reveling in her mortification would provide the answer. She pressed her feet against the floor, digging her toes in, trying not to think about how the next blow would feel.

She said, "You call that research? You're from Chicago. You must frequent every brothel in the city. You probably live on 4th Street. How else would you get a woman to tolerate you? Look at how swollen with courage you are now that you've got us tied down. I'll bet you're notorious for beating up women in all the houses in Chicago."

She tilted her chin higher, letting her eyes project contempt. "Something else, Mr. Grand Investigator. My mother is a madam, not a whore, and a very successful one at that. Besides, how can a pimp look down on a whore? You pimped me out to Nicholas Breedlove, didn't you?"

During this taunting, Ted's face turned deep pink, then crimson, before giving way to glorious purple. During this time too, Lily had intertwined her fingers and clinched her two fists into a solid ball. She confirmed her feet were set hard against the floor. She was ready. She was beyond ready. She fixed her eyes on the bead of sweat that ran along his upper lip. What was it going to take?

"Is that what got you upset, Ted? You didn't get your piece of Breedlove's money? What do you think, Sally? There's nothing lower than a pimp, is there?"

Ted flung the tumbler aside. It hit the carpet and rolled away without breaking as he stormed over to stand directly in front of Lily. He raised his arm well above his shoulder, his fist trembling. His eyes were dark slits, his mouth, a grotesque snarl.

"You know what, Ted? You're a whore. You're Madeline's whore. She pays you, doesn't she?"

"Whore's spawn," he spat and began the swing.

Using all the strength her savage desperation had summoned, Lily shoved her heels against the floor and the chair against the wall as she drove her fists upwards, directly into his groin. Another useful life-lesson from Effie.

Ted went down with a wail of pain. It took Lily several seconds to perceive that in the midst of Ted's howling, someone was knocking, banging, pounding on the door.

# Thursday, March 19, 1914
## HÔTEL DE PARIS

PAUL BURST THROUGH THE DOOR FIRST, JONATHAN hard on his heels. Jonathan hesitated when his eyes met Lily's, but Paul's charge towards Ted, who was still writhing on the floor, never faltered. He delivered a vicious kick to Ted's head, then two or three to his ribs, then one to his kidney, then back to the head.

"There's a gun," Lily yelled, but Jonathan was already snatching it up. He calmly watched Paul land a couple more blows, then put his thumb and index finger to his lips, shocking the room with an ear-piercing whistle.

Paul, suspending a kick mid-swing, blinked up at Jonathan.

"Stand down, Paul," he said.

"I'm not nearly done." Paul's breath came in short, audible gasps. "I've wanted to do this since the first day I met the man."

"You don't want to kill him," Jonathan pointed out.

Paul shot a look at Lily. "Did you tell him that?" he demanded. Then to Jonathan, "If so, it's a rank lie. He's alive only because my right leg is no longer the lethal weapon it once was."

Despite his words, much of the coiled fury seemed to

drain from Paul's body as he mopped his forehead with a handkerchief.

Lily couldn't tell if Ted, lying face down, was or was not conscious, but she wasn't going to risk falling on her face in front of Jonathan by hopping over for a closer look.

Paul returned the handkerchief to his pocket. He said, "Killing this hyena would count, at most, as a misdemeanor. Myself, I would categorize it as selfless public service." Flashing a triumphant smile at Lily, he took Jonathan by the arm. "However, I see your point. I shall not murder him until we have untied the damsels in distress. I might be embarrassed to learn that one of them has filed a prior claim to the right."

Using his pocketknife, Paul made brisk work of cutting the ropes tying Sally while Jonathan loosed the slip-knots binding Lily. She tried not to wince and shrink away as he gingerly probed her jaw. She would have liked to exhibit a phlegmatic air, one which declared her unfazed, one that said it wouldn't matter if this sort of thing happened to her every day. That was the attitude she would have liked to project, but in fact, it was all she could do not to lay her head on his chest and sob uncontrollably.

Kneeling beside Ted, who was now wearing the gag, Paul regarded the length of rope in his hand with uncertainty. "I never had the privilege of serving in His Majesty's Navy," he said. "Have you?"

Jonathan looked over his shoulder. "No," he said, "but I can execute a mean marlinspike-hitch."

While Jonathan set to work on Ted, Paul poured two large brandies. Lily had stood beside her chair as soon as she felt she could trust her legs, but Sally remained seated, arms wrapped around herself, slowly rocking with her head bent, her hair curtaining her face. She hadn't said a word since the cavalry dashed in and set them free.

Paul sat beside Sally and gently unlatched her arms, so he could fold her hands around the glass. He put his arm around her shoulders and leaned close to whisper in her ear. Sally's brow wrinkled in consternation. After he guided the tumbler to her lips, she took a stout swallow.

"I thought you weren't supposed to kick a man when he was down," Lily said. Her voice was obstructed by her thickened tongue and pounding pain.

"The Marquess of Queensberry was slow getting to my neighborhood," Paul said. "Is your jaw broken?"

"How can I tell?"

"How wide can you open your mouth?"

She was about to demonstrate when the polite knock of one of the hotel's staff sounded. Glances bounced around among the four.

"Yes?" Paul called, leaning down to retrieve his hat from the floor.

"Monsieur Wycliffe," a voice said, "is everything good? There were noises."

Paul pointed a finger at Sally and Jonathan, then held it against his lips. "Stand over there," he told Lily, pointing towards the liquor bottles. "Hide your bad side."

As soon as she was stationed, she heard the door open and Paul's hearty greeting. From the tail of her eye, she could see he had allowed the door to open only partially.

"Is Monsieur Wycliffe here?" the floor-waiter said.

Lily lifted a bottle, peered at its label, put it down, and picked up another.

"He is indisposed at present," Paul said. "Dreadfully sorry about the disturbance. The Victrola puts up a terrible noise, worse than an Alsatian giving birth. The lady and I were going through some dance routines, Tango. I am sorry to say that I am rather clumsy and dislocated some of the furniture."

Lily bent her head, letting the mess of hair knocked free from her bun further hide her bloodied face. That man would have to be a complete dolt if he thought she had gotten this disheveled dancing. Doubtlessly, Paul had included a man-to-man wink along with his explanation.

"Paul," she interrupted in a querulous tone, "we're out of gin. Tell him to bring some more."

"Her feet hurt from being stepped on," Paul announced cheerily. "Would you fetch a bottle of Bols? Mr. Wycliffe would be most appreciative."

"Of course, Monsieur."

"And some ice," Paul said. "Two buckets."

"Of course, Monsieur."

"Do we want something to eat, Lily?" Paul said. "What does Ted want?"

How about raw lizard turds?

When she didn't reply, Paul said, "Bring a plate of canapés, the largest plate you have. And some sandwiches, ham. Soup too, today's best. Wait until everything is ready and bring it all together."

# Thursday, March 19, 1914
## HÔTEL DE PARIS

PAUL PAUSED OUTSIDE TED'S BEDROOM DOOR TO return the handkerchief to his pocket while he stuffed down his satisfaction like a shirttail. The others were gathered around the table where the waiter had laid out the food. Sally was spooning soup into Lily's mouth.

"What took so long in there?" Jonathan said.

"I've always wanted to beard a man in his own lair," Paul said. "It was necessary to prolong the pleasure. That one has a coruscating wit. He continues to maintain his stout innocence, claims he was set up by these two conniving, thieving women. After dispatching that topic, I wanted to hear what he had in the way of stock-tips. I'm thinking of taking a little flutter on the Exchange. By the way, the sight of Wycliffe without his toupee is nothing short of astonishing. I expected him to be as bald as an egg. Not so, however, his hair does bear an alarming resemblance to mouse-fur."

"I hope you stuffed the filthy thing down his throat," Lily said, pulling back from the spoonful of soup. She held her hand against her jaw as she spoke.

"You need to learn to temper your violent tendencies," Paul said.

"I'm not the one who was longing to kick him in the ribs," Lily said.

"No, it would appear you had longings for another part." Paul gave Jonathan a sly grin. "Be careful around that one. She's got a fist on her like a mule-skinner."

By way of an answer, Lily picked up the ice-pack and applied it to her face after swiping back more of the tangled hair loosened during her ordeal.

Watching Jonathan finish a sandwich, Paul silently patted himself on the back. At least the boy didn't eat like he had been out haying.

Looking around, Paul said, "It must have taken Hercules to muck out this room. I presume he diverted the stream up at Beausoleil."

"Another part of his act," Lily said. "He doesn't have a limp either."

Paul smiled grimly. He, of all people, duped by The Hyena. Live by the con, die by the con.

Jonathan said, "Paul, I was explaining to the ladies how you and I showed up so promptly."

Paul said, "It might not stack up next to the relief of Mafeking, but I think we can take some satisfaction from our performance."

"You didn't trust me to come," Lily said.

"I was uncertain, and I didn't want to wait until two o'clock to find out. Gracious of Wycliffe to leave your room unlocked. The earrings on the table told me you had been there. The suitcases were strapped. I checked. They were full, yet it didn't seem you had had sufficient time to pack so completely. My thoughts naturally turned to him."

"What are we going to do with that creature?" Sally said.

"Hand him over to the police," Jonathan said.

"He's committed no crime the Monaco police will jail him

for," Paul said.

"No crime?" Sally said. "What about kidnapping and planning to murder Lily and me? What about beating up Lily?"

"Lover's quarrel. Happens every day," Paul said.

Sally's look of incredulity was replaced by one of disgusted understanding. "Right," she said. "The police think nothing of a man's beating his own wife or girlfriend."

"In Whitechapel, certainly," Jonathan said, "but in Monte Carlo?"

"Everywhere," Paul answered, setting aside the empty plates so he could bring out the deck of cards he had found while searching every cubic-inch of Wycliffe's wardrobe and drawers.

"Who wants to play?" he said, shuffling. "I think better when my hands are busy."

"What game?" Lily asked.

Paul resisted the impulse to suggest Old Maid. "Whist," he said.

"Bridge," she said.

"Hearts," Sally said. "Bridge takes too much concentration."

Paul raised his eyebrows in Lily's direction. Her eyes were closed, and she was drawing and expelling deep breaths while Jonathan pressed the icepack against her cheek.

"Hearts," Paul said and began dealing the cards.

"I confess this is a first for me," Jonathan said. "What does one do with a bound and gagged madman?"

"Can't we turn him over to the American authorities, the consulate or some such?" Sally asked. "Can't we bring charges as Americans?"

"No proof," Lily pointed out. "Only our word."

"What's wrong with our word?"

"Our word against his. Two women against a man."

425

Jonathan said, "The United States has no extradition treaties with any European countries."

"Neither does hell," Sally said. "Why don't we just poison the dog and be done with it?"

Paul looked up from his cards. He was starting to like that girl.

"What has he done beyond this lover's quarrel you had this afternoon?" Jonathan asked.

Lily pushed Jonathan's hand with the ice-pack aside. "He shot Mr. Murphy," she said, her voice thick and strained. "Claims it was Mrs. Murphy or some German fiend. He hasn't made up his mind, but it was him all right."

Jonathan said, "No proof again?"

Paul said, "Irrelevant. No prosecution can be brought. The man he shot was already dead. My apologies, Miss Holmes."

Jonathan said, "Are there other recently deceased persons with whom he can be connected?"

Paul understood the question and the look that accompanied it. "There was a notable suicide recently," he said. "But I know for a fact Wycliffe wasn't involved in that man's death."

"I see," Jonathan said.

Paul was certain Lily hadn't missed the underlying importance of the exchange. He avoided her eyes by frowning at the cards in the center of the table and taking the trick.

"Mrs. Murphy is to be here at four o'clock. We have to –" Lily interrupted herself to gather more breath. "Dispose of him before then. And we need to account for him. She's the only one who might put up an alarm when he goes missing."

"How can we know she's the only one?" Paul said. "How do we know what else he's been getting up to and with whom?"

Sally said, "Last night, during my intermittent spells

of consciousness, he couldn't stop ranting about Madeline, about her money, about his inheritance, some gibberish about patents and inventions. His complaint is against her. He wants to destroy her. I have no great fondness for Madeline Murphy, but she should be warned."

Paul found the idea of turning Wycliffe over to his cousin almost irresistible. She would make certain he did not escape with his manhood intact. Nevertheless, he said, "She would only be one more complication. If we can rid ourselves of him without involving her, so much the better."

"What should she be told?" Jonathan asked Sally.

"Everything," Sally said.

To Paul's raised eyebrows, Lily interjected, "She's my friend from San Francisco. You tell him, Sally."

"I mean everything that concerns Mr. Wycliffe. He thought I was piggybacking Lily's account, but that wasn't true. I have my own rooms."

Paul made a show of studying the cards in his hand before pulling one out to throw on the table. He was liking that girl more and more. She had immediately understood that they were not being perfectly forthcoming with Jonathan.

"Should she be told about Wycliffe's posing as Joseph Murphy at Winzig Krenz's?" Paul asked.

Lily nodded. In answer to Sally's inquisitive expression, he summarized what Lily had deduced at Villefranche.

"But, but why?" Sally said. "Why would he do that?"

Lily said, "Whatever it was, Mr. Murphy's death was supposed to put an end to it."

Paul said, "Thereby making retribution or recovery on the part of his accomplices impossible. Very shrewd, when you think about it, shoot Murphy and tie off whatever was going on at Krenz's."

"And get Mrs. Murphy charged with murder at the same

time," Lily said. She explained how both Wycliffe and Bridget Rose claimed Mrs. Murphy was in her rooms the night her husband was shot. "He planted clues to make it look like she was there. He wanted to frame her for murder."

Paul said, "What kind of clues?"

When Lily told about the false teeth in the glass and hair in the brush, Paul recalled the device for making wax-impressions of keys he had found in Wycliffe's bedroom. No doubt, the skunk could come and go in the Murphys' suite as he pleased just as he could with Lily's room.

"Also, she couldn't produce a railway ticket to prove when she had returned from Cannes," Lily finished, blinking back the tears forming in her pain-widened eyes.

"Are you sure your jaw's not broken?" Paul said.

"One more thing," Lily said, "Ted's convinced it was German spies who ransacked Mrs. Murphy's rooms. He's fixated on Germans."

"That must have spooked him as much as it did Mrs. Murphy," Paul said, relishing the thought. He now had a perfect understanding of why Wycliffe sought to close off the faux-Murphy's connection with his friends, the Germans.

Paul, Sally, and Lily focused on their cards. They knew it had been Hervé's crew looking for the military plans, but Jonnie didn't need to hear about that. Downstairs, Paul had shared with Jonnie the information about a probable scheme to arm Irish revolutionaries and told him Cyril's death was undeniably connected with Basil Zaharoff. But the Schlieffen Plan figured nowhere in the Irish scheme or in Cyril's death. There was no reason for Jonnie to appear more valuable than necessary to his superiors. It was time he got out of the spy-business and back to crime-reporting.

Sally sat with her chin in her hand, her eyes on Paul. She said, "Last night he was going on and on about the incontrovertible evidence he had proving not only that Joe and Lily were lovers but that they were involved in espionage schemes with Germany."

"Evidence?" Jonathan said. "He had evidence?"

Sally said, "He told Lily he used her journals to forge her handwriting. He already had samples of Joe's. He constructed piles of letters between the two of them. They're in Lily's room, waiting for the police to find them."

"That answers one of my long-standing questions," Paul said. "What he was doing with his spare time. A good forgery is not easy, even for a professional. And reams of it? One cannot help but admire the man's modesty. In the midst of all that boasting, he never once mentioned a talent for forgery."

Jonathan looked at the clock on the mantle. "It's after three o'clock. What's to be done with him?" he said.

The group fell silent as Paul shuffled and dealt the cards once more. "There can never be anything other than a Carthaginian peace with that maniac," he said, passing three cards to Sally. "We could chloroform him and return him to Krenz's cohorts, resurrect his Murphy-disguise. I apologize, Miss Holmes."

"Sally, if you please."

"Paul," he reciprocated, then continued, "Pin a note on his lapel. Let them know they've been played for chumps."

"That would be tantamount to murder," Jonathan said.

Paul grinned.

"We cannot be parties to a murder," Jonathan said.

"How can we be sure they would kill him?" Sally said. "What if he bought them off or convinced them he could be useful?"

"How would we get him there?" Lily asked.

Silence descended once more as each person looked at his cards.

"Ted can never go back to Chicago," Lily said. "He knows who my mother is. He knows where she is. I can hide from him, but she cannot."

Paul jerked his head back. "What a shock. All this time, I've been thinking you sprang fully grown and armored from the head of Zeus."

"Did you hear me?"

"Tell your mother not to open the door to strangers."

"That won't be possible. We have to decide something quickly. I'm leaving tomorrow. I should have left today."

Paul was pleased to observe that the statement came as news to Jonnie.

"Have him committed to an insane asylum," Sally said. "Isn't that what people do with their inconvenient daughters?"

"He could escape or buy his way out," Jonathan said. "Harry Thaw fled to Canada."

"Well then, is there some pest-infested, fever-ridden outpost where he can be sent to die a slow, miserable death?" Sally asked.

"We could package him up for a rest cure in the Belgian Congo or the Amazon Jungle. Both are famous for their salubrious climates and friendly natives," Paul said. "They could carve him into chops and steaks."

"Let him judge himself," Lily said. "Give him a pistol with one bullet in it."

"He's too much the coward," Paul said.

"We could hoist him on his own petard," Sally said. "Shoot him and claim it was suicide."

Lily was nodding enthusiastically.

"My, my, you girls are a bloodthirsty lot," Paul said. Looking at Jonathan, he said, "You object to a solution that promotes Wycliffe's end. That's a sound sentiment but bad judgment. Something has to give. That freak has committed

430

serious crimes, and if left to his own devices, he would have committed several murders this afternoon."

Jonathan folded his cards and laid them face down on the table. "Hoisting him on his own petard isn't such a bad idea," he said. "Why not set him up to be arrested for another crime, one with a very long jail sentence. Ensure the police have the right facts, so they will come to the right conclusion. Seems to me, if Devil's Island was good enough for Dreyfus, it should be good enough for Wycliffe."

Paul said, "The Russian exquisites know how to deal with a diseased rat better than the French do. A katorga could be just the thing. It never gets cold enough to kill some smells, but a slow, unheated train-ride across the Siberian Steppes should deprive Mr. Wycliffe of much of his stench."

Each person retreated into his own thoughts once more. A possibility began to form in Paul's mind, but it would take time to set up, and there was no time to spare in his plans for his immediate future. There would have to be a sidetrack where Wycliffe could be temporarily parked.

He said, "Usually, I disdain blackmail because of its lack of originality, but it could be a murder-free way of silencing him."

"How can we blackmail him?" Jonathan said. "If we have no evidence that would satisfy the authorities, we have no evidence with which to blackmail him."

"True," Paul agreed, "but we can disgrace him so thoroughly he will never show his face in Chicago again." Sicily's boy-calamites and a camera should ensure that outcome.

"What about his disguises?" Lily said.

"You have a point, but his name would be ruined."

"Not enough," Lily said.

Paul leaned back. He sat, motionless, his eyes three-quarters shut. The card game had served its purpose, simultaneously loosening and sharpening his thoughts. He believed he had struck on a solution that would satisfy everyone – everyone except Hervé and possibly even Hervé.

"Who will rid me of this troublesome leech?" he said, getting to his feet. "Unless we shoot him here and now, whatever we come up with is going to take time to put into action. Grant me an hour or so, if you please."

He pulled Sally's chair back and offered his arm. "Miss Sally, if you would like to lie down and take a rest, I shall be pleased to escort you. Perhaps it would be as well if Lily and Jonathan remain here to greet Mrs. Murphy. I concede. She should be apprised of her cousin's misdeeds."

At the door, he stopped. "I almost forgot. Lily, your earrings."

He removed them from his coat's inner-pocket and returned to place them on the table in front of her. "I would never think of leaving them unprotected."

# Thursday, March 19, 1914
## HÔTEL DE PARIS

As soon as the door closed behind Paul and Sally, Jonathan was on his feet. He filled a clean linen with fresh ice and placed it in Lily's hands. Next, he gathered the dishes and stacked them on the service-tray before accumulating the used glasses.

"Would you care for more soup?" he asked.

"No."

He placed the uneaten food along with the dishes and utensils on the tray and put everything in the hallway. He opened the bedroom door and looked in. Lily could hear muffled sounds coming from the room.

"How is he?" she asked.

"Looks like he's coming around after Paul's pummeling."

Good. She was eager to hear how Ted would go about explaining himself to his cousin. She was even more interested in hearing how Jonathan was going to explain himself to her.

"Do you need more ice?" he asked.

"No."

He withdrew his watch from its pocket, checked the time, then crisscrossed the room for no discernible reason before reseating himself. "You mentioned you are leaving tomorrow," he said.

She had no need to discuss that. She knew all about it. What she didn't understand was Jonathan and Paul. They acted like they barely knew one another, yet Paul had known she knew Jonathan. At the Hôtel Hermitage, he had said, "I will have Jonathan Chandler with me." Just like that, with the snap of a finger, he could produce Jonathan Chandler.

"How long have you known Paul Newcastle?" she said.

"I met him recently."

"At the conference?"

"No, that's – No. I was, that is, my employer told me to look him up."

She let the silence lengthen as an invitation for elaboration, but he failed to accept it.

"Do you trust him?" Lily said.

"Paul?"

"Paul."

Jonathan took some time before answering. "I could say I have little choice but to trust him. Do you know of a reason I should not?"

No, she knew of no reason Jonathan should not trust Paul. If anything, she should be gushing like Spindletop with praise. He had rescued her not once but twice in less than twenty-four hours. The second time, he had literally saved her life. No, she could not give Jonathan a reason he should not trust Paul. But she had every reason not to trust either of them.

"Did he tell you everything?" she asked.

That damned crooked smile again. A thin version of it, but nevertheless ....

"Without knowing what everything is, I am not in a position to judge."

This time, she was the one who ignored the silent invitation for elaboration.

"Would you like to tell me everything, so I can compare?"

Jonathan said. His eyes were watchful.

All at once, the enervating effects of pain, the aftermath of terror, and the residue of the predator Krenz's drug descended in concert. Fatigue swamped every particle of Lily's being, her mind, her muscles, her skin, her fingertips. Her hand released the napkin containing the ice chips, and she could no longer keep her eyelids from drooping.

Jonathan was kneeling beside her, his hands grasping hers. "You've gone deathly pale. Let me help you to the sofa. You need to lie back."

She extracted one of her hands from his grip and covered her eyes with it, her elbow propped on the table. She could not lie down. She must keep herself erect. She must. The only other choice? There was no other choice.

Since the calmness in Ted's room had been restored, with each renewed stab of pain, each time every instinct demanded she descend into hysterics, she had been stiffened by a memory, another memory from the early years in Chicago, the years before the move to the big house. It was a sultry summer morning when that man came to the door. He began by yelling at Effie, who stared at him wordlessly. Then he slapped her, hard. Effie had stumbled backwards until she hit a table and was stopped. The man surged into the room and landed four blows with his fists, one to each side of her head and two to her ribs. Everything happened so quickly that Lily, sitting on the floor playing with her ragdoll, was unable to react. She said nothing, did nothing, other than clutch her doll tighter. Effie had not resisted, but when the man raised his arm once more, she ducked beneath it, and in one swift motion, yanked Lily up and was pulling her out the door. Afterwards, they had walked the streets for hours and hours. They had walked and walked until well after nightfall.

Near the top of a very long list of things for which Lily

435

believed she could never forgive her mother had been her allowing that man to introduce violence into their lives. Yet today, for the first time ever, Lily realized that during the long, hungry, and thirsty hours they had trudged along Chicago's hot, crowded, dirty streets, Effie had never once let go of Lily's hand. And, Lily also realized, in spite of the blood on her head and the pain that caused her to stoop and to stop frequently for breath, Effie had never cried.

Jonathan was rubbing the back of her hand, the one encircled by his own. His face had lost all traces of geniality. "Earlier, I had to play the Devil's Advocate," he said. "Everyone's blood was up, and I've seen too much senseless tragedy as it is. But I will admit it in private. If you want, I will kill that man."

Lily pressed her palm against her mouth to prevent the smile that would have provoked another stab of pain. "How romantic," she said. "No one has ever proposed that to me before. Let's wait and see what Paul comes back with."

"Before he does, there's something I must say."

Lily felt her heart flutter with something like happiness.

He reached out to hook a long strand of her hair behind her ear. "You mentioned leaving tomorrow. I regret to say I must leave this evening on the eight o'clock. I must return to London immediately. It is unavoidable."

Lily's happiness collapsed into searing chagrin. She had expected him to beg her to stay another week, another day. Instead, he was going to beat her out of town.

"Exit, pursued by a bear," she murmured under her breath.

"I beg your pardon?"

Lily brushed off his confusion with a shake of her head.

He said, "What I wanted to say before then .... That is, I have many questions about ..... Not that I have the right .... Are you certain you don't want more ice? Never mind. I can call the waiter for more soup. Never mind. What I wanted to say — that is, what I am saying — is that I refuse to see this as an end. I very much would like for you to come to London."

His eyes were no longer searching. They were asking, offering, pleading, and Lily's difficulty in speaking was no longer due to the swollen jaw but to the pounding of her heart.

"I have work in Paris."

"Afterwards?"

"Don't." Her whisper had been so soft she wasn't sure she had said it aloud. She couldn't raise her eyes higher than his chin. She couldn't allow herself to be drawn into those bottomless, dark eyes. She had never known which world frightened her more, the one that was dangerous or the one that was indifferent. This man promised to relieve her of both. She had a sudden, terrible understanding of Sally's decision to throw it all over for Mr. Murphy.

"I would," Jonathan said.

"I couldn't."

"I would."

"I know."

The sharp knock on the door spared her. Neither Lily nor Jonathan moved.

It came again, louder, more insistent.

They looked at the clock on the mantle, ten minutes until four o'clock.

# Thursday, March 19, 1914
## HÔTEL DE PARIS

MADELINE MURPHY APPEARED TAKEN ABACK WHEN
Lily opened the door. "What happened to you? Did a horse
step on your face? And who fashioned your hair?"

"You're here to see Mr. Wycliffe," Lily said.

"Since this is his room, I think that's a safe inference."

Mrs. Murphy's gaze went from Lily to Jonathan and back
to Lily.

"Mrs. Murphy, may I present –"

"Are you the man from Schneider? You're about a week
late. Where's Teddy?"

Lily's eyes met Jonathan's. "Mrs. Murphy," she said, "may
I suggest you take a seat?"

It took several passes to convince Madeline Murphy that
there was no representative from Schneider et Cie or any
other aviation firm present and that she really should remove
her coat and accept a brandy. Only after they assured her
she would be allowed to speak with her cousin after hearing
what they had to say, did she agree.

Jonathan took the lead, and Lily gladly allowed him to
take the brunt of Mrs. Murphy's harsh questions. She filled
in only when they concerned details not covered earlier.
She was more than a little impressed by his perfect recall.

Even if Paul had coached him before they arrived, there had been little time for absorbing everything so thoroughly. The disclosure of a friend who was kidnapped from Lily's room was met with a sharp look of displeasure.

When Jonathan finished, Mrs. Murphy looked at Lily. "You believe Teddy intended to frame me for my husband's murder." It was a flat statement, not a question.

Lily repeated what Jonathan had related about the false teeth and the hairbrush. She didn't mention the missing railway ticket again.

"And he was going to murder me in this room," Mrs. Murphy mulled aloud, holding out her glass for a refill. She smiled warmly at Jonathan. "And you are not the man from Schneider. There never was a man from Schneider. It looks like I am very lucky Mr. Newcastle convinced you my cousin was up to no-good."

She reached out to pat Jonathan's hand and let hers linger a shade too long on his. Lily refused to meet his eyes. He was on his own. Mrs. Murphy fell silent, the gloved fingers of one hand drumming against the side of her thigh.

She inclined her chin towards the bedroom door. "He's in there?"

"Yes, ma'am," Jonathan said.

"If he told you he was doing this because he had some long-standing grievance against my father, it was just another one of his maggot-faced lies. What are you planning to do with him? Turn him over to the worthless Monaco police?"

Jonathan again did a masterful job of summing up the difficulties inherent in that question. He ended by acknowledging they were waiting for Paul to return.

"Mr. Newcastle believes he may have a solution," Jonathan said.

Mrs. Murphy gave the bedroom door a malignant look

and sniffed loudly. "I will have something to say about that," she announced.

# Thursday, March 19, 1914
## HÔTEL DE PARIS

Before Lily could ponder the significance of Mrs. Murphy's statement, their attention was drawn to the opening door, through which Paul Newcastle strode like Hector taking the field at Troy. He was followed by the perpetually vexed Jacques Barousse. Mrs. Murphy's features hardened.

"Good afternoon," Paul said, joviality spilling over in his tone "Mrs. Murphy, Miss Turner, I believe you know Mr. Barousse. Jacques, this is Mr. Jonathan Chandler, Miss Turner's friend whom I was lucky enough to enlist in our cause."

Lily fought back her impulse to answer with a farcical double-wink. *Sure. Sure. I get it. We're disavowing your acquaintance with Jonathan.* The charade seemed all the more ridiculous because, when Paul and Jonathan were together, the similarities in their appearances were glaringly obvious. Did no one else notice?

Paul said, "Mr. Barousse is in a position to help us out of our present difficulties."

"That will be the first time," Mrs. Murphy said.

Paul looked at her. "You have been informed of the situation?"

"Say what you need to," she returned.

He said, "Everyone agrees that Ted Wycliffe is an exceedingly dangerous man. There are no two ways about it. He must be got out of the way permanently. His cannon must be spiked. In order to have time for this to be arranged, he must be detained somewhere temporarily. Mr. Barousse has acquaintances of the official sort and, need I mention, the discreet sort, who are willing to escort our friend to an undisclosed location in France until such time as it is convenient for us to have him released."

"Released to whom?" Mrs. Murphy said.

"Those arrangements will be made with Mr. Barousse's friends."

"No, they won't," Mrs. Murphy said.

Lily felt her shoulders slump. She should have known nothing would convince Mrs. Murphy of anything she didn't want to be convinced of.

"You have it all wrong. You have it all wrong as usual. Be a dear and get me a whiskey and soda," she said to Jonathan. "I can only take so much of this syrup." She returned to Paul. "I'll tell you what's going to be done with my cousin."

Lily stamped her foot with frustration, but no one seemed to notice. She was tired of sinking in the unfathomable question of Ted Wycliffe's fate. At least Loveday Brooke's villains had the decency to kill themselves after the lady-detective exposed their perfidy.

"Before we get to that," Mrs. Murphy said, "I'm going to clear up a few facts. I told those two." She indicated Lily and Jonathan. "The idea that Teddy had a grievance against my father is ludicrous. My father gave his no-count brother, my uncle, large sums of money which he was never able to hold on to. After my uncle's death, my cousin came to my father and wanted to renounce all future claims to a share in our grandfather's estate for a premature payout. This exchange was instigated by him, but my father willingly agreed to it. Even after that abdication of his rights, my father repeatedly bankrolled other ventures for Ted Wycliffe."

She held her hand out for the whiskey and smiled up at Jonathan. "Let me tell you what his grudge is really about. Last year, Ted Wycliffe was indicted in Chicago on several counts of fraud and embezzlement. He swore he was innocent and begged me to advance the money to cover his legal fees. I loaned him the money all right, but I'm not as tender-hearted as my father was. I charged a suitable rate of interest and took liens on all his property to secure the debt. Before we left the United States, he told me he had been cleared of the charges and that he was almost ready to repay the loans.

"Perhaps I should have questioned it then, but I did not. I believed him because I wanted a relative. I have none other except him. However, after we got here, it started becoming clearer and clearer to me that something was not right with his story. In fact, it became clearer and clearer that a lot was not right with his story. I made my own inquiries. I sent wires from Beaulieu to my representatives in Chicago. I learned he not only had not been found innocent, he had never come to trial. He was out on bail, a bail I financed, and he had disappeared. I also learned he could not be extradited from Europe. At that point, I became certain he never planned to return to America."

Lily ran her fingers beneath the rims of her eyes, underlining her exhaustion and her amazement.

"That, gentlemen, was only the beginning of his fantastic string of lies to me. My cousin lured me here this afternoon using the same false pretenses he used to lure me away from Cannes the night he shot my husband. He told me he had arranged a meeting for me that night with a man from the

Schneider Company. He fed me some cock-and-bull story about the man, the Schneider agent. He said the agent was afraid our negotiations would be discovered by spies from Vickers, so I had to register under a false name in some out-of-the-way hovel in Nice. That must have put Teddy rocking with laughter. But it worked, didn't it? I couldn't prove I returned from Cannes Thursday morning, only from Nice. I decided I wasn't going to do that." She delivered the last sentence with a hard look at Barousse.

He in turn said, "Madame, if I may inquire, why were you seeking an interview with the Schneider firm?"

Indeed, Lily thought, especially since they don't sell tapestries or jardinières.

"I was coming to that. My grandfather was an inventor along the lines of that Tesla fellow and Thomas Edison. That is to say, he did a lot of tinkering with electricity and motors. You see, genius runs in our family, not madness. My cousin must have gotten that from his mother's side. Anyway, among the many patents registered under Grandfather's name at home and in Europe is one for a magneto ignition-switch, an invention whose time has come. It looks like it's going to be just the thing for the engines in those aeroplanes. The French have been mad about designing those things since one of theirs won the prize for being the first to fly across the English Channel. Teddy told me the Schneider Company wanted to purchase the rights to the switch and that he had arranged the meeting. He said I would be looking at hundreds of thousands of dollars in royalties. Note I said 'I' would be looking at hundreds of thousands of dollars in royalties, not Teddy. His rights to Grandfather's patents were among the things he signed away when he negotiated the premature payout from my father."

Her smile of satisfaction turned into a frown. "I wouldn't

be a bit surprised to find out I penned a new will after my husband's death, a new will naming my cousin as my sole heir."

"He did have a talent for penmanship," Paul said.

"Be that as it may. I'm not dead, and here's what is going to happen to Mr. Wycliffe. Once I found out the truth, I wired Pinkertons in Chicago. They're sending a man down from their European office who will escort him back to the States on the next steamer out of Monte Carlo. Another one of their men will meet him in New York City and take him on to Chicago. If nothing else, he's guilty of violating his bail-terms. I've begun the foreclosures on his property and garnished his bank accounts. By the time he gets there, I will have several additional iron-clad charges to bring against him. Pinkertons has great sway in Chicago. The Almighty Dollar has even more. You may consider his goose laced, basted, and cooked because I can promise you, he will never draw another free breath."

She addressed Barousse. "You may have him until the next White Star sails. That should be later this week. I don't care if you scourge and starve him. Just make sure there's something left for me to send back to Chicago." She got to her feet. "Now, I'm ready to speak to my cousin."

She threw open the bedroom door and spent a few seconds taking in the sight. "Ah, Teddy," she said, "you never did have any taste for half-measures did you? After all that time you spent dancing around me like a trained gorilla, this is where we're going to part company. The men who are going to be taking care of you from here on out will explain it to you. I don't have the time. The baroness has a nephew who has set up talks for me with Vickers. Her family, the Rothschilds, you may have heard of them, has connections all over Europe, banking and railroads and such. The young man is also

445

going to arrange a meeting with Farman Aviation. I'll ask him about Schneider too, now that I know they were never contacted. I should be able to get a better deal by playing them all against each other."

Turning away from the bedroom, she said, "Poor Teddy, he will always be his own worst enemy."

"Not while I'm alive," Paul said, none too quietly.

While Mrs. Murphy was speaking to Barousse and Paul as she made her way out the door, Jonathan said to Lily. "I regret I didn't get to know Mr. Wycliffe sooner. He seems to have an extraordinary faculty for making enemies."

"It's not too late. Stay another day." She hated herself as soon as the words were out of her mouth.

By way of an answer, he took her hand and squeezed it. When he released it, she realized he had deposited a calling card there.

"My address," he said. "My landlady's telephone number."

She buried her hand in the pocket of the blue dress as Paul Newcastle sidled closer.

He said, "Lily, you look like you could use a rest. There's no need for you two to wait here. I'll see to it that Mr. Barousse and Ted get on their way. And, don't worry. I'll lock up."

# Thursday, March 19, 1914
## VILLA ACHILLES

PAUL WATCHED THE TAILLIGHTS OF THE MOTORCAB disappear before he turned towards the twin Coqs Gaulois guarding the path to Hervé's door. He was certain his friend heard the vehicle. His ears would be sharply attuned to any coming or going this night.

After wordlessly receiving Paul, Hervé took his accustomed place on the divan while Paul helped himself to the whiskey. He was more than ready for a stiff drink. Unwilling to forfeit the sharpness of his perceptions or the domestication of his reactions, he had forborne spirits until now. Hervé passively regarded Paul as he tossed off the drink, preparing himself for the disquisition that was to follow.

"The documents you sought," Paul began, "they've had a tortured history of late. First, they were burned. Then, like a phoenix, they rose reconstituted from the ashes. Before you likewise resurrect your hopes, I regret to inform you they have once more gone out of reach."

Hervé listlessly waved off the comment. "So has Alexei. He has bolted." He paused. "But you knew that was coming."

"I was ninety-nine percent certain. Near the end of an affair, you always take on a Lear-like aspect."

"Alexei was no mere affair. He was different."

Paul did not doubt his friend's sincerity, only his memory. "A Menelaus-like aspect," he amended.

"Better. Are you going to raise the fleet?"

"Is he worth a thousand ships?"

Hervé gave a noncommittal shrug. "We had barely completed a truly magnificent *entrée* in our *pas de deux*, the finest of my life, when he abruptly discovered his calling as a choreographer. Because he is cursed with youth's indelible delusion that any world he touches will collapse without him, he was convinced he had destroyed Russian dance by abandoning the Imperial Ballet. In a perversion of restitution, he has decided to take it upon himself to save, resuscitate, or create — I am unsure which — the Italian School of Dance. Cerrito, Cormani, all must bow to the savior of their art. This will be accomplished in a matter of months with Antonio's able assistance. Antonio, who doesn't know his arm from his elbow. I foresee Alexei will end like the other great Alexander, weeping inconsolably over the deplorable lack of new worlds to be conquered."

Paul sipped at his second whiskey and thought how good it felt to be free of that string of spaghetti, Antonio.

Hervé said, "You may as well complete the tale. Did Miss Holmes have the documents?"

"She had been alerted to fact that I knew who was looking for them in her rooms. That it was you, she put together quickly enough. Murphy had told her about his visit to you, and she believed only the three of you knew what the papers signified. The problem was, we needed to extract certain concessions from Jacques Barousse, the manager of the Hôtel de Paris. She ultimately agreed to let the documents be used for such an exchange."

"My name was left out of the matter with Barousse?"

"Naturally. Miss Holmes was scarcely unknown to him,

but there was no reason for you to figure in it. I might note, however, that forgiveness for the damage to Miss Holmes' rooms was among the items included in the negotiations. There was no reason she should have to pay for what your idiots smashed."

"On whom did you lay off that?"

"It wasn't easy. I was tempted to blame the Mad Mullah of Somali, him or the Swiss Navy or the Hawaiian Hussars, but I dreaded the diplomatic storms that would be aroused by such charges. In the end, I suggested the Austrians. They're harmless enough."

"Barousse believed you?"

"He pretended to."

"What did the police conjecture?"

"They were not called for either incident, Miss Holmes or Mrs. Murphy."

Hervé stroked his unshaven chin. "Was money involved in this exchange?" he asked.

Paul shook his head. "Miss Holmes was adamant that the documents be placed in the right hands. To her, that meant the French government. She was also adamant they should not be sold."

Hervé leaned back and regarded his visitor with hooded eyes. "Naturally you honored that desire," he said.

"A man should do what's right every ten or twenty years, just to keep his hand in. Otherwise, he's apt to lose his touch."

"I understand. In all honesty, now that Alexei has fled, those were my intentions as well. I have had my eye on the rank of *chevalier* for some time. That was it? You traded my prospects with the *Légion d'honneur* for a few pieces of damaged furniture and a feeling of virtue?"

"Hardly." Paul outlined the day's events: Wycliffe's kidnapping of the young women with the intention of

449

murdering them and Mrs. Murphy, the need to keep him contained until he could be returned to justice in the United States, Barousse's connection with the French military intelligence.

Hervé rolled his cigarette holder between his fingers as he listened. Paul was encouraged by seeing the care-lines on his friend's face softening.

Hervé said, "Tell me, if you please, after you and Miss Holmes became intimates, did she confide in you the reason for Murphy's visits to Winzig Krenz? That is, the visits which were confirmed by Friedrich Hoffmeister?"

"There's an interesting twist to that."

Under the scrutiny of Hervé's steady, insightful gaze, Paul had to consider closely what he wanted to reveal. He had said nothing to his friend about Cyril other than to use his death as a signal of impending danger. A time would come for mentioning a possible rapprochement with Jonnie, but it would have to be when certain details, such as his work for the British Secret Service, were not crowding the edges of the disclosure.

After Paul finished describing Lily's discovery in Krenz's library, he said, "The way I figure it, Wycliffe's initial plan was simple. He intended to destroy his cousin by framing her for the murder of her husband. This plan fell apart when, after shooting Murphy, he learned the man had already died by another means. Consequently, Wycliffe had to come up with a new scheme for ruining his cousin. Upon learning that Murphy had cashed out of San Francisco, he took that fact and twisted it into a fantastic story about Murphy's plotting to buy weapons for the Irish. This, he ultimately escalated into a second plot against the American government. These lies were to be supported by forged letters."

He paused to take another slug of whiskey. "It is important

we remember that this string of falsehoods was manufactured well after the visits to Krenz's villa. Whatever was his purpose in posing as Joseph Murphy, it wasn't related to his original plan for destroying Mrs. Murphy simply by shooting her husband. And whatever that other purpose was, it obviously did not come to pass."

"Therefore, the visits to Villefranche were washouts, complete failures?" Hervé said.

"The truth of his intentions in going to Krenz's will be forever beyond our reach. Whatever he hoped to achieve obviously could not be pulled off. Perhaps his pigeons were less gullible than he expected. Without a shred of a doubt, he overestimated his charm and charisma. So he had to settle for those other half-baked tales and their fabricated evidence."

As Hervé murmured sounds of acquiescence, Paul could see his friend's mind was turning away from Alexei. Another month, sooner if an agreeable replacement appeared on the horizon, and this latest sorrow would be forgotten.

"Not so half-baked," Hervé said. "The Irish do exert considerable pressure on the British Government. Such a scheme, if uncovered, might tip the scales in that perennial Home Rule debate. Something else could take the headlines for a change."

"You and I know that. I doubt Wycliffe did."

"He apparently came across the information somewhere if he started using it. What if there were a grain of truth in his story?"

"I gave that consideration, but Miss Holmes convinced me she is the legitimate heir of Joseph Murphy's funds and that all were accounted for. Nothing was diverted for buying weapons like Wycliffe wanted the world to believe."

"He who pays the band calls the tunes," Hervé said. "It

451

is more likely the German government or its agents would furnish the money, not Murphy."

"True. However, that much cash would never be handed to a middleman. They would pay for the goods directly. Remember, Zaharoff was present at the same time."

Hervé smacked himself lightly on the forehead with the heel of his hand. "I should have thought of that," he said.

Paul helped himself again to the whiskey.

"Just for the sake of argument," Hervé said, "let us posit that the party with the leverage insisted on holding all the money. It would be an enormous sum to carry around in cash."

"Wycliffe might have insisted on holding the cash, but he would not have succeeded. The Germans are many things, but they are not sloppy."

"Again for the sake of argument, do you think this Wycliffe, also known as Joseph Murphy, would be such a consummate ass as to confer these services without compensation to himself? A man should want boatloads of money for bringing boatloads of armaments to Ireland. He would be purchasing not only arms. He would be transporting them, furnishing the contacts, putting himself and his capital equipment at risk."

Paul smiled indulgently. "That's only if you lend any credence to Wycliffe's fantasies. In the end, it was I who turned out to be the consummate ass." He proceeded to reveal in the strongest of terms how thoroughly The Hyena had taken him in. "I would be paltering with the truth if I didn't admit it outright. By making me despise him, he rendered me incapable of divining his true nature. He may be an idiot, but he's an *idiot savant.*"

A smile ghosted across Hervé's lips.

"Listen to that," Paul said. "A high-proof idiot, that's me.

I still cannot admit how cunning he was, how completely I was taken in by him."

Hervé said, "You have washed up on more shores than Odysseus and always managed to survive nicely. I am confident you will find some redeeming feature in this unfortunate experience. A man who cannot see that things often turn out for the best either has a short memory or an unforgiving heart. You mentioned a game you have going at Antibes. Finish it and come back here. You were always a good flywheel for me. I can run another table."

"I am much obliged, but a deck can be shuffled only so many times. I'm telling you, I've lost my edge. An old crow like me, getting caught in a pigeon trap, it's inexcusable. I'm going to cease my toil in the vineyard. I'll retire and live quietly on my savings, along with whatever I can pick up at a card game or two."

"It is a set-back, that is all, my friend. You always land on your feet."

"Even a dead cat will bounce if it's dropped far enough."

Hervé flung a gesture of defeat towards the ceiling. "So that is how you propose to spend the rest of your days, dozing on a porch at Brighton with the other pensioners, jaded by orthodoxy and stirring up an interest only for liver pills and laxatives?"

"I have to say, you do make it sound appealing."

Hervé straightened his arms over his head, flexed all his fingers, then slowly lowered them to pose with one fist curled in front of his face, studying his fingernails, the corners of his mouth twitching.

When Hervé raised his eyes, Paul met his friend's penetrating gaze with perfect insouciance. Hervé then exploded with laughter, slapping his palm repeatedly against the divan's cushion.

"You, an old, dead cat," he charged between gulps of air and more shouts of laughter. "Since the minute you walked in the door, you have looked like the cat who just feasted on the family's Easter bunny. You are no old, dead cat. You are an old fox, an old fox in the hen-house, no less."

# Friday, March 20, 1914
## GARE DE MONTE CARLO

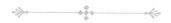

LILY TURNER STARED ACROSS THE EMPTY TRAIN tracks towards the scattered trees opposite. Beyond them, the morning sun, poised midway between the horizon and its noontime apex, spread its glow over the sea. Her eyes remained fixed straight ahead as Paul Newcastle lowered himself next to her and placed a Gladstone bag beside his left foot before removing his hat and setting it on the bench.

"Good morning," he said. His eyes took in the bruised jaw and blackened eye, only partially hidden by green-tinted spectacles. "I must say the colors become you, especially the indigo."

"You'll forgive me if I don't thank you for the compliment."

His voice grew softer. "Give it a couple of days and a little stage-makeup. You'll be fit for the drawing room once more."

"Is Ted gone?" she asked, still refusing to look at him.

"I tried to enter him in a claiming race for the White Slavers, but no one expressed an interest. So, yes, Barousse had him taken off yesterday, all done up like a kipper."

"You're sure Mr. Barousse can keep him contained?"

"Mr. Wycliffe may already be a cherished guest in a French prison. He will find the room-service deplorable, but then, so is the food. All we can do now is wait and hope for the worst."

"They'll bring him back? Nothing will be done to permanently prevent that?"

"You will recall Mr. Chandler expressly forbade such an extremity. Under no circumstances conceivable or inconceivable to the minds of gods or men would I betray a trust. It would be against my principles."

For the first time, she looked at him. He regarded her openly skeptical gaze. "Can a man make too much of his principles?" he said.

"You can."

"I have never lied to a friend or a cleric."

"I'm neither."

"Pshaw," he said as he playfully bumped her arm with his shoulder. "You know better than that. After all we've been through together?"

Lily's gaze returned to the vacant train tracks.

"What about the Gallaghers?" Paul said.

"What about them?"

"The Irish have an inbred sense of impending doom, but in Gallagher's case, I believe it is genuine. Are they to be left to the tender mercies of Mrs. Murphy?"

"I mentioned their plight to Sally. I didn't tell her about Bridget Rose and the poison, so she wants to make good on Mr. Murphy's commitment. She'll see to it they get to Belfast with some money in their pocket."

"That means you forfeited whatever it was you had coming for uncovering her as the poisoner."

"I never said –" She didn't finish the statement.

"There had to be something worthwhile in it, or you wouldn't have been pursuing it with such vigor."

"Knowing half of it belonged to you took some of the sting out of the sacrifice."

"*Touché*. That one is yours."

Paul sat with his hands flattened above his knees like a seated pharaoh. At length he said, "Miss Holmes tells me you're off to a new vocation as a private detective in Paris."

"What's that to you?"

"It's a good choice. You have more than a slender talent for sleuthing."

"How can you say that? I literally stumbled over my most important discoveries, Sally and Mr. Murphy, Ted's impersonation, even Jonathan Chandler."

"You were lucky, and that is one thing you should never discount. Do you know that whenever Napoléon was told of a new commander, his first question always was, 'Is he lucky?'"

"I'll keep that in mind the next time I'm about to invade Austria."

"I know you don't take advice, but listen to your Uncle Napoléon this one time. Most people have to navigate life with little more than dead reckoning to use for charting a course. Considering the obstacles that must be skirted – storms, sandbars, sea-monsters – most people think a man must be a superior calculator if he is not to founder and end up on the bottom. I'll grant you good calculations help, but in the gravest of extremities, it's not superior calculations a man needs. It's good luck."

The foot traffic around the pair was increasing. Some persons were trailed by porters with two-wheeled carts groaning beneath the baggage. Some persons carried flowers for greeting the arrivals from Nice and beyond. Several toted boxes from the confectionary to pacify the upcoming hours.

"Here endth the first lesson," Paul said. "For the next, why not go to London? You're an American, but he could do worse."

Lily kept her eyes on the ground for several long seconds.

Then she said, "Enough of the sweet talk, Paul. Are you Jonathan's father?"

His lips parted in speechless astonishment. "Why," he began but fell silent again. At last, he said, "No."

"Then you're the uncle, his mother's brother."

"Is that all you two talked about, family trees? Small wonder you're left sitting alone at a train station."

"Why the secrecy, the lies? It's not fair, your swanning around, knowing full well about him, but him, not knowing about you."

It was Paul's turn to develop an interest in empty train tracks and the scattered trees beyond. "It was not so much a lie as a protected truth," he said.

"What on earth is a 'protected truth'? That's just more of your malarkey."

"I mean, the undeformed truth can be vastly overrated. Even the exacting Augustine said it should never be used to injure. It's a good deal like your not telling Miss Holmes about Mrs. Gallagher."

"How is knowing he's your nephew going to injure Jonathan?"

"That's something I hope you will come to understand with time. Every choice is not black or white. Young people in particular often have difficulty distinguishing half-tones."

"Jonathan appears mature to me, and the Methuselah bit, if that's your only argument, is wearing thin."

"It's family," Paul said. "There's nothing in it that is logical. Those are depths that can never be sounded."

They simultaneously broke off the stares they had fixed upon one another, Lily tending to the right and Paul to the left. The distant shriek of the train's whistle announcing its departure from the station at La Condamine broke the impasse.

"What does your mother think about your going to Paris?" Paul said.

"She doesn't think anything. She doesn't know I'm going."

"Is that fair?"

"Is it fair? I don't know. I just know it's necessary I do it this way. It's only recently, since yesterday to be precise, that I've come to understand why that is." She opened her handbag and took out a handkerchief, which she folded and refolded before tucking it up one of her coat sleeves.

"All my life," she said, "most of it anyway, I swore that no matter what, I would never be like my mother. I swore that because I was mortally ashamed of her. Before she was fifteen years of age, she had me. Her husband, if my father ever legally assumed that title, made her a grass-widow by abandoning us in a boarding house in Omaha. Somehow, she never said how but somehow, she made her way to Chicago. That's where my memories begin, when I was around four. There she was, eighteen years old, straight from the cornhuskers, barely able to read or write, alone except for me, and caught in Chicago's merciless maw. There was nothing to distinguish her from the thousands of other women who, every day, find themselves in that same hapless, helpless, hopeless condition. Those are the thousands who eke out survival by slaving in sweatshops or by regularly being beaten senseless by brutish husbands or who walk the streets until disease or a criminal robs them of their lives. Those were my mother's brilliant prospects in 1897."

The tears hovering in Lily's eyes lost their hold. Paul leaned across and gently wiped them away with his thumb. She snuffled and straightened. "You should see Effie today. Granted, she'll never be elected president of the Garden Club, but within a couple of years after arriving in Chicago, she

459

was clawing her way to the top of the only profession that could offer material promise to a woman with her limitations. Today, she has seven women, thirteen servants, and half the policemen and government officials in Chicago on her payroll."

Lily removed the handkerchief from her coat-sleeve and dried the tinted lenses, then dabbed her cheeks. Remnants of tears clung to the thick lashes. "So that's it. That's what I had to admit to myself. I was never afraid of being like her. Instead, I've always known I could never meet, let alone exceed, her accomplishments. The truth is, if I could be one-half the woman my mother is, I would be one hell of a woman. And that's what I'm going to do in Paris. I'm not only going to survive; I'm going to succeed. After that, I'll tell my mother what I've done."

Up the tracks, the steam whistle sounded, signaling the locomotive's approach to Monte Carlo.

Paul got to his feet. He lingered in front of Lily without speaking, studying her face as though searching for something not visible on its surface, his jaw rhythmically clenching and unclenching.

"What is it now?" she said.

"I was thinking about salty chocolate, that's all."

"Why can't you ever be straight with me?"

The air pulsated with the hot energy and smell of burnt coal being pushed ahead of the engine making its way past the Casino to their right.

"That's yours coming into the shed," Paul said, placing his hat on his head. He turned to watch the smoking, sizzling, clanging metal-monster clamber into the station, couplings battering, brakes squealing. Heads protruded from the wagons-lits in the rear. Porters strategically positioned themselves where the doors should align. A voice was shouting to stand back for disembarking passengers. Everyone on the platform was in motion.

A look of panic shot across Lily's face.

"You'll be all right," Paul said, but his words were lost in the locomotive's final snarling hiss as it gathered itself for its heaving halt. In the midst of the noise and smoke and steam, he lifted his hat as a parting gesture.

When he had gone about sixty feet, Lily called out, "Paul!"

He pivoted on his heel but continued moving backwards. She held the obviously heavy bag he had placed at his feet. She pushed it away from her body, pointing at it with her other hand. Shaking his head and smiling broadly, he waved, then turned around and kept walking.

# Friday, March 20, 1914

PAUL STROLLED ALONG THE PROMENADE BELOW THE Casino's upper terrace, his hands buried deep in the pockets of his overcoat. A ship's horn wailing across the water didn't disturb the flock of gulls, circling low, cawing, calling above a school of fish. At the point where the promenade overlooked the Tir aux pigeons, he stopped. All quiet down there, the slaughter of the innocents temporarily suspended.

He smiled as he breathed the invigorating air of freedom. He had declared himself demobilized to the Casino's management late last night, and he would be bidding farewell to Madame Piggot, Olivier, and Pierre later today. Nothing which had happened in the last couple of days had tempered his need for a prompt departure. Because his lengthy disreputable past never would have borne close scrutiny, he had always avoided drawing attention to himself. That folly, however, had been committed several times during the past week. He would never feel confident that his role in providing the guest-lists to Cyril was unknown or unsuspected by Chief Inspector Gautier or the Commissioner of Police. For that matter, he would never feel confident Cyril hadn't kept written evidence of Paul's true identity among his papers as a form of life-insurance. Also, there was the knowledge of Barousse's connection to the Deuxième Bureau, which Paul had implicitly shown by going to him with the Schlieffen Plan. Given Barousse's abundantly demonstrated hostility, the next thing Paul might learn was that he had excited the curiosity of the French Sûreté. And if those weren't ample reasons for casting off, Friedrich Hoffmeister and his throat-slitting pals might show up at any time.

After Lily discovered it was Wycliffe, not Murphy, who had visited Krenz's villa, Paul had become ninety-nine percent certain a considerable amount of money had changed hands. Wycliffe's tale of arms for revolutionaries had stood up because it had the starch of truth. The theory was further stiffened by the idea that Wycliffe needed Murphy dead not only in order to disgrace and destroy his cousin but also to make the co-conspirators believe there was no possibility of recovering their investment. Also, Wycliffe was genuinely convinced the intruders were looking for money – not, as he claimed, the money Murphy cashed out of San Francisco, but the money the Faux-Murphy had been given to buy weapons that never would have been purchased.

However, in order for Paul to get his hands on the fortune Wycliffe had scammed, he needed Lily. Ironically, his scheme had mirrored Wycliffe's. He wanted her to lure The Hyena away from his room, so he could search it. When she left the Hôtel Hermitage yesterday, she seemed determined to leave Monte Carlo. Therefore, he didn't wait for her at the restaurant until two o'clock but went directly to her room. Not for anything would he have knowingly sent Lily into the jaws of death, but damned if she hadn't proved herself once more.

He was still wrestling with the feelings which had been resurrected at the train station. There was not one iota of similarity in their appearance. Lily was tall, large boned, bold featured, and aggressively present. Marie-Odile had been slight, petite, and she darted about like a forest-sprite. She would have been a subject only for a watercolor by an impressionist; whereas, Lily would have to be kept to a few strokes in impasto. Yet in their essences, they were identical. Both were as strong as reinforced concrete, and each was as fragile as a misty dream. At the train station, for several perilously long moments, he had seen in Lily what Marie-Odile could have been, if only life had dealt her one or two trump cards and if only she had lived long enough to play them. Back there at the station, for several perilously long moments, he had thought his heart was going to break all over again.

Hervé had called it correctly. The cash was heavy and bulky. Lily was given the larger denominations. Hervé could help convert the remaining notes into something more portable. Paul would also pass the talon for the Antibes game to Hervé. The mark had never seen "the expert," and there was no reason to let that exquisite Book of Hours go to waste.

Paul had considered playing out that game along with Hervé. The Murphy-episode had felt much like their old capers, creeping along like poured honey at the start and racing like a raging fire at the end. His nostalgia, however, was short-lived. Even after dividing the swag with Lily, he could live handsomely wherever he chose to drop anchor next. And if he had learned nothing else in a lifetime of riding the gains and losses, it was to quit while he was well ahead.

Paul interrupted these thoughts to tip his hat to the white-haired Hélèna, leaning on her walking stick, making her way to the Casino to claim a seat that would be sublet later. He regretted she didn't recognize him outside his element. He would have liked to assure her one last time of his everlasting sorrow over never having had an affair with her.

Putting Hélèna and the Casino behind, he continued down the Avenue de Monte Carlo towards La Condamine. He decided it was good he and Jonnie met again here. They would be starting from this point, not twenty-five years ago. Naturally, there would be questions, even a few recriminations. He would deal with those when the time came, perhaps with complete honesty, probably not. Some things should never be spoken except on one's deathbed, others not even then. As for justifying his conduct during the last twenty-odd years, well, he had never been any worse than he needed to be. Considering that necessity knows no law, he believed he had been granted a fair amount of leeway there.

He stopped to squint into the morning sun. He would prefer to see Jonnie far away from the heaving politics of Europe. If he could be talked into emigrating to Canada or Australia, Paul could use the money to set them both up. Anabatic winds had always deposited him and Hervé on some acceptable promontory. Surely he and Jonnie could manage as well. Then again, Lily might prove to be useful there. Perhaps she could convince Jonnie to emigrate to the United States. The last idea's appeal lasted only a matter of seconds, only until his thoughts turned to Madeline Murphy, Ted Wycliffe, Nicholas Breedlove, and the scores of other Americans he had known. Most of them ranged from the merely potty to the criminally insane. To follow Jonnie to America would be unthinkable. Another problem to be met when the time came.

The flock of seagulls, having lost interest or ambition or hope, ceased hectoring the water's surface and, pumping their wings in unison, rose, then banked to fly farther up the shoreline towards Menton. A single pair peeled off from the formation, soared higher, and glided away from the shore, out towards the sea. Paul watched them, pressing their wings against the unseen, using it for propulsion and support. His eyes followed the pair until they were absorbed by the brilliance of the noontime sun. Then he brushed his fingertips along the scar on his cheek and resumed walking.

# The End

# Author's Notes

SOME OF THE PLACES USED AS FICTITIOUS SETTINGS in this novel are based upon historical structures and places. These include the Hôtel de Paris, the Hôtel Hermitage, the Palais de Beaux Arts, the Oceanographic Museum, the Tir aux pigeons, the Gare de Monte Carlo, and the Hôtel Dieu, all in Monaco; also the Trophy of Augustus and the Hôtel du Righi d'Hiver at La Turbie; the rack-and-pinion railway to La Turbie; the villa Ephrussi de Rothschild (Villa Ile de France) at Cap Ferrat; and, of course, the Monte Carlo Casino. To see them as they appeared in 1914, enter that year or a nearby year in the internet search. (The results often are pictures used on contemporary postcards.)

Some of the persons referred to in this book were actual persons. These include Basil Zaharoff, Kate Warne, the Molly Maguires, the O'Donnell family, Sergei Diaghilev, Jean Juarés, Beatrice Rothschild Ephrussi, Enrico Caruso, La Belle Otero, Stanford White, Jane Addams. They do not appear directly in any scene, and they have been used in an entirely fictional manner in order to root the story in the period. More information about them as actual persons can be found in Wikipedia as well as in other sites on the internet.

The Von Schlieffen Plan, which formed the basis for Germany's invasion of Belgium and the beginning of World War I, is well known. According to Barbara Tuchman in *The Guns of August*, the German Army's intended use of reserve units for the invasion, which was a key feature of the Von Schlieffen Plan, was known to France's Deuxième Bureau in the spring of 1914.

In late 1914, Germany's Foreign Secretary was visited by an Irish Revolutionary, and a plan was laid to land 25,000 soldiers in the west of Ireland with 75,000 rifles. However, the German General Staff did not approve the plan.

Germany's offer to the Mexican government of a recovery of territory in the United States in exchange for an alliance against the United States is well documented. This incident is sometimes referred to as the "Zimmerman Telegram."

Questions? Comments?
See: www.monterenfro.com
Email: Spraguepublishingco@gmail.com
Write: Sprague Publishing Company
PO Box 873934
Vancouver, WA, 98687 USA

Made in the USA
Lexington, KY
22 January 2018